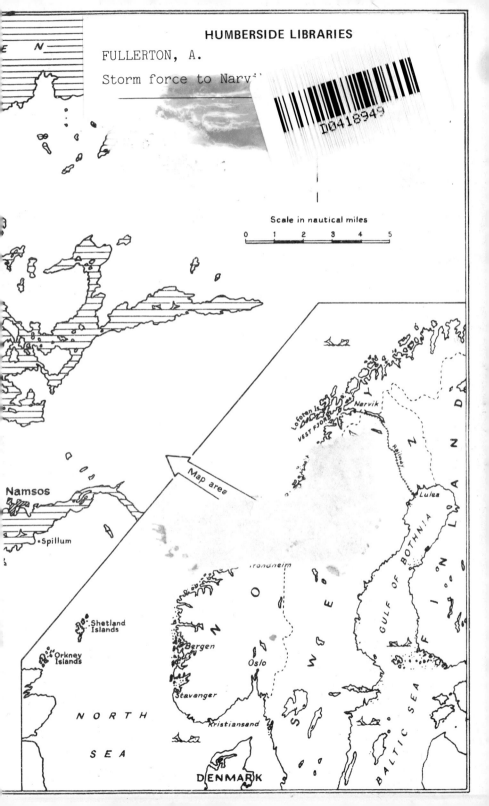

Scale in nautical miles

0   1   2   3   4   5

Map area

Namsos

•Spillum

Lofoten Is

Narvik

VEST FJORD

Railway

Luleå

GULF OF BOTHNIA

Trondheim

N   O   R   W   A   Y

S   W   E   D   E   N

F   I   N   L   A   N   D

Shetland
Islands

Orkney
Islands

Bergen

Oslo

N   O   R   T   H

Stavanger

Kristiansand

S   E   A

BALTIC   SEA

DENMARK

STORM FORCE TO NARVIK

April 1940. Nick Everard divorced and forty-two, is now in command of the destroyer, INTENT, trying to prevent a German landing in Norway: as the battle opens INTENT is crippled, with engine defects, lacking fuel, and with all her technicians dead. Limping into a Norwegian fjord to try and effect repairs Nick finds that the Germans have invaded. But INTENT needs fuel, and hearing of a German fuel-tanker in a nearby anchorage the crew plan to raid and capture it. Only by enlisting the help of a Norwegian steam yacht commander and his daughter can the raid succeed.

Books by Alexander Fullerton
in the Charnwood Library Series:

THE TORCH BEARERS
REGENESIS
A SHARE OF HONOUR
THE GATECRASHERS
STORM FORCE TO NARVIK

ALEXANDER FULLERTON

STORM FORCE TO NARVIK

Complete and Unabridged

CHARNWOOD
Leicester

First published in Great Britain in 1979 by
Michael Joseph Ltd.,
London

First Charnwood Edition
published August 1985
by arrangement with
Michael Joseph Ltd.,
London

British Library CIP Data

Fullerton, Alexander
Storm force to Narvik.—Large print ed.—
Charnwood library series
I. Title
823′.914[F]   PR6056.U435

ISBN 0-7089-8277-8

Published by
F. A. Thorpe (Publishing) Ltd.
Anstey, Leicestershire
Set by Rowland Phototypesetting Ltd.
Bury St. Edmunds, Suffolk
Printed and bound in Great Britain by
T. J. Press (Padstow) Ltd., Padstow, Cornwall

Author's Note

Storm Force to Narvik is a novel about the naval operations off northern Norway between 8 and 13 April 1940. The destroyers *Intent*, *Hoste* and *Gauntlet* are fictional, as are the events described as taking place around Namsos, but the general framework of the story and details of the two Narvik battles are drawn from history.

The last-published Everard story left Nick Everard at the Golden Horn in 1918, about to take a destroyer into the Black Sea in support of Russian White Army operations against the Bolsheviks. That story, and others of the 1914–18 period, will be told later.

1

GAUNTLET had opened fire. The port-side lookout had reported it and Nick Everard had seen it too, distant yellow-orange spurts of flame, small stabs of brilliance piercing the blanket of foul weather and dawn's greyness still lingering under heavy cloud. Part-lowering his binoculars for a moment he looked across *Intent*'s bridge as she tilted savagely to starboard and bow-down with the quartering sea lifting her from astern, and saw young Lyte with his hand extended to the alarm buzzer, excitement as well as enquiry on his boyish and now salt-dripping face: Nick nodded, and putting his glasses back to his eyes heard the Morse letter "S" sounding distantly but with dentist's-drill persistence through the ship. "S" for surface action stations. The destroyer was standing on her tail now, stern deep in white churned froth and her bow and "A" gun pointing at the cloud: jammed for support against the binnacle he put the glasses back on *Gauntlet* and saw her four-sevens fire again, rosettes of flame that bloomed and faded into smudges and were lost in the surrounding murk. The ship herself was almost invisible and her target, whatever it might be,

1

was completely so: visibility was patchy but at the most four miles.

"Port fifteen." Acknowledgement came hoarsely from the voice-pipe. He added, into the reek of metal polish and cigarette-smoke which not even a Norwegian Sea gale could clear away, "Two-five-oh revolutions." In normal conditions that would give her about twenty-four knots; in this sea it was doubtful whether such high revs could be kept on for long. On most courses it would be out of the question, but as she swung to port she was putting the force of the gale right astern; the dangers now would be of her screws racing as they came up into thin water when she pitched heavily bow-down, and of being pooped —overswept by big seas from astern.

Gauntlet was in action, and alone, and *Intent* had to get down there and join her.

"Sub!"

Sub-Lieutenant Lyte, on his way off to his action station in charge of the after guns, turned back, throwing an arm round one of the binnacle's correcting-spheres to hold himself in place as the ship stood on her ear: Nick told him, shouting above the noise, "If we look like getting pooped, secure 'Y' gun until we're on a safer course. And tell the first lieutenant I want him up here."

The second-in-command's action station was at the after control position; but until he knew what was happening, Nick wanted him within

2

easy shouting distance. He ducked to the pipe: "Midships!"

"Midships, sir!"

Men rushing to their action stations had to grab for hand-holds as they went, staggering for balance while the ship flung herself about. The helmsman reported he had his wheel amidships; Nick bawled down to him to steer one-four-oh degrees. *Gauntlet* had been just about due south of them and steering north, and she'd been firing to starboard; so this alteration of forty degrees to port—*Intent* had been steering south—was intended both to close the distance and at the same time to bring *Intent* up towards the enemy. Meanwhile communications were being tested, gun receivers lined up, ammunition supply readied, all the set routines of preparing for action being gone through for the second time in an hour. It was only that long since the ship's company had been piped to dawn action stations, no more than fifteen minutes since they'd been sent down again, and the alarm's buzzing would surely have turned the messdeck air blue with obscenities. The off-watch hands would have had breakfast in mind—not *this*. . . . Nick saw Tommy Trench, his outsized first lieutenant, oilskins shedding water in streams as he talked over the telephone to Henry Brocklehurst in the director tower, the gun-control position above and abaft the bridge; the tower and its separate range-finder were meanwhile training this way and that over an arc from north-east to south-east—like the raised head of some monster seeking prey.

"Sir . . ." Pete Chandler, *Intent*'s RNVR navigator, former insurance broker and yachtsman, fetched up in a rush against the other side of the binnacle. Tall, pale-faced, hooded in a duffle coat. "*Gauntlet*'s wirelessed an enemy report—two destroyers."

They'd intercepted her first signal, that she was investigating an unidentified ship to the nor'ard. There'd seemed to be some possibility of confusion then, that she'd been referring to *Intent*; they'd met at just about that time, exchanged the coloured-light challenge and reply and then swapped pendant numbers. But the puzzle was resolved now—partly.

"Tell the first lieutenant. Then see if anything else is coming through."

Chandler went slithering downhill to join Trench, who'd now tell Brocklehurst the Gunnery Control Officer what he was supposed to be looking for, and Brocklehurst could tell the guns' crews over their sightsetters' telephones. It would be damned uncomfortable down at the four-sevens, and by no means easy to shoot effectively or to handle heavy projectiles on slippery, wildly canting gundecks. . . . It could be argued, he realised—one thought overtaking another—that he should be ordering *Gauntlet* to wait for him to join her. But if he did, she might lose contact

4

with the enemy. If the Hun wanted to evade contact it would be all too easy in this weather, and if those destroyers were part of an invasion force, part of the expected German attack on Norway, they *would* want to. The priority therefore was to maintain contact at all costs: not only in order to engage but even more importantly, in the prevailing state of ignorance and confusion, to see what ships were here and then tell the C-in-C about them.

He focused his glasses again on *Gauntlet*. He'd picked her up, to his own and his navigator's great satisfaction, just a short while ago. Dawn, arriving after the four-hour dark period which was what constituted a "night" this far north, hadn't done more than change pitch black into dirty grey: but suddenly there she'd been, a needle in the North Sea haystack. He stooped to the voicepipe: "Port fifteen. Steer one-three-oh" —because *Gauntlet* had altered course again, gone round to about 090 degrees, east, which was the bearing of the nearest part of Norway. And there, in fact at three different points on that distant and of course invisible coast, close inshore, minelaying operations were in progress at this minute. *Intent* and *Gauntlet* and half a dozen other destroyers were at sea with the battle-cruiser *Renown* as cover to these operations, in case the Germans tried to interfere with them; but *Gauntlet* (Lieutenant Commander J. A. Hustie RN) had turned back to search for a

5

man lost overboard, and subsequently *Intent* (Commander Sir Nicholas Everard, Bart., DSO, DSC, RN) had been sent to find *her*.

God only knew what might be happening elsewhere—whether the Hun was about to invade Norway, or whether the British were. Troops had been embarked in cruisers and transports in Scottish ports, but they were just sitting there, waiting. For what? For the War Cabinet to make its woolly mind up?

And now the Home Fleet had sailed; the C-in-C, Sir Charles Forbes, had brought them out of Scapa last evening. But apparently they were staying out in the middle, not covering the approaches to the Norwegian ports at all. Surely if the Germans were invading that would be the place to find them?

Usual bugger's muddle, Nick thought. We haven't changed. At Jutland nobody knew what the hell anyone else was doing either.

Twenty-four years ago, Jutland had been. It felt more like last week. . . . At Jutland he'd been a sub-lieutenant, and since then he'd been many different things—including, for about eight years, a glorified labourer on his own land in Yorkshire. The peasant years . . . If it hadn't been for that break in his naval service he'd have been at least a post-captain now. He'd been promoted to the rank of commander—the three stripes they'd given him back now—as long ago as 1926.

Well—it had been by his own choice that he'd left. And in wartime one only needed a bit of luck to make up that sort of leeway.

"Course one-three-oh, sir!"

"Flag signal from *Gauntlet* sir!"

Acknowledging the wheelhouse report, he looked round: at the back of the bridge, starboard side, Leading Signalman Herrick had a telescope trained on the tiny patch of colour at *Gauntlet*'s yardarm. Herrick bawled, "Enemy —destroyer flag—bearing—"

He'd stopped, unable to read the numerals under that red-and-white bearing pendant. Blowing down-wind the flags were almost end-on, and when both ships were down in troughs between the waves they were completely hidden from each other. But now it ceased to matter: Trench was yelling with the director telephone at his ear, "Director has enemy in sight, one destroyer bearing green one-oh range oh-seven-five!"

"Open fire!" Nick called down to the coxswain, "Port ten." To turn her so that the after guns, "X" and "Y", would bear.

"Ten of port wheel on, sir!"

"Steer one-one-oh."

It would still be a converging course—with *Gauntlet*'s, and so presumably with the enemy's. Nothing about enemy course from Brocklehurst yet. And it was strange that "A" and "B" guns

7

hadn't started shooting. Nick shouted to Trench to ask what the delay was.

"Director lost target!"

He'd got the information at just that moment. Nick cursed, and put his glasses on *Gauntlet* again. She'd gone further round to starboard. Trench called, "Director reports enemy has turned away eastward, sir."

Running away. *Gauntlet* chasing him.

"Starboard fifteen." A sleet-shower was lashing across the bridge. Nick was thinking that two Hun destroyers would hardly be up here in 65 north latitude on their own. They had to be escorting or screening something bigger.

"Fifteen of starboard wheel on, sir!"

"Steer one-three-oh." He was watching *Gauntlet*, and although the distance between them had lessened somewhat she was becoming harder to see. This sleet didn't help, but where she was the visibility must have closed in during the last minute. . . . Escorting *something*, those Huns must be. Troop transports for Narvik, perhaps; or scouting ahead of bigger ships. It would be a normal destroyer tactic to turn away and lead a pursuer into the range of a heavier ship's guns; whereas it was most unlikely that any destroyer man would lead attackers towards a convoy that was in his own protection. This was the analysis that made sense: and you could add a further detail to the picture of probabilities: in

8

these weather conditions any encounter would take place at virtually point-blank range.

And consequently, this was the moment when the right decision for him as senior officer might be to call *Gauntlet* back, not let Hustie press on alone while *Intent* was too far astern to support him.

"Course one-three-oh, sir!"

Wind and sea were just about dead astern again, on this course. He'd acknowledged the coxswain's report: he called down, "Three hundred revolutions." If he ordered Hustie to wait for *Intent* to catch him up and contact with the enemy was lost, in this weather it wouldn't be regained. *Gauntlet* therefore had to be allowed to take her chances. Nick yelled at Trench, "Tell Opie to have his tubes on a split yarn. And Brocklehurst to load with SAP and open fire without further orders."

"Aye aye, sir!" Tommy Trench was a lieutenant-commander, twenty-nine years old, six-foot four in his seaboot stockings, a very experienced first lieutenant who probably saw his dug-out CO as some kind of ancient mariner. Possibly even as a supplanter. Nick had only taken command a fortnight ago and Trench, who'd been first lieutenant under the previous captain, might have entertained hopes of getting the ship himself.

The voicepipe on the left of the binnacle was

the one to the engine-room. Nick called down it to his commissioned engineer, Mr. Waddicor.

"We may need to make smoke at short notice, Chief."

"I'll be ready for you, sir!"

A Devon man, was Waddicor. Short and rather stout—well, say stocky—and always boisterously happy. Extraordinary . . . *Gauntlet* was out of sight, he realised suddenly. In the last few seconds she'd faded, merged into the thick weather, the soupy haze down there where the clouds' lower edges seemed to be throwing roots into the sea. She couldn't be more than 6,000 yards away, and she'd vanished. He was still searching, expecting her to appear again after being hidden temporarily in a squall—they'd endured rain, sleet, hail and snow since midnight —when he heard percussions, heavy as thunder only sharper, more clearly defined. From that easterly direction.

Trench was looking round at him, with a hand cupped to one ear. And there'd been a flash, a diffuse explosive brightness which had flared for about a second and was now extinguished, leaving only drab grey again.

Big-ship guns . . .

"Ask Brocklehurst if he can still see *Gauntlet*."

Trench turned, ducked behind the glass windbreak which topped the forefront of the bridge, taking the telephone down there with him. Perfectly timed: half a ton of green water burst

10

over, missing him as it plumped into the bridge, bursting in all directions and swirling inches deep to the level of the gratings before it drained away. Trench grinned at Able Seaman Hughes, who'd taken it fair and square and looked like an angry spaniel. Trench rose, slamming the hand-set into its bracket: "They've lost her, sir!"

Gunfire had become continuous, had thickened into a solid blast with no gaps in it. If Hustie had run into some big ship at close range his reaction would be to turn and fire torpedoes; and the enemy's reply would be to let rip with his big guns as the destroyer swung and exposed her vulnerable beam to him. Guesswork: but it was more than that: he could see it happening—with an accompanying thought in his mind that if *Intent* had been there with her, *Gauntlet* wouldn't have been getting all that vicious attention directed at herself alone. She was there alone because he'd *let* her be. . . . More gunfire: but less intensive, separate salvoes again. *Intent* pounding, battering towards the sound of them. Scream of the fans competing with that of the wind: different notes blending into a roar of sound punctuated by the rattling and thumping of the ship's fabric, the battering of the sea.

"*Gauntlet* on green two-oh, sir, on fire!"

Trench, hauling himself over to the starboard torpedo sight, gestured to the communications number, Hughes, to take over the director tower's telephone. And Nick had *Gauntlet* in his glasses. She was coming back, almost bow-on: he saw shell-splashes all around her. The fire was abaft her bridge, he thought probably between the funnels. But now she was beginning to make her own smoke, oily-looking black stuff oozing out and curling away down-wind just as another salvo plummeted down and one shell landed on her foc'sl, its flattish orange burst darkening into a red-brown haze with solid pieces flying.

No enemy in sight still. *Gauntlet* swinging hard to port though, lengthening and then shortening again as she turned, belching smoke, revealing the blaze amidships, mainmast gone and after funnel shot to ribbons. The wind was pushing the smoke away to port, between *Gauntlet* and her enemy: her course was something like south now so the German had to be to the east of her.

"Starboard fifteen."

"Starboard fifteen, sir!"

"Steer one-five-oh." He added, "Three-five-oh revolutions."

The gap had to be closed: the dangers of increasing to full speed had simply to be accepted. And *Gauntlet* was still visible to the enemy, despite the smokescreen: she'd been straddled again, shell-spouts lifting grandly, the wind blowing their tops off as they subsided. Nick saw Trench throw him a glance back across the lurching bridge with a can't-we-do-something appeal on his large, squarish face. He looked over at the suffering *Gauntlet*, waiting for Hustie to turn back behind his own smoke. He *would*, obviously, otherwise there'd have been no point in laying it: and the turn would bring him back towards *Intent*, who meanwhile was straining her steel guts and loosening every rivet in her plates by crashing flat-out across a sea in which normally one wouldn't have attempted more than twelve knots. But she and *Gauntlet* would be closing in towards each other fast once Hustie made his turn: the rate of closing would be the sum of their combined speeds. The enemy had to be somewhere on *Gauntlet*'s bow, since that was the only angle from which he could have her in sight. Unless he was seeing her *over* the smoke: seeing her foretop from his much higher one?

Gauntlet had begun to turn. *At last* . . . He watched her, counting seconds, for her to get behind that smoke barrier. It was already some distance from her, as the diameter of her turn added to the smoke's down-wind drift. But she was round: by now she'd be hidden from the German. Heading back this way. . . .

But—still under helm: continuing the turn?

Hustie was going right round, back into the smoke—*attacking on his own again*. . . .

"Port twenty, full ahead both engines!"

Maximum revs were already on the clock but "full ahead" meant emergency, sit on the safety-valves. He shouted to Trench, "Stand by all tubes port side!" Trench raised a hand in acknowledgement: he'd already crossed to the other sight,

13

having assessed the position for himself and seen that they'd be bound to fire on a starboard turn, since the enemy must be on a southerly course. If he hadn't been, *Gauntlet* wouldn't have laid out her smoke-screen that way. Nick called down, "Steer one-five-oh."

"Captain, sir." Chandler, with a signal log. "New one from *Gauntlet*. She's reported the enemy as a *Hipper*-class cruiser."

He was watching Hustie's ship straighten from her three-quarter circle and steady on a course of about 110 degrees. She'd be into the smoke before *Intent* could be: and it was too late to recall him. Partly because *Gauntlet* was further ahead but also because *Intent* would be entering this top end of the smoke—which, having been laid first, was further down-wind now than the rest. And thinner, too. He told Chandler, "Get a signal off, pilot. Same addressees." That meant the C-in-C in his flagship *Rodney* and Admiral Whitworth in *Renown*, repeated to Admiralty in London. He dictated, "In company with *Gauntlet* in position—whatever it is—about to engage enemy cruiser with torpedoes, *Gauntlet* severely damaged in previous attack."

"Course one-five-oh, sir!"

Tremendous racket: wind, sea, and turbine-scream . . . *Gauntlet* was vanishing into the smoke barrier. Nick yelled at Trench, "Tell Opie and Brocklehurst the target is a *Hipper*-class cruiser." The smoke seemed to be holding

14

together remarkably well, down at its southern end; but at this end it was breaking up, leaving gaps that were quite clear of it. *Gauntlet* was blanketed, but the disintegration of the smoke was spreading that way quite rapidly and it wouldn't cover her for long.

She'd have used some torpedoes, presumably, in her first attack; it was anyone's bet how many she'd have left to use this time. No smoke here now to speak of: just patches, and eye-whipping sleet again: and suddenly there was *Gauntlet*—a low, blazing silhouette glimpsed sporadically as she slam-banged through the waves. But the fact that he was seeing her didn't mean the German could. He took his eyes off her: it was the target, the *Hipper*, one had to look for now; and suddenly he heard—with interest and surprise because he hadn't heard it for twenty years and it had the sharp familiarity of something long forgotten suddenly brought to mind—the noise of shells scrunching overhead. Then "A" and "B" guns fired, their reports not much more than harsh cracking thuds because of other noise, the smoke and smell of cordite instantly whipped clear on the wind. Hughes, at the director telephone, shouted, "Enemy cruiser bearing green five, range—"

They'd seen her from up there because they were above the smoke and spray and had that extra height-of-eye: and the German must have spotted *Intent* even sooner. Then Nick had the

Hipper in his glasses too. Immense, and spitting flame, huge-looking with towering bridge super-structure and single massive funnel. Shell-spouts rose to starboard, a grove of them lifting almost politely from the sea as though rising to watch the destroyer pass: battle experience a quarter of a century old prompted Nick's order to the wheelhouse: "Starboard twenty!"

Jinking towards the fall of shot. The enemy GCO was bound to make his correction the other way. So you turned your ship one way while he sent his next salvo elsewhere.

But you couldn't dodge for ever: you had to get in close enough to have a fair chance of hitting with one or more torpedoes. . . .

Gauntlet: he'd been ignoring her while he watched the *Hipper*, but glancing to starboard now he saw Hustie's obvious intention: he was steering his ship right for her, going to ram!

He must have used up all his torpedoes in the first attack. So he had nothing left to hit the German with except his ship. Fifteen hundred tons throwing itself at ten thousand . . .

"Midships!"

"Midships, sir!"

He should have held him back. They should have been attacking together now, simul-taneously.

"Meet her. Steer one-six-oh."

And now hold this course. No more dodging.

Just a little gritting of the teeth. Salvo coming now . . .

It would miss. Because it *had* to. And before the next lot arrived he'd be close enough to turn and fire. A fan of ten fish from abaft the beam mightn't take all that much avoiding, especially with only one destroyer attacking on her own. You needed several, a co-ordinated attack. But —*bad workmen blame their tools*. He decided he'd fire the first five, the for'ard set, then hold on until the enemy began to take his avoiding-action, fire the rest when she'd committed herself and he could see which way she was swing-ing. There'd be punishment to take in that process. . . . Shells ripping over: that tearing-sailcloth sound. A violent jolt flung him forward against the binnacle and he realised she'd been hit aft. He shouted for the general benefit, "Nearly there!" No point looking round: there'd be flames and smoke and you'd seen all that before. Young Lyte would be looking after things if he was still on his feet: and Opie, please God, would be alive and with his two sets of tubes intact. Stink of burning paintwork and fire-heat in the wind: and Trench pointing . . . *Gauntlet* had rammed the German right for'ard near his starboard hawse-pipe and she was scraping and crashing down his side, ripping off armour-plating as she went. Nick ducked to the voicepipe: "Steer one-five-five." Up again: the *Hipper* had blasted off another salvo. Eight-inch shells would be in mid-

17

air now. *Gauntlet* had sheered away from the cruiser's side: she lay stopped, wallowing low in the sea and burning from end to end, and the German gunners weren't even bothering to shoot at her now because they knew she was finished.

They were shooting at *Intent* instead.

"Course one-five-five, sir!"

Shells would be arriving at any moment.

"Starboard twenty-five!"

"Starboard twenty-five, sir!"

Shot was falling close ahead, the splashes lifting like green pillars and from the nearer ones foul, smelly water streaming back across the ship as she drove through them—and beginning, *at last*, to swing. More fall of shot to port: one near-miss, the ship recoiling as from a body-blow. Heeling hard to port as she slammed around across wind and sea. Trench was stooped ready over the torpedo sight. Another crash back aft somewhere. But she was still turning, fighting her way round: in seconds Trench's sight would come on and the silver fish would leap away. More shells scorching down: and an explosion, aft again but—*inside* the ship? On its heels a *whoosh* of flame from aft and, overhead, a crack like a gun firing: then, drowning other noise, the racket of escaping steam.

She'd stopped her swing. Trench looking round, an expression of dismay on his big spray-wet face. A snow-shower sweeping over like a shroud and *Intent* was stopping, slumping in the

18

waves, surrendering to them like a stag pulled down by hounds. No swing now: the momentum of the turn was spent and the sea was beginning to punch her back the other way. She was stopped, and at the mercy of the cruiser's guns.

2

IN London there was no gale or sleet, but it was a blustery day and the tall, grey-haired civilian coming down St James's Street in dark overcoat and homburg strode briskly, keeping the cold out and, by his manner, enjoying the exercise too. An ebony cane with a silver knob swung from one gloved hand; it was a stick that might have gone with a naval uniform and perhaps once had, and as he turned left into Pall Mall he glanced up at the sky with the air of one accustomed to reading weather-signs and making his own interpretation of them. It was a useful knack to have, too, now that for security reasons there were no public weather forecasts.

He'd crossed the road, and presently he turned right into Waterloo Place, where he climbed a flight of stone steps. He was putting a hand out to push the glass front door open when a uniformed hall porter, reaching the door just in time, saved him the trouble.

"Good morning, sir."

The voice was Scottish, the inflexion faintly interrogative, the tone reserved for someone whom the porter didn't recognise as a member but wasn't *quite* sure about.

20

"Good morning. Thank you." He was looking interestedly at the porter. "Don't I know you?"

That solved one problem: he couldn't be a member. The porter was now battling with the new one. Concentrating, his brown eyes were narrowed to mere slits in a face which, with its corrugations and tan complexion, had something in common with a walnut.

The eyes suddenly lit up.

"Admiral Everard!"

Hugh Everard, nodding, raised the hand with the black cane in it. "Don't dare tell me . . . You were with me in *Nile*. In '16. And you were—in my gig's crew?"

"I was *that*, sir!"

Hugh was still nodding to himself as he regained pieces of lost memory.

"Robertson?"

"Aye, sir!"

"You were a dead-eyed Dick of a marksman, I remember. We were runners-up in the Scapa championships and you were in *Nile*'s eight. Am I right?"

The walnut seemed permanently cracked in that wide smile.

"Right enough, sir . . . Why, I'd never've— my word, it's twenty or more years—"

"I'll tell you another thing, Robertson." The blue eyes were smiling. "At Jutland you sustained a slight wound. A shell-splinter in the—er—"

"Aye, sir, I did." A hand moved as if to rub

21

one buttock, but was then needed for opening the door as some members came up the steps. Hugh Everard moved to the side. Robertson came back to him: "May I ask, sir—did ye hear anything ever of old George Bates?"

"Dead, poor fellow. Years ago, now. He came with me, you know, when I left the Service. Turned out he had a weak heart—Bates, of *all* men. Wouldn't have believed it, would you?"

"That I would not, sir. Why, us lads were the ones he gave weak hearts to!" He shook his head. "Sorry—very sorry indeed, tae hear . . ." Away to the door again: and now back, as Hugh began to unbutton his coat. Hugh murmured, "I'd give a great deal to have old Bates brought back to life. . . . By the way, I'm lunching here with Admiral Wishart. D'you know if he's in the club yet?"

"I'd say he's not, sir. But ye could take a seat i' the—" His voice tailed off; he was looking puzzled. "I'd have thought ye'd be a member here, sir. But unless I'm mistaken—"

"Never bothered to join, Robertson. Always plenty of pals here—and I've a club in St James's Street, d'you see."

Robertson nodded. "Aye . . . Sir—your nephew, was it, at Jutland in that destroyer? Is he—"

"My nephew Nick? Yes, he's at sea. He left the Navy earlier on—various reasons of his own —but he's back now. They've given him a

22

destroyer, one of the 'I's. . . . And would you believe it, his son's at sea?"

"Och, that's grand!"

"As an OD, what's more!"

"*Ordinary Seaman?*" Robertson looked shocked. Hugh nodded, smiling as if the thought of it pleased him. "Joined up without telling his father. A very independent young man, d'you see. Brought up in the United States—well, these last years, his school years, you know. Did you hear that my nephew married a White Russian girl in 1919, when he was messing about in the Black Sea? Well—cutting a long story short—she cleared off to the States and collared a millionaire. Took young Paul with her, of course. But when this war started he came over—worked his passage in some liner—and joined up right away. Didn't want to use his father's influence—or mine, he said. I told him, I've not a *shred* of influence, these days!"

"Well, I'll be—"

"What d'you mean, Robertson, you *will* be?" Another tall man: but younger and bulkier, and in uniform with a rear-admiral's broad and narrow stripe on each sleeve. He told the porter, "You *have* been. Frequently." He warned Hugh Everard, "Shouldn't pay attention to anything this chap tells you, Sir Hugh. Most awful line-shooter in the place." Robertson was smiling, shaking his head sadly as if he'd given up hope for Aubrey Wishart years ago.

23

Hugh told his host, "Robertson and I are old shipmates. *Nile*, 1916."

"Ah. Jutland." Wishart's eyes ran over the porter's 1914-18 medal ribbons. He had some of his own, and they started with a DSO. Robertson repeated softly, "Jutland. Aye." Wishart put a hand on Hugh Everard's elbow. "Come along in, sir. Sorry I'm a few minutes adrift. Fact, there's something of a—" he glanced round, and lowered his voice—"flap on. Looks like the balloon's going up, up north."

They'd ordered buckling for a first course, and steak-and-kidney pie to follow, with a bottle of claret to help things along. Aubrey Wishart glanced across the table at his guest: then, meeting his eyes, uncharacteristically looked away again. Ostensibly, he was looking for the waiter who served the tables at this end.

Hugh Everard was about old enough to have been Wishart's father. They'd met through Nick, at a shooting weekend up at Mullbergh in Yorkshire, several years ago; and Wishart's friendship with Nick dated from more than twenty years back, when as captain of an E-class submarine he'd taken the young Lieutenant Everard on a slightly hair-raising jaunt through the Dardanelles minefields to Constantinople. It was a solidly-rooted friendship which had survived Nick's years on the beach.

24

Wishart murmured, "Turns out it's a tall order you've set me, Sir Hugh."

"What, a sea job for a retired admiral? What's tall about it? Where'd an old goat like me be if *not* at sea?"

"Well, sir—"

"It's got you in a dither, I can see *that*."

Wishart, fiddling with a crust of bread, could feel those blue eyes opposite boring right into his skull. It was the rottenest day imaginable to have chosen for this lunch, and he was wishing he'd followed his first inclination—to telephone the club and leave a message expressing regrets that Rear-Admiral Wishart was unable to leave his office for the present. If it had been anyone but Sir Hugh Everard whom he'd have been letting down, he'd have done that; and conversely, if it had been anyone else he wouldn't have been feeling so much on edge.

Gauntlet and *Intent*: both gone. *Intent's* "about-to-engage-with-torpedoes" signal, and then—nothing.

"You see, the problem is—"

"My dear fellow, I know what the problem is. They'll say I'm too old. Falling to bits and probably a bit dotty too. Eh?"

"No, sir, not *quite*—"

"Look here. Let's talk about my little schemes later. I'm far more intrigued by what you said as we were coming in—about the balloon going up, 'up north', you said? Norway?"

25

Shouldn't one have the guts to tell him straight out what's happened?

But as well as cowardice, there was a strong unwillingness to hurt. Hugh and Nick Everard were more like a very closely-in-touch father and son than uncle and nephew. More like very good friends. Each, Wishart knew, had a profound affection and respect for the other. It didn't make this situation any happier.

Hugh Everard saw his host glance round to see who, if anyone, might be in earshot. *Let not thy left hand know . . .* But here in this panelled dining-room with the oil paintings of Nelson and Jellicoe glaring down at them, mightn't it be somewhat over-cautious, let alone rude, to refuse information to Admiral Sir Hugh Everard, KCB, DSO and Bar? Hugh saw—thought he saw—some such thoughts whisking through Aubrey Wishart's mind; then Wishart had nodded, and begun somewhat unhappily, "You'll know that Winston Churchill's been pressing Chamberlain for a decision to mine the Leads, to stop the Hun sneaking his blockade-runners, and particularly his iron-ore supplies, through Norwegian waters?"

Hugh nodded. "Heard that months ago. And it won't stop 'em, will it. Not on its own."

"The idea is to force them out of territorial waters so we can get at them. If they knew they always stood a sporting chance of finding mines inshore—"

26

"What the devil are the Norwegians *allowing* them in their territorial waters for?" Hugh tapped the table angrily. "They raised blue murder when we went in and boarded the *Altmark*—in their so-called neutral waters and stuffed with prisoners out of British ships—and they say nothing about letting the Germans treat the same waters like their own private river!"

"I gather they're going to enormous lengths not to offend the Hun, sir. Not to give Hitler an excuse to invade."

"While that damned fool Chamberlain daren't so much as cough in church for fear of offending anybody!"

"Yes, well—"

"I beg your pardon. Interrupted you. Were you going to say the mining is going ahead, at last?"

"It is. In fact it was authorised for the 5th, three days ago, and then postponed to today. I believe most of the reason for the postponement was to give time for mounting a contingency plan, called R4, which involved putting our own troops into certain key ports—to forestall the Germans if they look like doing the same thing—which they might, as a reaction to our mining operations. Troops have actually been embarked—in the Clyde and at Rosyth; although in fact—" He checked what he was saying. "No. I must stick to the point. That was the reason, I think, for the postponement. And the PM imposed a condition on this plan R4—none of the troop-carrying force should be allowed to sail until or unless Germany actually attacked Norway. He's —as you say—very much concerned to be *correct*, in regard to Norwegian neutrality."

"He's an old woman, Wishart, in regard to anything you like. . . . How would he expect to know German intentions in time to sail the troops?"

"Submarine reconnaissance. We've a number of extra patrols out, in the Skagerrak and Kattegat. And—talking of submarines—Max Horton's quite sure they're on the point of invading."

Max Horton was the Vice-Admiral commanding the Submarine Service.

"Denmark as well as Norway. He's convinced it's imminent."

"Their Lordships disagree?"

"It's a matter of how one evaluates and interprets the Intelligence reports. You've got to allow the Admiralty the fact there've been literally months of false rumours: they've been conditioned against crying wolf. Personally I'll admit to bias, because as a submariner and an admirer of Max I'd tend to see it his way. And I don't have the entire picture; I'm without any real base there now, just a sort of temporary hanger-on putting an ear to whatever's audible."

Hugh Everard looked surprised. "I thought you were setting up a new section to do with

28

convoy planning and Board of Trade liaison, Wishart?"

"That was the case when Nick wrote to you, sir. But there's been a change. We're all a bit at sixes and sevens, just now. And my own days with dry feet are strictly numbered."

"Sea job?"

"Mediterranean, is all I know. Andrew Cunningham's asked for me, apparently."

"*Has* he, indeed." Hugh sat back, smiling. "I'd say that sounded *very* promising."

"Can't think of a man I'd sooner work for." Wishart watched his guest helping himself to buckling. "And Italy'll be joining in against us shortly, soon as Mussolini feels convinced the Germans have got us licked." The dish came round to his side; he told the waiter, "We'll have some thin brown bread and butter with this, please."

"Of course, sir."

Wishart said quietly, "It does mean I'm less well placed than I'd like to be from the point of view of assisting *you*, sir."

"Obviously. I'm sorry—if I'd known—"

"No, I'd like to help . . . But the snags are the same irrespective of what *my* job is, of course. Frankly—"

"My age."

"Well, yes. Even for convoy commodores—"

"I did hear that Eric Fullerton has got himself back to sea?"

29

"But—with respect, he's not sixty-nine years old."

"Not *quite*. But that, Wishart, is simply a statistic. What they should ask themselves is *can this fellow do the job*? And I'm as fit as many other men ten or fifteen years my junior. I *am*, damn it!" He pushed the bread-and-butter plate across the table. "Eric, of course, has Kitty pulling strings for him."

"Oh now, that's hardly—"

Wishart checked whatever protest he'd been about to make. Kitty Fullerton was Jackie Fisher's daughter. He'd forgotten, for a moment, the story of Hugh Everard's treatment at Fisher's hands, treatment that had pushed him out of the Navy a few years before the 1914 war. There was a follow-up story too—again, retailed by Nick— of history repeating itself in 1919. Not Fisher's doing, this second time; Fisher by then had been out of it, an old, sick man with only a year to live. But—Wishart wondered, studying his guest with interest as well as sympathy—was Hugh Everard a disappointed, *bitter* man? It had never occurred to him before: but wouldn't it be surprising in all the circumstances if he were not?

There was no doubt he'd had a rotten deal. *Two* rotten deals. And no doubt that his nephew, Nick, was now the centrepiece of his life. Knowing this, the prospect of telling him now about what must have been a murderously one-sided action in that North Sea gale only a few hours ago . . . Wishart admitted to himself, *All right: I am a coward. . . .*

The mind shied away, turned to another difficult but less positively hateful problem. This notion Sir Hugh had of getting to sea as a commodore of Atlantic convoys. Quite a number of retired admirals were being recalled in that capacity, certainly; and as likely as not Hugh Everard *was* as fit as many younger ones. But the line had to be drawn somewhere, and an even worse snag was that he'd been ashore since 1920.

"Something the matter, Wishart?"

"I was—thinking around this problem—"

"Some difficulty you haven't mentioned?"

Only a little thing like your nephew being dead . . .

"None that wouldn't have occurred to you, sir."

"I've no ties, you know. No old woman to worry about me!"

Hugh Everard had been married once: before the first war, so Nick had told him. He'd been divorced not long after he'd left the Service. Wishart had expressed surprise: all those years, and all the women who surely would have been only too ready to fall for the good-looking, distinguished admiral with the famous name? Nick had said something about Hugh having had his reasons: there was an impression of there being one woman, one particular and unnameable woman, with whom his uncle had been

31

in love for years and who wouldn't or couldn't marry him.

Someone else's wife?

Sir Hugh put down his knife and fork. "*Very* good." He looked at Wishart. "You're thinking of the length of time I've been retired, I suppose."

"It's—a factor that's bound to be considered."

"I retired four years ago, Wishart."

"*Four?*"

"From an active directorship of Vickers. I have never been out of touch with naval matters. On occasion I have even been to sea. I dare say I could tell *you* a thing or two about modern warship design, equipment, weaponry, what-have-you."

Wishart nodded. "It's a good point. But it might be argued that sea-going experience, *command* experience—"

"Wishart." Hugh Everard beckoned to him to lean closer across the table. He whispered, "As they say in the vernacular—*balls* . . ." Wishart sat back, chuckling. Sir Hugh asked him, "Anyway, is command at sea so very much changed from my day? If so, in what respect?"

"Well, we now have Asdics—"

"Which virtually any retired officer would have to learn something about. They sent Nick on some course, didn't they?" Wishart nodded. "What else is new?"

Quite a lot was new. But it was all detail. The

basics were the same. Wishart surrendered the point.

"When one thinks about it—darned little."

"Exactly!" A finger pointed at him. "And look here. Even if the technical changes were far greater than they are, it's quite irrelevant. A convoy commodore's job is to organise his convoy as it were domestically, internally. It doesn't overlap with the job of the escort commander—that's *another* kettle of fish. The commodore has to jolly his merchant skippers along, get 'em to understand the scheme of things and then play to the rules. More like being chairman of a company —in a slightly unsteady boardroom, eh?" He pointed at his own chest. "I have all the qualifications and experience that's needed. What's more, Wishart my boy, I shall damn well *do* it!"

"Good. And to whatever extent I can help I'll certainly—"

"No, no." Sir Hugh swivelled round to contemplate the steak-and-kidney. "Thank you, but I've plagued you enough. Only got on to you because of what Nick told me, that it was in your new department. Since it's not your part-of-ship at all, however—" he was helping himself to the pie, and sniffing like a Bisto Kid at the aroma which he'd released from its crust—"since you're making a move that's entirely in the right direction and which I'm truly delighted for your sake to hear about—" he put the tools down in the pie-dish—"no, I'm grateful for what you've

33

already tried to do, but I don't want you going to any further trouble."

"It's absolutely *no*—"

"I'm considering my own interests, really. It's results I'm after, and I'll attack on a different front now—when I've thought it out. . . . This does smell good!"

"Let's hope it is. Thank you, waiter." He reached for the wine bottle. "Now then . . ."

When the vegetables had been dispensed and the waiter had finally moved off, Hugh came back to the subject of Norway.

"You said 'the balloon's gone up.' And 'there's a flap on.' Mind telling me what it's about?"

"Well . . ." The essential thing was, not to know about this morning's action. There was no reason why one *should* have known. And Sir Hugh would hear soon enough; to keep one's mouth shut now wouldn't be doing him any harm. . . . "Well, for some days—couple of weeks, I suppose—rumours of a German plan to invade Norway and Denmark have been getting stronger and louder. Personally I—well, there is *no* doubt that they've been contemplating it off and on. For instance, they were right on the point of launching an invasion when we and the French were making noises about going through Norway to help the Finns. Then when the Finns chucked their hands in, of course, we shelved our plans and we *think* Hitler did something similar with his."

Russia had attacked Finland, without declaration of war, on 30 November—about four months ago. They'd expected to make a quick and easy meal of it, but the Finns fought back magnificently; in fact they fought the Soviets to a standstill. Then in February, just two months ago, a new Soviet offensive opened—better-trained troops in enormous strength, and massed artillery; and while Britain and France were still making plans to send men and supplies through Narvik and over the mountain railway to Lulea on the Gulf of Bothnia, Finland capitulated, on 12 March.

"Vian's rescue of our chaps from the *Altmark* may have been another factor. They've certainly used it as an excuse—violation of neutrality by *us*, for heaven's sake. . . . Anyway, we've been getting reports of ships assembling and embarking troops, and yesterday we were hearing of fleet movements northwards out of Kiel and Wilhelmshaven. So finally the Admiralty's taking notice." He glanced round again: nobody else was listening to him. He told Sir Hugh, "The Home Fleet's sailed. Cleared Scapa yesterday evening."

"Deploying where? On the Norwegian coast?"

"Well—no. The C-in-C seems to be staying out in the deep field. I'd—" he nodded—"as you suggest, or assumed—*I'd* be more inclined to put the whole lot in the slips."

"But that could be a terrible mistake, Wishart. Even if Horton's right and the Hun's going into

35

Norway, he might well try to kill two birds with one stone—invade behind an offshore covering force which would then pass on out to the North Atlantic. Eh?"

A break-out by German heavy ships was the danger which had kept Jellicoe's Grand Fleet stuck in the wastes of Scapa Flow twenty-something years ago. And it was the same thing now. The sea-lanes to and from North America and the tanker routes from the Gulf, supply and trooping convoys to the Middle and Far East and Australia —the whole strategy of Britain's war depended on keeping the Germans boxed in and those lifelines intact.

"Of course, you're absolutely right, sir. And for Sir Charles Forbes it's a ticklish dilemma, I imagine. But it seems to me that if the Germans get the Norwegian ports our job in maintaining any sort of blockade is going to be twice as difficult. In fact that's probably what they *want* that coast for—as well as safeguarding their iron-ore supplies, which is just about as vital, if not more so. . . . But Trondheim, for instance, as a base—even just for U-boats?" He spread his hands. "My bet is, it's going to happen. While we're covering the Iceland–Faroes Gap and our War Cabinet's murmuring 'After you, Adolf . . .'?"

"If I were in Forbes's shoes, *I'd* stay well out to sea. I'd send cruisers and destroyers inshore, and keep the battlefleet's options open until the last minute. . . . But—in general terms, what we need is Winston at the top. I mean, as Prime Minister."

Wishart smiled into his glass. He murmured, glancing up, "That move wouldn't be at all unwelcome in the Admiralty."

"Ah." Hugh Everard nodded. "Interfering again, is he?"

By "again", he was harking back to Churchill's stint as First Lord of the Admiralty in 1914 and '15. He was back in the same job now that he'd had then as a young man—a *very* young man who'd driven Jackie Fisher, a very *old* man, half out of his mind and into snarling retirement and senility.

Wishart said quietly, "He wants to row every boat himself. Despite a tendency to catch crabs." He shrugged. "Talking out of turn, of course. And I agree, he'd make a terrific PM. A bit of hard drive at the top is just what the country needs: instead of a wet flannel. And Winston might not have time, then, to play sailors . . ." Wishart snapped his fingers, as a thought struck him: "Sir Hugh—about this ambition of yours to get to sea—"

"Winston?"

"If you had him on your side—and you probably would have, because what he'll go for every time is positive action—"

"Yes. Yes, indeed." Hugh Everard frowned,

considering the idea. Wishart put in, "I'm sure he'd see you, if—"

"I dare say. I dare say . . . But—you'll think I'm daft, I suppose, but—frankly, I don't like to ask a favour of a politician. They're not safe hands to let oneself get into. Even if one might be prepared to believe that Winston's a cut above the others. . . ." He shook his head. "I had some experience of politicians, at one time."

"In 1919?"

"Oh." The blue eyes sharpened. "Did Nick tell you about it?"

Wishart nodded. "In confidence, of course."

"Even in confidence, I'm—surprised."

"Nick and I are close friends, Sir Hugh."

Are: or *were*?

"I'll give your suggestion a bit of thought, Wishart." He poked with his fork. "This pie's as good as I've ever had here."

"You've had a good few meals in the place, I imagine, over the years?"

"For a non-member, probably too many." He watched Wishart topping up their glasses. "I've belonged to Boodle's since the year dot, you see. Nick uses it too. And like me, when he left the Navy he didn't feel inclined to—so to speak, to hang around the fringes."

"I can understand that." Nick had said much the same thing, he remembered. He thought of something else that would help to keep the conversation on safe ground. . . . "I meant to ask

38

you—Nick's son, your great-nephew—any news of him?"

"Yes. He's away at sea now, but he came to visit me a couple of months ago. You know he joined on the lower deck?" Wishart nodded. Sir Hugh went on, "He was in Portsmouth barracks then. Pleasant lad. Plenty of fire in him—very like his father, you see. Just as damn pig-headed, anyway. And there's a Russian streak in this one, too! *What* a mixture!"

"A Russian Everard in square rig. Ye Gods!"

They both laughed. Wishart added, "Nick told me he was trying to push him into becoming a CW candidate, and not getting much response."

"CW" stood for Commissions and Warrants. A CW candidate was a sailor marked as potentially suitable for commissioned rank after a probationary period at sea on the lower deck. But you couldn't be forced to accept a candidacy if you didn't want it. Hugh Everard muttered, "Nick would be wiser to let the boy reach his own decisions. He isn't the sort to be pushed."

Wishart was glancing back over his shoulder, trying to contact their waiter. The boy sounded like a chip off the old block, he thought.

"What about the other one, the baby half-brother who went to Dartmouth?"

"You mean Jack."

Nick's stepmother, Sarah, had surprised everyone by producing a son in 1919. She'd been only thirty-one then, but Nick's father, Sir John, had been a lot older; they'd been married since 1912 and if they'd ever thought of starting a new family there had certainly been no such expectations in more recent years. And it had not been a happy marriage. But Nick, returning from his Black Sea adventures in 1920 and bringing with him his Russian countess wife, was introduced to a year-old half-brother—who at an early age had opted for a career in the Royal Navy and was now just twenty-one and a lieutenant.

Hugh had joined his host in the attempt to catch the waiter. What they were after was a Stilton which had passed by earlier on. Hugh said, "Jack's done very well, from all I hear. And keen as mustard, apparently. But—" he shook his head—"even with twenty-five years dividing 'em, you wouldn't imagine he could be Nick's brother. Or half-brother either."

"What's he doing now?"

"C-class cruiser, refitting up north. He wants to specialise as a navigator, when he's eligible for the Dryad course." Hugh had spotted the Stilton, and it was coming this way; some people at a table beyond this one were obviously waiting for it. He told Wishart, "Coming up on your quarter. *Now.*"

"Waiter—we'll have some of that, please."

"Well done!"

"Good scouting did it." He gestured to the waiter, who pushed his trolley up beside Sir Hugh. Presently, as the trolley squeaked away on

40

its interrupted journey, he asked, "The OD— Nick's son—"

"Paul."

"Yes, Paul. You said he's at sea now?"

"First ship. *Hoste.*"

"*Is* he, by golly!"

Hoste was one of the 2nd Destroyer Flotilla, who were at this moment somewhere up near Narvik with *Renown.* And with the 2nd Flotilla on this operation were several other destroyers, including *Intent.*

Sir Hugh, with an eyebrow cocked, was waiting for an explanation of that "By golly".

Wishart told him, cautiously, about the covering force for the minelaying operations, Admiral Whitworth with the battlecruiser and destroyers screening her. Then he stumbled to a halt: faced with the problem of mentioning or not mentioning Nick's ship. And suddenly the dam burst in his mind: it was impossible to sit here and *not* tell him. . . .

"There's something—a subject—which I've been trying to avoid, sir. Largely because we've had only disjointed signals and no confirmation —we don't know for sure at all, but—well, this morning, roughly off Trondheim—"

"*Hoste?*"

He shook his head. "*Intent.*"

The older man's flinch was so quickly controlled that if you hadn't been face to face

41

with him and only three feet away you might not have noticed it.

Wishart told him quietly, "*Intent* and other destroyers were with the 2nd Flotilla for this operation. The other 'I's were doing the mine-laying, but *Intent*'s the only one of them not fitted for it, you know."

"I didn't."

"*Gauntlet* had to turn back—day before yesterday—to look for a man lost overboard. Hopeless in that weather, but—" He checked that. The hopelessness of survival in that kind of sea was obvious and hardly a point to dwell on, in the circumstances. "Nick was detached to go back and locate *Gauntlet*. Mainly I suppose because of the stream of reports about German units sailing or about to sail. This morning just after eight *Gauntlet* sent an enemy report—investigating unidentified ship. Then a sighting report, two Hun destroyers, and finally it became one *Hipper*-class cruiser and 'engaging with torpedoes'. Some little while after that *Intent* signalled—this was the first we'd heard from her —'Am in company with *Gauntlet*, about to engage enemy cruiser with torpedoes, *Gauntlet* damaged in earlier attack.' Since then—well, nothing. And no reply to signals addressed to *Intent* and/or *Gauntlet*." Wishart finished, "It's gale-force from the north-west and conditions are pretty awful." He paused, and looked into that blue, unblinking stare. "I'm—so *dreadfully*—"

One of the hands moved, stopping the offer of sympathy. And the waiter had paused beside them with the trolley, on his way back across the room.

"Touch more of the Stilton while I'm this way with it, sir?"

Hugh shook his head. Wishart cleared his throat: "No, thank you."

The waiter began to move the trolley on; Sir Hugh told him, "That contraption could do with a spot of oil."

In the ante-room, drinking coffee, Hugh asked him, "What's being done?"

"Whitworth's turned south with *Renown*, hoping to intercept the cruiser—*Hipper*, whatever the damn thing is—and the C-in-C has detached *Repulse* with *Penelope* and some destroyers."

"Where's Forbes now?"

"North-east of the Shetlands. He's left now with *Rodney*, *Valiant* and *Sheffield*, plus destroyers. But Admiralty has now ordered the cruisers out too—which means disembarking their troops first."

Sir Hugh stared at him.

"Disembarking them?"

Wishart nodded. "They'd been embarked for this plan I was telling you about—R4. The idea was to be on the top line for moving troops into the main Norwegian ports once the Hun showed his intention of invading. Now, R4 seems to have gone by the board. The First Cruiser Squadron's being sailed from Rosyth as soon as the pongoes are all ashore, and *Aurora* and her destroyers from the Clyde. *Aurora* was going to escort the transports that we've had sitting there full of troops."

"So if the Hun *is* invading, we're giving him a free hand once he gets ashore?"

"I suppose the object is to *stop* him getting ashore."

"And d'you think we'll manage that?"

"Not if we stay out in the middle of the Norwegian Sea—no, I do not. . . . But as I did say, I'm not as well-informed as—"

"Sounds like the beginnings of a thorough-going mess-up, doesn't it."

He said no to the offer of a glass of port. And since they'd left the dining-room he hadn't mentioned *Intent* or Nick. He sighed now, blinking, like a man wishing he could escape from his own thoughts.

"Well. Splendid luncheon, Wishart. Most enjoyable."

"Hardly that, sir, I'm afraid."

"I'd better let you get back to work now, though. But—if by any chance you did hear anything—"

"I'll telephone. You'll be at home this evening?"

"Later on, I shall be. I've a thing or two to see

44

to before I get back on the train. I may even be in the Admiralty myself, by and by. Twist an arm or two about a job."

"I wish you success, sir."

"But they may not give me any news, d'you see. And I can't prompt 'em, because then I'd be letting 'em know you'd blown the gaff. So—"

"You could call me. Here." Wishart found a card and scribbled a number on the back of it. "This is my extension—temporarily. I'll try to wheedle any news there is out of Max Horton, if I can get in to see him. He gets shown everything, of course."

"You've been very kind. I appreciate it."

"If there's anything I can do at any time—"

"Thank you." Hugh stood up. Looking round the room, taking long, slow breaths; he seemed to be searching for faces that he might have recognised. And to have drawn a blank: he turned to Aubrey Wishart.

"Nick will be all right, you know."

The calm, relaxed tone of voice made the assurance almost convincing. But Wishart had a mental picture suddenly of that wilderness of sea and the gale's howl, the ice-grey emptiness: in his mind it *stayed* empty, a wild and bleakly inimical seascape with only the screeching gale-driven gulls as proof that any form of life existed there.

3

HIS MAJESTY'S destroyer *Hoste*, 1,490 tons displacement and 34,700 shaft horsepower, was being tossed around like a toy in a bathtub. And Paul Everard, huddled in stiff, ill-fitting oilskins in the lee of "B" gun, was enjoying every minute of it.

It was the contrast. The fact that he was feeling well, superlatively well, when for the last three days he'd felt that sudden death would have been a mercy.

He'd felt so ill, so locked in sickness that nothing in life, past, present or future, had been anything but nauseating to think about. Taunts and jokes from his messmates and from the others of this gun's crew—well, five out of the six others, because Baldy Percival had been just as sick—had, after a while, become easy to put up with. Just noises in the background, merging into the rattling, thumping, crashing of the ship, pounding of machinery, wind and sea noise. *Try a lump o'pork-fat on a lanyard, Yank—swaller it then 'aul it up again!* You could oblige them with a smile before you grabbed for the bucket: buckets being infinitely safer in this weather than getting anywhere near the ship's side. But what was worse than the gibes was the inner depression, the hopelessness engendered in one's own thoughts and memories. He'd even begun to attach importance to his mother's contemptuous disparagement of his plan to come to England and join up. . . . "Paul, honey, you're no dull-witted sailorman! You're civilised, you're smart, you're going to be *rich* one day!"

He'd told her—fond of her, devoted to her really, but aware that they'd never see eye to eye in certain major areas—"I'm an Everard."

"The hell you are. And *if* you are—just a lick of Everard, and that's all it could amount to—do yourself a favour and forget it! Be a Dherjho-rakov! Be even a *Scott*, for Christ's sake!"

Dherjhorakov had been her family name. Grafinya Ilyana Dherjhorakovna. Grafinya meaning countess. She'd had a brother Pavel who'd been murdered by the Bolsheviks during their escape, and one of the earlier battles she and Paul's father had had—this was one of her lines of reminiscence, how she and her first husband had fought all the time—had been whether to christen their son Pavel or Paul, which was the name's English equivalent.

Scott was the man she was married to now. He had a machine-tool business and the war wasn't doing him any harm at all.

His father must have won that row about the name. Paul wondered whether he'd ever won another. He'd met his father briefly in London after he'd first arrived from the States, and then at Christmas at Mullbergh, the family place in Yorkshire; before this, the last time they'd seen each other had been in 1930 when Paul had been just a child. Ilyana had effectively prevented correspondence during the intervening years. Paul's impression—well, one of his impressions —of Sir Nicholas Everard, Bart., was that he was as different from the woman he'd once been married to as one animal species is different from another. It was impossible to imagine him and Ilyana storming at each other. In the face of her outbursts—frenzies, furies or raptures, and all totally unpredictable—wouldn't he just have clammed up, walked away?

If Ilyana's stories were half true, no, he wouldn't. Maybe he'd changed? Or he'd been in an unnatural state of mind: meeting his son, and knowing she'd have told him about the past? Paul wanted to do her justice. Ilyana wasn't anything like the driven snow and the things she said to people weren't always God's literal truth, but in a situation like this, talking to her own son about his father when she'd known they'd be meeting sooner or later, would she have sent up that much smoke without fire?

Listening to old Sir Hugh—Paul had visited him at his house in Hampshire—you wouldn't think there were any weak spots anywhere, on Nick Everard. But nice as he was, the old boy was also strongly prejudiced; he'd gone to considerable lengths, for instance, not to mention Paul's mother's name.

Stay out of it. Yesterday and for two days and nights before that it felt like the weight of the world sitting on your shoulders, and no way out from under. It doesn't have to be like that, though, it *isn't*, it's not your lock to pick. Let it *stay* locked. And render unto Caesar: accept that Commander Sir Nicholas Everard is a hell of a fine sailor and seems a more than ordinarily nice guy. So all right, she wants to project a different view of him, *let* her.

Dozing . . .

Jammed in as close as possible behind the gunshield; not much space between the shield and the gun itself, and several other bodies in there too. At least they all wedged each other against the fiendish pitching and rolling, upward staggers and downhill rushes. Jolting, battering: rather like being in a motor-car that ran into a brick wall several times a minute and, in between the crashes, bounced up and down on solid tyres.

The saying was that the Navy used to have wooden ships and iron men, and now had iron ships and wooden men. But nothing made of wood and getting *this* treatment would have lasted long.

"Oy, you, Yank!"

Waking: aware at once of the enormous pleasure there was in simply feeling *well* . . .

"How's that?"

"Got yer 'ead down, 'ave you, Yank?"

Bow-down, and the vibration of racing screws shaking the whole ship, humming in her steel. Ventilator fans roaring. Solid water smashed against the other side of the gunshield, slashed at the bridge's forefront and the wheelhouse above their heads. He yelled as *Hoste*'s bow began its upward swing, "Want something?"

It was Vic Blenkinsop, the sightsetter, who'd shouted at him. Vic was sitting under the gun's breech-end with his knees drawn up as far as possible into cover, and as usual he had a length of spun-yarn as a belt around his oilskins. He also wore a red woollen cap under his tin hat, and the earphones of the telephone headset were pushed inside it with the helmet jammed down on top of everything and the curved headpiece hanging down in front, looping under Vic's bright-red nose. With that narrow, bony face he looked like Little Red Ridinghood's grandmother.

"What's up, Vic?"

"Char's up, that's what. In the galley. An' you're the lad to nip aft an' fuckin' fetch it."

"Okay."

He might have argued, just for the sake of an argument, but he was feeling too damn *good*. Not just healthy, but exuberantly so. His spirits matched—it occurred to him as he struggled out of the heap of men and out behind the gun— matched the ship's dance, the gale's roar. He felt like doing a fandango of his own: or bursting into song. . . .

Steady, boy. That's pure Dherjhorakov!

The fanny, tin receptacle for tea: or rather, for the dark-brown paint-remover which destroyer sailors referred to as tea: Lofty McElroy was passing the fanny out to him. Tea from the galley was a new idea, some kind of dummy-run for something called Action Messing.

"Thanks, Lofty."

"Don't go over the side, lad, ay?"

"Lofty, I am profoundly moved—" he bowed, with a hand grasping the edge of the gunshield —"by your consideration for the safety of my person. Had I not heard this with my own ears—"

Ducking sideways to avoid flying sea, he'd staggered and fetched up hard against the loading-tray. If his ribs hadn't been padded by two sweaters and the oilskin, they'd have suffered worse. McElroy yelled, "All I'm considerin', Yank, is the safety of my fuckin' tea. Get a wriggle on, willya?"

Wind and sea were on *Hoste*'s starboard side. Checking on this before choosing his route to the galley, Paul looked out across a heaving grey-white foreground, saw other destroyers strung out in line abreast, battling through the storm. Two, he'd seen then: and far apart, so there'd be one between them and temporarily hidden in a trough. Eight altogether, he thought; there'd

51

been nine before, and now the battlecruiser, *Renown*, had left them and taken one destroyer with her. Nobody knew much about what was going on; and during the last few days he'd been too ill to care. All he knew was they'd come a long way north, so far north that there was hardly any period of darkness. In another month, in these latitudes, there'd be none at all. Land of the midnight sun . . . Well, presumably there *was* land not far off, but if it had any mid*day* sun, even, it was hogging it all to itself. He went down the port ladder, the leeward side, to the foc's'l deck, and turned aft—keeping close in against the wet grey-painted steel of the bridge superstructure—past the screen door and down the ladder at the foc's'l break. The whaler was creaking in its davits, straining against its gripes as the ship rolled over, over—almost *right* over —while he held on tight to the bottom of the ladder. If you went over the side, in this stuff, even if someone saw you go they'd never find you: you'd be *gone*, finished. Now she was rolling back: he reached the galley door, pulled the one retaining clip off it, climbed in over the foot-high sill and slammed and clipped the door behind him.

"Gawd, it's the stars and fuckin' stripes. An' better late than never. 'B' gun, is it?" Paul nodded. Perry, the duty cook, was too scrawny to be much of an advertisement for his own art. Crew-cut, and in a boiler-suit draped in loose

52

folds around him but sleeveless, sleeves torn off so that his long arms, stringy-muscled, extruded like white tentacles. A cigarette-stub was stuck to his lower lip. *Hoste* carried two ordinary cooks and one leading cook, and Perry was about as ordinary, Paul thought, as a cook could get to be. Although—when you saw him here in the galley —you had to admire anyone who could cook anything in this cramped black hole: even if the ship stood *still* occasionally. . . .

One of the arms came out, clawing for the fanny.

"Right then."

Two other men were in here, over on the other side. Green, a telegraphist, and a man called Cringle who was either a bridge messenger or a lookout.

"Did say 'B' gun, didya?"

"Absolutely, old pip."

It was intended to sound ultra-British and thus, from someone they all called "Yank", amusing. But it seemed to annoy Cringle.

"Tryin' to sound like 'is dad."

"Eh?" The cook, with Paul's tea-fanny under the urn's tap and brown liquid gushing into it in a steamy jet, looked over his shoulder at the messenger. "Whose Dad?"

Cringle jerked his head. "The Yank. 'Is guv'nor's skipper of the *Intent*. The one Sparks 'ere says 'as bought it."

53

Silence. Perry looking at *him* now as he turned the tap off. Cringle's words sinking in slowly.

"Now wait a minute." Questions were forming on top of each other, out of complete surprise and—already—an unwillingness to believe. . . . How did anyone know about his father? And *Intent*—was she around, even right here with them, one of the ships he'd been looking at? But then—*no* . . . That expression "bought it"; it was current slang, over this side, for *busted, shot*. Disliking Cringle, he looked at Green: all telegraphists were called "Sparks".

"What *is* this? D'you mind?"

Green shrugged, stared blankly at the cook. Perry looked at Cringle, who told him, "I 'eard 'em 'aving a natter on the bridge. *Intent* got sent off—yesterday, was it?" Green nodded, staring at Paul now. Cringle went on, "On account that other—*Gauntlet*, ain't she—'adn't showed up still. Forenoon today there's this palaver goin' on, skipper an' Jimmy, an' Jimmy asks, 'What about this Everard lad what's the son of *Intent*'s captain, the OD we got aboard 'ere?'—sort o' thing. Skipper rubs 'is nut a while, then 'e says no, 'e says, don't tell 'im, *Intent* might still turn up, no use warmin' the fuckin' bell, 'e says. Aye aye, says Jimmy. Well, later on I gets talkin' with Subby Peters, an' 'e says yeah, you're right, 'e says, but best keep your fuckin' mouth shut, see."

Paul took the fanny, hot and heavy now, from

54

Cook Perry. He rested it on his own end of the stove, holding on to it so it wouldn't slide or slop: and one hand on the door, so *he* wouldn't slide. He looked at Cringle as the ship dipped, jolting, stubbing her bow into the sea, shaking as if she was trying to bore her way into something solid.

Did that bastard know what he'd just told him?

"That's what you're doing, Cringle, is it? Keeping your fucking mouth shut? D'you do much of that, with your mouth? Maybe you've nothing *else* to do it with?"

Hate and rage were sudden, overwhelming. A cold rage. Not reasoning: just *there*.

"I'll shut *your* mouth, my little Yanky-lad!"

He was trying to push past Perry. Five or six years older than Paul, a head taller and a lot heavier. It made no odds at all. Everything contributed: the whole damn set-up, and the fact there was nothing he could do about it. What he felt—or did not feel—about his father was a background to the questions that weren't answered, only *raised*: like was any of this story true, had *Intent* been here and where was she now, what if anything had happened while he'd been spewing and feeling sorry for himself. You were born into a situation that wrapped itself around you and you couldn't influence or change: then other things developed out of it and you were still helpless, shut off, impotent.

He could do something about this bastard

Cringle, though. That thick, soft-looking throat: hit there first, then—

The cook planted a hand on Cringle's chest and pushed him back. The cook, like Paul, was a smaller man than Cringle; those stringy muscles must have had steel wire in them. One-handed, he'd not only stopped the larger man but actually moved him backwards—as if he'd had castors under him.

Paul said, "I'd be obliged if you'd let him pass."

"Don't give a tinker's fart about obligin' you, old son." Perry hadn't looked round. He told Cringle in just as pleasant a tone of voice, "Bugger off. Out me galley, pronto. An' when it's me on watch, *stay* out."

"Never mind your galley, chum, I'll shove you in your fuckin' *oven!*"

Cringle, half-turning his head, for some reason assumed that the telegraphist, Green, was joining the opposition. He swept an arm back, flinging Green against the starboard-side door as the ship rolled that way, helping him. . . . But she was holding that steep list. Altering course? Cringle had an upward slope to climb if he was going to reach the cook; he grasped the rail that ran along the front edge of the stove and began to haul himself along it. Paul was clinging to the other door, behind him, to save himself from being thrown downhill, and only Cook Perry, in the middle, was keeping an easy balance.

He'd also picked up a knife. It had a blade about nine inches long. Without looking down at it he was stropping it expertly on the horny palm of his left hand. He asked Cringle, "Comin', then?"

Silence, except for the racket all around them. The ship was still heeling hard to starboard. Probably had port wheel on, making a biggish change of course. Cringle was staring at the knife, immobile. Perry put it down.

"Your mates 'll be wanting their char, won't they." He looked round at Paul. "*You* better scram, too." He waved his arms, like shoo-ing chickens. "G'arn—sod off, the lot of you!"

"Hey—just a minute . . ."

"Now *look*, I said—"

"This stuff about *Intent*," Paul asked Green, "is it true?"

"Didn't you know?"

"For Christ's sake, how *could* I?"

One grey destroyer shape was very much like another. Particularly the G, H, and I classes, which were all practically identical. In any case, he hadn't been doing much looking.

"*Gauntlet* lost some sod overboard and turned back for 'im. Two or three days back. Then they reckon she shouldn't be on her tod like, so *Intent* goes to round 'er up. The pair of 'em fetch up against bloody *Scharnhorst* or something, they gets one message out, and *wallop*."

Paul stared at him. Why would anyone make up such a story?

"This true?"

It couldn't be. He *knew* it couldn't.

"It's the buzz." Green shrugged. "Well, more 'n a buzz, really. I don't see ciphers—we take 'em down coded like. But—you 'ear this an' that, and—"

He stopped talking: the cook, with his boiler-suited back to Paul, must have been making faces at him. Green looked at Paul now as if he was realising for the first time what it added up to.

"Sorry, Yank. If—" he jerked his head backwards—"if bloody Cringle 'adn't—"

"It's all right."

Perry turned round; both of them were looking at Paul with a mildly sympathetic interest. Paul couldn't remember exactly how the row with Cringle had started. He'd wanted to kill him, he knew *that* . . . He wasn't sure some of it hadn't been his own fault.

"I don't know why I lost my temper."

Perry nodded. "You want to watch that, lad."

The Dherjhorakov factor? He'd found it surfacing before, once or twice. And Perry was right, it did need watching.

Green said, "Buzzes don't always get it right. Shouldn't let it bother you too much."

"No, I won't." He picked up the fanny. "Thanks, Cookie."

"Oy!"

58

"What?"

The cook told him, "We've altered course. Best use the other door."

"Taken your time, Yank, ain't you?"

"Slight problem in the galley."

"Yeah?"

"Nothing much." He stooped, pushing the fanny in towards McElroy. "It's still hot, anyway."

"I should fuckin' 'ope so!"

He sat down on the deck with his own mug of the so-called tea. At least it warmed you. He had never, he realised, given much thought to being sunk or blown up. One should, he supposed; there was obviously a reasonable chance of it happening, and if you thought about it in advance it wouldn't take you so much by surprise. You might even subconsciously have some ideas mapped out so that when or if it did happen you'd react without panic or too much dithering. . . . He—Paul—happened to be an unusually strong swimmer; at prep—Taft, in Connecticut, where the Scott home was—he'd captained the school team; and swimming hadn't done him any harm, he thought, in Amherst's acceptance of him after he'd graduated from Taft. As it turned out, he spent less than half a year at Amherst, which had been his stepfather Gerry Scott's old Ivy League Alma Mater. Scott had been very decent, despite that, about Paul's insistence on dropping out and coming to England, to England's war. His attitude had been one of regret but resignation: a marked and welcome contrast to Ilyana's hysterical opposition. But it hadn't been a choice, for Paul. And less impulse, he thought now, than instinct, a kind of personal compulsion.

Would a German ship stop to pick up survivors?

You heard and read conflicting stories. He thought it would most probably depend on the character of the individual commander, and perhaps also on the circumstances, whether he'd feel safe in stopping to pick them up.

He remembered an incident he'd read about, where three British cruisers were torpedoed in the English Channel, in the last war, by one U-boat. It had got the second and the third when they were lying stopped, saving men from the first. It had always seemed to Paul quite extraordinary—to treat human beings like bugs, things of no importance, flies to be swatted. . . . And if that was the way they were fighting *this* war. . . .

Face it. You no longer have a father.

Running on from that, another thought: Ordinary Seaman Sir Paul Everard, Bart.?

The idea was laughable, but he couldn't raise even an inward smile at it. Why, though, should the prospect be so—*disturbing*, to one who'd had no contact with his father in nearly ten years and perhaps wouldn't have been about to have any now if this war hadn't started?

Jammed just inside the edge of the gunshield, half in cover as *Hoste* flung herself about and sea lashed continuously against the shield, ringing hard like hail, he thought about the two days he'd spent at Mullbergh at Christmas. His father, standing more or less eye-to-eye with him—Paul had been surprised to find he wasn't taller, having always thought of him as a big man—saying, "For what it's worth, this place'll be yours one day. If it still belongs to us at all."

"Must be quite a—quite expensive to maintain?"

"It is. Even *half* maintaining it as we are now. Costs always tend to rise faster than revenue, you know. But at least the estate's in sound order now, the farms show profits and their tenants have roofs over their heads that don't leak. To that extent we've stopped the rot—given ourselves a bit more time. That's what's kept me busy since I left the Service—making the old place earn its keep."

"Didn't your—my grandfather, I mean— didn't *he*, in his time?"

"No." Nick kicked a log in towards the flames. "No, he did not. He put nothing back, ever, just took out all he could. To no good purpose whatsoever. Well, he ran our local pack of hounds, and paid for it all out of his own pocket."

Nick shrugged. "Some people would call *that* a good purpose. I don't know."

Ilyana had told Paul that Sir John had been a sweet old guy. He himself barely remembered his grandfather at all.

"I can't give you much of the family history in just two days. What's more, they'd be better spent enjoying ourselves. And for you, getting the feel of the place. Don't suppose you remember it very clearly, do you? But—" his hand closed on Paul's arm—"there really is the dickens of a lot to talk about, things you ought to know and understand. When time and Their Lordships permit I'd like you to come here for a good long stay. I suppose that means when you and I have long leave simultaneously." He raised his eyebrows: "*If.*"

"Or we might win the war, then *really* have time?"

"Better still." His father had smiled. "It won't be done in just a year or two, I'm afraid. But tomorrow, I'll show you round the whole estate. Also tomorrow, I have to attend Morning Service. Perhaps you would too?"

"Please."

"Good. Now then, Paul. I'm not—how shall I put it—I'm not very well house-trained, at this juncture. Domestic and family routines, I mean —I've lived here alone, pretty well, since 1930, and I've acquired—degenerated into—bachelor

62

habits. You may find me a little—well, *rough*, in some ways—"

"Isn't—my step-grandmother, do I call her?"

"Sarah?"

"Sure. Isn't she around—kind of a feminine influence on things?"

"She's 'around', as you call it, in the sense that she lives in the Dower House, about half a mile away. I had it done up for her when my father died, and she and her son Jack have lived there ever since. Remember Jack?"

"Ah—not *well*, but—"

"You'll be seeing him this evening. They're dining here—he was due to arrive some time this afternoon, I think Sarah said. But you were asking whether Sarah's presence hasn't kept me civilised—"

"Not, if I may say so, that I've noticed anything *un*civilised, so far."

His father had smiled. "Early days yet, old chap. But you may be right, Sarah may have stopped me running *completely* to seed. But what I was going to say, Paul—this Christmas business, I'm no use at wrapping things up, sticking candles on trees, all that business. But I do have a present for you. As a matter of fact I've been keeping it for you for quite a long time and rather looking forward to handing it over. So—just come along, would you?"

He'd led the way out into an ice-cold corridor and along it for about forty yards and then down a short flight of steps to an oak door. The room they went into was even colder than the corridor.

"Gunroom." Nick pointed. "As you see."

Most of one wall was occupied by a glass-fronted cupboard which had a whole rack of firearms in it. Nick Everard said, turning a key that had been in the lock to start with, "We still have some good shooting here—even with only one keeper who should have retired five or six years ago. My father had him and three others under him—*and* they were kept busy. D'you do any shooting over there, Paul?"

"Oh, I've hunted a little. With a college friend whose father—"

"Delighted to hear it. But I was asking about shooting."

"Oh. Well, we call—I guess what you call shooting, over there is called hunting?"

"How extraordinary." Nick turned round. He had a shotgun in each hand, double-barrelled twelve-bores that looked as if someone had just been cleaning them. Gleaming, beautiful-looking guns. His father said, "These are yours. Made by Purdy. It's a pair that was your grandfather's. You won't find better guns anywhere in the world."

"Why, they're—*lovely!*"

He took one, turning it in his hands, feeling its balance. "I—really, I don't know what to say. Except 'thank you' . . ." He put it to his shoulder. "Seems about right, too. I—"

"Should be. You're about the same build. But nothing'll beat a Purdy, and this is a particularly fine pair. Look after them, Paul."

"I sure will!"

"They're quite safe here, for the time being. For ever, if you choose to keep them here. . . . D'you realise that if I should get drowned or something silly of that sort, you'd just walk in here and it's yours?"

He'd said something of that kind a short while ago. Must have it on his mind? Paul said, "I'd prefer it if you did not."

"Eh?" Over his shoulder, as he put the guns back in the rack.

"I'd sooner you did *not* get drowned."

"Very decent of you." Turning back, he smiled. Paul thought it was the first real, deep smile he'd seen on his father's face; he realised too that he was returning it—because it was natural and he couldn't help it. Nick Everard said, "But it could happen. So there are one or two things you must know about. There's a lawyer-chap in Sheffield, for instance, who's supposed to know all there is to know. And a lot of detail, of course, Sarah could put you on to. . . ." He shook his head. "Later, all that. We'll get back to the fire now and have a snifter before it's time to change. . . . You do drink, I hope?"

They were relieved at 1600 by the crew of "A"

65

gun, who however took over on "B" gundeck. At this "degree of readiness" one gun was kept manned for'ard and one aft; torpedo tubes were manned and ready and so were the depthcharge traps and throwers, but two of the four-sevens were considered enough, and "B" and "X", being on raised gundecks, were the obvious ones to use.

Paul went down to the seamen's messdecks, two decks below the foc'sl, to shed his wet gear and clean up, warm up. To get to the messdeck you went down the ladder and aft to the screen door that led in below the bridge, and across to the starboard side and then for'ard along a narrow passage which had doors off it to such things as the wireless office and the TS, transmitting station. Then you passed a sliding steel door that led into the washplace, and at this point you were entering the messdeck.

Low-roofed, cluttered, foul-smelling. Lockers ran along the ship's sides port and starboard, and there were racks above them for bulky gear like kitbags and suitcases. Scrubbed-wood tables on both sides, and each pair of them constituted a separate mess. The nearest was 5 Mess, and the next was 4; then came the central, circular support of "A" gun, and for'ard of that interruption were numbers 3, 2 and 1 Messes, number 1 being right for'ard where the compartment began to narrow. Paul belonged to 3 Mess, the one just past "A" gun's support.

You had to stoop to avoid slung hammocks. It

was like groping your way into a long, narrow, highly mobile cave. The movement was greater here, of course; the further you went from the centre of the ship, the bigger was the rise and fall. The smell was of dirty clothes, *wet* clothes, unwashed bodies, cigarette-smoke, vomit.

Home.

Dripping oilskins—Paul's, for instance, and other men's when they came down off watch—didn't make it any drier. Rubbish—cigarette packets, sweet-papers, crusts, tea-leaves—drifted in a scummy mess, to and fro as the ship rolled. There was an attempt at a clean-up every now and then, but the place was too crowded with men and gear to be got at effectively, when the ship was at sea. Especially in this kind of weather.

"You're in luck, lads." Brierson, leading seaman of 3 Mess, pointed at the tea-urn. "Only just wet it." Brierson was a thickset man with curly yellow hair and rather battered features; he was sitting on the lockers at the end of the table, on the ship's starboard side, reading a torn, week-old copy of the *Daily Mirror*.

"Nice work, Tom." But he waited, to let Baldy Percival—Baldy being a messmate as well as one of the crew of "B" gun—help himself first. This was Baldy's first ship too; he was as green to the Navy as Paul was. He smiled courteously; he'd been a Boots librarian, in civvy street.

"After you."

"Okay."

Brierson glanced up, stared at Baldy, winked at Paul, looked down at the strip-cartoon of Jane again. On the near-side of the table Randy Philips said to Whacker Harris—they were both regulars, as opposed to "HO", Hostilities Only ratings, like Paul and Baldy—"After *you*, Claud."

"Oh *no*, Wilberforce, after *you*."

Brierson glanced up again. "You're after *every* bugger."

The ship climbed a mountain, tottered on its crest, rolled on to her port side and dropped like a stone. Harris said, "Gettin' bumpy." Paul took his mug along behind him and Philips and sat down near the leading seaman.

"Have a word with you, Tom?"

"S'a free country."

There was noise enough to allow one to talk quietly, at close range, without being overheard. Paul asked him, "D'you think I could get to see the skipper?"

Brierson put his paper down, lifted his mug and took a long, noisy sip of tea. Then he smacked his lips, and rested the mug on his knee, tilted his head sideways and stared at Paul.

"What for?"

"It's private. But—okay, but in confidence?" The killick nodded. He told him, "There was a destroyer with us, not one of our lot, one called *Intent*. My father's in her. But she's not with us now, and there's this buzz that she's been in action and—well, could have been sunk or—" he shrugged—"something."

"Don't want to believe all the buzzes you hear, lad."

"I know. But—I could ask the skipper, couldn't I?"

"S'pose you could." Brierson swallowed some more tea. Then he pointed aft and upwards. "Nip up to the Chiefs' mess, see the cox'n, tell 'im what it's about. 'E might take you to Jimmy, more likely than the skipper."

"Jimmy" meant the first lieutenant.

"Okay. Thanks."

"What is he, your guv'nor?"

"He was out of the Navy, now he's back in for the war."

"Yeah, but I mean, what *is* he?"

"Does it matter?"

"Eh?" Brierson looked surprised. Then he shrugged. "No. Not to *me*."

"Thanks. It's just—"

"No skin off *my* nose."

"Wait here, Everard."

"Right, Chief."

CPO Tukes had brought him up to this lobby which was one level down from the compass platform. A door in the for'ard bulkhead led into the signal and plotting office, and the two on the other side were chartroom to port and captain's sea-cabin to starboard.

69

By the feel of it, *Hoste* was steaming more or less into wind and sea. Or possibly—judging by the amount of roll—the main force of it was just on her bow. The roll, combined with violent pitching, was giving her a sort of corkscrew motion. He propped himself against the after bulkhead, between the two doors. There might be a long wait now, he thought; he'd heard that the skipper hardly ever left the bridge at sea, particularly in rough weather and with other ships in company, and you'd hardly expect him to come rushing down immediately just at the request of some OD.

This was a *hell* of a motion!

Someone was coming up the ladder from below. . . .

It was Sub-Lieutenant Peters. Dressed for watchkeeping, by the look of him. Peters was short, round-faced; he paused between one ladderway and the next, and looked at Paul.

"You're Everard, aren't you?"

"Yes, sir."

Peters was disconcerted. He knew about *Intent* —that fink Cringle had discussed it with him— and who Paul was, but he didn't know that Paul knew. It was awkward for him. Paul said, to give him a hint and make it easier, "I'm hoping to see the captain, sir. Cox'n's asking him if I can."

"Oh." Peters nodded. "Right you are, then." He started up the ladder to the bridge. Probably quite a pleasant guy, Paul thought. His own age,

70

near enough. As, of course, was Lieutenant Jack Everard. And if he—Paul—encountered his "half-uncle" Jack at sea, he'd have to call *him* sir, too!

On the evening before Paul had left home, Ilyana had gone off the deep end about lots of things, including Jack and Sarah. A surfeit of dry martinis had paved the way; then he'd happened to mention Jack, whom he'd last seen when they'd both been children—and come to think of it, hadn't got on with too well. . . . Ilyana had accused him, "You don't *believe* me about your father's darling little Sarah, huh? Don't like to think it of your daddy? Well, you listen, Pavvy boy—if Baby Jack's your father's brother and not his *son*—sure, you heard me—if Jack's not Nick's *son*, so help me I'm the Pope's aunt! When I first set eyes on that kid—and listen, I was bigger than a house with *you*, at that time—I just turned around to Nick and yelled '*Snap!*' And guess what? Little Sarah turned the brightest shade of pink you ever saw!"

But Jack Everard, at Mullbergh this Christmas, had turned out to be quite *un*like Nick Everard. He was taller, slighter, and different in manner and personality too. He had a rather plummy way of talking, and his manner had been condescending, with a sort of shallow jocularity which Paul had found irritating. It was so obviously false. Paul *knew* that Jack resented him; resented his being here, and probably the fact that he was

71

the heir to Mullbergh; this last he only guessed at, because there had to be some reason for that disguised but almost palpable hostility. And as for Sarah—well, what Ilyana had said about her could only be a product of that wild Slav imagination. Sarah was dry, thin-lipped, with a figure like a broomstick and not even a speck of powder on her pale, shiny face. Grey hair drawn back severely into a bun . . .

Sarah was *nobody's* "little darling". She never *could* have been!

She obviously doted on her son—in a stiff, school-marmy way—and was spinsterishly diffident with Paul. Small, frozen smiles, little bursts of talk for talk's sake. About her late husband, Paul's grandfather; what a fine judge of a horse he'd been, what a great master of hounds, how the whole county missed him. And about local charity committees and war work: she ran some bunch of women who were knitting seaboot stockings and sweaters and sending them off to ships at sea. And decorating the church for tomorrow's service . . . The meal would have been a lot more enjoyable, Paul had thought, if there'd been any possibility of truth in Ilyana's accusations—which all too plainly there could not be. In fact it seemed to him that there was a kind of wall between his father and Lady Sarah: and also as if Jack was a puzzle to Nick, a cuckoo in the nest whom he'd given up trying to fathom.

Paul was certain it had been as much of a relief

for his father as it was for himself when Sarah and Jack said goodnight and went back to Dower House. They were alone then: Nick had sent his butler, a very old man named Barstow, away to bed an hour ago. He'd explained, "I want the old chap to last as long as possible. Shan't ever be able to replace him."

He suggested now, "Nightcap?"

Paul had thought he was being offered something to keep his head warm. His father thought this was very funny.

"A final drink before bed, old chap. I'd suggest —I've a rather splendid malt here. Know what that is?"

"I can't say I do."

"Your education's been neglected, in some areas. We'll have to fill in the gaps. Starting now. A malt is a real Scotch whisky, as opposed to the cheap blends, which are a comparatively modern innovation. This particular malt is called Laphroaigh—and I'll lay you half a crown you can't spell it. . . . What d'you make of Jack?"

"Jack. Well . . ." Paul stooped to do something unnecessary to the fire. "I hardly talked enough with him to have much of an opinion."

"Hmm." Nick had some bottles on a sidetable. He said, with his back to the room and to Paul, "He's done extraordinarily well, in what you might call the early promotion stakes— courses, exams, and so on. Infinitely better than I ever did. Tell you the truth, I hated every minute of my time at Dartmouth. But he loved it, you see. Extraordinary." He turned, with a glass of brownish liquor in each hand. Remembering the moment, Paul could see him as if he was looking at a snapshot: a man of medium height, wide-shouldered, a fighter's build. Dark hair with no grey in it yet. A stern, even harsh expression; but it was a harshness that broke up and vanished when he smiled.

"Now then. Try this."

Liquid gold, he remembered: golden fire. Nectar. Glorious. He'd said, "If this is how I get educated, I can stand a lot of it." Thinking back to it, to the whole *ambience* and feel of that evening, made him long to be beside that great log fire again with his father lifting a glass and murmuring, "Here's to us, Paul."

Oh, Christ . . .

Like cold grey sea washing over your mind.

And seaboots were clumping down the ladderway. He pushed himself off the bulkhead, pulled himself to attention as CPO Tukes snapped, "Ordinary Seaman Everard, sir!"

Paul saluted. The skipper—he was a lieutenant-commander and his name was Rowan —said, "All right, cox'n. Thank you. Come in here, Everard." He slid back the door of the chartroom and went inside, and Paul followed him. "Shut the door, so we'll be left in peace." He pulled back the hood of his duffle, then took his cap off and flung it on the settee which the

74

navigating officer, at sea, used as a bunk. Rowan was swarthy, brown-haired and brown-eyed, in his late twenties or thirty, thirty-one. He told Paul, "For God's sake, stand easy."

"Aye aye, sir."

"Stand easy, Everard, means relax."

"Yes. I'm—very grateful to you, sir, for—"

"I know what it's about. I only wish I was in a position to give you some kind of reassurance. But—well, all I *can* give you is as much information as I have myself."

Paul nodded. It couldn't be as bad as he felt in his bones it was going to be. If it was, he didn't want to know. . . .

Don't be stupid. You have *to know.*

"Here we are." Rowan pulled one chart out of the way, clearing the one that had been lying under it. Paul saw its title: *NORWAY: Lindesnes to Nordkapp.* Rowan pointed with a pair of brass dividers. "Here's Trondheim. Not so far off it— here—*Intent* and *Gauntlet* were in action between 0800 and 0900 this morning with what *Gauntlet* reported as a *Hipper*-class cruiser." His pointers moved up the chart. "We're here. Roughly a hundred and fifty miles farther north . . . Everard, I'd give my right arm to be able to say to you, 'Don't worry, your father will be all right.' I can't say that, though, because all I know is that the pair of them were about to make a torpedo attack on this enemy cruiser, and from then on we've heard nothing. You must realise—

I'm sorry, but it's best to face it—it *could* mean the worst. I'd be lying to you if I pretended anything else."

"Yes. I appreciate—"

"But it's possible they were damaged and can't use W/T. There've been air searches for them during the day, but in this weather it'd be fifty to one against finding them. We do know *Gauntlet* was badly damaged in the early stages of the engagement—no such indication about *Intent*. There could easily be some good reason for her being off the air."

"If she'd been sunk—" Paul heard the artificiality in his own voice, the result of trying to sound unworried—"would there be much chance of some of them surviving? The action first, and then being rescued?"

"Yes. To both questions. But—it's guesswork, obviously."

Paul met his captain's eyes. "On what's known, sir—it's *probable* they were sunk?"

Rowan grimaced: disliking the question. Then he shrugged.

"That's the guess one would make if one had to, Everard. But truly, you can't be sure at all. And remember too—when ships get sunk, nine times out of ten there *are* some survivors."

"Yes." He thought, *That's it, then.* And then, *For God's sake, what was I hoping he could tell me?*

Rowan tapped the chart. "We're here now,

76

as I said. Steering west—on this course. This pencilled track, d'you see?"

They seemed to be heading a long way out from that indented and chewed-up-looking coastline.

"We were supposed to stick around in the entrance to—here, this place, Vestfjord. At the top of it, you see, you come to Narvik. For various reasons Narvik's of particular strategic value, and we don't want the Hun getting any ships in or troops ashore. But now—" he pointed again at the pencilled line—"we've had an order direct from the Admiralty in London to come out and rendezvous with *Renown* again. She went off southwards, earlier in the day, in the hope to finding this cruiser we've been talking about— the one that was in action with *Gauntlet* and *Intent*. With this new order, though, she's turned about in order to come back up and meet us."

"Nobody's left to watch the entrance to the fjord now?"

Rowan, staring down at the chart, sighed.

"A good question, Everard. But ours is not to reason why." He looked at him. "I'm extremely sorry about your father. About the uncertainty, that is . . ." Then he changed the subject: "I'm told you expressed no enthusiasm for being considered as a CW candidate. Is that right?"

It was an effort to switch one's mind. . . .

"Well, sir, I felt I'd sooner not put in for it right away, that's all. I'd rather—well, if I could

77

get there on my own showing, so to speak, I'd feel I'd *earned* it."

"A CW candidate does earn it, Everard. He has a probationary period at sea, and during that time he's under observation. Only if he comes out of it with the right recommendation does he go through for his commission."

"But wouldn't I have been selected in the first instance on account of—well, my father, and—"

"No, you would not. You'd have been selected because you look like suitable material. We've a huge construction programme, an enormous expansion of the fleet—small ships particularly—sloops, corvettes, destroyers. So we're going to have to train a lot of new officers, and the kind we want are those with the educational background to pick up knowledge quickly and the intelligence then to use it effectively. One or two other qualities as well—some of which, you may be surprised to hear, *are* very often passed from father to son. . . . It's not what would or would not be nice for *you*, Everard, it's a question of what the Navy needs."

Quite a new angle. If you could keep your mind on it. . . . Rowan said, "Think about it. And meanwhile, anything I hear about *Intent* I'll—"

"Bridge, chartroom!"

Disembodied voice squawking from a voice-pipe on the centre-line bulkhead. Rowan had slid over to it.

"Chartroom. Captain speaking."

"*Renown* bearing red three-oh four miles steering north, sir!"

It sounded like Peters' voice. Rowan snapped, "I'm coming up." Paul slid the door open and stood aside as the skipper snatched up his cap, shot out and bounded up the ladder.

4

*I*NTENT was coming sluggishly round to the new course, rolling more violently as she turned her quarter instead of her stern into the north-westerly gale. She was a cripple, crawling to find shelter where she could lick her wounds.

And *Gauntlet* was sunk, as likely as not with all hands. Should he have held her back, taken charge of the attack, risking loss of contact with the enemy?

"Course south seventy-three east, sir!"

"Very good." Steering by magnetic because lack of generator power had put the gyro out of action. What would a court martial decide, he wondered: that the loss of *Gauntlet* was at least partly due to his, Nick Everard's, negligence?

Wind and sea astern had helped *Intent* to make good an average of just over five knots throughout the day. It was 1800 now, 6 pm. That tripod and beacon marking a shoal to port was Nylandskjaer light, and if CPO Beamish managed to keep the screws turning for a few more hours, in about a dozen miles they'd be at the entrance to Namsenfjord.

Beamish was *Intent*'s Chief Stoker. He was in charge of her machinery now for the simple reason that all the other senior men were dead. Mr. Waddicor, Chief Engineroom Artificer Foster and ERA Millinger had all been killed when that shell had struck and burst in the engine-room. Leading Stoker Brownrigg had also been killed outright, and the only other men who'd been in the compartment, Stoker Hewitt and ERA Dobbs, weren't going to live. So the doctor, Bywater, said. They were in his sickbay, two ladders down below the bridge. Dobbs wouldn't have been in so bad a state if he hadn't stayed below long enough to shut off steam in an attempt to save the others: he'd been wounded to start with and on top of that scalded almost to death before they'd got him out.

Pete Chandler, Nick's ex-yachtsman navigator, came back to him from the chart. "Twelve and a half miles, sir."

They'd have to turn down a bit before they entered the fjord, as there was a shoal right in the middle of the entrance. It wasn't an obvious danger on the chart, but the Sailing Directions contained a note that in bad weather the shoal was often awash. And this *was* bad weather. The helmsman was finding steering difficult with the following sea—in which low revs didn't help, either. The sea was overtaking them all the time, great humped rollers racing up astern and lifting her, tilting her this way and that, dropping her back again as they ranged on shorewards; the biggest ones were higher than the ship, so that between the troughs visibility was nil. Grey-green seas mounting, rolling on with spray streaming down-wind from their crests, then toppling and spreading into a wilderness of white where, ahead and on both bows now, the ocean hurled itself against rocks and islands, leaping sometimes against obstructions to a hundred feet or more. *Intent*, with the force of the gale on her port quarter, was like some hard-driven animal with a limp, staggering harder each time to the right than to the left. Funnel-smoke, carried into the bridge by the stern wind, was acrid, eye-watering.

Who'd receive them in Namsos, he wondered —Norwegians, or Germans?

In the first seconds and minutes after the German shell struck and exploded inside his ship, Nick had been preoccupied with two questions. First, whether in her immobilised condition he might still get his torpedo tubes to bear on the enemy, and second, how long it might be before the next salvo smashed down on them.

"A" and "B" guns, meanwhile, were still firing; but the answer to that first question—and obviously, seeing it in retrospect, to the second as well—had come in a blinding, smothering snowstorm which swept down like a blanket, cocooning the destroyer in her own agony, hissing into the fires leaping from her afterpart.

The guns ceased fire. Brocklehurst reported

by telephone from the director tower, "Target obscured."

It was no good thinking about getting any signals out. The fore-topmast had collapsed half over the side, taking both the yards and the W/T aerials with it. MacKinnon, the PO Telegraphist, aided by PO Metcalf, the Chief Bosun's Mate, and his henchmen, had rigged a jury aerial since then, using the stump of the foremast and the diminutive mainmast aft, but there'd been no question of trying to transmit. For one thing there were at least one enemy cruiser and two destroyers in the vicinity, and with any luck the Germans were under the impression that *Intent* had been sunk. They must have thought so, because otherwise they'd have arrived through that snowstorm to find her and finish her. So it would have been stupid to have risked alerting them to her continued existence. But in any case, with the ship's main generating plant out of action MacKinnon doubted if they had enough power on the set for it to be heard even five miles away.

The PO Tel was a tall man, black-bearded, with the soft lilt of the West Highlands in his voice. "It's voltage we're lacking more than aerial height, sir."

"Have you been listening out since you rigged the jury?"

"Aye, sir, but all we're gettin' is a load o' German."

There were no British ships anywhere near

83

enough to have a chance of receiving them. And the signals that really mattered, the enemy reports, had been sent out before the action started.

"All right, MacKinnon. Pick up whatever you can, so we hear what's going on. We'll be in shelter in a few hours' time—we'll fix the generator and step a new fore-topmast, and you'll be in business again."

"We've no spare topmast, sir."

It was hard to concentrate on one issue for so long, when there were fifty other things to think about. Plugging slowly south-eastward: pitching like a see-saw and losing oil-fuel all the time. The stern tanks were leaking as a result of the main damage, and the port-side tanks for'ard were also leaking, presumably from near-miss damage slightly earlier. So now the only sound fuel tanks were the starboard pair for'ard and the smaller auxiliaries amidships. They were going to need oil as well as repairs.

"D'you know what that topmast was made of, PO Tel?"

"Would it be Norway fir, sir?"

"It would." Nick pointed. "And that's Norway."

But this conversation had taken place several hours later. At the start, with the ship stopped and on fire and no report yet of her machinery state or count of dead and wounded, there'd been no time for anything but coping with such emergencies as one knew about and getting ready for such new ones as might be expected. Like the weather clearing suddenly and the cruiser opening fire again. There'd be nothing to do except to shoot back—for as long as the ship floated.

Tommy Trench had gone aft to take charge of damage-control and fire-fighting. The snow still hid them, hid everything *from* them. Mr. Opie, the torpedo gunner, was still standing by his out-turned tubes, and Nick had sent down for Cox, the RNR midshipman, to come up to the torpedo sights, in case visibility *did* lift suddenly and reveal their enemy. If that happened and one was quick enough . . . Well, he knew the cruiser wouldn't be lying stopped as *Intent* was; in fact the probability was that she'd be a long way off by this time. But she might be picking up survivors from poor *Gauntlet*?

Thinking of the possibility of *Gauntlet* survivors, he wondered about sending a boat to search in the direction where they'd last seen her. Both ships had been immobilised, so if there were any that was where they'd be. There'd be none alive in the water, but there might be a Carley float, something or other. . . . Risk sending away the whaler in this sea? Throw sound lives after doubtful ones?

Ten or fifteen minutes after the shell had hit them Sub-Lieutenant Lyte hauled himself into the bridge with a report from Tommy Trench.

"Engine-room's a shambles, sir. Chief Stoker's

85

trying to sort things out—*says* it's not as hopeless as it looks. There's a lot of electrical damage, but the LTOs are coping. Only the auxiliary generator's operable—or will be, Beamish says. And we're losing a lot of oil-fuel aft, so he's shut off those tanks. Other damage is comparatively minor—except for the hole in the engine-room casing—first lieutenant's getting that covered with timber and tarpaulins. But everything's in hand, sir, really." Lyte was panting: he'd paused, getting his breathing under control. "The four men who were killed are in the officers' bathroom for the moment, sir, and the two wounded—ERA Dobbs and Stoker Hewitt—are in the sickbay."

"Are they going to be all right?"

"No, sir." Lyte clung to the binnacle as the ship was lifted and flung on to her port side. "Doc says not a hope."

"On your way down, tell him I want a report as soon as possible."

"Aye aye, sir." He hadn't quite finished *his* report yet. "Most upper deck gear's smashed or burnt, sir. The only boat we have left intact is the dinghy. Whaler and motor-cutter are just charcoal. Even the Carley floats have had it. And —Mr. Opie asked me to tell you he had to ditch several depthcharges, when everything was burning."

That seemed to be the lot.

"All right, Sub. Thank you."

No boat for *Gauntlet* survivors, then; *that*

problem had solved itself. No boat for anyone else either. Lyte told him, "Chief Buffer's clearing away the wreckage of the topmast, shrouds and stuff, in the waist port side, sir, and he's got all the wire inboard now."

"Good." Metcalf's first thought would have been for trailing steel-wire rope that might get wrapped round the screws. *If* the screws were to start turning again.

"Sub, I want to know from Beamish, *one*, how long he's going to be, *two*, what revs he thinks he'll be able to give me?"

Visibility was lifting. The snow was changing to sleet and thinning. A minute ago you couldn't see more than ten yards but he could see the ship's stem now—about a hundred feet away. And the sea beyond it, too . . .

"Lookouts!"

Gilbey on the port side and Willis on the other. He told them, "Keep your eyes peeled now. Weather's thinning. I want to know if anything's there before it sees *us*. . . . Mid!"

Midshipman Cox faced round. "Yessir?"

"Ask Lieutenant Brocklehurst if he can see anything."

Cox had picked up the 'phone. He was short, sturdy, with a nose like a lump of putty and skin scarred by acne. He'd been a Merchant Navy cadet until 3 September 1939, and he was now just eighteen. His action station was in the plot, below the bridge, and most of the time he was employed as "tanky", assistant to the navigating officer.

He'd shoved the 'phone back on its bracket. "Director tower reports nothing in sight, sir."

"Keep a smart lookout yourself now, Mid."

Young Cox was a problem. Chandler wanted to get rid of him. But for the moment, the foreseeable future, there were more pressing problems. . . . Visibility had stretched to about half a mile, and there was still nothing to be seen. Only the sea heaving green and angry and the clouds pressing low as if they were trying to smother it, and here and there the flurry of a passing squall. *Intent*, soaring and dropping, swinging whichever way the waves and wind pushed her, felt inert and lifeless, with no will of her own.

Some time later, Tommy Trench's mountainous form had dragged itself off the ladderway and slithered across the bridge to join him. Pete Chandler had come up behind the first lieutenant; he was carrying a rolled chart which he took to the small chart-table in the front of the bridge. It was a sort of alcove, like a dormer window's recess, with a grey-painted canvas shield that could be let down to keep the weather out and, at night, the light in.

To the left of it, in the port fore corner of the bridge, steps led down to the tiny Asdic compartment.

Trench reported, "I've got the hole in the engine-room casing adequately covered for the time being, sir. Timber and tarpaulins with a wire lashing to hold it down. The work'll go more easily down below now; Beamish reckons another hour and then slow speed, revs for three or four knots."

"I see." He'd been hoping for better things than that. He asked Trench, "Is it going to be a permanent repair—at that reduced speed—one we can rely on?"

"Afraid not, sir. To make a job of it he says he'd need several days with the ship on an even keel and—well, he's not *up* to it, sir."

"No."

It wasn't any of CPO Beamish's fault that he wasn't. He was a stoker, not an artificer.

"I doubt if it was an eight-inch shell that hit us, sir. But in any case it didn't get far in before it burst. Hence the size of the hole."

It could have been a shell from the cruiser's secondary armament, a four-inch. It had already occurred to him that a direct hit from an eight-inch would almost certainly have sunk them. The engine-room was the biggest compartment in the ship: if it was flooded, she'd go down, to where poor *Gauntlet* was.

The thought of *Gauntlet* was a weight inside him. He thought that in the same circumstances he'd have made the same decisions, but he knew it was arguable and that there'd be plenty of post-mortem experts who'd take a different view.

"How far to the Shetlands, pilot?"

"Roughly—" Chandler hesitated—"five hundred miles, sir. D'you want a more accurate—"

"No." It *would* be about five hundred. And it might as well have been five thousand. He looked at Trench. "Five hundred miles at three knots—no, not as much, revs for three knots but beam-on to this gale—and with a chance of the engine packing up on us altogether. . . ." He shook his head. "Hardly."

"Might whistle up a tow, sir?"

Nick asked Chandler, "How far are we from Trondheim?"

"We could just about *drift* there, sir."

"Let's have a look at it. Take over, will you, Number One."

You could see a couple of miles now: see *nothing* over a radius of about that. Thank God, he thought, for vast mercies. Despite *Gauntlet.* And don't count on getting many more, not even small ones. Luck, even if one thought of it as intervention by the Almighty, was always a rationed commodity. When you'd had a fairly large issue of it you'd be stupid not to expect some of the other sort thereafter. But for the moment there was still no enemy about. The lookouts and the snotty were all hard at it with binoculars at their eyes, and overhead the director tower was slowly, constantly, traversing around.

So far—*Gauntlet* apart—things might have been a lot worse than they were, he thought. He was staring up at the swaying director tower. Trench glanced up at it too: the motion up there as the ship rolled was terrific. Trench observed, "If Brocklehurst was a churn of milk he'd be cheese by now." Best not to dwell on the *Gauntlet* business. Nick knew that *Intent*'s present problems demanded all his concentration. Later, *Gauntlet*'s fate and his own part in the action would be examined through a dozen microscopes, some of them with bureaucratically hostile eyes behind them. If one got through as far as "later". . . .

Chandler was waiting for him at the chart table.

"DR's here, sir, and here's Trondheim."

He'd already taken the major decision—to seek shelter and repairs in Norway rather than risk losing the ship and all her company in attempting the very long, rough passage homeward in this unseaworthy condition. With enemy units known to be at sea, and probably a lot more of them than were *known* to be, to stagger off into the gale hoping to find assistance—a tow—wasn't a justifiable gamble. At best, if it worked, it would take other Royal Navy ships from their operational functions, add to the burden of other men's responsibilities. He hunched over the chart: the decision to be made now was which bit of Norway to aim for.

Trondheim was close at hand. It was a major port with full repair and fuelling facilities, and at first sight it seemed the obvious choice.

His eye ran up the jagged coastline, the mass of offshore islands and indentations, the long reaching arms of sea called fjords—narrow, twisting, deep-water channels. He reached to the back of the table for dividers.

Namsos, he was looking at. At the head of Namsenfjord. The approach to it—from Foldfjorden—was about seventy miles north of the approach to Trondheim. He checked the distances to both places from *Intent*'s present DR position. Nothing in it: they were as close to one as to the other. The only significant difference was that the course to Namsenfjord—he ran the parallel ruler across and saw it would be about 130 degrees—would be exactly down-wind.

Passing a hand around his jaw, he was reminded that he hadn't shaved since yesterday morning.

"Namsos might be our best bet."

"Wouldn't repairs be easier at Trondheim, sir? And more likely oil fuel?"

"Let's see what the pilot says. Send Cox down for it."

Now—think this out . . .

If the Germans were invading—which you could bet on—they'd make landings at four, five, possibly six strategic points. Oslo obviously. Trondheim was probably the next most obvious target. Stavanger for its airfield. And—Kristiansand, Bergen, Narvik. If they had ships and men enough that would be the bones of it. And it made a powerful argument against taking *Intent* into Trondheim. Wherever one went, admittedly there'd be some risk of getting stuck; Namsos *might* be occupied and presumably would be eventually—its strategic position in relation to Trondheim meant it couldn't be left alone for long—but for openers the Hun couldn't spread his forces too thinly, he'd have to concentrate on the more important places.

So if repairs could be made in just a few days there'd be a better chance of getting them done in Namsos and getting away again than there would be at Trondheim.

"Right. Thank you." Chandler took the *Norway Pilot Vol. III* from Cox, and looked up Namsos in its index. Then he was riffling over the pages. "Here we are . . ."

"The crucial requirements are repairs and fuel."

"Yes, here it is . . . 'Small repairs can be executed.'" His finger moved on, stopped at another paragraph. "'Fuel oil is available.' Seems we could do worse, sir."

"Is that a fairly recent issue?"

"Looks new enough." The navigator turned to

the front and checked the publication date. "Yes. 1939."

"Namsos it is, then." Nick touched the wooden surface of the chart table. "*If* our chief stoker can get us that far."

Nylandskjaer was well astern now. One bit of bad news since Beamish had got her going had been the discovery that oil was leaking from some of the for'ard tanks as well as the after ones. Problems of that nature could only be cured in dry dock: even if there was a dock in Namsos and engineers who could take on such a job he wasn't going to risk his ship being high and dry when the Nazis might arrive at any moment. So however good a job Beamish might do eventually in the engine-room, with or without shore assistance, *Intent*'s range was going to be reduced by almost half. And she'd only have *that* if the harbour authorities in Namsos came up to scratch with a couple of hundred tons of oil.

Sufficient unto the day, he told himself. For the moment she was, at least, *afloat*.

Trench, lumbering up, caught hold of the binnacle on Nick's left. "Burial party is standing by, sir."

"Right. Thank you." He called to Chandler, who was at the chart table. "Pilot, come and take over."

"Aye aye, sir." The navigator's long, bony frame began to back out of the alcove, letting the canvas down across it to make sure his precious charts stayed dry. He'd got the larger-scale inshore chart of Namsenfjord and surroundings up here now. Midshipman Cox was still at the front of the bridge keeping a lookout, and the watchkeeping lookouts had been doubled up so that there were two each side. The only food anyone had had throughout the day had been corned-beef sandwiches, mugs of soup, and kye. "Kye" meaning cocoa. Nick stared round, seeing the low encircling rock-grey coasts white-blotched and hung with spray in a continual mist.

Intent had her stern up, foc'sl buried deep in sea. . . . The navigator, joining Nick, wiped spray from his long, pale face. Chandler was a cricketer; it was a burning interest which he shared with Tommy Trench. "With your permission, sir, I'd like to come two degrees to starboard now."

"All right." He turned away. "She's all yours."

"Then it's six and a half miles to Namsenfjord, sir."

An hour and a half, he thought. "How far up the fjord for shelter?"

"Bit less than twenty miles, sir." Then he re-heard the question, and shook his head. "Sorry. That's the distance up to Namsos itself. There are sheltered anchorages long before that."

If they were lucky they'd be met by a pilot boat or some kind of patrol craft who'd lead them in. A pilot was essential, by normal standards, but it might be unwise to count on getting one. For one thing, the ordinary way of getting him would be to radio the nearest pilot-station; and even if the W/T was working he'd no intention of using it. But also, if the Norwegians were expecting to be invaded they'd be chasing their tails a bit—and might not relish being seen playing host to the White Ensign. In fact going on recent form they'd scream blue murder at the sight of it. So—if no pilot was available, as the distance to Namsos was twenty miles and *Intent*'s speed say five knots, they'd be in that narrow fjord when the dark period hit them. Therefore, he'd have to reckon on anchoring before the light failed: and as the fjords were deep—the chart revealed that most of Namsenfjord had more than two hundred fathoms in it—an anchorage would have to be selected in advance.

Well, there'd be time to do so. Now, there were five men to be buried. Five because Stoker Hewitt had died, as the doctor had said he would. Dobbs, the ERA, was surprising him by holding on, and Probationary Surgeon Lieutenant Bywater was staying at Dobbs's bunkside and practically counting every heartbeat. Six months ago Don Bywater had been a student at Bart's.

Nick told Chandler, "I'm going aft. When it's over I expect I'll visit the engine-room and then the sickbay."

A small crowd of men had assembled near the for'ard set of torpedo tubes. Mr. Opie was there

—spidery-thin, grey-stubbled, touching his cap to Nick and then immediately resuming the massage of that long, thin nose. Lyte too— looking soberer, less boyish than Nick had seen him before. This morning's engagement, he realised, must for the majority of officers and men have been a first experience of action. . . . Had *he* been changed, he wondered, by his own rather dramatic blooding at Jutland? In career terms, certainly, because at Jutland he'd won himself— by accident, pure chance, he still felt that was all it had amounted to—a future, which he'd not had before. But *personally*?

He didn't think so. Success, approbation, had given him some confidence. That was about all. . . . He was looking round at Trench's dispositions for this funeral: at four bodies sewn in canvas and lying under the shelter of the tubes, a fifth on the launching-plank which had been rigged athwartships with its outboard end protruding over the ship's side. Spray flew from mounting curves of green sea, higher than the ship's side: Nick told PO Metcalf, "Mind you drop 'em in the troughs." Otherwise they might get dumped straight back aboard. The gunner's mate, PO Jolly, reported, "Firing party ready, sir." Four sailors with rifles. The body lying on the plank was shrouded in a Union flag, and the same flag would cover each of the other four as their turns came. Men in gleaming oilskins clung to whatever was solid and in their reach; mostly to the tubes and the gear around them and to the ladder and other projections on the searchlight island. The searchlight itself was *kaput*, non-existent, and the platform it stood on was blackened and twisted out of shape. Nick took up a position under the platform's overhang. One hand for himself, the other for the prayer-book. He was going to have to shout the prayers, to be heard over all the surrounding noise.

I am the resurrection and the life, saith the Lord: he that believeth in me, though he were dead, yet shall he live: and whosoever liveth and believeth in me shall never die. . . . We brought nothing into this world, and it is certain we can carry nothing out. The Lord gave, and the Lord hath taken away; blessed be the name of the Lord.

The language was fine but its value here and now was less obvious to him. It wasn't a matter of not believing; more one of believing and caring too much for these ritual mouthings to carry the weight of regret which he felt himself and sensed from the men around him. He looked up from the book: he wanted to say something more personal and more apposite, something these sailors could identify with in their own hearts. Defeated in that, he looked down again. . . . In the midst of life we are in death: of whom may we seek for succour, but of thee, O Lord, who for our sins are justly displeased? Familiar verbiage: reminding one of other such occasions. A Dover scene, for instance: Christmas of 1917, destroyer men in ranks under a grey drizzly sky, and the flag on the castle at half-mast while a bugler sounded the Last Post. Here there was no bugler, only PO Metcalf and his bosun's call. Metcalf had the little silvery instrument ready pressed between fingertips and palm, and he kept wetting his lips as if he was worried that the prayers might stop suddenly and find him unprepared, lips dried by the wind. Nick paused, to make sure the side-party were ready; then he looked down again and read, Forasmuch as it hath pleased Almighty God of his great mercy to take unto himself the souls of our dear brothers here departed: we therefore commit their bodies to the deep, to be turned into corruption, looking for the resurrection of the body when the sea shall give up her dead. . . .

For each man the pipe shrilled and a volley of rifle-shots crackled into the sky. Five splashes, and within seconds of each there was nothing to be seen in the boil of sea. He read the Lord's Prayer: and that was it. . . . But he saw Tommy Trench staring at him hard, imparting to him by the stare that there might be something else expected of him.

He told them, "These were our shipmates. When they were alive we took them for granted. Now we know how valuable they were—to us and to the ship. Let's remember it—because it applies here and now to every one of us: we are

99

all dependent on each other, and every single man has his own value and importance."

Those five had been more valuable than most. *Intent* was not only wounded, she was chronically short of doctors, engine-room staff, technicians. The thought reminded him of ERA Dobbs; he turned the prayer-book's pages back quickly to *Visitation of the Sick*.

"A prayer now for ERA Dobbs. Surgeon Lieutenant Bywater is with him now in the sickbay, but he does not have—very good chances. . . . Oh father of all mercies, we fly unto thee for succour on behalf of thy servant George Amos Dobbs, now lying under thy hand in great weakness of body . . ." Taking a breath—this shouting was hard work—he saw with dismay that the words which lay ahead were about "unfeigned repentance" and Dobbs's "pardon" and a request that he should be granted "a longer continuance amongst us". It wouldn't do; he was stopped, totally unable to bawl such stuff into the face of present reality—a crippled ship and a battering sea on a coast which might already be swarming with the enemy, and a man lying close to death because he'd taken it on himself to try to save his mates. It wasn't Dobbs's fault they'd died anyway. The words came suddenly and naturally and with a kind of anger: "Save him, please God, for us and for this ship and for his family at home. Give him the strength to recover from his injuries. *Please* God—let him *live!*"

This time the "amens" came sharply, res-
onantly. And shutting the prayer-book, Nick
was suddenly aware of plain *liking* for the men
around him: of understanding and respect for
them. Instinct told him too that the empathy was
two-way: he'd reached them, and they were
beginning to feel they knew him. He hadn't
thought of it or remembered it until this moment,
but it was a phenomenon he'd encountered before
and was recognising now from twenty-something
years ago. He could see it reflected back at him
from a couple of dozen different faces as he
looked round at them. They were seeing him as
a human being: in time, liking would grow into
confidence. It didn't matter whether or not they
knew it. The marvellous thing was that it was
there, to be tapped and to be built on.

He told them, "We're going into Namsenfjord,
and up to the town of Namsos if the engines hold
up long enough, to find shelter and some help in
patching up our damage. We need oil-fuel too,
and I hope to find some there. It's possible the
Germans are on the point of invading Norway;
they may even be there ahead of us. In that case,
we'll be somewhat up the creek. But—" he went
on, over a burst of laughter—"but *they* won't be
expecting *us*, either."

A snow-shower obscured the headland. In about
half a mile, though, they'd have it on the star-

board beam, and the shoal would be well clear to port, and they'd turn down into the fjord.

"Kye, sir?"

"Thank you, Mid."

Midshipman Cox was offering him a mug of cocoa. It was a pleasure to accept it. The kettle was plugged in on the starboard side of the bridge, on a brass-edged step there. Cox went back to prepare another mug, making a paste of cocoa powder, sugar and condensed milk and then adding the hot water. The cocoa powder was produced beforehand by scraping a block of pusser's (Admiralty-issue) chocolate, and old sailors reckoned that in a good cup of kye the spoon should stand up straight without support; but this involved the addition of custard-powder as a thickener, and was a taste for connoisseurs.

Cox was a problem that Nick would have to tackle sooner or later. Chandler said he was lazy, untidy and sloppy at his work—work which consisted largely of correcting charts and other navigational publications. Also, he was hopeless as a navigator and uninterested in it; a star-sight took him an hour to work out and was usually all rubbish when he'd done it. What made this particularly surprising was that he was RNR, and Royal Naval Reserve officers—even embryo ones, which was what a midshipman really was—were usually the best navigators you could get. Conway, Worcester and Pangbourne, all the merchant-navy training establishments seemed to be way ahead of the RN college in injecting the navigator's art into their cadets.

Nick thought Cox was the only exception to the rule he'd ever come across. And worse than the incompetence was—according to Chandler— the boy not seeming to give a damn about it.

"Aircraft green one-seven-oh!"

Think of the devil. . . . Cox had yelled it. Rising from his cocoa bar he'd caught a sight of it, put a mug down and snatched up binoculars. . . . "Almost right astern, sir. Moving left to right, angle of sight—five degrees."

To be visible under the cloud it would have to be pretty low.

"What does it look like?"

Nick and Chandler were both out on that side, looking aft, and not seeing it yet. Cox said, "Passed astern, sir." Meaning it had gone out of his sight. He was moving—uphill, at the moment —over to the port side. He answered Chandler's question: "Can't tell what it is, sir. In and out of cloud and—" He had it in his glasses again and so did both the port-side lookouts. Then: "Flown into cloud, sir."

It had been flying up-coast, northwards from the direction of Trondheim; or it had come from seaward and was doing a leg along the coastline. It could have been Norwegian, or German, or an aircraft catapulted from one of the Home Fleet's big ships and doing an inshore reconnaissance. Whatever it was, if its pilot had seen something way off on his starboard side that was very small and grey, foam-washed and not moving fast enought to be noticeably moving at all, he'd have had no way of distinguishing it at that range from about half a million rocks.

"Well sighted, Mid." Credit where credit was due. And the corollary too: he called back to the starboard after lookout, "*You* should have seen that first, Kelly." It had stopped snowing, and the entrance to Namsenfjord was opening out, its westward coast seeming to fall back as the vista opened. The entrance here was about two miles wide; at the limit of present visibility he could see where it narrowed to less than half that. But —he wiped the front lenses of his binoculars and tried again—you could see beyond that too, to a further broadening.

"Can we come round yet, pilot?"

"In about ten minutes, sir."

A bit stiff-necked, was Pete Chandler. Very good at his job, but sometimes *unnecessarily* meticulous. He'd drawn a pencil track and he was going to stick to it: well, that was his intention. Nick suggested mildly, "We don't have to go smack down the middle, do we? Isn't it all deep water?"

"It is, sir."

"Let's come round now, then."

"Aye aye, sir." Deadpan . . . The navigator stooped to the voicepipe. "Starboard fifteen."

If that had been a Home Fleet aircraft, Nick

thought, it would not, probably, have been searching for *Intent* or *Gauntlet*. They'd have written them off, hours ago. C-in-C and Admiralty and the Vice-Admiral Battlecruiser Squadron —Whitworth—had every reason to assume that both ships had gone down.

How long would Admiralty wait before they notified next-of-kin?

Aubrey Wishart was in the Admiralty and, being Aubrey, would have his ear to the ground when anything was happening. He'd know of that early-morning engagement, the enemy reports and the ensuing silence. And since Nick had recently put Uncle Hugh in touch with him he'd get to hear about it too. He'd keep his mouth shut, though, as long as there was any doubt; basically he'd always been an optimist, and he'd been in love with his young sister-in-law Sarah for—oh, twenty-five years?

Honourably, of course. He'd have kissed her cheek a few times, sometimes touched her hand and found the experience thrilling, something to think about when he was lonely. . . . After his brother, Nick's father, had died, Nick had half expected Hugh to propose to her. But he'd overlooked the existence of the Table of Affinity, of course: *A man may not marry his brother's wife.*

She'd have refused him, anyway. Her husband's death hadn't done anything to remove Sarah's hair-shirt, that ghastly outcome of past sins and present rectitude. . . . Whoever put that

Table of Affinities together could have expanded it in some directions: he could for instance have added *A man may not go to bed with his father's wife?*

Incredible—to know her, see her now. And she'd been like this—to him—ever since he'd returned from the Black Sea in 1920. Coldly formal, untouchable—actually and figuratively. And at that time she'd still been young and pretty, she hadn't succeeded in turning herself as she had now into an old maid. Caustic, dried up . . . Although Uncle Hugh still seemed to regard her as a raving beauty. . . . At first he'd seen her transformation as an act, a cover-up aimed at making sure no one ever guessed the truth: even to *destroy* that truth, erase it from his mind as well as from her own—the truth being that Jack, supposedly Nick's half-brother, was actually his son. But even if that was how it had started, as a deception that was supposed to last for ever and to cover events that wouldn't be referred to by either of them even if they'd been alone on some mountain-top, it had changed into something stronger and less rational. Now, she hated him. For what he'd done all those years ago, and again for what he'd done more recently.

Above all he remembered the loathing in her eyes ten years ago, on the wide front steps at Mullbergh when they'd returned together from the church, from burying Nick's father, her husband. He'd muttered, speaking his thoughts

106

aloud more than talking to her, "I feel as if I'd killed him." Her hand on his arm stopped him, halfway up the steps, and her eyes blazed in that dead-white face inside its frame of black: she hissed, "*Didn't* you?"

Grey-green mounds of following sea still unending, lifting her and tilting her on their summits before they allowed her to slide back and down again and rolled on disdainfully as if they hadn't noticed her or felt her weight.

"Midships!"

"Midships, sir. Wheel's amidships, sir."

"Steer south fifty-two east."

"South fifty-two east, sir!"

The engine's thrum had seemed to falter. Chandler had noticed it too, looked round quickly towards Nick. . . .

Steady again, and plugging on. He let out a breath of relief. This lee shore would *not* be a place you'd choose for breaking down.

Sarah loathed him, he thought, as a symbol of her own guilt and shame. But there'd been some basis for that accusation.

In 1929, in the autumn, he'd come up to Mullbergh on his own in order to break the news of his impending divorce from Ilyana. He'd been executive officer of a battleship in the Mediterranean Fleet for the previous two years, and now he'd been appointed to the staff of the Senior

Officers' Tactical Course at Portsmouth, but he had some leave due to him first. Much of it was to be spent conferring with lawyers and providing Ilyana with "grounds". Providing *her* with them, for heaven's sake!

His father had been furious, utterly opposed to allowing a divorce in the family. Nick had expected *some* fuss to be made: as a boy he'd been aware of frightful upheavals at the time of his Uncle Hugh's divorce. But that had been so long ago; divorce in these days had become far more commonplace, acceptable.

Not to Sir John Everard, though. And certainly not when it was his own son and heir who was instigating it. A son and heir whom he could not, incidentally, disinherit, in terms of the entailed estate. He made it plain that he regretted this. Nick might have left at once, but it happened to be the Mullbergh pack's opening meet next day, and it was a long time since he'd ridden to hounds; also, he had the faint hope that if he stayed another day or two some opportunities might arise to make his father understand how he had absolutely no option in the matter of the divorce.

Which was to involve this stupid sham of a convention, that *he* should provide the grounds, allow Ilyana to divorce *him*. . . . After Malta, for God's sake! And after—he had to face it now —ten years of shirking the truth. . . . He kept remembering a remark he'd overheard at the time

108

of his marriage to her. The marriage had been contracted primarily to save her life, since the Admiralty had decreed that no more White refugees were to be brought out of Russia in HM ships. The only way to get round this had been to turn Countess Dherjhorakov into Mrs. Everard: but in any case he'd been in love with her. Or infatuated. Or that and also influenced by the circumstances, the approaching horror of the Red advance and knowing what they'd done elsewhere, the unspeakable savagery and the sheer impossibility of leaving the tiny, exquisite and fantastically *brave* Ilyana to the butchers and the rapists. The fact they barely knew each other hadn't counted: she was there in front of him, he could *see* her, he knew what she'd been through already and what struck him most forcibly was the combination of ultra-femininity and high courage: all he had to do, he'd thought, to make a go of it, was measure up to her. And that snide remark—one young Russian nobleman had said it to another, in French and in Nick's hearing— Ilyana Dherjhorakov? Yes, I know who you mean. Here, is she? The one they say used to ride horses, until she discovered men?—he'd dismissed it as clever, cruel, unfounded gossip. It was the way those people talked. Only much later did he remember it and recognise its accuracy. And the last time had been in Malta: where his own captain had summoned him to the cuddy for pink gins and spoken of forbearance, wisdom, the folly of cutting off one's nose to spite one's face; and then an admiral with a famous name had talked paternally of the good name of the Service and the reputation of the Everards. Again it had been a nobleman, of sorts—but an Englishman and a senior officer. The Mediterranean Fleet had gone on its summer cruise; Nick had been with it in his battleship. Back in Malta afterwards he'd found that Ilyana, only just returned to the island, was evasive, uncommunicative, peculiar in manner. It had been the start of Paul's schooling, his first term at prep school in England; she'd gone to collect him and bring him out to Malta for his summer holidays; but she'd left early, the day after the fleet had cleared Valletta, and gone not to England but to a villa at Menton. The villa was owned by a White Russian cousin and had been lent to a certain British officer, a man with aristocratic connections, who until recently had been in Malta. There'd been a photograph in a glossy magazine, and a letter to Malta from someone who'd seen them at some princely party; and then a few more bits and pieces and suddenly it was common knowledge all over Malta, from every gunroom and wardroom in the fleet to the Union Club and the governor's palace. . . .

He remembered the admiral, himself not unconnected in high places, telling him uncomfortably—the interview had obviously not been arranged on the admiral's *own* initiative—

110

"You've a brilliant record, Everard, and potentially a great future in the Service. A little caution now, a few second thoughts, would certainly not be harmful to your prospects. I'm bound to warn you on the other hand that a scandal of such dimensions could be—frankly, disastrous . . ."

The scandal could be avoided. The divorce could not.

In fact he didn't hunt, that day at Mullbergh, and neither did his father. In the morning the head groom came to report that he couldn't saddle Sir John's stallion. The animal wouldn't let him into its box, and it was kicking the place to bits. Nick's father flew into a rage: he shouted at the groom that he was sacked—as of that moment, with no wages, notice or reference. In the first place he didn't know his job, in the second he was a coward; in the third, if the horse was in such a state it was his own, the groom's, fault to start with. Sir John stalked out, taking a crop with him. Five minutes later, with the same groom's help, Nick managed to get his father's unconscious body out of the loose-box. He had extensive bruising, some cracked ribs, a broken wrist and slight concussion.

None of which kept him quiet for long. Within a few days he was shouting from his bed that Nick's behaviour had always been a source of annoyance and embarrassment, and that if he continued with his plans for this divorce he needn't bother to come back to Mullbergh until he—Sir John—was dead.

"All right. If that's how you feel."

But there was no train he could take that day. And a few hours later, passing by to tell Jack—who was in the sickroom—that Sarah wanted him downstairs, he heard his father lecturing the boy about his future in the Navy. Jack had already expressed the wish to try for Dartmouth.

Sir John was instructing him, "Model yourself on your half-brother David. If David had lived he'd have been well on the way to becoming an admiral, by now. Brilliant—brave as a lion—why, there's not the slightest doubt he'd have gone to the very top!"

The boy put in, "I'd like to be like Nick. Get medals like he has. If I could be like Nick—"

"Arrant *nonsense*, Jack! Nick was lucky, that's all—in the right places at the right time! That's nothing to do with *staying power*—which was what David had in such abundance. Determination—grit! And something else—it's called *integrity*. He'd have lived like an Everard, not a creature sliding in an out of marriages and law courts, muck-raking and—"

"I beg your pardon." Nick stood in the doorway. The door next along from this one he'd seen smashed down—by his father, in a drunken fury, when he, Nick, had been a child and woken in the night to Sarah's screams and come rushing down to help her. . . . Today there'd been the

112

earlier row—accusations, threats, and Sarah's tight-faced, mute hostility: and he was looking at a man now who'd never in his life lifted a finger except to please himself. Even in the war he'd found himself a comfortable, safe niche. . . . One's own father: a life-long sham! Nick told him, "David was a coward and a weakling. At Jutland his nerve broke completely—it was the first time he'd been shot at and he couldn't face it. What that padre told Hugh was a lot of bunkum. I heard the truth from a man who was in *Bantry* and took charge towards the end. He had to detail a brother officer to look after David, save him from disgracing himself too obviously in front of the sailors."

The truth, he'd given him. Like a bullet between the eyes. It was something he'd sworn to himself he'd never tell a soul.

Sir John had his first heart attack that evening. He lived for a few months after it, but that had been the start. Nick had suffered ever since from the knowledge of what he'd done. There'd been no point in it, nothing achieved; he'd let go for a moment, surrendered to a fit of temper. He'd done a dreadful thing. Worst of all was that he'd said it in front of Jack, his own son. All right, *half-brother*. But Jack, who—although one tried hard not to see it—*was* in so many ways like David.

Nothing seemed to be on the move except the sea

and the clouds and *Intent* bashing doggedly in towards the land. And a variety of screeching gulls. Namsenfjord lay open now on the starboard bow and Pete Chandler had just taken some bearings for a fix. He came back from putting it on the chart.

"We could come round to south thirty-eight east, sir. Then fifty-five east after two miles."

"All right. Take over, and bring her round."

He had to work it out now—times, distances, and the dark period. He went to the chart and leant over it, resting on his elbows. From about midnight to 4 am were the hours when fjord navigation without either a pilot or local knowledge would be too dangerous; so he had two hours—say ten miles—before the ship had to be tucked up in some safe anchorage.

Chandler had laid off courses all the way through to Namsos. Checking on where a two-hour run on that track would take them, Nick found a small, almost circular dead-end of a fjordlet off the main one and on the starboard hand. Hidden and well sheltered. Hoddoy, the island which shut it in was called. But—checking —he found that the run of it would be just *over* the ten miles.

Nearer, then. *This* place . . . He looked up the reference in the Pilot, the book of Sailing Directions. Quay with mooring rings: and inside the distance, certainly. But he didn't want to tie up to the shore: and anyway it was too open to

114

the main channel of the fjord. One had to think of a German invasion force arriving with the dawn, and *Intent* caught there without a hope in hell. She wasn't in a condition to win battles anyway, but if he had her hidden when the enemy arrived there was at least the chance he'd be able to sneak her away later when the repairs were done.

The messenger of the watch brought him a cup of kye. Then Trench joined him.

"Problems, sir?"

"Picking an anchorage." Glad to share his thoughts with him, he ran a pencil-tip down the length of the fjord. "If we tried to get right through, the dark period would catch us about here. No good. I'm reckoning on two hours' steaming and then dropping the hook for four to five and pressing on again. Which means *this* is about as far as we can manage."

"How about here?"

Vikaleira: a bay on the northern shore. Nick dismissed it. "No anchorage, according to the Pilot. And it's visually exposed."

"I take that point." Trench added, "But— thinking on much the same lines—if we're at Namsos and the Huns arrive, won't we be in a trap?"

Nick straightened, to drink some kye. "My hope is to get what we need and then away again before the bastards come." He shrugged. "We won't get any oil anywhere *short* of Namsos,

Tommy." He put his mug down. "But for this temporary stop—here, this is the hole I'd like to sneak into, other things permitting." He was pointing at that gap to the west of Hoddoy, and the anchorage it led to—Totdalbotn. "In there we'd be tucked away nicely out of sight, and what's more we'd have an alternative exit—this channel, out around the island. But unfortunately it's just outside our range, and that bit's so very narrow that I couldn't risk just not quite making it in daylight."

Trench thought about it. He suggested, "Might we persuade Beamish to give us another knot or so?"

It was one answer, perhaps. But Nick didn't want to pressurise his chief stoker into going beyond what his own judgement told him was safe. With Mr. Waddicor or Chief ERA Foster it would have been different, but Beamish was less sure of his ground and might agree to something out of ignorance.

But Totdalbotn would certainly be the place to hole up.

"I'll see how he reacts to the suggestion." He went to the engineroom voicepipe, and got the chief stoker on the other end of it.

"How's it going, Chief?"

"Holding up, sir. All parts bearing an equal strain."

"D'you think all parts might bear just a little more?"

116

"More revs, d'you mean, sir?"

"If you could give me one more knot for slightly less than two hours, Chief, I could then give you five hours at anchor. What d'you say?"

"I'd say it's a deal, sir!"

"Good. Up twenty-five revs, then."

"Well—I'd thought twenty, sir, really—"

"If twenty-five felt like too much you could always come down a bit."

"I'll see how she takes it, sir."

There wasn't much shelter yet, because Namsenfjord opened right into the direction of the gale. But as soon as *Intent* rounded the point which the chart called Finsneset she'd begin to get some respite, and it was coming up now on the starboard hand. It was half an hour since Beamish had cautiously increased the revolutions, and so far all seemed well.

To port, eastward, the fjord opened into a V-shaped inlet called Altfjord. It had an island in the middle and the depth of the V was about two and a half miles. What you couldn't see from here but was clear on the chart was that the V's apex was also the narrow entrance to an inner fjord, an almost totally enclosed piece of water that went off at right-angles for about a mile and a half. It would be like a lake, a lagoon in there. He thought, looking at it and wishing he could make use of it, that if only he had some artificers a hideaway like that would be perfect. Nicely

117

hidden, completely sheltered, and just a stone's throw from the open sea.

Lacking artificers, he had to get to Namsos, where there'd be at least *some* kind of engineering help.

Chandler was watching the bearings of the left-hand edge of Altoy Island. When it was abeam he brought the ship round a few degrees to starboard.

"Four miles on this course, sir. Just under eight altogether."

It was just past ten. *Intent* had been making better than six knots, and as she'd be in calmer water now one might reckon on as much as seven. So they'd be dropping an anchor in that little bay west of Hoddoy no later than 11.30, and sitting down to a hot meal about midnight.

If there was enough power to heat the galley stoves.

"Number One." He beckoned, and Trench came over to him. "When we've anchored I want small-arms put out where they can be got at quickly. Revolvers in the chartroom. Rifles and bayonets—well, let's have three or four dumps in convenient places."

"Aye aye, sir." Trench was looking at him trying to read his mind. He was like that: he'd work it out, avoid asking a question if he could. Chandler was quite different: he asked immediately, "Expecting unfriendly natives, sir?"

The engineroom voicepipe squawked: and

118

simultaneously the note of the turbines began to drop away. . . . Nick was already at the pipe.

"Permission to stop engines, sir?"

"*No!*"

"It's bad trouble, sir—"

"Chief, for the moment you *must* keep her going."

Back into Altfjord, anchor behind the island? He was studying the coastline, remembering the alternatives he'd studied and checked on in the Sailing Directions. Chandler pointed to starboard, where the coastline fell away, opening the fjord to a width of about two miles. "There's an anchorage in there, sir. Fairly sheltered."

"Bring her round. And let's have the book."

Expecting the engines to stop at any second. He bent to the pipe again. "One mile, Chief, to where we can anchor. We *can't* stop sooner, d'you understand?"

"I can *try*, sir, but—"

"Just *keep her going*."

He straightened, threw a glance at the rocky lee shore not half a mile away. If the engines stopped now, that was where she'd go, and it wouldn't take long, either. She was under helm and coming slowly round to starboard, and Chandler was telling the helmsman to steer south forty-three west. There'd be at least partial shelter in there, because they'd be in the lee of Finsneset, the last point they'd rounded. He remembered the name of the village near the

119

anchorage—Lovika. He lowered his binoculars: Trench had fetched the Sailing Directions and found the place.

"Lovik?"

"That's it." Give or take a syllable.

"Twelve to seventeen fathoms, sand and clay bottom."

That sounded all right, so far as it went. He told Trench, "Leadsman and cable party, then. I imagine you'll have to work the capstan by hand. And I want Jarratt on the wheel." He put his glasses up to examine that little bight of coast towards which his ship was creeping. Dying: as if blood instead of oil might be seeping out of her. Anchored there, she'd be in full view of anything passing up or down the fjord. There weren't likely to be any marine engineers in those tiny houses either.

5

THIS afternoon Hugh had tracked down one key man and worried at him for an hour like some importunate old terrier; and this evening he'd dined another at his club. Now it was pushing midnight and he was listening to the night-time London silence in an ante-room where 150 years ago a young half-pay captain by the name of Horatio Nelson had waited in vain for an audience with the First Lord. Nelson had been after a sea appointment too.

Hugh Everard had made better progress than Nelson had achieved *that* day. But the commodore's job wasn't what he was here for now. It was still important, and if the worst came to the worst in the matter of Nick and *Intent* it would be vital, would become absolutely imperative to get away to sea. Bad enough to be stuck ashore with things as they were now: but if Nick had gone—he shifted jerkily on his stuffed chair, the thought provoking a sort of stitch—he wouldn't be able to stand it another day.

Cling to hope. There'd always been *such* hope. Getting afloat again would be a kind of escape: he could see that but he saw no reason to be ashamed of wanting it. He could handle it all so much better there than he'd be able to cooped up like an old dog in a kennel.

There was *still* hope, damn it!

He glanced at his watch again, and sighed. Either young Wishart had forgotten he was here or there must be the devil of a lot going on the remoter depths of this labyrinthine building. People forgot that the Admiralty was an operational headquarters as well as an administrative one. The public probably still thought of it as a place where ancient sea-dogs sat behind vast tables and signed parchments with quill pens: whereas actually there was an Operations Room upstairs, probably going full-blast at this very moment.

Wishart had said on the telephone, "I'll be here all night, sir. If you'd tell the porter to let me know when you're free, I'll get down to you in my first spare moment."

Hugh had booked himself a room at Boodle's. One had to keep busy, and in touch. He hadn't liked the idea of the train journey down to Hampshire and then a night at home without news—without a *hope* of news, because nothing could be said over an ordinary telephone these days. He'd have had to have come up again in the morning; there'd have been no point in it.

Strange to think of Nelson kicking his heels in this gloomy hole. He'd failed in his attempt to see Lord Chatham, and hurried over to Wimpole Street to call on Lord Hood instead. Hood had seen him, but told him no, he would *not* intervene with the First Lord. Might one ask why not? Certainly. The admiral had never been a man to shirk an issue. It was because His Majesty had formed an unfavourable opinion of Captain Nelson.

The King, Hugh thought, wouldn't give a damn whether Admiral Sir Hugh Everard succeeded or did not succeed in transforming himself into Commodore Sir Hugh Everard RNR. He'd probably never heard of him. . . . But then, he might have. As Prince Albert—or rather, in the alias of "Johnson"—His Majesty had served as a junior turret officer in *Collingwood* at Jutland: and Hugh had made a bit of a name for himself in that battle. Yes, he probably *would* have heard of him—and forgotten him again long since. . . . Anyway, string-pulling, arm-twisting and general brow-beating had worked wonders this afternoon and evening, and it would be surprising if in a day or so he wasn't summoned to a medical check-up. He'd pass that as A1, he knew.

Well—near enough A1. . . .

The achievement was less exciting than it should have been. He'd have swapped all hope of it for a reassuring word about Nick.

"Sir Hugh, I am so dreadfully sorry—"

"What?"

He'd jerked upright in his chair: in a kind of shock . . .

"—to have kept you waiting all this time."

"Oh." Getting hold of himself again. "You do seem rather busy, Wishart—for a man with no job to do here?"

"Well, yes. Quite." The rear-admiral had pushed the door shut behind him. He flipped open a silver case as he crossed the room. "Cigarette?" Hugh shook his head. Wishart told him, taking one for himself and lighting it, "I'm helping out on Max Horton's staff." His eyes held the older man's as he flicked the match into what must once have been a cuspidor. "I'd better tell you right away that we've no news of any sort of *Intent* or *Gauntlet*."

Hugh realised he'd known there wouldn't be. He was aware also that it was a case of no news being bad news. Wishart knew that too, of course. He sat down in a chair facing Hugh's.

"I'll tell you what's going on. The first thing is—we were right, they *are* invading. The first really solid confirmation of it came this afternoon —*Orzel*, a Polish submarine, stopped a Hun transport, *Rio de Janeiro*, and ordered her crew and passengers into the boats before she sank her; then some Norwegian craft came and picked them up. But the passengers were German soldiers in uniform, and they made no bones about it— on their way to 'protect' Bergen, they said." Wishart added, "On top of a lot of other reports, it doesn't leave any room for doubt. But nobody here—" he pointed upwards—"seemed to take

124

much notice. And the Norwegian government won't believe it. They won't even mobilise!"

Hugh commented drily, "Must have some politicians of our kind over there too, by the sound of it."

He saw it suddenly: this was going to be the start of the *real* war. We were about to be shown up—to ourselves—as unready and ill-led: it would be so obvious that even the War Cabinet would see it. Britain would get a bloody nose, lose men and ships and strategic advantage: *and be woken up.* . . .

An old man's musings . . . The picture seemed real, though. He asked Wishart, "What *are* we doing? Anything?"

"Well." Wishart leant forward. "Early this afternoon a flying-boat 200 miles ahead of the Home Fleet sighted a German force steering west. One battlecruiser, two cruisers, two destroyers. So the C-in-C turned north-westward—to block any Atlantic break-out, of course. He sent off another aircraft—catapulted from *Rodney*—but it never reported back. Either went into the sea or landed in Norway." He shook his head. "If only we had a carrier up there. If the Nazis grab the airfield at Stavanger—"

"Have we *no* carriers?"

"*Furious* is in the Clyde but she's not fit for operations yet. *Ark Royal* and *Glorious* are in the Mediterranean. But—other happenings, now . . . Well, first, *Renown* and her destroyers—

including *Hoste*, by the way—are heading out westward, for the same reason the C-in-C is. To cut off that force which the flying-boat reported. So Narvik is now left open to the enemy." He saw Hugh Everard's look of surprise, and nodded. "I know. I know. And now, anyway, Whitworth's been ordered to turn back and concentrate on blocking the Narvik approaches. It'll take him quite a while to *get* back, though, as it's blowing a real rip-snorter and the destroyers can't make much speed in it. Now—what's next . . . Oh —at about three this afternoon our attaché in Copenhagen reported that two cruisers with either *Gneisenau* or *Blucher* had entered the Kattegat, northbound. Since then two submarines have sighted the same force and one of them made an unsuccessful attack on it, off the Skaw. . . . Anyway, it's prompted Sir Charles Forbes to turn south again with *Rodney* and *Valiant*, largely because Admiral Edward-Collins's Second Cruiser Squadron is pretty well in the path of that northbound force, and unsupported. But Forbes has sent *Repulse* and *Penelope* with some destroyers to join Whitworth in the Narvik area."

"So we've one German force in the north and another to the south'ard."

"I think others too that we haven't heard about. After all, we know they *are* invading— and there must be inshore forces, assault parties for the different ports. . . . But that's the state of things. Admiralty has signalled to the C-in-C that his priorities must be (a) to stop the bunch in the north returning south, and (b) locate and engage the southern force." Wishart shook his head. "Between ourselves, I'd say we're making a frightful mess of it. The places we ought to be watching are the Norwegian ports—because that's where the Hun's going, *must* be. In fact we've three cruiser squadrons up there and all out in the deep field, and when the C-in-C just a short while ago ordered the First and Second Squadrons to get into position to start an inshore sweep at first light tomorrow—*really* inshore, in sight of land—our Lordships here in the Admiralty cancelled the order over Forbes's head."

"That's—incredible . . ."

And utterly depressing. What must it be like for Sir Charles Forbes, the C-in-C?

Wishart drew heavily on his cigarette. Hugh Everard thought, He's telling me all this to get my mind off Nick. . . .

"I imagine you're staying at your club tonight, sir?"

"What?" He looked up. "Oh, yes. Yes, indeed." He frowned. "I'm being a damn nuisance to you, I'm afraid."

"You're being nothing of the sort. I only wish I could—" He broke off in mid-sentence, shook his head as he stubbed out the cigarette. "Sir Hugh, if you were to telephone me here during the forenoon—say about eleven—then if there's

127

any news we could arrange to meet, here or else-where, whatever's handy?"

"Very good of you, Wishart. I'll make my call at eleven sharp."

"You said you'd had some success today, in this scheme of yours?"

"It's a matter of the supply-and-demand balance being tipped my way, I believe. Nobody's admitted it, but I suspect they need more chaps than they've got fit and able to do the job. So—yes, as far as that's concerned it's been a well-spent day."

Would the day have been missed all that much if the sun had failed to rise?

Careful, he thought. If you get too fanciful they'll rule you out as old and dotty, senile. . . . He shivered suddenly: it was a shiver of the mind but it came out through his nerves like a sign of fever. To cover it, he moved quickly, standing up.

"I'll telephone. I am—*most* grateful to you."

"B" gun's crew took over their own gun from "A"'s when the watch changed at midnight, and by this time the gale was said to be easing. Down from Force 9 to Force 8—*that* kind of easing. Trying to sleep on the messdeck had been like talking one's ease in a tin that was being kicked around by a mule; and in spite of it Paul hadn't only *tried* to sleep, he'd slept.

Waking had a new pattern to it. First there was

128

a feeling of relief, of escaping from a disturbing dream. Then the truth bore in: it hadn't been a dream at all, *Intent* was lost and almost certainly her captain would have gone down with her. Reality confirmed itself sickeningly while he dressed for the four hours of the middle watch: sweaters, towel round the neck, oilskins. Depression: this unwashed, unshaven feeling: and the sense of isolation. . . . It wasn't only his father's death—he'd lived to all intents and purposes without him, and he could do so again —but the consequences of it, the prospect of becoming a baronet, with Mullbergh to cope with and Sarah and Jack and—*oh, Christ.* . . . It wasn't only depressing, it was frightening. Then, feeling the ice-cold sweat, he told himself to snap out of it: *stop acting Dherjhorakov.* . . . Old tennis shoes: they were already on his feet but not laced up. He slept in them. Rubber soles were best on the gundeck, when you had to stagger around with projectiles or charges in your arms and the ship was doing its best to dump you overboard. . . .

Up top, out of the screen door and in the howling bedlam of the gale on the port side of the foc'sl deck—the wind was on *Hoste*'s starboard bow—he paused with one foot on the ladder and both hands stretched up overhead as high as he could reach; when she started her roll back to starboard he began climbing, up to the top and over the edge of the gundeck quickly, across into the lee of the gun. He clung to the edge of the gunshield, peered round at the sea and as much as was visible of other ships in company. *Renown*'s biggish stern-on shape ahead was a black smudge framed in white; and to starboard in another patch of broken sea another destroyer banged along on *Hoste*'s beam. . . . Then he realised how wrong he was. In the dark, with your eyes not yet adjusted and your brain only half awake, sizes and shapes were confusing. That wasn't *Renown* ahead, that was a destroyer; the battlecruiser would be ahead of *her*. Or even *two* up . . . *Hoste* and that ship on her beam each had at least one other destroyer ahead of them; the rest would be strung out astern and invisible from this gundeck.

Bow down, stuck deep into the sea: the ship quivering, shaking, as if she was trying to wriggle or bore her way into it. . . . "That you there, Yank?"

Dan Thomas, gun captain and breechworker, a three-badge killick whose home town was Swansea, was checking to see he had his crew complete. Vic Blenkinsop the sightsetter told Paul, "Shifted course to nor'-west during the First, Shortarse 'Iggins says. Ride out the worst o' the blow like, 'e reckoned."

"Which way we goin' now, Vic?"

"*Every* fuckin' way, mate." Blenkinsop spat down-wind, over Johnno Dukes's shoulder. Dukes was gunlayer. Blenkinsop asked him,

"'Adn't you noticed?" He settled the headphones over his ears, easing his balaclava over them before he turned the mouthpiece up and reported to the TS, "'B' gun closed up."

"No 'B' gun bloody ain't, you bloody ullage you!" Dan Thomas bawled it from inside the gunshield. "If 'B' gun's closed up where's that bald-'eaded bloody bookworm then?"

"I'm—if you mean me, I'm—*here*. . . ." Baldy Percival launched himself from the head of the ladder and came slithering across the canting gundeck. Bow out: water streaming back—solid, battering against the shield. She was rolling viciously to port: Paul grabbed an arm and held on until Baldy had his balance and was more or less at rest. . . . "Sorry—er—Dan. Fact is I lost a boot, couldn't find it *anywhere*, then—"

"Next time come up wi'out the bugger!"

"Ah—yes. Yes, I will." He crouched down, close to Paul who was edging his way further into shelter, past the sightsetter. The ship was acting like a mad thing: it was a marvel that she was holding together. If it had been worse than this, as apparently "Shortarse" Higgins—one of "A" gun's crew—had indicated, it must have been pretty frightening. Percival told him, "This boot's soaking wet inside—all slushy round my foot. I think—it sounds *ridiculous*, but—I think someone must have peed in it."

"'B' gun!" Blenkinsop was answering a call through his headset. He was listening now, and

131

the men round him waiting for the message. Then, "Aye aye. But if I'm not 'ere when you next call, mate—ah, shurrup yourself . . . ." He pushed the microphone away from his mouth, and told them, "In five minutes, ship will be reversin' course—turnin' right around like. They reckon she'll roll like a bastard an' all 'ands is to 'ang on an' say their prayers. . . . 'Ear me, kiddies?"

Baldy Percival was muttering, close to Paul's ear, "All squelchy round my toes. Honestly, some filthy—"

"Who'd have *peed* in it, for Christ's sake." He was fed up with Baldy's fussing. He should have kept his boots on his feet, like anyone else did if they had any sense. He was thinking about this change of course they'd just been warned about. It was a north-westerly gale and they had it on the starboard bow, so *Hoste* was steering west, and reversing course would mean coming round to east. Heading back towards Narvik, then. Or Vestfjord, whatever it was called.

Having left it for long enough for some Germans to sneak in?

He remembered Lieutenant-Commander Rowan's *Ours not to reason why.* If it wasn't for a ship's CO to reason why, it surely wasn't for a raw OD . . . He still did, though. He wanted not only to know what was going on, but to understand it. He'd always had such a need: it irritated him to have to act blindly, or to be fobbed off

132

with shallow explanations that didn't fit or make sense in his own mind. (Shades of childhood: *Because I tell you to, that's why!*) None of his messmates seemed to share this urge; most of the time they didn't even know which way the ship was heading, let alone what for. But in training, the instructors talked about "initiative": and how could you use initiative if you didn't know what the hell was happening in the first place?

"Here comes the Rose an' Crown!"

Johnno Dukes yelled it: it was his rhyming slang for *Renown*. He'd been looking out through his sighting port, the window in the gunshield above his laying handwheel. Paul shifted back out of the crush, craned his head round the edge of the shield into the buffeting, thumping wind. Eyes more settled to the dark now: in fact it *wasn't* really dark. Baldy Percival squeezing out beside him. Must be more of a kook than one had realised, to suspect messmates of pissing into his boot, for heaven's sake. . . . *Renown*—he saw her suddenly, a black mass surrounded by a welter of white: she'd come about and she was pounding back on an opposite course to the destroyers'. Getting on for 40,000 tons of ship—colossal, like a floating town 750 feet of her and Lord only knew how many decks below the waterline. About a third of that 750 feet was foc'sl, and all of that, as she ploughed bow-down, was buried in the sea: now, rising, bursting out immense, fantastic in size and power: the very size and weight of it made the upswing of that long sweep of bow seem to be happening in slow-motion, breaking out and throwing up a mountain of sea to stream back over her massive for'ard turrets like so much confetti flying on the wind —only it wasn't confetti, it was solid sea, as much as a hundred tons of it tossed back as effortlessly as a man might flick a peanut. The night sky turned blacker with her bulk across it as she thundered past, turrets and superstructure and twin funnels seemingly one mass, bow-wave high and bright underscoring it, curling away aft to pile and then spread out into the morass of foam astern. Bow *down* again now, that enormously long, powerful-looking forepart dipping in with the same slow-seeming grace: there was a look of grandeur, impressive and somehow emotionally inspiring too: it triggered some thought-process at the back of his mind and it was important, a personal thing he had to come to terms with. . . . Dan Thomas yelled, "Inside and 'ang on, lads!"

Paul moved in, shoving Baldy in ahead of him. Thomas was right, of course. The destroyers which had been next-astern of the battlecruiser would be following her round now, and soon it would be *Hoste*'s turn, and when she was beam-on to this murderous sea she was likely to do just about everything except loop the loop. Even crowding in here and jammed tight as they were might be quite hazardous, if a big sea decided to demonstrate its power, to reach in and winkle a few bodies out.

"'B' gun!"

Blenkinsop taking another call. They waited to hear what was new. Probably a warning again, stand by for the rough stuff. Tom Brierson, the leading hand of 3 Mess, had said he'd been in a destroyer when she had her foc'sl deck flattened and pushed in by a sea no worse than this one. There'd been stooping-height only in the upper messdeck, he'd said; and it had happened only a few miles outside Scapa Flow.

"Aye aye." Vic Blenkinsop shouted. "Secure the gun, clear upper deck!"

The skipper must have been having second thoughts, seeing just how tricky this turn-about was going to be. Dan Thomas was yelling at them to do this and that; Paul, clear of the scrum, checked that the lids of the ready-use lockers were screwed down tight. The lockers held cordite charges; the projectiles were in open racks, since it didn't matter how wet they got.

"One at a time to the ladder, now. Percival— you first—*move!*"

Baldy went slithering to it, crab-like. One at a time made sense; there wasn't anything much to hold on to at the top of the ladder, if you'd had to wait there. "All right, Yank!" He shot across, and swung over the edge. Below him Baldy yelped as Paul's foot coincided with his ear or nose, and above Paul's head boots were already

135

clumping down relentlessly. He kept his hands on the ladder's sides, clear of the rungs where fingers could get crushed. Then he was off it and tight-rope walking aft, reaching from one support to the next, vividly aware of the sea roaring fury at him on his right and only a few feet away. The screen door was open, Percival holding it open for him: he pushed inside, and Lofty McElroy leapt in behind him. Paul knew what it was that had been in his mind when he'd been watching *Renown* pass them: the CW business, going in for a commission: what the skipper had told him and also, linking with that, the fact of being alone now, a feeling that one had to move in *some* direction.

"How's the time, Yank?"

Paul shifted aching limbs. A steel deck got to you, after a few hours, and a tin hat didn't make much of a pillow. He squinted at his watch, and was vaguely surprised that there was enough light to make out the positions of the hands. He told Dukes, "Half three."

Baldy Percival, mummy-like with the white anti-flash gear covering his head and face, twisted up and on to his elbows. "What? What's that?"

"Go back to dreamland, Baldy."

"My foot's *frozen*!"

"Oh dear, oh dear!" The high-pitched exclamation came from Harry Rush, the rammer. He began to warble in a falsetto voice, "*Your*

136

tiny foot is frozen. Let me wa-arm it in the fire. . . ."

"Shut up, you fuckin' idiot!"

Dan Thomas's growl, from the huddle of duffel coats and oilskins inside the shield. Rush murmured, "Charming. *Suave*, you might say . . . 'Ow you makin' out, Yanky lad?"

"I'm okay, thanks."

"Can't you bastards bloody *kip*?"

"No, we soddin' can't. Too bleedin' comfortable up 'ere, for the likes of us. We ain't used to such soddin' luxury, are we, Yank?"

"Sea's gone down a little."

"Bloody 'ell it 'as. Just the course she's on."

You could feel the way the following sea was driving her along, lifting her from astern, the destroyer surfing over the big seas and seeming to drop back as well as down as each small mountain rolled on ahead of her. Still going east, Paul realised. Narvikwards. Vibration and ventilator-noise suggested they were doing revs for about twelve knots, something like that.

McElroy mumbled, half asleep, "Fuckin' 'oggin. Nothin' but mile upon mile of fuckin' 'oggin."

"Never knew you was a poet, Lofty." Vic Blenkinsop shifted, pushing himself upright and adjusting the headset under his balaclava. "Sheer delight to listen to you . . . *What* fuckin' time d'you say it was, Yank?"

"Minute or two past three-thirty."

The sky was brightening ahead. In streaks here and there, where the black storm-clouds had cracks between them, were rifts with a new pale, gale-driven day glittering through. If any Germans had got into Narvik during the night they'd have been damn glad to get inside, he thought, into the shelter of those fjords. He wondered what it would be like inside there. Like a river, probably: flat calm, reflecting the mountain-sides, beautiful. What a change from *this* . . . Keeping one's thoughts on solid things, on present and immediate-future subjects: the aim being to stop oneself indulging in the luxury of worrying, of trying to find an angle that would make everything all right and as it had been. It was *not* all right, and this was something one was going to have to accept and live with, recognise as existing, permanently, behind all the other facts of life.

If the Germans had got into Narvik, what could this force do about it? Sit the gale out in Vestfjord, wait for the Hun to come out and fight?

Couldn't hang around and wait for ever, though. Have to fuel some time. Some time pretty soon, he imagined.

"We're in Indian bloody file again." Dan Thomas had stepped over some sprawling bodies, crossed behind the breech; he was leaning against the inside edge of the gunshield and staring out over the port bow and ahead. He yawned: it sounded like a donkey braying. . . . "Like a lot

138

of bloody ducks followin' mother . . . *Hey*, what the—"

Vic Blenkinsop screamed, "Alarm bearing red one-oh, all guns follow director!"

A split second while it hit them and penetrated drowsy brains: then everyone was dodging and barging to the various positions round the gun. Everything happening at once: alarm-buzzer honking away below to get the other watch up, and the sound of the engines changing, turbine-whine rising and the roar of the fans increasing; the ship was swinging to port—but steadying already, course about due east. . . .

"All guns with SAP load, load, load!"

SAP stood for semi-armour-piercing, and Baldy Percival, who was the projectile supply number, snatched one of the right kind from the ready-use rack and clanged it into the loading-tray. Paul dropped his cordite charge in behind it and Harry Rush rammed shell and charge home into the breech. The block slid up automatically, its concave curve of silk-smooth steel pushing his fist clear as it rose, and Dan Thomas had slammed the interceptor shut.

"'B' gun ready!"

No fire order yet. Anti-climax. Thomas told them, "Dirty great battler out there."

"What, *German*?"

"Wouldn't be fuckin' Chinese, boyo, would she."

The ship that had sunk *Intent*? But that had been a cruiser, not a battleship. . . .

"'Aving you on." Dan Thomas laughed. "All I seen was *Renown* swingin' off course. Some fuckin' HO on the 'elm, I thought. . . ."

Paul had another charge ready in his arms. Until yesterday he'd been the projectile supply number and this job had been Baldy's: they changed you around so you'd learn the different jobs and be able to take other men's places in an emergency. In other words, if some of them got killed. Handling the cordite charges was a lot easier than lumping shells. *Hoste* was in a hurry now, slamming across the rollers, rolling savagely as she plunged in the wake of her next-ahead. She'd have to alter course, he guessed, before they opened fire. The enemy—whatever kind of enemy it was—was somewhere right ahead, blanked off from them by the leading ships. It had to be so, or the guns would have been trained out on some other bearing. He was pulling on his anti-flash gear one-handed and with the tin hat gripped between his knees while he leant sideways against the gun for support. They were supposed to wear the anti-flash hoods and gloves all the time when they were closed up at the gun, but nobody did—except for Baldy. . . . Blenkinsop shouted, "Target is *Gneisenau* with one *Hipper*-class cruiser astern of 'er. Course will soon be altered to port and enemy will be engaged to starboard!"

"Bloody *Gneisenau*, for Gawd's sake!"

"'Ere, Dan, you was fuckin' *right*!"

"I'm *always* fuckin' right. . . ."

Hipper-class cruiser, Rowan had said. Here it was again. *Here it was!*

Why couldn't *Renown* have opened fire? Nothing ahead of *her*, was there? Well—she'd want to get her after turret into it too, of course, fire broadsides, not just use the for'ard guns. . . . Lofty McElroy bawled, "Next-ahead's goin' roun' tae port!" He'd be seeing it through the port in the gunshield in front of him. He and the gunlayer on the other side each had one, an aperture with a shutter on it for keeping wind and wet out. In Director Firing—the normal system, which they'd be using now—neither layer nor trainer had to see outside or even know what the target looked like; all they had to do was keep one pointer lined up on another in a brass-cased dial. The director layer did the aiming for all four guns, from up there in the top.

Renown opened fire. Rolling crash of fifteen-inch guns and a flash like lightning flaring briefly, a splash of brilliance overtaken immediately by the dark, which seemed all the darker for it in the racket of wind and sea and the ventilators' roaring, and the turbines' scream. Paul stood with his feet braced well apart, rubber-soled shoes gripping the wet steel platform, one shoulder against the gunshield. Another salvo erupted: explosion and flash, black curtain clamping down

141

again. The ship was swinging, leaning hard to starboard as port rudder dragged her round and turned her port side to the gale's force. Plunging, shuddering, staggering round. As she turned, the gun trained out, staying on the bearing of the enemy. Twenty knots now? Third salvo: count to five and another sky-splitting crash. . . . He wondered if the Germans had been caught on the hop: it was possible, with those cloud-cracks in the east putting a light behind the bastards, showing them up to the British battlecruiser who would herself be still hidden in the westward gloom, storm-darkness. Two more salvoes had hurtled away: *Renown* had three twin turrets of fifteen-inch, so they'd be three-gun salvoes, and a fifteen-inch was a huge projectile. *Hoste* was steady now on what must have been a northward course, wind and sea deafening and violent on her port bow, gun trained out on the beam.

"Commence, commence, commence!"

Clang of the fire-gong: then the ear-slamming explosion: recoil, breech open, reeking cordite fumes flying as Dan Thomas jerked the lever to send the breech-block thumped down, projectile and charge in, breech shut, interceptor made: fire-gong—*crash*—second salvo, all four guns firing together and a ripple of the other destroyers' guns all down the line and the deeper thunder of the battlecruiser's salvoes in a steady rhythm now, flaming into the dawn-streaked east. No time to look at anything except this job, the

142

loading-tray and the breech, charges and projectiles coming up from below now through an ammo hatch in the deckhead of the Chiefs' and POs' mess under their feet and, before they got that far, from hand to hand up through two messdecks below that. The ship was trying to knock herself to bits, jolting and hammering across the sea, thrashing and flailing like a salmon on a line. The firing was constant now: breech open—filled—shut—*crash*, and flinging back—open. . . . Baldy seeming to be in the throes of a little dance as he banged his rounds in and lunged around for the next: it *was* like a dance, a kind of seven-man reel. . . .

"Check, check, check!"

Stone deaf. Skull ringing. Dizzy from noise and dazed by flash, muscles aching. Dan Thomas's fist hitting Paul's bicep had stopped him as he was about to drop a fresh charge into the loading-tray. The gun's crew was still now, only swaying and weaving to the ship's wild motion. And she was slowing, while from ahead *Renown*'s guns still boomed out, sound muted by distance as well as by one's own temporary deafness. *Renown* had obviously drawn well ahead of the destroyers; so if *Hoste* had been making twenty knots—which in conditions like these was fairly unthinkable, despite the fact that it was what she'd been doing—the battlecruiser must have been working up to—what, thirty?

143

Enemy running away? *Renown* cracking on full power to stay inside gun range?

They'd run from something their own size, Paul thought bitterly. Different when it had been just two destroyers. . . .

Hoste was swinging to starboard. Slowing, and turning back to her former eastward or south-eastward course.

"Secure from action stations."

Dan Thomas yelled to Lofty McElroy, "Train fore-an'-aft!" Baldy Percival's eyes gleamed at Paul through the gap in his anti-flash hood. He panted, "D'you realise, we've been in *action*?"

"Yeah. I suppose . . ."

Action was supposed to be something terrific, though. Like getting married or circumcised or something. This had been like a gun-drill. He hadn't caught a glimpse of any enemy and he certainly wasn't aware of having been shot at or in any danger. Technically, Baldy was right—they'd been in action: asked whether one had fired shots in anger, one could now answer in the affirmative. But he didn't feel it counted, really. And it certainly wasn't the kind of action that *Intent* must have been in. . . . He was looking out towards the destroyer on their starboard bow —he thought it was the flotilla leader, *Hardy*, Captain (D)'s ship—and there was a signal lamp sputtering dots and dashes from the back end of her bridge. The flotilla—ships from more than one flotilla here, actually, there must have been

144

about nine or ten destroyers altogether—seemed to be in the process of rearranging itself into the two-column formation.

"Right, then." Blackie Proudfoot, "A" gun's layer, had come up the ladder and lurched across into shelter. Blue-jowled, scowling, chewing gum. "*Right*, then! Bugger off, you shower o' fuckin' amacheurs!"

Shouts of ritually insulting welcome greeted him. Paul checked the time: it was well past the watch-changing hour, and therefore "B" gun-crew's watch below now. Lovely! A mug of tea or kye, he thought, whatever's going: then head down, kip until breakfast-time. . . . Proudfoot was grumbling, "Waste o' fuckin' ammo, wasn't it?"

Inside, on their way down to the messdeck, they met Sub-Lieutenant Peters, and Rush stopped him, asked him something about the action. Peters told them, "The second German wasn't a cruiser, it was *Scharnhorst*. GCO thought she was a *Hipper* when he first saw her —but we've been engaging two pocket battle-ships." He seemed delighted by it. . . . "Last we heard, *Renown* had scored three hits—including one in *Gneisenau*'s foretop, and it's put her main armament out of action. So *Scharnhorst*'s laying smoke now to cover their withdrawal."

"Mean they're scarpering, sir?"

Peters nodded to Harry Rush. "Our own gun-flashes will have helped to put the wind up them.

They couldn't know we're only destroyers, you see. If they *had* known, they could have got stuck in and knocked the be-Jesus off *Renown*. They're both twenty years newer than she is, you know."

"They'll 'ave the legs of her, then."

"Oh, they'll outrun her, I'm afraid." Peters' round face was scarlet from the wind. "Unless she's lucky and lands another one in some vital spot."

Paul asked him, "What are we doing now, sir?"

Peters turned to him. "We've orders to patrol Vestfjord, Everard. But if we're lucky—well, there's a signal just in from C-in-C to Captain (D) that he's to send some destroyers up to Narvik. That means right up through the fjords. Apparently some Huns have got in while our backs were turned."

"Bit late to be much fuckin' use, then." Rush was pulling a wet-looking pack of cigarettes from some inner pocket. "I mean, if the sods are *up* there, settled like—"

"*Un*settle 'em, boyo!" The gun captain struck him violently on the back. "We'll bloody *un*settle 'em!"

6

"CAPTAIN, sir!"
Dragging himself out of sleep . . .
"Unidentified ship approaching, sir!"
He was off the bunk, snatching duffle-coat and cap: *really* awake now, hearing the alarm buzzer sounding surface action stations. Across the lobby outside his sea-cabin, on to the ladder and up it to the bridge.

Very cold, and already daylight. It was four-twenty: he'd had about one and a half hours' sleep. Before he'd turned in the telegraphists had picked up an English-language broadcast announcing that Denmark had been overrun and was now in German hands and that the forts in Oslofjord were being bombarded by German warships.

Tommy Trench was waiting for him on the bridge. He pointed—over the starboard bow.

"Sure she's Norwegian, sir. Better to be safe than sorry, I thought, but—out of the last century, by the looks of her."

"And practically alongside." This reproof came as a reflex as he settled his glasses on her and found her so startlingly close. Trench was explaining that when she'd come into sight around the point she'd been only a mile away. A

147

small ship with the lines of an old-fashioned yacht, two raked masts and one high, thin funnel. Clipper bow, cut-away stern, gaffs on both masts and a white painted wheelhouse just for'ard of the funnel. Abaft it there was a longer, lower, dark-coloured deckhouse with ports all along its length. What ought to be a saloon. One could imagine its dark mahogany, red velvet, brass. She was flying the Norwegian ensign and there were no guns on her that he could see. He glanced up over his shoulder and saw that the director tower was trained on her. The four-sevens would be too.

He lowered his binoculars. "Warn Brockle-hurst not, repeat *not*, to open fire without orders. Signalman—give me the loud-hailer."

Obviously she *was* Norwegian. But since the Germans had taken the whole of Denmark in about half a dog-watch it wasn't inconceivable that they could have pinched a few Norwegian ships by this time. On the other hand he couldn't imagine Germans bothering with such a delicate-looking, totally unwarlike craft; or for that matter that even if she was packed with Nazis from stem to stern she'd pose much of a threat to a well armed, albeit immobilised, destroyer.

He took the loud-hailer from the signalman—who'd plugged it into the socket that was more often used for the kye kettle—and lifted it, aimed it at the stranger. Clearing his throat produced a

148

sound like a seal's bark, fairly cracking across the fjord.

"Do not approach any more closely. Stop and identify yourself!"

He repeated it: his voice boomed over the water and echoed back from the land behind him. Whatever that floating antique was, she must have come round the headland—Finsneset—from seaward, perhaps en route to Namsos, then spotted *Intent* lying at anchor in the shallow bay and turned down to investigate her. *Intent* was lying almost parallel to the shore, with her cable growing straight out into the incoming tidal flow. Beyond the Norwegian—he hadn't stopped yet and he was still heading straight for the British ship—you could see white-topped waves and a drifting haze of spray that was being whipped off their crests, but here in the lee of the point there was no broken water and the ship's motion as she rode to her anchor was comparatively gentle.

He aimed the hailer again.

"Stop, or I shoot!" He glanced at Trench. "Tell Brocklehurst to load one gun with practice shell."

A warning shot across the bows was a good way to short-cut any language problems. A practice shell was solid, non-explosive. But he'd no wish to aggravate this Norwegian. If it was true that the Nazis were invading, then Britain and Norway were now allies with a common enemy. And this strange-looking craft might prove to be

Intent's saviour, a means of getting shore assistance for the engine-room repairs.

He put his glasses up again. The newcomer was altering course, turning to starboard, and the ripple of bow-wave at her shapely forefoot was diminishing as she slowed. Her captain was doing things his own way, in his own time; either he didn't understand English, or he was deaf, or he was demonstrating a spirit of Viking independence. And these were, after all, Norwegian waters. . . . His ship was beam-on to *Intent* now, and stopping; two hands had gone for'ard to let go an anchor. They were visible only from the waist up, on account of the ship's high, white-painted bulwarks.

The anchor splashed down and its cable rattled out; at the same time a man in what looked like naval uniform emerged from the wheelhouse, and waved.

Nick waved back. He told Trench, "Fall out action stations, but keep one four-seven and the point-fives closed up. Better send the hands to breakfast while things are quiet."

The Norwegians were preparing to lower a boat. It was a motor skiff, slung from davits abaft the mizzen mast, and some men were hauling on tackles to turn the davits out on this side.

She was unarmed, and the rigging on those masts and gaffs indicated that she had sails and was equipped to use them. Training ship? Around 200 tons, he guessed, and roughly 120 feet long.

No weapons anywhere, not even a machine-gun. But she'd be capable of getting into Namsos and bringing out some plumbers, all right.

He asked Trench, "Any progress in the engine-room?"

"None at the last enquiry, sir. Beamish is still at it but he's not exuding much optimism. . . . MacKinnon's improved the W/T reception though, and he's picked up two or three signals addressed to Captain (D) 2, they tell me. I've been leaving the deciphering until the doctor's had some zizz."

Nick had told MacKinnon to take in everything he could pick up. He wanted to know what was going on: especially any details of the Hun attack on Norway. But they'd only be able to decipher signals intended for ships of their own size, more or less. Admiralty messages to and from the C-in-C, or signals between flag officers, would be in ciphers which a destroyer didn't carry.

"Have you had any sleep, pilot?"

"Yes, sir." Chandler took the point of the enquiry. "I'll make a start on the deciphering."

"Lyte or Cox can give you a hand." You needed one man to read out, another to look up and write down. He asked Trench, "How's Bywater's patient?"

"Stronger, he said. That's why he decided he could get his head down. . . . We're about to have visitors, sir."

The skiff was in the water with two men in

her, and the one who'd waved was climbing down to join them. Nick focused binoculars on him. Three stripes: or two and a half. A burly, biggish man. Trousers tucked inside seaboots. Now he was in the boat's stern-sheets, and as he turned around Nick saw a crumpled-looking cap pushed well back and a reefer jacket unbuttoned over a high-necked sweater. Lowering the glasses, he thought he already had a fair idea of the sort of character he'd be dealing with.

"Let's give him the red carpet, Number One."

Trench nodded. "I'll have it unrolled, sir." He went down to organise a Jacob's ladder and a side-party, and Nick sent a message to Leading Steward Seymour to get his day-cabin straightened—after the rough weather it was bound to be in a mess—and to lay on coffee and biscuits. Then Lyte, the sub-lieutenant, came up, sent by Trench to take over anchor-watch on the bridge, and Nick went down to see what was happening in the engine-room.

Beamish and his henchmen looked just about done in. Dull, red-rimmed eyes, faces grey under coatings of oil and dirt. Listening to his laboured explanation of the problems, Nick told himself that one had to allow for that tiredness as a factor in the chief stoker's defeatism. Beamish was winding up his depressing report by explaining what he intended to do about the blast-hole overhead. It was a large, jagged hole; as Trench had said earlier, the shell must have exploded virtually

152

as it pierced the thin layer of steel. And yet the explosion had sounded as if it had been right inside. Echo-effect, perhaps . . . Beamish's plan was to use two of the steel floor-plates, weld them over the hole after the uneven edges had been cut away.

"What'll you stand on, without floor plates?"

"Timber staging, sir. Chief Buffer reckons he can knock some up for us."

"Sounds reasonable."

"It was the middy—Mr. Cox—as thought of it, sir."

"What's it to do with *him*, for God's sake?"

"Well, he's been lending us a hand, sir."

"*Has* he . . ." Extraordinary. But he'd ask Cox about it, not Beamish. "Just one question, Chief. Could we move now if we had to?"

"Oh, *no*, sir!"

"Second question, then. Do you anticipate that at some later stage we'll be in a condition so we *can* move?"

"I—s'pose so, sir. Somehow or other, like. But—"

"At this stage you can't guarantee it."

"No, sir." An oily hand passed round an already well-oiled jaw. "No. I'm sorry, sir, I—"

"It's not your fault. Anyway, we're about to be boarded by a Norwegian, and with any luck I'll persuade him to carry on into Namsos and bring out some shoreside help."

The Norwegian would damn well *have* to.

Otherwise *Intent* would still be sitting here when the Germans came.

PO Metcalf's bosun's call shrilled as the man came over *Intent*'s side. He was a lieutenant-commander, and in his late forties, Nick guessed. A rugged-looking character with greying hair showing under the battered cap. Wide-set blue eyes in a tanned, muscled face scanned the reception committee and returned to Nick. The salute was casual, friendly.

Nick shook a wide, meaty hand. "My name's Everard, and this is His Majesty's Ship *Intent*. Glad to welcome you aboard."

"I am Claus Torp. Kaptein-Löjtnant, Naval Reserve. My ship there—" he jerked a thumb— "is *Valkyrien*."

"A very handsome ship, we've all been thinking." Nick introduced Tommy Trench. Torp asked him as he shook his hand, "You got many of such size?" Trench laughed; Nick asked Torp, "Are you from Namsos, Commander?"

"I—yes. But *Valkyrien* I am bringing from Mo i Rana to Trondheim. Then I am hearing on my radio the Boche is already there, so—"

"The Germans are in Trondheim?"

"I think they are in *every* damn place, you know?"

They could be here at any moment, then. . . . It wasn't really a surprise—only confirmation of existing fears. At least he'd been wise not to take her into Trondheim.

"Will you come below, Commander, and discuss the position over a cup of coffee?"

"Sure, thank you."

"Join us, Tommy?"

"Thank you, sir." Nick saw Henry Brocklehurst emerging from the screen door, the entrance to the wardroom flat. Short, neat—he'd just shaved—a little cock-sparrow of a man, smart enough for Whale Island, the gunnery school, to which he hoped to return soon for his "long G" course. Nick introduced him to Torp: and beside Trench, Brocklehurst really did look like a sparrow. Torp grinning down at him and glancing at the bigger man, obviously thinking something of the same sort. Nick told him, "I'd like you to keep an eye on the bridge, while we're below. Lyte's up there, but we aren't in the safest of spots."

Brocklehurst nodded. "Aye aye—"

"Have you had any sleep yet?"

"I kipped in the director, sir."

"My God . . ." Leading the other two down to his day-cabin, Nick asked *Valkyrien*'s captain, "D'you have any details of what's happened in Trondheim?"

"The forts are fighting but the town is captured. One cruiser, *Hipper*, and four destroyers with her, they are through the Narrows before alarm was given." He snorted angrily. "We are not ready for the bastards, I think. . . . Is your wireless not working, Captain?"

"We lost our topmast. Messed things up somewhat. We're on reduced power too." He led into the cabin and saw that the coffee was already there, set out by Leading Steward Seymour, together with a plate of shortbread from his private store. "Sit down, please." Seymour came in behind them, and stood hovering; Nick told him he wasn't needed. He explained to Torp, "We were damaged in action with a German cruiser. *Hipper*-class—perhaps *Hipper* herself, if she's in Trondheim now."

"You are lucky to be afloat, I think. Against *Hipper*? One H-class destroyer?"

" 'I', as it happens. For *Intent*."

" 'H', 'I'—who's giving a damn!" A forthright character, this Norwegian. "From one look I see what you are. Otherwise I am turning round to run like hell, you bet. *Valkyrien* has no guns, you understand, she is for boys' training. I bring her now from Mo i Rana to Trondheim so they put guns on her for patrol work in Trondheimsfjorden." He'd stopped his prowling inspection of the cabin in front of a portrait that didn't belong in here. It had strayed—thanks no doubt to the steward's "straightening"—from Nick's sleeping cabin. Torp let out something between a hiss and a whistle: "This is your wife, Captain?"

He'd pronounced it "vife". Nick told him no,

it was not, and invited him to sit down. Torp said, lowering himself into an armchair, "I suppose you did not hear what has happened in Oslo?"

"Only that Hun ships were bombarding the forts."

"So." The Norwegian accepted coffee. "Thank you . . . Patrol boat *Pol III*, with commander my friend Wielding Olsen—also naval reserve—is in Oslofjord. Sight Boche—make challenge—no answering, so open fire. *Pol III* has one gun—forty millimetre, *one*. She was whaler—very small . . . You know what ships she is fighting? *Blucher, Lutzow, Emden*! Also torpedo boats and minesweepers. Wielding has ram one torpedo boat, then—finish. He himself—listen, I tell you —he is blown in half, his legs—all from *here*. . . . He roll himself overboard so the men do not see him and stop fighting. Huh?" Torp's jaw-muscles bulged: his eyes closed, opened again. . . . "Wielding Olsen. My *friend* . . . I have this in Norwegian broadcast. Also our government—listen—they have ordered now to mobilise—and they are sending the calling-up orders today, *by post*!"

"I don't believe it."

Torp looked at Trench. "Believe everything, my friend. Anything. So long as a German is not telling it, believe it. We have *idiots* in our government. You too, I think. I think your Navy could—could have been around—not *laying mines*, God damn it, but—"

"Quite." Nick put his cup down. "The point is, to decide what we're going to do *now*. And the first thing is, Commander, I very much want your help."

"Okay, you have it. But the *first* thing is you must move up the fjord much higher. Here you are exposed all ways. If the wind veer one point you have bad conditions and lee shore southward. Also, if I was enemy, I come round the point here and before you can see who I am—*boom!*"

"The problem is that we *can't* move. This is as far as we could get. The cruiser—*Hipper*—hit us in the engine-room. Not only has it done us a lot of damage, but it killed all my artificers and I've no one left who can put us right. What I'd like to ask you to do, Commander, is go to Namsos as fast as possible and bring off some engineers. With whatever gear they might think they'd need. Would you do that for us?"

"Sure." Torp nodded, munching shortbread. Then he took a swallow of coffee to wash the crumbs down. He blinked at Nick across the table. "I also have wish to go to Namsos. I *must* go there. But for you maybe I have better plan." He took a cigarette from the case that Trench was offering him. "Thank you. I think first I send my boat to *Valkyrien* for bringing my engineer to look at your troubles. You agree?"

It seemed an obvious preliminary. But it would

use up *time*. . . . And what sort of old Scandinavian shellback would be the engineer of that museum piece?

"Every minute counts, Commander. With the Germans in Trondheim—what, seventy miles from us—"

"Halvard Boyensen is damn fine engineer. This is why I have been taking him to Mo i Rana. That old *Valkyrien* don't work for just any damn-fool mechanic. So I take young—" he tapped his forehead—"*smart* fellow—"

"All right." It might *save* time, in the long run. "Let's have him over."

"Good." The Norwegian pushed himself up. "You stay. I tell them."

Waiting, finishing his coffee, Nick saw Trench glancing at the portrait. Fiona Gascoyne—a rich man's widow. Thirty, thirty-one. Girl-about-town, and now in the MTC—Mechanised Transport Corps. Hence the existence and presence here of the photograph. She liked the look of herself in the MTC uniform—made for her, of course, at Huntsman. Nick had told her the obvious thing—that he preferred her out of it—and she'd said, "You're not getting one of me like *that*, my pet!" But there'd be quite a number of those portraits around, he knew that. She made no secret of it, she was far from being a one-man girl. She wouldn't be, she'd added, at least for quite some while. She'd been tied down all her life: she'd been very young when she'd married old Gascoyne, and the marriage had bored her stiff, but now she was free and rich enough to please herself—until she tired of it. . . . Which from Nick's point of view was perfectly all right. What seemed to be his mark were brief affairs or longer but essentially light-hearted ones. The long struggle with Ilyana and the continuing background of blind enmity from Sarah—whom he'd loved, twenty-plus years ago, to a degree beyond distraction—well, what was the point, when everyone ended up hurt?

Trench murmured, "We're in a bit of a spot, sir, aren't we, by and large."

"Oh, I don't know, Tommy. If this plumber's all he's cracked up to be, we might be running lucky again."

There'd been some Norwegian sounds up there; now Torp came back into the cabin. "I have send for Boyensen." He dropped into his chair, stubbed out the cigarette-end. "You guess what year my old *Valkyrien* is building?"

Nick made his guess and knocked a few years off the age before he spoke.

"Nineteen hundred?"

Trench said less gallantly, "Eighteen-ninety."

"Not so bad." Torp nodded. "Ninety-one."

Nick heard the motor skiff chug away from his ship's side. He told his guest, "There's one other urgent requirement we have, and that's oil-fuel. I imagine that once we're fixed up and can get into Namsos—"

160

"Sure." Claus Torp shrugged. "If the Boche stay away that long."

It was a lot to hope for. But there wasn't anything one could do *except* hope for it.

"I suppose there's no chance of a tanker coming out to us with some oil?"

"Yes—"

"What?"

"I say yes—no chance. No tanker."

Trench asked him, "Have you heard anything of Hun activity elsewhere than Trondheim and Oslo?"

"Sure. Stavanger. Around midnight, one Norwegian destroyer sink one German transport full with guns—artillery. And there were being—" he moved his big hands about above his head—"landings by parachute, you know? For the airdrome, I think. Well, of *course* for that . . . But also Narvik—one report say ten or maybe twelve big destroyers—"

"*German* destroyers?"

"Ja—twelve, big ones—on approach to Ofotfjord . . ." He aimed a blunt forefinger at Nick: "You hear what our government have been saying, that Germans come because you British laying your damn mines?"

"They can say whatever they like. But they're talking through their hats and we all know it."

The large hands spread. Now that he'd removed his cap you could see that he was completely grey. Nick had amended his estimate

161

of Torp's age, from late forties to early fifties. Torp said, "*I* do not know it."

Nick thought, *Then you're an idiot. . . .* He wasn't sure of him yet: whether there might be a useful ally under that rough exterior or whether he might be backwoodsman all through. He had no enormous hopes, consequently, of the engineer. Torp had a high opinion of him, but what was Torp's opinion worth?

He'd have the answer to that one soon enough. He explained, "This invasion—Denmark, then most of your ports—is obviously part of a well-planned operation. Separate assault forces, naval covering forces—you can't launch such a project in twenty-four hours. In fact the troops must have been assembled several days ago—let alone the planning before that, the mustering of stores, equipment—"

"Sure." Torp nodded.

"Well, our mining operation was carried out yesterday morning. At least, so far as we know, it *would* have been. So how can it be said to have precipitated the German assault?"

"Maybe they learn what *you* have been planning and move first, very quick?" He glanced at Trench. "Is there more coffee?"

"Might be." Trench felt the pot's weight. "Yes. Here . . ." He took up the cudgels while he poured out the dregs. "You realise we *had* to lay those minefields—that you Norwegians made us do it? To stop the Hun routeing all his

162

blockade-runners and ore-ships through your precious territorial waters while your government weren't doing a damn thing to stop it?"

The Norwegian stared at him, half-smiling. He glanced at Nick, then back again at Trench.

"You want to make some fight with me?"

"Lord, no. We want to fight *Germans* with you, Commander."

"All right." Torp nodded slowly, still looking hard at Trench. Then he glanced at Nick. "You got a good man here, I think."

Chandler had sent Midshipman Cox aft with some deciphered signals, and Nick looked through them while he and Trench waited on the upper deck for a verdict from the engine-room.

Renown had been in action only about an hour ago against *Gneisenau* and a cruiser. Then another signal referred to *Scharnhorst* as being in company with *Gneisenau*. That one faded out: the fault of *Intent*'s poor reception, no doubt. Both were from Vice-Admiral Battlecruiser Squadron—Whitworth—to his destroyers—the 2nd and 20th Flotillas, under Warburton-Lee and Bickford. Then there was another from Admiral Whitworth ordering them to proceed to Vestfjord and patrol to cover approaches to Narvik; Whitworth, presumably, was chasing off in pursuit of those two German ships. So the destroyers would be patrolling Vestfjord on their own.

He turned to the last of the batch of ciphers. It was from the Commander-in-Chief to Captain (D), 2nd Flotilla: Send some destroyers up to Narvik to make sure no enemy troops land.

But Claus Torp's information was that there were a dozen Huns up that fjord already. If Warburton-Lee sent just a few ships of his flotilla up, and they found themselves ambushed by twelve of those bigger, newer, five-inch destroyers the Germans had—in fact even if the *whole* of the flotilla went up, because there were only six of them, including *Hoste* with Paul in her. . . .

Not a comfortable thought. *So don't think about it. . . .* In any case, Torp's rumours weren't necessarily better founded than whatever reports had reached the C-in-C. In this kind of fluid, not to say *muddled*, situation you had to take everything you heard with a pinch of salt.

"Here." He passed the log to his first lieutenant, and asked Cox, "That's all we've got?"

"Afraid so, sir."

"When you go back, ask the PO Tel to come and see me."

"Aye aye, sir."

"Is the doctor up and about yet?"

"Yes, sir. He thinks ERA Dobbs is going to pull through, sir."

Marvellous. And good for Bywater. But if Dobbs hadn't elected to be such a hero he might have been more than just "pulling through", he might have been on his feet and directing the repair work. The highly recommended Halvard Boyensen hadn't at first sight inspired much confidence; he looked more like a farm-hand than an engineer. Red-faced, with a heavy jaw and small, deep-set eyes. He and Torp had gone straight below with Beamish, after the skiff had brought him. Nick looked at his watch again; it felt like an hour that he'd been waiting.

Trench handed the signal log to Cox. And Nick remembered what Beamish had been telling him. . . . "Mid. You've been giving our chief stoker some technical advice, I hear."

"Oh, no, I—" Cox had turned pink. "I only —mentioned an idea, sir—"

"What made you go down there in the first place?"

"Just—wanted to see the shape of things, sir."

"D'you have a mechanical bent, then?"

"I've always—well, I like using my hands sir, and"—he glanced down at the signal log—"that sort of thing."

"You made yourself useful, anyway. Well done."

The boy looked surprised. Perhaps he'd expected a reprimand, for trespassing in a department that wasn't anything to do with him. "Thank you, sir."

Trench murmured, "They're coming up, sir."

Claus Torp, leading Boyensen and Beamish,

was wiping his hands on a lump of cotton waste. He stopped in front of Nick.

"In Namsos, alongside, with power from the shore, all that, he fix all good as new in one day." He raised two fingers, then four. "Twen'y-four hour, okay? But right here, working with your ship's men, *two* day." He pointed at Boyensen. "He say he can do this, but—" a shake of the head—"two day here, too damn dangerous, I think."

"You're thinking of towing me to Namsos?"

"Sure."

"But is he certain of what he's saying? Can I count on it a hundred per cent?"

"Yes. I tell you, he is damn fine engineer."

He still didn't look like one.

"I want to be sure of this, Commander. Your man's saying he could do the job here, without other help or gear?"

"Sure. But much better in Namsos, with other help, tools also, and shore power. I think also very bad here if Germans coming."

Against that, it was also obvious that in Namsos they'd be in a dead-end, trapped. But the priority must be to get the ship back into a state of operational fitness as quickly as possible. If he took the chance of getting bottled up at Namsos, she'd be mended in a single day—and fuel at the same time. . . . For fuel, she'd have to go to Namsos anyway.

"What's your ship's speed?"

166

"Six knots, full speed. We tow at maybe three. You think?"

Behind the Norwegian loomed the burly, bearded figure of PO Telegraphist MacKinnon. Sent aft by young Cox, of course. Mr. Opie the torpedo gunner had appeared too: shaved and spruced up, pulling at his nose while he tuned his ears to the proceedings. Nick was thinking that from here to Namsos was about fifteen miles. Five hours then; possibly only four, then twenty-four alongside. Say thirty hours in all.

"All right." He nodded to Claus Torp. "I'd be grateful for a tow."

"Up and down, sir!"

It meant that the ship was up to her anchor so that the chain cable was vertical. Trench, in the front of the bridge, acknowledged the foc's'l report; he glanced enquiringly at Nick, who nodded and told him, "Weigh."

The cable began to clank again as the foc's'lemen recommenced their circling, leaning on the capstan bars. Weighing was by hand because the auxiliary generator would have been hard put to it to provide enough power. Internal lighting, communications and fire-control systems had priority. Young Cox was down on the foc's'l with Lyte; Nick reckoned he'd been shut away with fine nibs and coloured inks for too long.

Off to starboard, *Valkyrien* was displaying her

cut-away stern, and white water under her counter showed that her engine was chugging ahead, already putting some strain on the towing wire which had been led through *Intent*'s bullring and had its eye fast on the starboard Blake slip. Black coal-smoke leaked from the Norwegian's tall, pipe-stem funnel as she kept enough pull on the wire to hold the destroyer's bow from falling off landward when the anchor broke clear of the seabed. To start with, Trench had sent one end of a floating Coir rope over to *Valkyrien* with the skiff on Torp's return trip to his ship; then the Norwegians had winched it over with a stronger hemp cable attached to it, and finally the hemp had been dragged across, pulling behind it the towing hawser of flexible steel-wire rope.

"Anchor's aweigh!"

Hanging over the flared edge of the foc's'l, Lyte had seen the cable swing, proof that the hook had been wrenched out of its clay-and-sand bed. He'd got back now, out of the way of a man with a hose and another with a broom; it was their job to clean the muck off the chain as it clanked up towards the hawse-pipe. If it wasn't cleaned there'd be mud and weed collecting in the chain-locker down inside the ship, and before long there'd be a fearful stink as well.

Torp had got Nick's signal, and the white at *Valkyrien*'s stern was spreading as she put on more power. Funnel-smoke increasing simultaneously . . . The towing hawser came up out

168

of the water, rising and lengthening as *Intent*'s inertial weight came on it. Trench yelled down at the foc's'l, "Stand clear of the wire!"

Cox and two seamen jumped away from it: and Lyte, who should have seen it before Trench had, was lecturing them about it. A steel-wire rope under strain was a lethal thing if it parted and found human flesh and bones in the way of its scything recoil.

"She's swinging to starboard, sir."

"Very good."

Chandler was watching the ship's head in the compass, checking her response to the pull on her bow. This was the tricky bit—getting her moving, and particularly at this angle, turning her out across the direction of the wind and the up-fjord tide. On the port side of the foc's'l a sailor crouched with a sledge-hammer over the slip on the port cable; if the towing wire snapped he was ready to knock that slip off and send the anchor plunging down. With no engine power of her own to call on, *Intent* was entirely dependent on *Valkyrien* and on that wire.

"Clear anchor!"

Lyte had yelled it. It meant the anchor was high enough to be visible and it was on its own, not caught in some submarine cable or wreckage. Chandler said, "Ship's head north thirty-five east, sir."

Nick had put starboard rudder on to help her round: he didn't give a hoot what the ship's head

169

was. Torp could see to that. She was turning steadily now and the wire looked all right, still had a springy sag in it. They heard the thud as the twenty-eight hundredweight anchor banged home into its hawser-pipe: the rhythmic clanking ceased. Now they'd put the bottlescrew slip on that cable—because the Blake was in use as a towing slip—and veer to it until the slip had the anchor's weight.

Claus Torp could be seen on the roof of his wheelhouse, out on its starboard edge, with binoculars trained aft on *Intent*. Might have done a lot worse than run into Torp, Nick thought. It was a pity his ship had no guns and wasn't capable of more than six knots. A waste, in present circumstances, of such a man.

But there might be guns ashore that could be mounted in her. Or some less ancient craft that could be taken over and adapted.

"Midships."

"Midships, sir!"

CPO Jarratt, the coxswain, was on the wheel. Chandler's head bobbed up and down like a hen drinking as he switched his glance between the compass and *Valkyrien*'s stern. Completely unnecessary. If Torp went the wrong way what could *they* do about it? Chandler was—or might be, in some ways, Nick thought—a bit of a pompous ass. Perhaps not the right man to deal effectively with a lad like Cox. A fed-up youngster needed to have enthusiasm imparted to him,

170

not constant disapproval. Enthusiasm, and in extreme cases, chastisement as well. Having spent some years as a fed-up midshipman oneself, one *knew* it.

"Swing's easing off, sir. Steadying towards south eighty east."

"All right, pilot. I can see what's happening for myself."

On this course *Valkyrien* would take them out into mid-fjord, where they'd then go round about fifty degrees to starboard. And now that the pull was from directly ahead *Intent* was beginning to pick up a little speed. With no engine noise or fans sucking, the rustle and slap of water along her sides was a peculiar, rather spooky sound.

Spooky was right. Ghost-ship. She'd have been written off as lost by this time. He stooped to the voicepipe: "Keep us in the middle of *Valkyrien*'s wake, cox'n, and use as little wheel as possible."

She'd be in rougher water in a few minutes, but only for half an hour. Then they'd turn a corner into a more sheltered part.

MacKinnon had reported that he'd sharpened up the W/T reception, but there was no possibility of being able to transmit over any worthwhile range. Nick wouldn't have used his wireless anyway, even if they'd had full power. One signal out would be enough to bring Germans *in*. Or— worse, or at any rate just as bad—*over*, with their aircraft. If the bastards had been capturing airfields the sky would be thick with their dive-bombers before long. For the time being this low, dense cloud was a blessing, but it couldn't last for ever.

Patience—for one day. Well, thirty hours. Patience and a touch of fortitude. Then, fighting fit, sneak out during the dark hours with either Claus Torp or some other Norwegian as pilot. When *Intent* was well offshore he'd break the self-imposed W/T silence. She'd have generator power and a jury fore-topmast by that time.

There was more motion on her, and on *Valkyrien* too, as they crept out into the less protected water in the middle of the fjord. Chandler was taking bearings—of Sornamsen light structure on the Finsneset headland, and Altoy Island, and a sort of beacon on the Otteroy coast almost right ahead. And now here was young Bywater, the doctor—skinny, dark-haired, smiling his rather boyish smile as he anticipated Nick's question.

"ERA Dobbs is sleeping peacefully, sir. It's a downright miracle."

"Not medical genius?"

"Ah—perhaps just a *touch* of that, sir."

"Fishing-boat green three-oh, sir!"

Valkyrien was making the turn at this point, and the towing hawser was angling away to starboard. Jarratt could handle it. . . . Nick had the boat in his glasses. Blue-painted, bouncing northward—as they were turning, it would be on the *port* bow in a minute. Nearly ahead now, and for a while it was going to be out of sight. But *literally* bouncing: a beamy, double-ended boat with a wheelhouse amidships painted a paler blue, and the boat was travelling in sheets of spray, moving quite fast, fairly smashing through the lumpy sea. . . .

Jarratt had done it well. *Valkyrien* had steadied on the up-fjord course and *Intent* was smack in the centre of her wake.

That boat was in sight again, on the other bow. It looked as if it had sheered away to starboard: and several figures had come out of that little box amidships to stare at the oncoming ships. They'd know *Valkyrien*, presumably. Claus Torp was up on his platform again, waving his cap and his other arm as well, apparently calling the boat towards him. . . . Message received there, evidently, and similarly interpreted: the boat was turning, plunging round and heading—by the looks of it—for *Valkyrien*. Perhaps its coxswain had been unsure of what *Intent* was, knowing there could be Germans in the offing?

There was a lot of waving going on, between Torp's ship and the boat. And now a light was flashing from *Valkyrien*. Nick lowered his glasses and looked round. Clash of the Aldis: Signalman Farquharson was ahead of him and had also beaten Herrick to the draw. From *Valkyrien* the calling-up signs ceased, and Nick read the laboriously spelt-out one-word signal: STOP?.

"From *Valkyrien*, sir—'Stop'."

"Very good."

He warned Jarratt of what was about to happen. Meanwhile the blue fishing-boat was closing in towards *Valkyrien* and Torp had put his helm over, altering round to starboard as his ship lost way. Giving the boat a lee on his port side, Nick supposed. One of the boat people was still on the outside beside the wheelhouse, waving frantically: a man in a bright blue oilskin, much brighter than the paintwork of the boat itself. He put his glasses up: it wasn't a man, it was a woman. What he'd thought to be a sou'wester was a lot of dark hair blowing about in the wind. Then the boat vanished, behind *Valkyrien*, who'd gone round about forty-five degrees to starboard, obviously so that the boat could go alongside in that slight shelter.

Trench cleared his throat. "Popsie in that boat, sir."

"Yes. I noticed." He put his glasses up again. The towing cable was sagging to the water but not much more than that. *Valkyrien*, being almost beam-on to the wind now, would drift faster than *Intent* was likely to, so the wire should be kept reasonably taut. He hoped they weren't going to be kept waiting long; he wanted to have his ship alongside that quay, have the work start below, get some oil-fuel flowing into her sound tanks. There was a biting urgency to get her operational again.

Before the bloody Germans come . . .

There was activity now on the Norwegian's

174

upper deck, around her mizzen mast. Several people were clustered on that far side, where the boat would be. He took his eyes off the binoculars to glance again at the hawser; Chandler murmured, "All's well so far, sir." Mustn't take too critical a view of Chandler, he told himself. Lumbered with a bloody-minded snotty for an assistant, he'd quite understandably lose patience with him. The more of a perfectionist one was oneself, the more one disliked sloppiness in others; and Chandler as a navigator *was* something of a perfectionist. What else did one want from a navigator but perfection? It was simply that he, Nick, happened also to have some sympathy with bloody-minded snotties.

"By the way, pilot—"

"Sir?"

"I've decided to take Cox out of the tanky job. I want to shake his ideas up a bit by pushing him around to other parts of ship. I think later he'd better come back to you—not as tanky, probably, but just to knock some navigation into his head. All right?"

"Suits me, sir."

"Tommy."

Trench came back to the binnacle. Nick said, "You've got this CW candidate—Williamson, is it, on the searchlight?" Trench nodded. Nick paused: he'd just seen a patch of bright blue on *Valkyrien*'s deck. He focused his glasses on it: and he'd guessed right, it was the girl. He told

Trench, "Your popsie, Number One, has transferred to *Valkyrien*."

"I've lost her, then. Some chaps have all the luck."

Torp, he meant. And one could, indeed, imagine. . . . Nick said, "This CW, Williamson —how would he take to a spell as tanky, to widen his experience?"

"I'd say the idea's bang-on, sir."

"Except—" Chandler put it—"that at this stage I hardly need one."

"You will when we get home and you find a whole raft of Notices to Mariners to deal with. More importantly, it might be good for Williamson."

When we get home . . .

The boat was leaving *Valkyrien*, nosing out round her stern and turning into the wind, sending up sheets of sea again as she picked up speed. Heading towards *Intent*? It looked like it: and it also looked like Claus Torp standing amidships beside the wheelhouse doorway with one arm inside to steady himself against the roller-coaster motion. . . . It *was* him. He was shouting at someone inside and pointing with his free arm towards *Intent*. But if he was planning to come alongside—well, Nick hoped he wasn't. He couldn't give the boat any shelter, unless *Valkyrien* elected to pull her round, and Torp might not appreciate how flimsy a destroyer's plating was, sideways-on.

The boat was turning in towards them. Trench suggested, "Shall I put a ladder and fenders over, sir?"

"I'd rather not encourage him. Hang on." The last thing he wanted was that heavy-timbered craft bashing up and down against his ship's side. But it had swung to port and it was heading directly for *Intent*, its stunted mast rocking like a metronome as it rolled, beam-on to the waves. *Damn it* . . . He opened his mouth to tell Trench to get fenders over quickly: then saw the boat going round again—about forty feet from the ship's side, turning to point her stem into the weather, and slowing to a crawl as she came up level with the bridge. Torp had ducked inside: now he was out again with a megaphone.

Trench snapped, "Loud-hailer, signalman!"

"*Intent*, ahoy!"

Nick got up on the step and put a hand to his ear to show Torp that he was listening. Below him, Herrick was plugging in the loud-hailer. Torp bellowed through his megaphone, "There are Boches in Namsos!"

Silence . . .

Implications spread quickly through the initial shock. Primarily, no repairs in Namsos. No oil . . . What ships have they got there, for Pete's sake? He'd got the loud-hailer up.

"How did they get there?"

"There was one merchant vessel empty for loading cargo. In Namsos lying three day. This

177

morning before light two hundred Boche soldier with guns come out from ship's hold—all surprise, no time for defending. They have control now—*all*."

Wooden Horse tactics. And Namsos was German. *Intent* wasn't capable of going anywhere. She couldn't stay where she was, either.

He lifted the loud-hailer again.

"What do you suggest we do?"

"I think I tow you into Totdalbotn."

Totdalbotn. Something familiar about that name. Some small port on this coast? But Torp's earlier remark echoed in his brain: *I think they are in* every *damn place, you know?* Chandler had gone quickly to get the chart and bring it to him. And before he'd looked at it, he remembered—that enclosed anchorage right inside Hoddoy Island. Very sheltered and well hidden. The spot he'd been aiming to reach last night, before the engines packed up. Nearer to Namsos than one would have chosen to be, now that the Germans had taken over, but if they'd come in a freighter and had no naval units with them it might be possible to get away with a short stay —long enough for Halvard Boyensen to work some miracle in the engine-room.

No oil, though. But then, there'd be none— none that he could get at, now—*anywhere* up these fjords. Once the ship was repaired she'd have to sneak out again on as much fuel as was left in the tanks, and when he'd got her well away he'd wireless for a rendezvous with some big ship from whom he could refuel.

It had taken about fifteen seconds to cover that much ground, and to realise that while this was a major setback it didn't have to be exactly doomsday. And in any case his options weren't all that numerous. He pointed the loud-hailer at the fishing-boat, which was holding its station abreast the destroyer's bridge, stemming wind and tide while Torp waited for an answer.

"All right. We will do as you suggest. Totdalbotn."

Torp bellowed, "Okay! Very good!"

The conference was over. The blue boat began to surge ahead and swing away to starboard for its trip back to *Valkyrien*. Torp had disappeared inside it. Nick got down off the step, and Leading Signalman Herrick took the loud-hailer from him. Chandler said, looking at the chart, "Nice private little anchorage, but it's awfully close to Namsos, sir."

Nick barely heard him. He was staring up-fjord, thinking about the Germans and the ship they'd come in. "Merchant vessel", Torp had said, but she might be armed; she wouldn't have displayed weapons any more than she'd advertised her cargo.

He told Trench, "We'll go to action stations, please."

7

"**B**OAT'S coming off shore, Vic."

"Yeah?" Blenkinsop's eyes were squeezed half shut in the gap in his balaclava. "What you got, Yank, telescopic eyeballs?"

"Damn it, look *there*!"

"Blind as a soddin' bat." Rush glanced critically at the sight-setter. "Too much you-know-what. Oughter leave it *alone* for 'alf an hour, give the poor bloody thing a chance." Rush looked shorewards at the tight huddle of houses and the tall, black-looking light-tower, where *Hardy*'s boat had gone in and from where it was now returning. They were in Vestfjord, the inner part of it, the funnel-shaped entrance to Ofotfjord and to Narvik.

"B" gun's crew weren't much of an audience for Rush's jokes this evening. There was increasing tension in the ship as the time for action neared. Paul could feel it in himself: excitement touched with fear, and also an element of frustration at not knowing what was happening or why they were hanging around here, why the flotilla leader had sent that boat inshore.

The buzz was that the tiny village with the lighthouse was called something beginning with "T" and that it was the pilot station for this area.

That would explain the boat being sent in—to bring off a Norwegian pilot for the tricky passage up to Narvik. Particularly if it was true that they'd be making that passage in the dark.

Black water, and a streaky blackish sky. Snow patched the land and blanketed the inland mountains, mountains rising white and steep dramatically against dark sky. Intermittently falling snow was quickly filling the non-white patches; before long there'd be nothing *but* white, anywhere. Because of the cold, most of the gun's crew were wearing greatcoats instead of oilskins. Here in Vestfjord, with the sheltering arm of the Lofotens making a seventy-mile barrier between themselves and the North Sea violence they'd come from, there were no leaping seas to wet them. Only the snow-showers and, in place of discomfort from salt water, the biting cold.

Hostile, who'd been on some detached duty, had just rejoined the flotilla, so now all six destroyers were present. *Hardy*, the leader and Captain (D)'s ship, had moved close inshore, and the rest of them had cruised around further out, waiting. Leading them now was *Hunter*; then came *Havock*, and astern of her, *Hotspur*. *Hoste* had dropped back to last place, in order to let *Hostile* slip in ahead of her. *Hoste*'s CO, Lieutenant-Commander Rowan, was junior to the other five captains.

Paul was thinking of applying to join submarines. The idea had been triggered by a broadcast which the skipper, Rowan, had made about an hour ago over the ship's tannoy, telling them about things that had been happening up and down the Norwegian coast. Among the items of news had been details of British submarines' successes off southern Norway, in the Skagerrak and Kattegat. Paul had been left with the impression that the submarines were the real front-liners: in enemy waters and sinking Germans while the Home Fleet in all its glory was —apparently—parading up and down well out to sea.

And something else influenced him too, towards the submarine idea. The talk at that dinner-party at Mullbergh had turned in that direction, and Paul's father had told him how he'd always regarded them not as ships but as *devices*—and nasty, dirty ones at that; but in 1918 he'd had to take passage in one through the Dardanelles to Istanbul, and while he would not, he'd said, want to do anything like it again, he'd come to understand the submariners' fascination with their trade. At this, Jack Everard had definitely sneered. In his opinion Nick's original view had been the right one. Submarines weren't ships, they were *things*: and not the *sort* of thing that one had wanted to join the Navy for. Strictly for oddballs and technical people. . . .

So if one did join submarines, Paul thought, one might be fairly sure of not running up against Jack Everard?

182

There was a superciliousness, an assumption of superiority, in Jack's manner, which he found extremely irritating. There was also resentment, he thought, directed at this half-foreign interloper, an outsider who'd one day take Mullbergh away from Jack Everard the True Blue. Something like that.

He might have to face that hostility very soon. If he was now Sir Paul Everard—HO, OD? There'd be Jack's mother to deal with too. Really a nightmare prospect.

"We're off, lads!"

Harry Rush had made the announcement. There was a light flashing from *Hardy*, the flotilla leader, and *Hunter* up ahead was leading these other five destroyers round to starboard, turning shorewards and right round, reversing course. *Hardy* herself was gathering way westward. You could see her bow-wave rising; her motorboat was inboard, up on its davits and in the course of being secured there.

The light had stopped flashing. Paul guessed it might have been an order to form up on her. The way she was taking them was *away* from Narvik. . . . Then he guessed that if the plan was to go through in the dark tonight, it would be much too early to start now—he checked the time —at 1750.

What would close action be like, he wondered. Being shot at; seeing men hit, killed, wounded. He'd asked his father, on the last day he'd had

183

at Mullbergh, what it felt like, the first time you were in it.

"Well . . . You've swum in competitions, inter-school stuff?"

"Why, sure, but—"

"Nervous before the starter's gun, then too busy to do anything but get on with it?"

He saw the point, and nodded. "I guess so."

"That's how it is, Paul. The fright comes *before* the action."

He'd been satisfied with this answer, at the time. Up to a point. With the mental reservation that when he'd swum in inter-College matches nobody had shot at him, and that this must make, surely, *some* difference. . . . But now it didn't feel anything like that kind of pre-contest nervousness, it felt more like—*well, damn it*, he told himself, *it's like he said, it really is! This is the "before", and okay, so I'm worried; and he can be right about the "after" too, can't he?*

In a tizz now, a Dherjhorakov-type tizz, with himself. Recognising it and trying to stifle it . . .

His view of the village—Tranoy, that was the name they'd mentioned—was suddenly fading as if a curtain was being drawn across it. He went back into the shelter of the gunshield and told Baldy Percival, "More snow coming." *Hoste* was heeling as she turned behind the rest of the flotilla; she was on *Hostile*'s starboard quarter and from this angle there was a view of the other five ships of the flotilla, in line ahead and all

184

exactly alike, grey ships gliding through the quiet water. Sturdy, powerful. They looked good, he thought; they looked *terrific*. Baldy Percival muttered, "It might become pretty hot, you know, up that fjord."

"*Hot?*"

"The fighting—"

"Oh . . ."

"And going up it in the dark?"

"Not *our* worry, Baldy."

"It will be when we get up there. *Then* we'll be—"

"Worse for them than it'll be for us. Catch 'em on the hop, with any luck." He looked at him, smiling. "Hell, Baldy, this morning you were glad you'd been in action. You said—"

"Don't you think this is likely to be rather different?"

Paul shrugged, peered out into the falling snow. It was gathering on the gundeck, whitening the whole ship. Ahead, the fjord widened, white-covered mountains receding into a haze of cloud. *Hoste* heeled again as the flotilla began to zig-zag —to upset the aim of any lurking U-boat.

Vic Blenkinsop answered his telephone headset with his customarily sharp cry: " 'B' gun!"

Listening . . . Then—"Ah now, bloody 'ell mate, that's a bit bleedin' much—"

Someone had shut him up.

"What's up, Vic?"

He pushed the mouthpiece aside, and told

them, "Ship's company will be piped to action stations at 0030 hours."

It sank in slowly. This watch now ending was the First Dog; they'd be relieved in about one minute, at 1800, off-watch for the Last Dog, on again for the four hours of the First watch at 2000. That trick would end at midnight. And half an hour after *that* . . .

Rush complained, "Fuckin' 'ell-ship, this is. The 'uman body 'as certain simple wants—"

"We know about *your* 'orrible body's wants!"

"—such as more 'n five minutes fuckin' kip per fortnight—

"Don't call yourself *'uman*, do you, 'Arry?"

"If you can't take a joke, boyo—" Dan Thomas summed it up with an age-old naval admonition—"you shouldn't 've fuckin' joined."

In *Hoste*'s chartroom, Alec Rowan re-read the operation orders which Captain (D), Captain Bernard A. W. Warburton-Lee, had signalled from *Hardy* to his flotilla.

Final approach to Narvik: *Hardy* will close pilot station which is close to Steinhos Light. *Hunter* will follow in support. *Hotspur* and *Havock* are to provide anti-submarine protection to the northward. Ships are to be at action stations from 0030. When passing Skrednest Light *Hardy* will pass close to shore and order a line of bearing. Thereafter ships are to maintain narrow quarter-line to starboard so that fire from all ships is effective ahead. On closing Narvik *Hardy* will steer for inner harbour with *Hunter* astern in support. Germans may have several destroyers and a submarine in vicinity. Some probably on patrol. Ships are to engage all targets immediately and keep a particular lookout for enemy who may be berthed in inlets. On approaching Narvik *Hardy*, *Hunter*, *Havock* engage enemy ships inside harbour with guns and torpedoes. *Hotspur* engage ships to north-west. . . .

Rowan leant over the chart. It was the best they had on board but he should have had chart 3753, the harbour plan, and it wasn't in the folio. It was only now, to study in advance, that he'd have liked it. He knew that once they got in there there'd be no time for looking at charts of any sort.

Hostile and *Hoste* had freelance roles. They were to be ready to join in the action here, there or anywhere, depending on how it developed.

He read the last part of the orders. . . .

Prepare to lay smoke for cover and to tow disabled ships. If opposition is silenced landing parties (less *Hotspur*) when ordered to land make for Ore Quay unless otherwise ordered. *Hardy*'s first lieutenant in charge. Additional visual signal to withdraw will be one red and one green Very light from *Hardy*. Half outfit of torpedoes is to be fired unless target warrants more. In order to relieve congestion of movements all ships when turning to fire or opening are to keep turning to port if possible. Watch adjacent ships. Keep moderate speed.

Clear enough, Rowan thought, and about as detailed as could be practical. When they got in there, everything would be happening at once and in all directions. They'd be like foxes in a hen-run—except that the hens would be twice their size and better armed. . . . He'd turned to the next signal on the log, the one which in fact had preceded the operation orders and in which Captain (D) had passed to Commander-in-Chief and to Admiral Whitworth the information obtained ashore at Tranoy. According to the Norwegian pilots there, there were at least six big German destroyers and one U-boat up at Narvik. The destroyers were of rather more than 1,800 tons, and had an armament of five five-inch guns apiece.

Surprise was going to be important, Rowan thought, to balance that German superiority in fire-power. It was a factor which Captain (D), Warburton-Lee, must obviously have weighed up and accepted, since he'd ended his signal to C-in-C with the words *Intend attacking at dawn high water.*

High water would help to carry them over any moored mines which the enemy might have laid. But then again, mines wouldn't be the only hazard on the way in. Ofotfjord was long and narrow, and despite the *Hardy* officers' attempts at persuasion, none of the pilots from Tranoy had been prepared to come along.

There was a SITREP—situation report—just in. Rowan skimmed through it: noting as he did so that it had not, by and large, been the best of days. The Home Fleet had been under heavy air attack from German squadrons using captured Norwegian airfields. *Rodney*, Sir Charles Forbes' flagship, had been hit—though not hurt, thank God. Several cruisers had suffered minor damage, and Stuka dive-bombers had sunk the destroyer *Gurkha*. Off southern Norway, German air superiority was total; effectively, only submarines could operate against German seaborne traffic down there. Had *anyone* realised, Rowan wondered, until this proof of the pudding was flung in their faces, how impossible it might become to operate surface ships without air cover?

The carrier *Furious* was with the Home Fleet now. But they'd sailed her in such a hurry that she'd come without her fighter squadrons.

He pulled on his duffle coat and left the chart-room, climbed the ladder to his ship's bridge. He told Mathieson, the first lieutenant, "You'll find Captain (D)'s orders on the chart table, Number One. Read, mark, learn, etcetera. Then start getting us ready fore and aft for towing and/or being taken in tow. And I want smoke-floats placed on the foc's'l and quarterdeck. And—now

—I want to see Gardner and Peters and Mr. Stuart—and Mr. Braithwaite, please."

Lieutenant Gardner was his gunnery control officer, and Mr. Stuart was the gunner (T). Braithwaite was a commissioned engineer and Peters was officer-of-the-quarters on the after guns. When he'd seen them, Rowan intended to have the coxswain and the gunner's mate and the chief buffer up for a chat. There were various arrangements to be made: for instance, the ship's company were going to have to be fed at their action stations during the Middle, so they wouldn't be going into action hungry as well as cold.

He moved up to the binnacle. His navigator, Tubby Wellman, was using the hand-held station-keeper, a pocket rangefinder, to check *Hoste*'s distance astern of *Hostile*. Lowering it, he glanced at his captain.

"Right on the nose, sir."

Rowan didn't comment. He was thinking about those Norwegian pilots, the ones at Tranoy who'd been unwilling to risk their skins. Might it be because they considered this force too weak for the job and hadn't wanted to be associated with losers?

Supper on the messdeck was beef stew, bread without butter, and tea. The duty "cooks" of each mess had prepared the food by cutting up the meat ration and carrots, and peeling the spuds, earlier in the day; they'd delivered it to the galley for cooking, and now they'd brought it back hot and steaming. There was enough gash gravy to soak your bread in; since 3 Mess had only about five spoons left that was the only way to get it up.

Whacker Harris pushed his empty plate away. He'd wiped it so thoroughly with bread that it looked unused. He mumbled, lighting a cigarette, "The condemned man ate an 'earty meal."

"No foolin'." Randy Philips nodded at him. "Should've been condemned years ago, you should." He leant sideways, sniffing the air near Harris. "Strike a *light*. 'E's fuckin' *rotten*."

The killick, Brierson, told them, "There'll be corned dog an' kye dished out sometime in the Middle, lads. Jimmy's orders to the cox'n. 'Eard it meself. So this ain't *quite* your last repast on earth, Whacker ol' son."

"Yeah, well . . ." Randy turned to Baldy Percival. "Bein' HO an' only at sea five fuckin' minutes, Percy, I don't suppose you'd appreciate the significance of an issue of corned dog an' kye in the Middle, would you?"

"Well—no, not in any *particular* way . . ."

They never tired of pulling Baldy's leg. It was so easy. He'd demonstrated this on his first day on board when he'd obediently gone trotting along to the chief buffer to ask for some green oil for the starboard navigation light.

"It's extra rations, see. They're takin' a chance

191

there won't be no further stores drawn, like. When it's an odds-on chance of the old 'ooker gettin' sunk, they reckon to build you up for the swim, like." He shrugged. "Waste o' time in your case, o' course."

"What d'you mean?"

"We'll, 'ardly last two minutes, in water as cold as they got up 'ere. I mean, all bones an' bugger-all else, ain't you. . . . Smoke, Yank?"

"Thanks."

He'd noticed that the old hands liked to have such offers accepted. They were gestures, more than offers. Philips probably wouldn't care if he *ate* the cigarette, so long as he took it. In fact, he lit it too. Randy said, "We 'eard about your guv'nor, Yank. Tough luck, an' all. Don't want to let it get you down, though."

He nodded. Several men had glanced at him and away again, as if embarrassed. Obviously they'd discussed it, and Philips was speaking for them all. Paul exhaled smoke. "Yes. Thanks, Randy."

"Might turn up yet, lad." Brierson was wiping his plate with a crust. "Never say die." He swallowed, reddening, and began again, "I mean—"

"Sure, Tom. I know what you mean."

Baldy Percival said, "He could easily have been picked up by the Germans. It's really *likely*, when you think about it. And it would probably be quite some while before the news came through."

"Well, bugger me!" Whacker Harris smacked

192

the table. "First sensible remark our Percy's made since 'e's been aboard 'ere!"

It was time to get ready for the next four hours on the gun-deck. And really, Paul thought, one could snooze up there almost as easily as down here. *Almost* . . . When they got up top, the gun's crew all looked as if they'd put on a stupendous amount of weight, with the extra sweaters under their greatcoats. Paul was three-quarters asleep when the flotilla went about, heading back towards Ofotfjord, and when the watch changed at midnight they were nearing Tranoy again, the place where *Hardy* had sent her boat in. This time, there wasn't any stopping.

Getting towards 1 am. Pitch dark, and snowing hard. The five destroyers ahead were showing light-clusters on their sterns; without them, it would have been near enough impossible to maintain the line-astern formation.

Alec Rowan leant with his left side against the binnacle. Wellman and Mathieson were vague shapes hunched against the bridge's starboard side, straining their eyes into cold, wet darkness. The flotilla was approaching the island of Baroy, which was on the south side of the entrance to Ofotfjord; when they sighted it, it would be quite close on the starboard bow. The gap between Baroy and Tjeldoy to the north was roughly 4,000 yards.

There was a light on Baroy, but it was unlikely

the Germans would have left it shining, even if the Norwegians had. It was mounted on the end of a white timber-built house: which might or might not show up, now that the land behind it would be snow-covered. It would be an advantage to pick it up, because the Sailing Directions described it as the best mark for entering Ofotfjord, and with no pilot or local knowledge one couldn't afford to waste any such aids. It was *Hardy*'s job to lead them all in, of course, but each ship still needed to know where she was; otherwise if the flotilla became separated from each other you'd be lost and groping.

There was nothing to be seen at all except for *Hostile*'s stern cluster and its bluish glimmer on her wake, and the snow like a curtain all round. Thrum of the turbines, subdued humming from the ventilators. *Hoste* was doing revs for about ten knots but the tidal stream would be outflowing and speed of advance would be more like eight. The snow was like a soft, soaked blanket, giving an impression of deep silence all around. Men spoke briefly and quietly, if at all. Below, guns' and tubes' crews slept around their weapons, while in the messdecks and other compartments ammunition-supply and damage-control parties lay on the decks or sat propped against steel bulkheads, dozing or playing cards.

You could only use binoculars for a few seconds at a time; then the front lenses would be clogged with snow and you'd have to wipe them clean. It was a better bet to search with the naked eye. Less time-wasting. And the glasses would still be wet and smeary even when you'd wiped them.

"Captain, sir?"

The voice belonged to Graham Jones, *Hoste*'s surgeon-lieutenant. "New one from Admiralty to Captain (D), sir."

Warburton-Lee must be getting a bit tired of London's chat by this time, Rowan thought. From 1,300 miles away they seemed to imagine that only they could direct this operation. The exchange of messages had been going on all through the night; and if the great men back there at home were poking their fingers into other sections of the pie as well, the Commander-in-Chief must be just about frothing at the mouth by now.

He didn't want to spoil his night vision, reading yet more signals. Once you'd lost it, it took about ten minutes to get it back. He told Graham Jones, "Read the bloody thing to me, will you?"

"Aye aye, sir." The doctor went to the chart table, and leant inside its canvas hood, He called out, "Norwegian coast defence ships *Eidsvold* and *Norge* may be in German hands. You alone can judge whether in these circumstances attack should be made. We shall support whatever decision you take."

He'd switched the light off, and backed out. "Looks like the decision is we carry on, sir."

195

It looked, Rowan thought, like a touch of cold feet in high places.

Mathieson called suddenly, "Baroy Light, sir. At least I *think*—"

"Where?" Wellman's tone was sharp. Navigators liked to be the first to pick up their marks. The first lieutenant told him, "It's not lit, but there's a light in the house itself and you can just make out the actual structure. Left from where you're—"

"Yes, I've got it."

"Well?" Rowan asked him, "*Is* it Baroy?"

"Yes, sir, I believe it is."

Wellman had recognised it from the little sketch of it in the Sailing Directions. So now they were entering Ofotfjord, and Narvik was about thirty miles ahead.

"Hey, what the—"

He'd been kicked, or trodden on—and it had nothing to do with Mullbergh or—

"Breakfast in bed, you lucky bastards!"

Harry Rush seemed to be talking gibberish. Paul wasn't out of the dream yet. A long, disturbing dream in which—

He'd forgotten, lost it; a second ago it had all been in his mind. Extraordinary. He was sitting up, feeling the ship's movement and the tremble in her steel, feeling the cold too and seeing the swirl of snow outside the gunshield, flakes drifting in and then out again in a kind of spiral.

196

The gun's crew were packed in here like over-dressed sardines. Harry Rush announced, "Kye an' butties. Any bugger don't want 'is, *I'll* 'ave it."

"Soddin' 'ell you will." Vic Blenkinsop's tone was cheerful, though. He added, "Dump the fanny 'ere an' shove them mugs along."

"Who asked for *your* 'elp, Victoria?"

"Ah, bugger off, then!"

"Boys, boys . . ." Lofty McElroy wriggled out, feet-first, past Paul. The kye and sandwiches had been fetched from the galley by Rush and Percival, Paul gathered. McElroy was questioning how many sandwiches there were per man, and whether Rush had scoffed a few en route. Paul, remembering what they were here for, where *Hoste* was going, was checking the time, peering at the faintly luminous dial of his watch and seeing that it was twenty-five past two. If they were still expecting to get to Narvik at first light, that would mean some time after 0400; so there was plenty of time yet. He felt himself relax enough to become aware of the cold again: of the wet steel deck inside here and the snow-plastered superstructure abaft the gun.

"Yours, Yank!"

He stretched forward, and his hands closed on thick hunks of bread. Then a tin mug so hot he could barely hold it even in the anti-flash glove. Rush mused, "Wonder if the bleedin' square-'eads know we're after 'em."

197

McElroy mumbled with his mouth full, "They best *not*."

"Why?"

"Well—be ready for us, wouldn't they."

"So what? Ready for *them*, ain't we?"

"Yeah, but—" there was a long sucking noise as the gun trainer started on his cocoa—"there's more o' them than what there is of us, an' they're bigger bastards too."

"What sod told you *that*?"

"Well, it's the buzz, ain't it."

"*Your* buzz, Lofty?"

That had been Dan Thomas's voice, from the other side. McElroy told him, "What they're sayin' on the messdecks."

"Talkin' through their great fat arse-'oles then, aren't they."

Silence—as if that had settled it, revoked the buzz. *Hoste* had a gentle motion on her, a little rise and fall resulting from the fact that she was moving through sea disturbed by the five ships ahead of her.

Dan Thomas had evidently been brooding on that estimate of enemy strength. He reopened the subject now.

"Wouldn't matter if there *was* more o' them than there is of us. Not if they was bigger boats an' all. We'll be *surprisin'* the bastards, won't we. Likely as not they'll 'ave their 'eads down when we get to 'em. That'll be why we're comin' up in the bleedin' dark, see. . . . All right, Lofty?"

"Yeah, well—"

The ship swung, heeling, suddenly. She'd been put hard a-starboard, slanting over. Turbine noise rising sharply: she was shuddering, probably screws full astern, or one astern and—

Rush squawked, "What the *'ell*—"

Both screws, Paul guessed, were going astern. Rush and Percival had moved: he did too, rocking forward on to his knees then pushing himself up: outside the shield he held on to Baldy, peered out round him into the night. He saw one ship about thirty yards to port and another on that same bow with her starboard quarter towards *Hoste*; and a larger but less distinct shape ahead was probably two destroyers overlapping. *Hoste* was going astern, all right; he could see the shine of black, white-flecked water sliding away for'ard.

"Well, strike a soddin' light!"

Harry Rush was pointing. Up ahead, beyond that mixed-up group of destroyers, an enormous white headland towered across black sky. A whole mountain-side—and the flotilla had nearly steamed right into it.

Perhaps if the snow hadn't stopped falling they *would* have?

Hoste's screws had stopped. You could hear the water whispering and thumping along her sides. Those other shapes were drawing away, re-forming into line; and *Hoste* began to swing herself round behind them—starboard screw astern, port ahead, the hum of the turbines and the rattling vibration dispelled those few minutes' unnatural quiet. Then the starboard screw had stopped: you *felt* it, when a certain element in the vibration cut out. She was moving ahead now —still swinging, gathering way eastward behind the others.

"All guns with SAP and full charge load, load, load!"

Baldy slammed a projectile into the tray and Paul thumped a charge in behind it. Harry Rush lugged the tray over with his left hand and rammed charge and shell home into the breech with his gloved right fist. The breech slid up with a metallic whisper and Dan Thomas had banged the interceptor shut.

"'B' gun ready!"

Its crew, tin-hatted and like Frankenstein monsters in their anti-flash gear, waited. Keyed up, tense.

Quiet . . .

Mutter of machinery, swish of sea. The stern lights had been extinguished. Dark, and snow still falling. But it seemed to be thinning out, Paul thought, might even be about to stop. And ahead—he was standing with his feet well apart and the next charge ready cradled in his arms, with nothing to do for the moment except wait —ahead there were seams of brightness showing through dark-grey haze.

"All guns follow director!"

200

"B" gun was trained round on the starboard bow, at about green four-oh. No elevation that Paul could see: flat trajectory for point-blank range.

Rush sang out, "For what you are about to receive, thank—"

No time for thanks. Dawn split into flame and deafening sound as ships ahead opened fire. Gun-flashes, shell-bursts: the sky flickered with red and yellow, orange, white, and suddenly with a much deeper, thunderous explosion, an enormous orange brilliance upwards and outwards. He thought, *Torpedo hit* . . . And immediately, another. A huge roar of sound—torpedo in some German's magazine or fuel tank, he guessed— and the sky ahead seemed to have caught fire. *Hoste*'s guns still silent; but looking across to port, behind the breech and Rush's and Thomas's dark silhouettes, he saw the beginnings of inferno, a whole jumble of ships racked with flame and exploding shells and clouds of smoke billowing out, and in that moment another torpedo struck, an eruption like a vast bonfire suddenly projected skyward. In the light of it he saw the victims—a tanker with a destroyer alongside her, both of them shattered and ablaze.

Fire-gong: "B" gun fired, recoiled. Reloaded, breech shut: clang of the gong again, and *crash* . . . No idea what they were shooting at. The noise had become continuous, a solid roar instead of individual bangs; in every direction there were

201

ships on fire, exploding, sinking. Two more torpedo hits: a gush of flame as one broke in two. The snow had stopped and daylight was growing rapidly; charges flowed into his arms and out again: he swung to and fro feeding the gun as it belched, recoiled, drew breath, belched again. Ears ringing, eyes half blinded sometimes by the flashes and the sting of cordite; he glimpsed, as he pivoted to snatch another charge from Billy Mitchelmore, one of two stokers who were at the sharp end of the ammo-supply chain, a large merchant ship alongside a jetty blowing up, her centre turning bright red and brightening more, then erupting upwards out of her. Ammunition ship? *Hoste* was swinging and the gun was firing on an after bearing now, so that he and Baldy were going to have to pass *in front* of it to get each charge and shell from the supply numbers at the ammo hatch. You had to duck right down below the level of the blast but there was still nothing between your brain and the explosion except rubber plugs in your earholes.

"Check, check, check!"

Run out of targets?

Just as noisy though. He wondered how long they'd been in action. Narvik's harbour was in flames, with a couple of dozen ships on fire, sinking, exploding. By the looks of it, the flotilla had achieved complete surprise and no small victory. You could only get an impression, though, see this bit of it or that, there was no chance to make sense or a pattern of it. Noise deadened, slowed the thinking-process, and Dan Thomas had them ready and standing-to, gun loaded, layer and trainer following the pointers in their dials, Vic Blenkinsop keeping his range-dial set to TS-transmitted range, deflection-dial the same, everything lined up and ready as *Hoste* swung—heading, presumably, for some new target or target area.

Mist, and drifting smoke. Over the harbour it was dense.

Fire-gong: *crash!* And the same again. How long had the pause been—half a minute, ten minutes? He'd glimpsed two of the flotilla, their two-funnelled silhouettes as familiar as old friends in a crowd of strangers, guns flaming shorewards. It was full daylight—and again the time-element was puzzling. . . . He banged a charge down, swung round for another, swinging back a second or so behind Baldy's swing with the heavier burden: the gun had fired, flung back; as he slammed the next charge in he felt the ship lurch violently. As if she'd hit a rock. But the impact had felt as if it was somewhere aft. Another round in, gun fired—firing ahead now, target invisible, hidden by the gunshield. That ship passing was *Hardy*, coming out from the harbour area: she'd been out and gone in again for her second smack at them already. Giving the others a turn or herself a rest, he thought, as he dropped a charge into the tray and swung away and the gun crashed—it was four guns you heard, of course, not just this one, four fire-gongs that rang each time just before the director-layer's trigger completed the electrical circuit that fired the guns. Paul saw a German destroyer with its bows blown off: it was slowly tipping forward into the sea, sliding in. He thought exultantly, *Us? Did we do that?* Hell, this *was* a victory! Swinging back with another charge he found he was having to take a new position on account of the slanting gundeck, a list the ship had developed. And she was slowing. Stopping? You just kept at it, seeing things in glimpses, shut into the confines of your job. "B" gun fired, recoiled, he slung in another helping and turned back for more, saw *Hardy* passing, going in there again, her leader's pendant snapping in the wind, ensign tattered, her for'ard guns already back in action and a stream of tracer racketing from her point-fives, probably dealing with some gun on shore. They must be field-guns landed from these merchant ships. *Former* merchant ships: wrecks now. *Hoste* was stopped, and the slant on the gundeck had increased. Her engines had stopped, but in fact she had just enough way on to maintain this slow turn to port. Dense smoke drifting; while the noise of battle hadn't lessened except intermittently in surprising pauses, the amount of flame and flash had. More smoke now than anything else. Daylight, of course, and fires having burnt themselves out, burning ships gone down . . . Recoil—breech open—stinking gush of fumes. His eyes were streaming from that reek and he and the men around him were moving completely as machines now, robot-like. Again it was on an after bearing that they were shooting, he and Percival having that quick rush to make for each round, into the muzzle-flash and the mind-crippling concussion. On the bow—starboard, and behind his shoulder as *Hoste* continued her turn to port—two of the flotilla were turning away from some shore target they'd been blasting.

"Check, check, check!"

Hardy was coming out again: that was three separate attacks she'd made. Two others of the flotilla were angling in to form line astern of her. *Hoste* still listing—she'd been holed, he realised —that jolt he'd felt. An hour ago? But she was under way again, moving ahead through the water: to tag on astern of those three, perhaps: or leaving a gap for that other pair to come in ahead of her. Withdrawing? He checked the time, fumbling to push back his greatcoat sleeve and pull down the anti-flash gauntlet. . . . Five-thirty. One hour, then, since the action had started. It could have been ten minutes: he'd had no idea. He was looking at those other two— *Hostile* and one other—when beyond them he saw a new group of German destroyers emerging from Herjangsfjord.

Three of them. Big, almost like light cruisers.

Jesus Christ Almighty . . .

Fire-gong: *crash*: recoil . . .

Engaging those three now. The flotilla must have sunk or smashed up five or six Hun destroyers already, and now here were three more —fresh, undamaged, with full outfits of torpedoes. All the Second Flotilla ships were engaging them, forming into something like a rough quarterline, fighting as they withdrew westward. Shot from the Germans' guns was whooshing over now—a hoarse, rushing sound— and splashes had just risen about a cable's length to starboard.

Check, check, check!

For God's sake, *why*?

Then he saw. The gun would still bear—just, on that after bearing—but *Hostile* and the destroyer with her—*Hotspur*?—were coming in between *Hoste* and the oncoming Germans, masking her fire. Not for long: they were crossing, turning to port, heading as if to form up astern, or just to get out of the way, clear the range.

And laying smoke, now . . .

Hoste was gathering way. Paul guessed they'd be following on astern of *Hardy* and those other two. Water sliding away faster as she picked up speed, still with the drunken list on. Shell-spouts rose again to starboard, leaping tall and white, collapsing with slow grace. The after guns were in action again. Baldy's eyes were bloodspots and what showed of his face around them, in the gap in the anti-flash mask, was smoke-blackened like a nigger-minstrel's. *Hoste* quivered to explosions aft: not gunfire, shell-bursts. And she was slowing again: you could feel the vibration ease—and then stop, as her propellers ceased driving her.

"'A' and 'B' guns follow director!"

She had enough way on to be answering her helm, swinging to allow the for'ard guns to bear on the enemy astern. "B" was now trained as far aft as it would go, right up against the stop; and loaded, ready.

Fire-gong: *crash* . . .

Back at it again. Like pressing a switch and starting up a machine. Eight working parts: seven men, one gun. It fired again, plunged back, breech opening and stink flooding back: projectile, charge, tray slamming over. . . .

Crescendo of gunfire up ahead, where *Hardy*, *Havock* and *Hunter* were leading westward.

"Check, check, check!"

A very short spasm, that one had been. Paul took a look round the edge of the gunshield; there was nothing to see except smoke. Which presumably was why they'd ceased firing. You could hear *Hostile* and *Hotspur* still in action, though; fighting a rearguard action to hold the attackers off, it must be. The list on *Hoste* was more pronounced and an easterly breeze—the wind had shifted right round during the night— brought a smell of burning. From aft, on this ship? But the whole fjord by this time would stink of burning. Harry Rush, who'd been standing with his back to the gun and looking out the other way, westward, had begun to shout: Paul and Dan Thomas joined him to see what was so exciting.

Hard to see *anything* . . .

Dan Thomas snarled, "Look at them *bloody bastards!*"

Two more big German destroyers were racing out of a side-fjord to the south, tearing across to cut them off.

How many did they *have* in here, for God's sake?

Hardy, *Havock* and *Hunter* were already engaging the new arrivals. It was all gun-flashes and drifting smoke, groves of shell-splashes around both groups of ships. Paul, Baldy, Rush, Dan Thomas and Vic Blenkinsop were staring out that way when *Hardy* was hit, her bridge smothered suddenly in a gush of flame and smoke. A flag-hoist had broken at the flotilla-leader's yardarm a couple of seconds earlier: the flames reached up to it and the bunting began to flare. *Hardy* swinging hard a-port: and *Hoste*, steadied from her own swing, was moving ahead through the water again and starting to turn back the other way. It seemed possible that Rowan was taking her to the assistance of his damaged leader.

Paul tried to get a sight of his watch. One gun aft was firing now. *One?*

"'A' and 'B' guns follow director!"

Leaving that after gun in local control to engage the Germans coming up astern? He'd only had the barest glimpse of the watch's face but he thought the hands were at just after six: and the fire-gong had clanged, they'd resumed the seven-some reel. Firing directly ahead—at the two new ones. Nothing to see, though; the gunshield limited one's world. Picking up speed: and shaking, rattling more than usual. Heat and stink of burning paintwork—from aft. One of the stern guns must have been knocked out. Fire-gong: *crash* . . . Sounds muffled in numbed or flattened eardrums. Eyes blurred, and mind blurred too. The clang of shells into the loading-tray and of the tray as it was swung over to the breech was totally inaudible, like a film when the sound-track's out. Arms were pistons, hands were claws, the gun was the master of seven men who served it. *Hoste* was listing still more steeply, he thought, than the last time he'd noticed. You got into a way of expelling a breath through your mask as the breech opened and the stench flew back. *Crash* . . . Jet of red flame, then black smoke pluming up and back. On "A" gun, he half realised—below them, just down there. . . . "B" fired, threw back; shell-spouts rose to port quite close, and another explosion down for'ard with a similar jetting flash upwards and sideways out beyond this gunshield. Foul black smoke reeking and flooding back aft. He'd dropped another charge in and turned in that lunging motion to grab the next from Mitch: something slammed into his back with tremendous force and he was aware of sound—*different*, unidentifiable —and tumbling helplessly, the kind of fall that woke one up in nightmares: then darkness and a sense of personal removal, a feeling that one had become a spectator of some battle being continued now at a distance. . . . He'd been unconscious, and he came-to in the act of getting to his feet. The ladder to the ammunition hatch and the sight of Mitch told him where he was: he'd been knocked down here, into the Chiefs' and POs' mess. Mitchelmore had been up the ladder and come back down it; he was shouting, "Whole bloody lot's 'ad it. *All* of 'em!" Shells and charges were arriving from below and piling up. Mitch said, "'A' gun's the bloody same. Christ, what are we—"

What are we *something* . . . Paul was climbing the ladder and getting out of the ammo hatch. "B" gun was a twisted wreck and the gun platform itself was slimy, slippery. At first glance it looked like oil but it was blood. He saw bodies and parts of bodies wrapped in the shreds of clothes, and everything burnt black. And some more or less intact. Baldy was one of them: but he wouldn't be putting stickers in any more library books. Guns were firing: a lot of them at a distance, and one much closer. One of the after guns here on *Hoste*, he thought. Over the flare, the leading edge of the gundeck, he saw that "A" gun had become scrap. One body had been smashed against its breech, which itself had been knocked sideways; it dripped, festooned with what had been the fabric of a man. He saw a leg sticking out of a seaboot, and part of a torso like something on a butcher's slab wrapped in blood-soaked cloth, and one body intact but flattened as if something huge had stamped on it. Turning away, glancing upwards—for relief, perhaps, the only safe direction you could look—he saw *Hoste*'s bridge blackened and smoking, a flicker of flames appearing here and there as the wind fanned them up. Then disappearing, flickering up again . . .

"Yank?"

He whipped round. The voice had come from down there below him, on "A" gundeck. But they were all—

"*Yank . . .*"

He jumped from the edge of the flare to the distorted top of "A" gunshield and from there in another two-footed hop to land jarringly on the foc'sl deck. Then he came round to the rear end of the gun. It was worse at close quarters, and that voice he'd thought he'd heard could only have been a grisly joke perpetrated by whoever arranged this kind of thing. . . . Then—inside the shield, port side—something moved and caught his eye.

A hand. He saw the arm attached to it and a

body attached to that, and blood all over everything. Crumpled, flung into that corner; and a dead body which had evidently been smashed down across the layer's handwheel was right above this live one, the corpse's arms dangling down to it and blood flowing in a thick, black-looking and quite slow-moving stream. The hand which had moved and caught his attention was the living man's, attempting to push those dead hands away from his face where they swung to and fro with the ship's motion. Paul knew he had to get in there, get the live one out. *The part one had to play.* It wasn't the kind you'd choose. He'd stepped over an intervening horror and he was dragging the broken and crushed remnants of a human being off the handwheel. Moving it was less difficult than he'd expected it to be. But to be able to reach the man who was alive and pull him out of the corner he'd been jammed into, he'd have to get this one right outside the gunshield, out past two others. The explosion must have been behind the gun, at the base of "B" gundeck's superstructure; that and the jutting flare above, the angled projection of the gundeck's front edge, would have contained it so that the whole blast would have been *into* "A" gunshield. Paul let his burden down on the deck and went back inside.

It was Blackie Proudfoot. He rasped, as Paul knelt to get hold of him, "Can't move me fuckin' legs. Can't feel 'em."

"Okay. I'll get you to the Doc."

"Good lad, good—"

"Try to hang on round my neck?"

Prising him up out of it. Blackie was coated in blood—that other man's. Probably shouldn't be moving him: but the doctor couldn't have got to him in that corner, he *had* to be brought out. Blood—clothes saturated—except where he'd been lying, his back on the steel deck. And even *there*—as he began to edge out, dragging the heavily-built gunlayer with his arms locked round him and Blackie's hands clasped together behind his own neck—Paul felt a damp hollow in the small of the man's back. The greatcoat was torn and sticky round the edges of the tear. That was Blackie's *own* blood.

Christ, but I'm lucky to be alive!

The thought hit him so suddenly and strongly that it just about made him stagger. The realisation that he *shouldn't* be alive . . . He got Proudfoot up in a fireman's lift, without having had to look at the wound in his back. The layer had groaned once, and muttered something; either he was incredibly tough or there was some failure of the nervous system and he wasn't feeling anything. Shuffling aft with the heavy body across his shoulders Paul thought not only had the list increased, but *Hoste*'s forepart was higher in the water. Meaning she was down by the stern? Well, obviously there must be some flooding somewhere, or she wouldn't have the list.

213

Screen door just ahead. Where the hell were the doctor's first-aid parties, he wondered. Weren't they supposed to—

"Who's that?" Someone stopping in front of him, peering into his face. Lieutenant Mathieson, the first lieutenant. Tall, fair-haired . . . "Everard?"

"Yes, sir. I—" His voice was like a croak— "this is 'A' gunlayer, Able Seaman Proudfoot. I'm taking him down to sickbay for—"

"The doctor's in the waist, Everard, by the searchlight platform. We're mustering all wounded there. She won't float long now, I'm afraid."

Not *float*?

"Are you all right, Everard?"

"Yes, I'm—"

"We thought everyone on 'A' and 'B' was killed." Mathieson jerked his head. "Get him along there quickly now. They'll find a job for you."

He went in through the screen door. Paul moved on—to the head of the foc's'l-break ladder, and slowly, awkwardly down it to the iron deck. Then continuing aft . . . "Hang on, Blackie. The doc'll fix you up." Maybe. The for'ard funnel was all chewed up. No fires seemed to be burning now: just smoking, smouldering wreckage. Passing the engineers' store. The point-fives were a tangle of junk on a burnt-out pedestal. Past the second funnel, which had only one shell-hole in

214

it that he could see, to the tubes. They were turned out: but not to fire, because there were no torpedoes in them. To make space on the deck between the two quintuple mountings, he realised. Wounded men lay or sat around. There was a Carley float alongside to port; Petty Officer Rowbottom and a few seamen with him were lowering a stretcher-case down into it.

"Sir—doctor—"

Graham-Jones was fixing a splint to a broken leg. Glancing up, he snapped sharply, "Put him down, man, put him down!"

A couple of other wounded sailors pulled aside to make room. And Mr. Stuart, the gunner (T), came to help. Stocky, red-faced, ginger-headed. Blackie Proudfoot slid into a bloodstained heap which had then to be straightened out. The doctor asked, "What's his trouble?"

"Hit in the back, I think, sir. He said he couldn't feel his legs."

"X" gun was still in action, in local control. Sub-Lieutenant Peters was up there, standing out on the side of the gundeck and giving visual spotting directions, watching the fall of shot through binoculars. Paul heard him yell, "Right eight—shoot!" The gun flamed, flung back, and the black-faced men around it went into a spasm of the dance and then froze to the cry of "Ready!" Paul wished he'd been kinder to Baldy, swapped places with him after half an hour or so of the action, switched to handling the projectiles and

215

given Baldy a break with the much lighter charges —nine pounds a time instead of forty-five. *Sorry, Baldy . . .* Graham-Jones had checked Blackie Proudfoot's heart and breathing, after one look at the hole in his back. He told Paul flatly, "This man is dead."

Peters howled, "Up four hundred, *shoot!*" Stuart had asked Paul something, and now he'd grasped his arm: "Eh?"

"Sorry, sir, I didn't hear—"

The hair was red but the stubble on the jaw was grey. Eyes grey too and rather close together. Stuart must have been about Paul's father's age but he looked ten, fifteen years older. Up the hard way and a lifetime of naval service, one of the tiny minority who by the standards of the lower deck had made it, to warrant rank. . . . "I asked can you swim, lad?"

"I'm a very strong swimmer, sir."

"Aye, well, you'll have a chance to prove it now. One bloody float's all we've got. We could fill the bastard three times over wi' just wounded men, but she'll sink long before that, d'you see. Most of 'em's going to have to swim, an' it's a hell of a long bloody way and colder 'n *that*—so they'll need help, right?"

"Right—" he corrected himself—"Aye aye, sir."

Staring at the rocky, snow-covered coastline. Three or four hundred yards, he thought. Ice-water, and then snow. *Then* what—Germans?

216

Stuart told him, "Check they're all wearing lifebelts and see they're inflated—right?"

Rowan, the skipper, was dead. Everyone on the bridge and in the director tower had been killed. *Hardy* had run ashore, five or six miles east of here, and *Hunter* had sunk out in the deep water. The other ships of the 2nd Flotilla had withdrawn westward now, and Mr. Stuart had said he didn't think the Huns had followed up very far. The Huns had their own problems, he'd said; he reckoned they'd lost three destroyers sunk and at least another three badly damaged, as well as half a dozen store-ships sunk inside the harbour.

So it *was* a victory, after all. Paul, looking round at the waiting wounded and the discarded dead, had thought of the Duke of Wellington's much-quoted words about battles lost and won. Here was vivid proof of it. *Hoste* sinking, while Stuart, Mathieson and Peters chatted to the men, keeping spirits up. And they *had* been up: there'd been singing, jokes, leg-pulling.

The loaded Carley float was clear of the ship's side, being paddled slowly shorewards.

"Right then. You lot with webbed feet—over the side, and we'll get these lads down to you." He remembered stripping off his greatcoat and sweaters and the tennis shoes. A scrambling-net had been rigged over the side, for men to climb down. Paul and about a dozen others who reckoned they were better-than-average swim-

217

mers were going to shepherd a whole crowd of poorer swimmers and lightly wounded men to the shore. He was going to take one man, a torpedoman with a broken arm, on his back.

Now this was his third trip. Third and a half, really. He'd got his first man ashore and then swum out again about a third of the way to help with stragglers from the group. Two had given up, and drowned; several others had died on the beach. The cold was unimaginable: in the first minutes of the first swim he'd thought he'd die of it, then he'd become used to it and stuck it out more easily, and now it was right inside him, killing. . . . *Don't think about it.* He'd told himself more than once that the sole survivor of two guns' crews didn't have much to complain about. On his second trip he'd been out to the ship and brought back that fellow Cringle, the man he'd had the barney with. Cringle had a head wound and some cracked ribs, and he hadn't seemed to know who or where he was or what was happening. Third trip now. *Hoste* was slanted steeply in the water, stern right down. She'd be gone soon. Lieutenant Mathieson and Mr. Stuart had still been on board, making a final search for anyone left alive, last time he'd been out to her. They'd be able to look after themselves, he guessed, but there'd been men in the water here and there, two or three who'd dropped out, or rescuers who'd gone out again and not come back.

This *bloody* cold. The other thing that was slowing him was the pain in his back—where whatever-it-was had hit him before he'd fallen into the hatch. He'd be bruised all over from that fall, he knew, but it was his back that worried him.

He saw her going. Bow rising slowly and then faster as her afterpart filled, up-ending her. . . . He saw a body in the water—about three yards ahead. Frozen black water, liquid ice. Like swimming in a cocoon of ice, a tight skin of it, and it was inside you too, in bone-marrow and veins, all through. The body was hunched, suspended in its lifebelt. Face grey and shiny, like a seal's. Graham-Jones's voice echoed in his brain: *This man's dead.* Looking away from him, seeking others who might *not* be dead, Paul saw that *Hoste* had gone.

He didn't realise at first that she'd been his marker, giving him direction, and that now he'd lost her. He swam slowly to his left. Slow, painful breast-stroke, slower than he wanted it to be. Cold put a brake on you. And he was lower in the water than he had been: to see any distance he needed to get his head up higher. Tremendous effort—just for one second—down again with sheer agony in his back. Can't do *that* again too soon. Relaxing thankfully now in the icy strait-jacket. Arms and legs moving so slowly that it was like swimming in frozen treacle. The mind swam slowly too. It asked him, *Take a rest? Just a little one?*

He wasn't sure which way the coast was. He'd been circling to the left, but he didn't know how much of a circle he'd completed. He tried again to get his head up, catch a glimpse of that snow-bound hillside.

No. Not *this* time. Only falling snow.

Rest. Try again in a minute. He'd strained his back and he had to rest it and gather some strength by relaxing just for a little while: a short rest in this black enclosing ice. Come to terms with it, don't fight it. Face-down, arms outspread —like gliding. Only for a minute.

8

DAWN had come poking over the low hills, spreading greyish light across Sundsråsa, fingering the southern shore of Hoddoy and applying the beginnings of a shine to the flat, quiet surface of Totdalbotn. Nick had been on deck in plenty of time to watch it happening. Pacing his ship's quarterdeck, hearing an occasional thump or clatter from the engine-room where work had been going on all night, and from time to time still having to push the girl out of his thoughts.

She did have an excuse for getting into them. The plan he was forming in his mind had to involve *Valkyrien* and Claus Torp, and so it had to involve her too.

This wasn't a very extensive deck to pace. About sixty feet each way, from the stern where a sentry with a rifle stood beside the bare ensign-staff, via a slightly curving track to skirt around "Y" gun and the after superstructure on which "X" gun stood, to a turning-point at the port-side depthcharge thrower. He'd been up since four and it was getting on for six now. Subtracting from those two hours one short visit to the engine-room—from which he'd learnt precisely nothing—and a much longer spell in the chart-

221

room, allowing for those intervals he must have been pounding this strip of deck for at least an hour. The officers whose cabins were directly under the area of perambulation, if they weren't exceptionally sound sleepers, would be cursing him; their bad luck in having him on their side of the ship was the result of *Valkyrien* being secured alongside to starboard and having a quartermaster of sorts lounging on her stern, hawking and spitting and crunching what sounded like lumps of coal. When Nick had appeared once on that side the man had gone to great efforts to engage him in conversation, despite the fact that he spoke no English and Nick spoke no Norwegian.

Enough distraction without that. The girl kept slipping into his mind, getting between him and the things he *had* to think about. A replay, over and over again, of the impact she'd had on him, and the reflection of it that he'd seen at once in her eyes. Blue eyes, rather wide apart—just like her father's, he'd realised afterwards. But he'd been somehow caught off-balance, taken by surprise, and he'd seen that same reaction, mirrored.

It was partly why he'd turned out this early. There'd come a time, and probably quite soon, when he'd need more sleep than he could get, and then he'd look back with regret on this waste of opportunity. But the girl wasn't the only reason he'd come up on deck. His mind was jumpy, he'd felt an urge to be up and doing. Prowling around,

222

churning the part-formed plan in his brain. The crux of it being that, Germans or no Germans, there was fuel in Namsos.

She'd probably felt nothing at all, he told himself. He'd imagined it. But even if she had, even if she'd been stirred by the most outrageous emotional or sexual upheaval at the mere sight of him—which he didn't flatter himself was likely —this would be neither the place nor time to respond to it. Perhaps one was suffering from the malady to which Fiona Gascoyne sometimes referred as "sex starvation": which incidentally was something he felt sure *she'd* never had much trouble with. But watch out, he thought: or you'll make an idiot of yourself . . . .

He had enough on his plate already. His own share of responsibility for *Gauntlet's* end, for instance, still nagged him. This *present* situation was what one had to concentrate on, but— Hustie's action had been crazy. If he'd been alone —all torpedoes gone, no hope of his ship surviving, ramming the only way left to him of inflicting damage on the enemy: *then* his action would have been justified, even heroic. But he had *not* been alone.

So Nick as senior officer should have held him back, taken him under his orders and co-ordinated the attack?

However much he thought about it, the conclusion he came to was that in similar circumstances again he'd act as he'd done two days ago.

223

Basically because if he'd held *Gauntlet* back and as a result they'd lost contact with a still unidentified enemy, he'd *undoubtedly* have been called to answer for it. . . . So then they'd ask why he hadn't stopped Hustie making his last attack, signalled him to wait behind the smoke: and the answer was that no order should have been necessary. It had been natural to assume certain intentions on Hustie's part: and inessential signals in action were only a distraction, to be avoided if they could be.

But men had been hauled over the coals before this, for doing the right thing. One could think of a dozen cases. . . .

Claus Torp's quartermaster had begun to sing some frightful Scandinavian dirge. Nick tried not to hear it. There were quite a few things to keep one's mind off: including the question of what might or might not have been happening up at Narvik, if Warburton-Lee had carried out the attack. There'd been an Admiralty signal in the early hours telling him that the decision was his own, and that he'd be backed whichever way he decided. Nick thought Warburton-Lee would have gone ahead, as long as the odds were reasonable. He didn't know, and there must have been a lot of signals that *Intent*'s operators had missed; but what might reasonable odds be, to himself, say, if he were in that position? Two to one against? It obviously hadn't looked like *even* odds, or the Admiralty wouldn't have sent that up-to-you signal.

The singing had stopped, thank God. There was a mutter of Norwegian conversation over there now. A relief quartermaster taking over, probably.

Gauntlet and *Hoste* apart, the more immediate problems weren't exactly bagatelles. Namsos was in German hands and less than ten miles away by water. Less than eight as the crow—or the Stuka —flew. With a garrison already planted there, it was obvious the Huns would send some kind of naval support as soon as they had craft to spare; they'd send a torpedo-boat or a minesweeper or two up from Trondheim, perhaps. And putting oneself in the shoes or boots of a torpedo-boat commander, one's first sensible move on arrival in a place like this would be to search all the fjords and inlets and hidden anchorages, not only for enemies but also for craft which might be commandeered and used for occupation pur- poses. Meanwhile, *Intent* was immobilised and helpless, and her chances of becoming oper- ationally fit depended on this one Norwegian, Boyensen. Well, assuming he was as good as he was cracked up to be, he'd mend her. But then —here was the biggest problem of the lot—she'd have fuel for only a few hours' steaming, and there was no source of fuel open to her and within her likely range. His earlier idea, of sailing with near-empty tanks and then signalling for help,

225

had collapsed when he'd subjected it to closer inspection. You needed a big ship to refuel from, so in effect he'd be asking for a cruiser to be sent inshore. The odds were that with the German air superiority which was implicit in so many of the signals they'd intercepted, he'd be asking for the impossible.

Hence the birth of the hare-brained scheme. In the circumstances, he thought it might be near-enough impossible to think up any scheme that was *not* hare-brained. He'd begun to toy with this one—fancifully, not really believing in it then—during the tow down Namsenfjord.

Meanwhile, and looking on the brighter side, this anchorage might have been tailor-made for present purposes. *Intent* lay in ten fathoms, in the inlet in Tötdalbotn's southern shore. (Botn, Kari had told him, meant "head-of-fjord", the equivalent of the Scottish prefix "Kinloch".) About a mile eastward there was a projecting hook of land, marked on the chart as "Skaget", which effectively hid the ship from anyone passing up or down the main waterway to or from Namsos. Unless a German ship actually came up into this backwater, the only real danger of being spotted would be from the air. And that was no immediate worry, with cloud-cover intact again.

It was higher cloud, though, and thinner. After such a large shift in the wind direction it was quite possible that the day might clear, later on. And that would be—*not* so good. *Intent*'s point-

226

five machine-guns, two four-barrelled mountings side by side on their platform between the funnels, were her only defence against dive-bombers; and they were short-range weapons, effective up to no more than half a mile. The main armament of four-sevens had a maximum elevation of forty degrees, which made them useless in an AA role. But in fact no matter what guns she'd had, *Intent* would be finished if they once found her here. Even if she'd been mobile, in these restricted waters she wouldn't have a hope.

The point-fives were manned now, and so was "B" gun. A lookout was being kept from those points and from the director tower and from the bridge, and there were sentries on foc's'l and quarterdeck. Also, a shore lookout had been established on Hoddoy, on a 500-foot ridge a bit less than two miles from this anchor berth. It was manned by Norwegians, a family from a farm somewhere in that area. Nick had picked the spot, after a study of the chart and a careful binocular inspection of the surroundings. From that hill, there'd be a view over land and water from north-west to south-east; really only Namsos port itself would be shut off, by some intervening high ground on the island of Skjerpoy. His idea had been to send young Cox and an OD to camp there, but Claus Torp had suggested local people might be persuaded to do it and be less conspicuous than British sailors.

He'd arranged it yesterday afternoon, when he'd gone ashore in his motor skiff to check on telephone communications and pick up what news he could.

They'd got into Totdalbotn early yesterday afternoon. By 4 pm *Valkyrien* had been secured on *Intent*'s starboard side, and by 4.30 Boyensen had been at work.

There was movement and voices up near the point-fives; and a sailor in a greatcoat and a webbing belt was coming aft, exchanging greetings with *Valkyrien*'s quartermaster. He'd be coming to relieve the sentry: which meant it was now six o'clock.

If there'd been an attack on Narvik at first light, as last night's signals had indicated there would be, it would be all over by now. And if *Hoste* had been in the attacking force—which presumably she would have been—Paul would have some answers of his own by this time to the question he'd asked not long ago at Mullbergh— what did action feel like. . . . Nick remembered vividly his own first taste of it: the awful period before it started, when one had been scared stiff of not coming up to scratch; then the relief when there'd been a lull in the fighting and time to realise that one had been in it and not had time to be frightened, only been totally immersed in doing one's job. He wished Paul that sense of relief. He hoped he'd be enjoying it at this minute. Paul's reappearance in his life was the

228

best thing that had happened to him in years: the boy had become a personal reason to want to live, to survive the war—in order to spend time with him, get to know him, have Mullbergh in good shape to pass into his hands.

And simply for the fact that he existed!

If he hadn't turned up, if he'd stayed with his mother in the USA, would there have been *no* reason to care much about survival?

Well, things were different now, and there was no need to think about how they *had* been. But thank God, anyway, for Paul's arrival on the scene. His half-Russian son . . . They had a lot in common, Nick thought. They didn't look much alike—Paul was more athletic-looking, generally *better*-looking than Nick reckoned himself to be—but inside, one sensed the similarities, the common wavelength. The basis of it was that you felt you knew how he'd react to given circumstances or problems: that given the knowledge, training, experience, whatever it took, he'd react very much as one would oneself.

It was something to hold on to, all right. It was a hell of a *lot* to hold on to.

After *Valkyrien* had berthed alongside yesterday, and ropes and wires had been secured and a brow put over from *Intent*'s waist to an entry-port in *Valkyrien*'s bulkhead, Claus Torp had invited Nick to go aboard. So he'd gone over, leaving Trench to see to essentials in the destroyer. Torp had met him at the gangway, and

229

as he'd arrived he'd seen the engineer, Boyensen, and two other characters come sloping aft with tool-boxes. It was more than he'd hoped for, that they'd get on to the job so quickly.

Torp sketched a salute as Nick stepped off the gangway.

"You are welcome aboard, Captain. I have to tell you, however, that since I have only twelve men on board, passage crew you see, with no cook or steward—"

"For heaven's sake—"

"What I do have is Aquavit. Also scotch whisky."

"Not for me, thanks. But I'd like to talk to you."

"Sure. Come, please."

Valkyrien's saloon was very much as he'd thought it would be. Mahogany, and a dark-red carpet, brass lamps in gimbals. Curved-backed swivel chairs were bolted to the deck around a central table which was covered in a green-baize cloth.

"Captain, I introduce my daughter."

She'd come towards them from the other end of the saloon. Dropping a book—it looked like one of the yellow-jacket English thrillers—on the table as she joined them. This was obviously the female in the bright-coloured oilskins, Tommy Trench's "popsie". He'd forgotten about her, until now. Torp was saying, "Kari, this is Commander Everard of the Royal Navy."

She wasn't conventionally "pretty". But she took all his attention immediately. She was—*very* attractive, in a way that might be difficult to describe, he thought. Except for the striking contrast of dark hair and light-blue eyes there was no feature you'd say was all that special. Very un-fussy, *natural* . . . He felt—immediately—*involved*, and off-balance at feeling any such thing: he saw the same kind of surprise in her face, and then the emergence of that stunning smile.

"Welcome to Norway, Captain."

"You're very kind." He glanced at Torp, if only because he felt he had to take his eyes off her for a moment. "So is your father."

"Oh, he's not such a bad fellow."

"You talk very good English, if I may so so."

"You may say so as often as you like."

Torp informed him, "Kari is a teacher. Of English, among other subjects. *My* teacher, of English."

"Must be a very good one, then."

"Thank you . . . Knut Lange, the man with the boat—the blue boat you saw?—was bringing her from Namsos to a village; it is called Skorstad, where we have friends. After, he would have come out to stop *Valkyrien* as I am coming into the fjord."

"I see." He asked Kari, "Will you teach me Norwegian?"

"If we have time, of course. But first—" she pointed—"won't you sit down?"

He laughed. Sitting, he asked Torp, "Your friend with the boat was still going on to this village, was he, when he left us?"

"Sure. And other places not so far from there. He had two other passengers, who had been in Namsos, to be taking to their homes. But he will come back to us here tomorrow, he was saying." Torp added, by way of explanation, "He is our good friend."

Knut's boat might come in very handy, with the lunatic plan that he was tinkering with. It was going to need a lot more thought before he'd be ready to discuss it with anyone else, though.

He asked Kari, "Can you tell me what's happening in the town?"

"In Namsos? Our little village, a town?"

"I beg its pardon."

"Oh, it would be honoured. . . . But I was not there myself, you see, I was with cousins who are at a small place called Hals. There is a bay where Knut brought in his boat. What is happening is the Germans have taken everybody by surprise, before daylight this morning. It was an empty ship, they thought, but out of it suddenly came soldiers, guns—"

"What kind of guns?"

"Big, on wheels."

"Field guns."

"And also some motor-cars—trucks."

Nick looked at her father. "All highly organised, prepared weeks in advance. Just sitting there, waiting."

Torp nodded. "*Now*, we know it."

"It must have been planned very well." Kari said. "They ran directly to the mayor's house and to the railway station, customs office, police station—to the main roads too, the crossroads have barriers and soldiers—all that. Now all the people must give their names and details for lists to be made and so on. They are being told the Germans are friends of Norway who are come to defend us against you British. This is what I have been told by people coming out of Namsos. Quite a lot of the young men—some old ones too—are making away for the mountains, to organise resistance, join an army or—will your British army come now to drive out the Germans?"

What a question, he thought. Did Britain have enough of an army and weapons, equipment, aircraft, to have held on to the Norwegian ports even if we'd stepped in first, he wondered? Let alone to drive out an entrenched occupation force. Most of the British army was in France, waiting for the war to start, while the French sat behind their Maginot Line, morale crumbling—one heard—almost defeated before a shot was fired. . . . *What* army, and who'd send it? Had the War Cabinet in London had a request submitted in quadruplicate, ratified by the League of Nations or initialled by the Almighty?

233

Nick had some questions of his own. Where had the field guns been set up, was the Trojan Horse ship herself armed, how might the German troops be deployed around the harbour area?

Kari didn't know. Torp said he might be able to find out; he'd go ashore to a farmhouse at Totdal, where he had friends—or one in Sveodden, which was nearer and where he also had friends—and see if the telephones were working. It was too soon for anyone who'd been in Namsos since the arrival of the Germans to have come this far—except by water, which no one had. . . .

"They're bound to have taken over the telephone exchange."

Torp nodded. "I will be careful." The Norwegian asked him, "Why do you want to know about the guns and defences?"

Nick wasn't ready to discuss it. Particularly if Torp was going to be ashore this afternoon, telephoning his friends. He answered vaguely, "Well, if that ship's armed—"

"I am sure she is not."

"Like you were sure she was in ballast?"

"I think they have painted false draught-marks, you know?"

He told them, "I imagine we *will* send troops. So any information we can get while we're here will be useful. If—" he looked at Torp—"if the repairs to my ship go as we hope, and we can get away from here, what would *your* plans be?"

234

"To sail with you, I think."

"In *Valkyrien?*"

"Why not in *Valkyrien?*"

"Would she have the range to reach—well, Scotland?"

Kari said, "She could be sailed there. With her *sails*."

"Yes." Torp agreed. "But steaming, she would have range to go where on our coast your army is landing."

"I'm only trying to understand your intentions, you see, how they fit in with mine. It seems to me you're as much at a loose end as I am. More so—you've no operational command in existence, so far as we know, and to the Germans you're an enemy just as I am."

Torp nodded. "Yes."

"So we're in it together. Do you accept the fact that I'm the senior officer here?"

"It's obvious." Torp glanced at Nick's three stripes. "You are in command. Although, since I don't have one single gun—"

"That's something we can think about later. But my point—the question of your leaving Norway, coming to England—you accept that it may be necessary?"

Kari told her father, "I'd like to go. It wouldn't be for *ever*. We'd come back, with—"

"You can go. But if there will be fighting in Norway I want to be here." He told Nick, "*She* could sail *Valkyrien*. She has done so before—"

Kari put in, "Illegally, but frequently."

"—and she has been sailing boats since she is a very little girl."

That idea seemed a bit far-fetched. But then, it was a day—an epoch, perhaps—for far-fetched ideas. . . . He asked Torp, "What about your crew?"

"They are reservists. They do what I tell them."

That seems to clear the ground. He could regard the Norwegians, for all intents and purposes, as part of his own force. One snag was the girl: if he was going into Namsos to get his oil, which was bound to be a slightly hazardous operation, he didn't like the idea of having her there with them. But he'd need *Valkyrien* for a landing-party. . . . Or perhaps Knut's boat, instead?

"Deep thoughts now, Captain?"

Kari, smiling. He asked her, "Do you have any close relations or dependants here, whom you'd be leaving behind?"

"No. Only cousins." Torp had answered the question. Kari told him, "He was asking do I have a mother, I think."

"My wife died when Kari was quite small." Torp explained, "It is why I left the Navy, to look after her in our home."

"Consequently he's a big noise in Namsos." Kari was teasing him as well as giving Nick the information. "Some great sacrifice, this leaving

236

the Navy was. Timber-merchant, ship chandler, shipping agent, auctioneer—"

"Good man to pick for a father, then. And perhaps with his interest in timber he could get me a spar that we could shape for a fore-topmast and a couple of lighter ones for yards—d'you think?"

"Sure." Torp thought about it for a moment. Then he snapped his fingers, and told his daughter, "From old Jens. He will have some already trimmed. If the telephone is working, I give a message to the Korens, and they tell Knut when he is there with his boat, and he will bring them to us tomorrow."

"Sounds like a smooth piece of organisation."

"You must tell me lengths, diameters—"

"Yes." Trench, with Metcalf as consultant, would provide those details. "But one other thing. If my men bring cables over, would you be prepared to run your steam generator and feed us with power?"

"Perhaps. If I can do it and not make a lot of smoke, I think so. I must speak with Boyensen."

"I'm most obliged. For *all* your help."

"You may end with doing some things for *us*, I think."

"Well, I hope so." Nick checked the time. "And to start with, may I offer you both dinner tonight, in *Intent*?"

"Morning, sir." Trench saluted as he joined him

237

on the quarterdeck. Quarterdeck and CO in one salute: a reasonable economy. Nick looked at his watch, and saw that it was six twenty-five.

"Bright and early, Tommy."

"Not as early as *you* were, sir, I'm informed."

"What's this, your intelligence service?"

"Something of that sort." The big man fell into step beside him. "Thank you for a most enjoyable evening, sir."

That supper party with the Torps as guests, he meant. It hadn't been exactly a gourmet's delight —canned pilchards, followed by what the wardroom chef called "cutlets", which meant shapes of minced corned-beef cooked in breadcrumbs, and a savoury of bacon-wrapped prunes on toast. Afterwards, green Chartreuse, and the men smoked cigars. They'd listened to the BBC news broadcast, which had spoken of air attacks on German shipping in Norwegian ports and of German dive-bombing of the Home Fleet offshore. The Norwegian King and the government had left Oslo in order to direct the fight against the Nazi invaders from a new headquarters. . . . Or words to that effect. It wasn't news, actually, since Torp had been getting Norwegian broadcasts during the day. The government and the Royal Family had moved up to a place called Hamar, about a hundred kilometres north of Oslo; they'd moved out only one jump ahead of the Germans, who'd chased them in armoured cars and then bombed and machine-gunned their transport from the air. In order, presumably, to clear the ground for this Norwegian traitor—a Major Quisling—who'd since been heard on Oslo radio announcing himself as the country's new ruler.

Nick had proposed King Haakon's health, and Torp replied with a toast to King George. Nick showed Kari the lovely colour of Chartreuse, the green variety, when it was lit and burning; in the low, yellowish lighting with which *Valkyrien*'s generating plant was providing them, the flame on the glass filled the cabin with an eerie, subaqueous glow. Then for the entertainment of their guests they turned on the Tannoy to a programme of light music, "Forces' Favourites", and "A Nightingale Sang in Berkeley Square".

Kari sighed, "That's a *lovely* song!"

"As a matter of fact, I know the man who wrote it."

Eric Maschwitz and his wife were friends of Fiona Gascoyne's. The club which Phyllis was opening, the Gay Nineties, was to be in Berkeley Street, a nightingale's warble from the square. He was telling her about it when Torp asked, "The photograph of the lovely lady dressed up as a general has been removed, I think?"

Nick saw Trench smother a smile. He told Kari, "That song's a great hit in a London show called *New Faces*. It's been running months now and it's still packed out every night. Well—every *evening*—our theatres start at six now, because

239

of the blackout. But if you do end up in England, Kari, you should see it."

Torp asked, "Have there been air raids on London?"

"No. We expect them, though." Trench asked Nick, "Have you had a chance to see *Me and My Gal*, sir?"

"No, I haven't . . ." But it was incongruous—he'd been about to say "not yet"—to be discussing those areas of frivolity as if one was so sure of getting back to them.

"If I did come to London one day, would you take me to some theatres?"

It wasn't obvious which one of them she was talking to. They both looked at her, and at each other. Nick told her, "Either of us would be delighted to, Kari."

"I suppose," Torp growled, "that if Mrs. Everard does not mind you going about the world with your cabin full of pictures of different girls—"

"There is *no* Mrs. Everard, Commander."

Kari, in a dress, had seemed quite different from Kari in slacks and a thick sweater. She had not only a lovely face now, she had a figure too. One could imagine her—just—in London, dining, theatre-going. . . .

Torp had achieved his objectives ashore in the afternoon. He'd arranged for Knut Lange to bring the spars, and he'd got through by telephone to some fishermen friends near the fjord

240

exits, chatted about fish long enough to confuse or bore any eavesdropping Germans, and then asked his friends to telephone to Sveodden if Hun ships entered the fjords. The message would be, "Tell Claus the animals are on their way." They were people he'd known for years and he was confident they'd do it. Chandler had christened it "Torp's Early Warning System", short-title TEWS.

Six-thirty. Wail of a bosun's call, and a muffled bellowing from for'ard. Calling the hands: the duty PO would be roaring through the messdecks, Wakey wakey! Rise and shine! Heave-ho, heave-ho, heave-ho, lash up and stow! Show a leg, show a leg, rouse OUT! Nick didn't have to hear it for the noise to start ringing in his head. He'd been thirteen when he'd first woken to those barbaric cries. At Dartmouth: where for sheer bloody hell . . . He shook his head, disliking even the memory of it. He wondered how Paul was taking to the crudities of messdeck life. At least his introduction to the Navy, at nineteen, wouldn't be nearly as unpleasant as his father's had been at a much more tender age.

Trench said, breaking a few minutes' silence, "My intention is to get the ship cleaned up, sir, during the forenoon. Starting with the messdecks. Do you want to keep one gun and the close-range closed up all day?"

"Yes. And lookouts on the bridge, and the

director tower manned. One officer on the bridge and a quartermaster on the gangway. We can do without sentries, though, in working hours. When the spars arrive, let Metcalf have as many hands as he wants. Did he finish the staging for the engine-room, d'you know, in place of the footplates they're using for the patch?"

"He did, sir."

"Good . . . Tommy, we'll fly no ensign and no Jack. For the time being, let discretion be the better part of valour."

The shaping, rigging and stepping of a new topmast was a job to be completed as soon as possible, because once Boyensen had done his stuff below and the generator was back in action they'd have full power for wireless transmitting, and the proper aerial height would be needed. If the raid on Namsos went badly at least it would be possible to let the C-in-C know what was— or had been—happening. If it went well, he wouldn't let out a peep. If the Germans could be taken completely by surprise, and if communications between Namsos and the rest of Norway could be cut before the action started, it was possible—with a reasonable share of luck—that *Intent* might get her oil and be away before any alarm went out.

He told Trench, "I'll be calling a meeting in my cabin this afternoon. I'll ask Torp to attend, and I'll want you, and also Chandler and Brockle-hurst. I'll let you know what time."

He'd have this forenoon, barring interruptions, to work out some details, formulate one cohesive plan out of the jumble of ideas. It could have been done more quickly: if *Intent* hadn't been immobilised, it would have been. As things were, there was time to plan it with some care. And by this afternoon, Boyensen might be able to forecast a time for the completion of his work. If his first estimate had been right, it would be done by some time tomorrow. So tomorrow night for the bust-up. Move in the dark hours: attack in the dark too, if Torp agreed that it could be done. Otherwise, at first light; but the night would be better, in order to get out of the fjords while it was still dark. Check the tides, and the shape of the harbour, and whatever the Sailing Directions had to say. It might be sensible, he decided, to talk it all over with Claus Torp before letting the others in on it. Torp, after all, did know the area and the port.

"Number One." He stopped near the super-structure door which led down to his own quarters and to the wardroom. "I'm going down for some breakfast. I'd like you to give Torp a message—not now, but after you've dealt with the hands at eight, say. My compliments, and would he join me at eleven for a cup of coffee."

"Just him alone, sir?"

Nick glanced at him sharply. Trench began to look as if he wished he hadn't asked the question.

"Yes. Just him."

He was in his bathroom, shaving, when at 0700 he heard the pipe "Hands to breakfast and clean." Scraping the lather off his face, trying to ignore the racket going on up top where engine-room hands were drilling bolt-holes ready to take the steel patch across that hole, and pondering on what part *Valkyrien* might play in the attack on Namsos. He thought the best use for her might be as an escape vehicle, for the landing-parties and others, if *Intent* should—God forbid—get scuppered somehow. *Valkyrien* could then stay clear of the rough stuff; and Kari could be in her. For landing-parties he could use *Valkyrien's* two motor skiffs or Knut's boat—if Knut was prepared to join in the operation.

Leading Steward Seymour knocked on the bathroom door. "Surgeon-Lieutenant Bywater would like a word, sir."

"All right. Hang on there." He put his razor down and went out, half shaved and with a towel round his waist, into the day cabin. "How is he?"

"Coming along very nicely, sir, I'm glad to say."

"Well done . . . He'll be laid up for quite some time, I suppose?"

"Yes, sir. To his own annoyance, he will. I've

244

taken the bandages off his face now—it's nothing like as bad as we thought at first—and he's talking—mostly about the engines and how he ought to be down there getting on with it, etcetera."

"Good for him."

"What he needs most is rest. But he'd appreciate a visit from you, sir, if you could spare the time."

"As soon as I've had breakfast. Anything else?"

"Only this, sir. It's the only one since last evening's SITREP."

Nick read the signal. It was from Vice-Admiral Battlecruiser Squadron to *Penelope*. The cruiser was being told to take four destroyers with her and proceed immediately to the support of the 2nd Destroyer Flotilla in Ofotfjord.

It didn't look too good. If Warburton-Lee needed support . . .

"We aren't getting much, are we." He passed the signal log back. "Anything of interest from the BBC?"

Bywater shook his head. "There'll be a news at eight, sir, of course."

When Nick had dressed he went back into the day cabin, where Seymour had his breakfast ready. Cornflakes, and bacon with fried bread.

"Are we out of eggs?"

"I'm afraid we are, sir."

He decided he'd ask Torp whether there'd be any chance of getting fresh provender ashore

245

here. The invaluable Knut might round up supplies from somewhere. Fresh milk, if there was any to be had, would be a change from this tinned stuff. One wouldn't want to take food from the mouths of Norwegians, but it wouldn't be any crime to put the Hun garrison on short rations.

Seymour had retired to his pantry, which had a service hatch connecting through the after bulkhead, near the door to the wardroom and cabin flat. Nick began to think again about Operation Namsos.

If the attack could be made in the dark hours, there were the alternatives of opening with a couple of rounds of starshell lobbed over the town to light up their objective and/or enemy strongpoints, or of keeping as quiet as possible, concentrating the attack on the oiling jetty alone, silencing any sentries or gunners without disturbing the garrison as a whole. It would be the neatest way of doing the job. Without a shot or a light: only some sentries to be found later with their throats cut—or discovered to be missing, if one took them prisoner—and fueltanks lighter by a few hundred tons, *Intent* slipping away to sea before the light came. . . .

Dobbs' face wasn't a pretty sight, smothered in some kind of ointment. But it was amazing to recall that such a short while ago he'd been so nearly a customer for that launching-party in the waist. Nick remembered his own impromptu prayer, and he said another now in his mind as he looked out of the sickbay's scuttle across still grey water towards the north-western shore of Totdalbotn: *Thank you, God.* Perhaps it was only a way of hedging one's bets: certainly he couldn't have said whether or not he believed that God might have taken a hand in Dobbs' recovery. But since one had asked for that intercession and then seen—almost miraculously, according to Bywater —the desired result, it would be churlish not to follow through.

He'd talked to Dobbs about Boyensen, and his hope that he'd have the ship fit for work by some time tomorrow.

"Only wish I could be on the job meself, sir. Seems *daft*—"

"It's fretting about it that would be daft. The more you can relax and rest the sooner you'll be on your feet. Right, doctor?"

Bywater confirmed it. Dobbs said he knew it: he still hated lying around when there was important work to do, *his* kind of work.

"You made a very stout effort, and it'll be in my report. . . . Got anything to read?"

"Be difficult to 'old a book, sir—or turn the pages, like."

Both his hands were wrapped like an Egyptian mummy's. Nick suggested, "If you had a rack of some kind—fixed or suspended about here . . . Then to turn the pages—Doctor, a marline-spike would do it. A spike shoved through a cork. You

247

could wedge the cork inside the outer bandage and he'd just prick the pages over?"

"Yeah, if I had *that* . . ."

Bywater was doubtful about how the rack could be fixed up. Nick said, "We have one *amateur* mechanical genius on board who might turn his talent to it. And who probably hasn't nearly enough to keep him busy at the moment. Midshipman Cox."

Dobbs grinned. It hurt him: he winced, and straightened his face. "He's a good lad, sir, is Mr. Cox. Very chummy with Mr. Waddicor— well, he *was*."

"I didn't know that."

"Both Devon, you see, sir."

Both West-Countrymen, and both with interests in things mechanical and oily. Waddicor, the commissioned engineer, had been a cheerful, easygoing character. A clear contrast to the fussy, very *proper* Pete Chandler. It made sense, all right, and no wonder the boy had enjoyed escaping to the engine-room.

He told the doctor, "I'll send him along to you."

Three weeks ago, he reminded himself, he hadn't known anything about anybody in this ship. You began to see them individually, like so many separate pieces of a jigsaw, and then you saw how they fitted in, with the ship's function and with each other, linking this way and that to build the whole picture, the community that was

248

a ship's company. The whole being enormously greater than the sum of the parts.

One of the parts being Randolph Lyte, whom he found on the bridge in charge of the lookout watch. Lyte hadn't shaved yet, he noticed.

"Morning, Sub."

"Oh—morning, sir!"

He'd made him jump. He asked him, "Had breakfast yet?"

"Not yet, sir. My relief's somewhat adrift."

For the change of watch at 0800, presumably. But Nick's watch told him it was still only three minutes to the hour. Then he remembered: just before he'd left the sickbay he'd heard the pipe "Hands fall in"—and that would have been sharp at eight.

"What's the time exactly?"

"Five and one-half minutes past, sir."

He'd missed that news bulletin. But someone would have heard it. . . . He asked Lyte, "Everything all right up here?"

"Very quiet and peaceful, sir."

"We'll change *that*, soon enough." He focused binoculars on the hill where Norwegians were supposed to be keeping a lookout over Namsenfjord. If they saw anything that looked German, they were to wave a red flag. It would probably be a petticoat, Torp had said. A white one after that would mean "all clear".

"You're keeping an eye on that hill?"

"Yessir. Starboard lookout's alert to it as well, sir."

"Good . . . When you go down, Sub, tell Cox there's a job I want him to do for the doctor. In sickbay."

"Aye aye, sir."

Pete Chandler was in the chartroom and on the point of going up to take over from Lyte. It was unlike Chandler, to be late like this. Nick asked him, "Did you hear the eight o'clock news?"

"Yes, sir." He seemed cheerful this morning. "*Good* news, for a change. Fleet Air Arm 'planes have sunk the *Konigsberg* in Bergen harbour, and destroyers have smashed up a whole bunch of Huns at Narvik."

"Tell me what was said about Narvik."

"German losses were two destroyers sunk and five so damaged as to be unseaworthy. So they're stuck there and presumably we can bomb them —or attack again and finish them off . . . . Plus six supply ships sunk or burnt—destroyed, anyway—and one large ammunition ship which our chaps met when they were withdrawing down Ofotfjord. It blew up with an explosion that sent flames to three thousand feet, the man said. British losses were two destroyers."

"Two *sunk?*"

"One sunk, one beached, sir."

"Didn't name them?"

Chandler shook his head. "It said a large number of survivors were thought to have got ashore." He shrugged. "Sounds as if we won by an innings."

Nick was silent, leaning over the chart, giving the appearance of studying it, reading without actually taking into his mind what the words meant, Namsenfjorden: from the Norwegian government charts of 1900. With additions and corrections to 1931. He heard Chandler say, "Good show knocking off the *Konigsberg*, sir." Six ships, he was thinking, in that flotilla. Two lost. One chance in three. Or rather—he switched to the other way of looking at it, in the process of getting a grip on this—two chances in three that *Hoste* was now out in Vestfjord. Probably fuelling from *Renown* or one of the other big ships they had up there.

"Pilot, I'm going to borrow this chart and the Sailing Directions and the tide tables. Better have the Nautical Almanac as well." For times of sunset and sunrise. He added, "We'll be having a meeting some time this afternoon, down in my cabin, and I'll need to have you there."

Chandler nodded. "First lieutenant did mention it, sir."

Six bells: and he had his notes roughed out well enough to go over them with Torp. He had a list of questions for him too. Torp should be here at any minute. From for'ard Nick heard the pipe "Up spirits!" and from the pantry Steward Seymour's murmured response, "Stand fast the

'Oly Ghost." Same old jokes, day after day and all over the world's oceans for—what, two hundred years?

Mr. Opie and the coxswain and a few other stalwarts would descend now to the spirit room —it was one deck below this and further aft, between the after magazine and the tiller flat, the steering-gear compartment—and draw the raw Jamaica rum which would then be mixed with water: one gill of water to half a gill of rum. Chief Petty Officers were allowed to draw it neat, and Paul, being under twenty years of age, wouldn't get it at all.

British losses, two destroyers . . .

There was a knock on the door, and he called "Come in." Trench announced, "Lieutenant-Commander Torp, sir."

"Thank you, Tommy . . . Come on in, Commander."

Torp said as he entered, "I must thank you for a wonderful dinner party." Trench withdrew. Nick told the Norwegian, "I'm all set to give you a few shocks, to make up for it." He called to Seymour, "Coffee please, steward."

"Shocks, eh?"

"Better sit down and prepare yourself." He pointed towards the open hatch. "It can wait for a minute or two."

"Then while we are waiting, I have an invitation for you to lunch with us, please, in *Valkyrien*. And before you make excuses I warn you we have fresh-caught fish and that Kari is the best cooker of fish that was ever born."

"No excuses, then. I accept with the greatest pleasure." Seymour had put the coffee in the hatch and he was on his way round—out of the pantry into the cabin flat and then in by the door through which Torp had entered. Nick said, "I was wondering—talking of fish—whether we could buy any fresh produce for the ship while we're here. Fish, eggs, vegetables, meat? One snag is we've only British currency on board."

"That would not matter. Only how much time there is. To arrange now for sufficient—is it for your whole crew?"

"Yes. Hundred and sixty-five."

"Well." Torp looked doubtful. "If it had been last week you were asking—before the Boche came—"

"You'd have told me to get the hell out of it. For trespassing in your neutral waters."

Torp frowned, blinking, watching Seymour carefully setting down the tray. He decided, apparently, to let the point go; he said, "Halvard Boyensen tells me his work goes well. I think you will not wish to stay here only to have provisions? If he finish maybe tomorrow midday—"

"I want to sail tomorrow night. About midnight."

Seymour could take *that* buzz for'ard. Nick saw it register—the steward's quick, interested glance. Sailors on the messdecks expected occasional buzzes from the wardroom stewards, and stewards lost face if they couldn't provide some from time to time. Nick told him, "I shan't be on board for lunch, Seymour."

"No, sir. I 'eard."

"And we shan't need anything else now. Shut the hatch, would you, before you leave the pantry?"

A minute later it slid shut, and then they heard the pantry door shut too. Nick told his guest, "I can't sail without taking in some oil-fuel. You are certain, I suppose, that there's some in Namsos?" Torp nodded. Sudden interest in the blue eyes. Kari's eyes, in that broad, entirely masculine face. Slight pouches under them and thickly matted brows above. Extraordinary . . . Nick pointed at the table on which last night they'd dined and on which he'd now laid out the chart and reference books and signal pads for making notes on. He asked Torp, "Would you make me a sketch of the harbour layout, quays and oiling jetty, and so on? Use the back of that chart, perhaps, so we can have it on a nice big scale?"

"I think, Kari, I can say without exaggeration or flattery that I've never eaten such fish as this. The sauce is—well, *what* is it?"

"It's secret."

"She makes up such secrets by herself." Torp pointed at her with his fork. "When you see she has a—what d'you call, a *goof* look?"

"Goofy. But I'd hardly—"

"No, you would not, would you. But goofy, yes. She is thinking then about food. Why she is not fat like a pig I do not know."

"Or why *you* aren't, if she gives you meals like this one very often."

"He's *quite* fat, don't you think?" Kari poured herself a glass of water. "Tell me about the plan you've made?"

Torp had produced the sketch which Nick had asked for, and provided answers to all his questions. Then they'd gone over the plan in detail, and made changes here and there. Biggest of all was that instead of an advance party going in by skiff to land and cut the telephone wires leading out of the town—it was a necessity, but it had worried Nick, because of the danger of the men being caught and the Germans alerted to the likelihood of an attack—Torp believed that his friends in Totdal, who had an old Ford truck, would agree to making the journey by road to Sjoasen and from there north up the main coastal highway to a place where the wires could be cut three or four miles south of Namsos itself. The whole road trip would be about forty kilometres, fifty at the outside. And from the torpedo stores the Norwegians could be provided with fitted charges and fuse, to make a real job of it. The rest of the plan hung together with only minor changes, all the result of getting answers to those questions, and by the time they'd come over to

Valkyrien for this lunch it was cut and dried, ready for presentation to Nick's officers this afternoon.

The oiling quay was on the western side of the harbour. It was made of concrete and about a hundred metres long. There was a railway line connecting to it. Another concrete quay of about the same length was being constructed just beyond it, but was in too rough a stage now, Torp felt, for any guns to have been mounted on it. Plenty of cover, though, among the heaps of sand and concrete blocks. The other jetties, all to the east, were smaller and made of wood, used mostly for loading timber from local sawmills. To the east again was the timber pond, the storage area, and the shallows on that side of the town dried out at low tides.

Kari had asked him to tell her about the plan. Nick glanced at her father. Torp shrugged. "Why not. You don't want her at your meeting, do you?"

"Well—no, I suppose—"

Kari asked him, "*Why* don't you?"

"Because—" Torp answered her—"our friend Commander Trench might not be paying attention to the right teacher."

"Oh, you're ridiculous!"

"I think he's right." Nick added, "And Tommy might not be the only one." Torp chuckled. Kari was looking at Nick, waiting for some more serious explanation. He said, "We'll

256

tell you about it now, then this afternoon we can use foul language if we want to."

"Sure." Her father nodded. "*I* want to."

"In a nutshell, Kari, we're going to raid Namsos, take control of the oiling jetty, and hold it for as long as we need to fill our tanks with fuel. Roughly for an hour from the time the oil starts flowing." That would be CPO Beamish's department, getting the oil in. Beamish would land with the assault party on the main quay. Nick went on, "While we're doing it—well, look, here's the town and harbour. This is our approach, up Namsenfjord. In this headland here, which is three thousand yards from the quay we'll be at, is a little cove, with a point called—?"

Torp supplied the name: "Merraneset."

Kari said yes, she knew it, of course.

"That's where you wait, with *Valkyrien*. This ship will be the way out, the escape ship in case *Intent* should get sunk or stuck there. We're borrowing your two motor skiffs, and we're also going to ask Knut Lange if he'll join us with his boat. If *Intent* has to be abandoned we'll blow her up and the survivors will escape by the boats to *Valkyrien*."

Torp added, "It would be for you then to take her out and maybe sail her to Scotland. I'll give you a course to steer. The Royal Navy would perhaps find you before you had gone so far."

She asked him, "You will be in the destroyer?"

"Sure. As pilot. We do all this in the dark, you see."

"Who will be with me in *Valkyrien*?"

"Martinsen on the engine, and Kristiansen and Rolf Skaug on deck. Perhaps also young Einar."

"The old ones and the baby."

"Exactly. Also any others who do not wish to volunteer. Maybe some of Knut's crew—it depends."

"Volunteer for what?"

"Halvard Boyensen will remain in the destroyer, because they have no engineers. Others—well, you see, Commander Everard's plan is to put ashore two parties of men with rifles and Thompson sub-machine-guns, one on the half-built quay and the other on the most western timber jetty. From there they will cover the approach to the oiling quay also, and maybe derail a railway truck at the inshore end. But the ship's guns will also be used, so for landing-parties we must give more men."

"Yes." She nodded. "More beans?"

"No, thank you." He told her, "We'll be tying up loose ends this afternoon. When it's all settled I'll give you some details on paper. Signals, for instance. We'll use Very lights, red and green, to tell you when we've finished and are casting off —so you can then up-anchor and start out—or if things are going wrong and the boats are coming to you. That sort of stuff."

"I am in charge of *Valkyrien* while you are doing these things?"

"Yes. Your father thinks you'd be better at it than any of his other people."

"All right."

Extraordinary. As cool as if she'd been asked to take the history class this afternoon. Nick would have liked to have got up, walked around to that side of the table and kissed her. He had a positive feeling, suddenly, that he was going to end up kissing her in any case; and it wasn't because she'd volunteered so readily. He looked at Claus Torp. "You've got quite a girl here."

"Well." Torp shrugged. "We'll see how she makes out."

Kari said, ignoring her father, "I am sorry there is no pudding now. Only these." Pointing at a bowl of apples. Torp pushed his swivel chair around and got up. "Boyensen will be eating lunch now. I will ask him how is the repair progressing."

"Take an apple with you?"

She'd tossed one to him. Nick declined. The door shut behind Torp, and Kari began to peel her own, concentrating on it as if she was alone and engaged on some particularly intricate task.

"You're terrific, Kari."

She didn't look up. "I am glad you should think so."

"I'm looking forward to taking you to those theatres."

"You must make sure your raid is successful, then." She was trying to keep the lengthening strip of peel unbroken. "It's going to be very dangerous, isn't it?"

"It might be, but it might turn out to be easier than we expect. Depends on a lot of things. How old are you, Kari?"

"Twenty-seven." Munching apple. "You?"

"Forty-three."

Mental arithmetic going on. Sixteen years was the answer, and it was an uncomfortably high figure, he thought. But Fiona Gascoyne was only four years older, at thirty-one, and she didn't seem to regard him as decrepit, exactly.

"You don't look as much. I'd have guessed thirty-eight, at very most forty."

"Call it thirty-eight, then there are only eleven years between us."

"Okay." At least she was looking at him now. "Why are you not married?"

"I was. I was divorced quite some while ago. My former wife lives in the United States and has an American husband now."

"Did you have children?"

"One son. He's nineteen, and he's at sea. Up off Narvik somewhere, to be precise."

"In a—" her apple-hand moved in the direction of *Valkyrien*'s port side, where *Intent* was— "destroyer?"

"Yes. One called *Hoste*. She's one of a flotilla that was in action at Narvik very early this

260

morning. They sank a lot of German ships, but two of our destroyers were lost in the process." Kari had stopped chewing: she was watching him intently. He'd already noticed that she was quick in the uptake. He told her, "The news bulletin didn't mention *which* ships. But—"

He'd stopped because he'd felt her hand on his. She'd leant forward, reached to him across the table.

"I'm so sorry. Of course you are worrying now. But he'll be all right, you'll see. It will not have been *his* ship that—"

"Ah-hah!"

Torp, in the doorway of the saloon, was wagging a finger at them.

"You hold hands, eh? This is what's happening when my back is turned?"

Kari had neither withdrawn her hand nor looked round. She told Nick, "Your son will be all right. I'm *sure* he will."

It would have been wonderful to have been able to take her word for it. She truly, genuinely wanted him to: he could see it, feel it. She may even have believed it herself: or been determined to, as if by creating that certainty in herself and for him she could *make* it so.

"Son, did she say?"

He looked up at Torp. "He's in one of the destroyers in that flotilla up at Narvik. The action we talked about this morning."

"I see." The Norwegian crossed two sausage-

261

sized fingers. "That is for him. For—what is his name?" Nick told him. Torp repeated it: "Paul. Good luck to Paul." He swung a chair round and let himself down on to it. "Boyensen says tomorrow noon."

Nick looked round at them: at Trench on his left, Henry Brocklehurst beyond Trench, Claus Torp at the end of the table and Pete Chandler on the right.

"That's the picture, then. Summing it up, the timetable will be as follows." He glanced at his notes. "*Intent* will weigh at 2300 tomorrow and proceed at six knots with *Valkyrien* following close astern and with both motor skiffs on our davits and turned out ready for lowering. We may also have the blue fishing-boat in company. At 0100/12th we'll be off Merraneset, where *Valkyrien* will be detached to remain hidden in that cove. The skiffs will be manned at this point, and *Intent* will increase to twenty knots for the last one-and-a-half miles to the target area. At 0105 we will stop engines, lower the skiffs and slip them, and they will proceed to points A and B as shown on that sketch, land their parties and remain with them in case resistance is such that either or both have to evacuate. Alternatively to bring off any wounded men or messages. The fishing-boat, if we have it, will remain alongside —port side, as we'll be starboard side to the wall —and will be employed as circumstances dictate.

262

"H" hour, for the skiffs' arrival at A and B and *Intent*'s at the oiling berth, will be 0110. Allowing for berthing and connecting up and roughly an hour's fuelling, I would hope to have recalled the landing-parties and be casting off *by* 0230. . . . Are there any questions, now?"

Trench nodded. "You say telephone lines out of Namsos are going to be cut, sir?"

"At 0100, we hope. Commander Torp is going ashore later this afternoon to make arrangements for it. Which reminds me, Number One—Mr. Opie is to provide two one-and-a-quarter pound fitted charges and a good length of Bickfords and some igniters—and a pair of pliers, while he's at it. As soon as this meeting's over?"

"Aye aye, sir."

Brocklehurst suggested, "Might it not be as well to blast any shore guns we can see as soon as we do see 'em, before we get alongside, sir?"

"If they open fire on us, yes. Otherwise I'd rather we took them with our assault party, fairly quietly and without waking up the whole town and garrison."

Tommy Trench was going to lead the assault on the oiling quay. He'd have a dozen men with him. Two of the twelve would constitute CPO Beamish's personal bodyguard until he was back on board with the fuel-hose connected.

"Do you think there's a chance of keeping it all that quiet, sir?"

Brocklehurst again. Nick admitted, "Not of

263

keeping it quiet. But with a bit of luck we might get the oil flowing before the opposition becomes too obstreperous. And they might not realise, then, what we're doing."

"You mean it may not occur to them that we're fuelling."

"Exactly. They're pongoes, after all."

Everybody laughed. Nick looked at Chandler. The navigator said, "Since we have a highly experienced pilot, sir—" he bowed towards Torp —"I don't think I've any navigational problems at all. But the plan for the withdrawal does bother me a little. If we're intending to pick up *Valkyrien* and take her with us—" Nick shook his head. Chandler, who hadn't been looking at him, didn't see it. Torp did though, and raised his eyebrows, staring at him down the length of the table. Chandler was saying, "—her best speed being six knots, if we cast off at your estimated time of 0230, sir, we shouldn't be out of Namsenfjord until something like 0700. As we'll have kicked up quite a rumpus by then it seems to me that such a leisurely withdrawal would be asking for the sort of trouble we can't easily handle. Aircraft attacks, for instance. Even if the telephones are out of action we've no way to stop them screaming for help by wireless."

"Well." Nick made a note. "Perhaps we *have* . . . But—you're right, of course, there's no question of withdrawing at six knots. It's a point which I and Commander Torp haven't gone into yet—although I do have a proposal for him."

Torp stirred. "What is it?"

"*Valkyrien* will be there in case we fail. If we succeed, she then has no function to perform. We embark everyone from her, and the last man out opens her seacocks."

"*Scuttle?*"

"If we don't, it's odds-on the Germans will. And *Intent* with her."

"No." Torp's face looked as if it had turned to wood. "I am glad to accept your command, sir, but—no. I don't sink my ship."

Nick had expected trouble on this issue. It was something for him and Torp to settle on their own.

"I understand your reluctance, Commander. Perhaps we can talk about it after this meeting."

"Wait. I tell you what I can do." Torp got up, came round to lean on the table between Chandler and Nick, pointing with a blunt forefinger at the chart. "Here we will be, off Merraneset. I will come here from shore not in your ship but in one of my skiffs. Or in Knut's boat maybe. I and my own people will board *Valkyrien*. You in this ship can go at your own speed straight out Namsenfjord to the sea." He put a hand on Chandler's shoulder. "There are no dangers if you keep your eyes open. Fifteen miles—even at fifteen knots you are out in the open sea at maybe

0330, with darkness for one more hour. Not bad?"

"Not bad for us. But—"

"I take *Valkyrien* this way. Up Lokkaren, Surviksundet, Lauvoyfjord, Rodsundet or Seierstadfjorden. The Germans will be hunting after you and *this* way, not for some old yacht up here."

"How long will it take you to get clear?"

"Three, four hours. From Flottra then I steer west, five knots. Departure Flottra 0630. When you signal your people you tell them this and they can send a few battleships for escorting me, huh?"

"Of course. The entire Home Fleet."

But seriously—he *might* get away with it. Nick still had one reservation. He told Chandler, "Pilot, when we break this up, ask the PO Tel to come and see me, would you. I want to talk about jamming any German transmissions while we're alongside. That was a useful point you made." He looked across at the GCO: "Once the shooting starts, we may want to use some starshell. Have one gun lined up for it, with starshell in its ready-use racks."

"Aye aye, sir." Brocklehurst made a note.

There was a knock at the cabin door: Nick called, "Yes?"

Cox stuck his head in. "Sorry to interrupt you, sir. The blue fishing-boat's just coming through the northern channel."

"Thank you, Mid." The head withdrew, and the door shut. Nick said, "One item not yet detailed is the composition of the two skiff landing-parties. We'll go into that as soon as we know how many Norwegian volunteers we have. Otherwise, I think we've covered everything?"

"Very good." Torp rose, stood rubbing his behind. "Sitting so long, I been getting a sore arse."

Trench murmured, "Excuse me, sir?" He'd want to see to the reception of the fishing-boat.

Nick told him, "Best if he berths on *Valkyrien*, Tommy."

"*My* paintwork, eh." Torp slapped him on the back. "First you say I should sink her, now to scrape off the new paint." Trench had gone up; the others were collecting their notes as Nick and Torp left the cabin. Torp's suddenly raised spirits, Nick guessed, were symptoms of pre-action elation. Something happened to the glands, the blood-stream, with some kinds of men. Some got jumpy and others—Torp's kind—got happy.

Cold air, grey water: the blue boat was carving a broad white track across it, approaching *Intent*'s stern where Trench and the buffer, Metcalf, were waving to Lange to tell him to come around to the inshore side. He'd see what was wanted, because he'd have seen *Valkyrien*'s raked masts and tall funnel sticking up behind the destroyer.

"Claus." Nick put a hand on Torp's arm. "One

suggestion I'd like to make, in regard to this plan of yours, that back-door exit you mean to take. . . . You know and I know that while you *may* get away with it, there's a good chance you won't. The Germans aren't all stupid, and they know there's more than one way out to the sea. If I had to bet on it I'd say you'll either be stopped by some incoming surface craft, or strafed from the air. Anything that's moving seaward, after the attack on Namsos—"

"Yes, it is possible."

"So you'll reduce your crew to a minimum?"

"I guess so. You take the others?"

"Of course. But what about Kari?"

"I thought so." Torp glanced at him, and away again. He either sighed or took a deep breath. "She has to be in *Valkyrien* during the attack."

"But she could transfer after it."

"Such delay, for one person—"

"Instead of coming off by skiff, you come with me, all of you. I'll put *Intent* alongside *Valkyrien*, and you can make a quick transfer, and away we go."

"You worrying for Kari, Nicholas?"

"Nick."

"What?"

"Short for Nicholas. Friends call me Nick."

"Ah. *Sir* Nick, I think."

"Who told you?"

"Boyensen. He is talking with your stokers down there. You worry for Kari, Sir Nick?"

"You've admitted the risk. You don't have to run it, you could scuttle your ship. My opinion is you *should*. But at least you don't have to put your daughter's life at risk."

The blue boat was slowing, chugging in alongside *Valkyrien*. They could see the spars lashed to the cabin-top and along the side. They looked enormous: but Metcalf and his assistants would be paring them down with adzes before they shaped and fitted them. The heel of the new topmast would have to be squared with chamfered corners, and slotted right through for the top-rope sheave; and at two places above that they'd make "stops", narrowings of the diameter where copper funnels would be fitted to take the upper yard and the rigging. Under the funnels there'd be another slot with a sheave in it for gantlines; and that was just the topmast, the yards would need shaping and fitting too.

Nick said to Metcalf, "You're going to have your hands full, Buffer, to get it done in time." Petty Officer Metcalf nodded. "Keep at it all night if we 'ave to, sir." The boat was alongside and its lines were being secured. Torp said, "You take care of her for me?"

"If you'll allow me to."

"Sure." The meaty hand patted his arm. "That is what we do, then." He broke into Norwegian as he moved forward, answering a yell from Knut Lange which even to a non-Scandinavian ear had

269

asked something very much like Where the hell's Claus Torp?

They were talking now. Or rather, Lange was. Unshaven, crop-headed, a triangular face that looked as if it might be all bone under the reddish stubble. He was down on his boat still and Torp was leaning down to him over *Valkyrien's* bulwark. Lange talking quickly, urgently. Kari had come out of the deckhouse and she was listening: Nick could guess from her expression that whatever this news was it wasn't good.

The spars were being unlashed. Torp straightened, moved aft past the skiff which was still inboard. He'd caught Nick's eye, jerked his head, and now he was waiting for him in the stern.

"We have company." He pointed northward. "Three Boche destroyers. They enter Altfjord last evening. At night, two are leaving, one stay at anchor behind the island. Knut told the people not to telephone—he thinks too much risk, better he tell me himself. But this morning one of the bastards is in Rodsundet. One now still anchored there, off Saltkjelvika, the other is going back out into Foldfjorden. Not fast, only—how you say, hanging around."

The picture was clear enough. One destroyer on each of the two main exits and another one outside. But—it didn't mean they'd still be there tomorrow night. Also, there was still one other bolt-hole.

Torp was as gloomy as he'd been elated a

few minutes ago. Scowling, watching some of *Intent*'s sailors manoeuvre the first spar up over *Valkyrien*'s side.

He swung round. "No raid on Namsos now, I think."

Nick met the blue stare doggedly. "There *has* to be."

"So you get your oil."

"Exactly. I can't move without it."

"If you are lucky, okay, you get it. Then you have three Boche destroyers waiting for you. What good is *that* for you?"

More good, Nick thought, than sitting here and waiting for the Stukas.

9

"HOW are you now, Everard?"

The short answer might have been, alive. . . .

Mathieson, *Hoste*'s first lieutenant, wearing fearnought trousers, a woman's embroidered blouse and a tattered red cardigan, was standing and looking down at him, and Paul—wrapped in a blanket—was sitting with his back against the classroom's wooden wall. The schoolhouse was —incredibly—centrally-heated; it was even conceivable now that they wouldn't all die of cold, which a couple of hours ago had seemed almost certain. He told Mathieson, "I'm okay, sir, thank you." Trying to get up, because he thought he should: the pain shot through his back, crippling him. It was only bruising and pulled muscles, Graham-Jones had said, nothing permanent or fundamental. Mathieson told him, "Stay where you are, man." Randy Philips was singing "The Last Time I Saw Paris". If Paris could have seen Randy it would have died laughing: he had on a skirt and a woman's overcoat, a tight, waisted garment of blue woolly stuff. Mathieson was moving on, looking for someone or other in the long, narrow, crowded room, one of several rooms in the schoolhouse into which the ship's company had flowed with the delight and disbelief of men transferred from hell to paradise. They'd trekked seven miles to this place—Ballangen, it was called, and it was about twenty or twenty-five miles from Narvik, someone had said—over rough, snowbound country, the snow in places six feet deep, guided by some Norwegians from the little timber houses near which they'd come ashore. The Norwegians had been marvellous: torn up their own clothes for bandages, deprived themselves of just about everything they possessed—clothes, food, bed linen, blankets. . . . Like angels of mercy in a frozen purgatory which had begun for Paul on the rocky beach with Timson the SBA—sickberth attendant, Surgeon Lieutenant Graham-Jones's assistant—kneeling astride him and pumping ice-water out of his lungs. About half of Ofotfjord was gushing out and *Christ*, it had hurt, that bastard Timson crashing up and down on his spine which already felt as if it had been sawn through. There'd been a dream which he remembered clearly—if one could have *clear* recollection of something so nebulous. Less dream than series of delusions. As if he was his own father: or with him, but at times actually *him*, Nicholas Everard: and drowned, knowing himself to be dead, which had meant that Paul Everard had also to be dead, to be here with him and part of him. The pumping and the pain had gradually taken over —and even worse, the *cold*. . . .

Mathieson had turned back. He had a list of some sort with him and he'd been checking names off, for some purpose. Tall, fair-haired, yellow stubble glinting on his jaw. He said, "Mr. Stuart and I were doing some figure-work, Everard. Your score seems to have been seven."

He didn't know what the man was telling him. His face must have displayed that lack of comprehension; Mathieson explained, "Seven men you personally brought ashore." He added, when Paul didn't react, "Bloody good effort." He'd turned aside, gone to talk to Perry, the cook, who was nursing a broken wrist. These injuries didn't count as wounds; the wounded were in the little hospital, which was the reason for having come to Ballangen in the first place. That and the fact that it was farther away from Narvik and its German troops.

Whacker Harris growled, "You'll be gettin' a fuckin' medal if you don't watch it, Yank."

"Oh, sure."

More jokes. All the time, from this pair.

"Reckon you might at that." Randy Philips didn't look as if it was anything he could approve of. "You 'eard what Jimmy said. Commen-bloody-dation, that was." He sighed, glancing at Whacker. "Bloody HO, not at sea ten fuckin' minutes, an' they're talkin' to 'im like *that. I* dunno."

"I don't either." Paul really didn't. All he'd been told was that Mr. Stuart the gunner, aided by PO Longmore the GM, had been bringing the Carley float inshore for the last time, after *Hoste* had gone down, and they'd found him wallowing face-down in the water. They'd been searching the ship one final time for any surviving wounded who might have been missed in previous searches, and drawn a blank, then loaded the float with small-arms and boxes of ammunition and got clear about a minute before she sank. When they bumped into Paul they'd thought he'd drowned, but pulled him into the float anyway and paddled ashore. After he'd been pumped out and had regained some appreciation of where he was and what was happening, Mr. Stuart had torn him off a strip.

"What you got between your ears, lad—solid bone? There's a time to start and there's a time to bloody stop, an' there's such a thing as 'aving the gumption to know when you're done in. What you want's a bit o' bloody savvy, you daft clown!"

Now Mathieson had been congratulating him. One might wonder who was daft and who wasn't. As far as Paul was concerned, the two cancelled each other out. Wondering more about that dream and his father, whether on some other plane they could actually have been together, in such close communication that they'd been virtually one spirit, and then by slipping back into life he, Paul, had deserted him. . . . *More* delusion, he told himself. But it had seemed so real: more real than this present scene seemed to

275

him: and the sense of desertion was horrible. Might his father know that it hadn't been his *choice*?

He told Philips, "I was just helping out, same as everyone else was. I do happen to be good at swimming. Nothing else about it's special that I can see."

"Yeah, well, Jimmy reckons it was special. An' it's what 'e reckons sticks, ain't it." He looked at Whacker. "Besides, if 'e *did* pull seven blokes out—"

"Way we got 'im trained." Whacker shrugged. He had a mauve shawl around his shoulders. "Brought 'im up right, ain't we. Now 'e'll go through for C bloody W an' all that 'ard work's fuckin' wasted, ain't it. . . . 'Ullo, 'swain!"

"All right, 'Arris, you foul-mouthed bastard." The coxswain said it quite pleasantly. "And you, Philips. Jackson, you fit? Course you are. 'Aven't 'ad a dose this year yet, 'ave you? On your feet then . . . And you, Barker. Smith—Daley—Woolley—"

"What's this in aid of, Chief?"

"Guard duty, Smith, that's what. Lovely, out there in the snow. Dream of a white Christmas, can't you. Long as *I* don't catch no bugger dreamin'. . . . 'Old off the bloody Germans, lads, that's your job now."

Paul was struggling to get up, to go along with the others. CPO Tukes told him, "You stand fast, Everard. On the sick list, aren't you?"

276

"Hell, Chief, I'm not *sick*, I—"

"Germans, 'swain?" Green: the telegraphist who'd given Paul his first news about *Intent*. He asked Tukes, "Coming, are they? Jerries coming ' ere?"

"Green."

"Yes, 'swain?"

"Does your mother cry every time she sets eyes on you?"

Green's mouth opened and shut: he looked round as if for help. The coxswain told him, "You make *me* want to cry, Green. . . . All right, you lot—in the 'all, draw rifles an' webbing from Petty Officer Longmore, then fall in outside. Shake it up, now!"

Germans: presumably they would come sooner or later, Paul thought. So those rifles and revolvers might come in handy. Although the enemy would be busy around Narvik, one might guess, repairing damage and looking after their own casualties and defences. . . . Mathieson was coming back this way. Tom Brierson, who'd been the killick of 3 Mess, went up to him.

"Excuse me, sir. What's likely to 'appen next? I mean, are we staying 'ere?"

"For the moment, yes. It's on the cards there might be a second attack, you see. Even a landing. After all, we gave them quite a hammering, and it wouldn't take much to finish the job off. Also, we'll have to put some troops ashore some time, some place—at least I imagine

277

we will—and Narvik would be as good a place as any. Specially as we've softened it up for them."

Davis, an Asdic operator, asked him what they'd do if there was *not* a second attack or a landing.

"Make tracks for the Swedish border, before the Huns come for us. As the crow flies the border's only about twenty-five miles, but the way we'd have to go—because of the mountains —it'd be about forty. That's according to a Norwegian here who says he'd guide us." He turned towards the door. "But it does depend on the Huns too, of course. Bastards could show up at any minute."

Brierson came over and sat down beside Paul.

"'Ow's it going, Yank?"

"Not bad, Tom, considering."

"Done yourself a bit of good, they say."

"I don't know how. What was I supposed to do, sit on the beach and watch?"

"Some might. Goin' through for CW, are you?"

"I don't know that, either."

"*I* would, in your shoes." The killick shook his head. "Bloody shame, skipper buying it. Good 'and, old Rowan was."

Nick, on *Intent*'s bridge, was studying the hill where the lookout post was. Or where it should have been. Not a sign of any movement there. There could be, though: now that German ships had arrived in the outer parts of these fjords it was only a matter of time before some of them came up to visit Namsos. But for the moment that hill slumped grey and lifeless, with the westering sun vaguely brightening this side of it.

Claus Torp had gone ashore to Sveodden to see about the wire-cutting expedition. And Knut Lange had left them again. He'd taken his boat away through the northern channel with the intention of crossing Namsenfjord and landing near a village called Skomsvoll, in a wide, open bay marked on the chart as Vikaleira. There was a road junction near the village, and Lange's plan —he'd worked it out with Torp—was to send some of his crewmen overland up the east coast of Otteroy to the narrow strip between Altbotn and Lauvoyfjord. From Arnes on the east coast and from the neighbourhood of Alte on the west they'd be able to see into both the anchorages in which the enemy were—or had been—showing interest. From where *Intent* lay now to Lange's landing place was less than five miles, and the trip would only take him twenty or thirty minutes. The hike overland would be roughly another five, for which Claus Torp reckoned one should allow an hour each way, as quite a bit of it was hilly.

"Good for young men." He'd patted his gut. "Not for old gentlemen. For them—easy."

Lange would stay with his boat and send three crewmen ashore. Two would keep watch on the anchorages—or elsewhere, if the German ships had shifted their berths—and the third would be the runner to bring news back to him. He'd return here to Totdalbotn before dark tonight, to let Nick and Torp know how things were shaping up to that time, but he'd go back again during the night to receive his men's first-light report.

Nothing to do but wait. And see which way the cats jumped. The cats were on the exits from the mouse-holes: big cats with five-inch guns. . . .

Torp didn't think they'd pull it off now. Nick saw two angles, in the light of this enemy naval presence. First, stealth became much more important. He thought it was just conceivable that the fuelling might be completed without firing a single gun. It wasn't likely, but it was possible, and he was making it his aim now. Cutlasses and bayonets, not bullets; bullets only after—if—the enemy opened fire. The other point he had in mind was that the fact of Hun destroyers having been there earlier in the day didn't mean they'd be there *now*—let alone tomorrow night. Of course, it was also true that by tomorrow night they might be up at Namsos: in which case. . . .

Well. *Sufficient unto the day . . .*

His mind jumped three hundred miles: to Narvik. There'd been a signal just after noon from Vice-Admiral Battlecruiser Squadron to the light cruiser *Penelope*, saying Present situation.

Enemy forces in Narvik one cruiser five destroyers one submarine. Troop transports may be expected. Your object is to prevent reinforcements reaching Narvik. Establish destroyer patrol across Vestfjord. . . . So *Penelope* was there now, with some unspecified number of destroyers; and Narvik—if this signal spoke the truth—was still bristling with Germans. It didn't mention whether the destroyers were now operational or still suffering from punishment administered to them by the 2nd Flotilla: it seemed to Nick that if there was a whole clutch of damaged ships in there, anyone in his right mind would nip in double-quick and polish the bastards off.

Guesswork. But carefully not guessing about *Hoste*. One had to keep one's mind on present circumstances, on what had to be done *here*. And whatever had to be done, he'd be running it— men's lives would rest on his decisions. It was necessary to be fit for that, not lose sleep worrying over *private* matters.

He heard a voice behind him: low-pitched, no doubt because *he* was up here. Turning, he saw the snotty, Cox, leaving the bridge, presumably having given some message to Brocklehurst, who had the afternoon watch. Nick called him back.

"Mid—did you fix something up for Dobbs?"

"Yes, I did, sir." Cox came over to him. "Wasn't difficult. I made it out of thick wire, just bent to shape and with a couple of screws in the bottom of the upper bunk to hold it."

"Well done. What are you doing now?"

"Helping with the new topmast, sir. At least, seeing how it's done."

"Progressing well, is it?"

"Seems to be, sir."

He put his glasses up quickly: he'd thought he'd seen a movement on the hill. But if there had been, there was nothing to see now. . . . "Mid, we aren't going to allow you to *give up* your navigational studies, you know."

"No, sir."

"You must understand that whether it's an activity that appeals to you or not it's as essential to be able to use a sextant and arrive at a decent fix as it is to be able to tie a knot or steer a boat. It's part of your stock-in-trade as a seaman. If you put your mind to it, not as a school lesson but as a practical tool that you've got to master, you may find it a lot easier than you think."

At Cox's age he'd been pretty hopeless at it himself. Probably for much the same reason: sick of instructors, the Dartmouth atmosphere which, so far as junior officers' training and gunroom life were concerned, lingered on when at sea. He'd been about as bloody-minded, when he'd been fresh out of Dartmouth, as anyone could have been. Then at Jutland—*after* Jutland, when he'd found himself sole surviving officer in his destroyer and that he had to get her back to England, he'd begun to realise that if he'd been less pig-headed in recent years, if he'd ignored likes and dislikes and states-of-mind and just damn well *learnt* it. . . .

He was trying to explain this to Cox. Not mentioning the fact that, bringing the shattered destroyer home after Jutland, he'd not known for sure whether he'd hit England or Scotland or miss the lot.

"Yes, sir. I understand that."

Nick could see that he was *trying* to understand it. He asked him, "In your cadet days, did they talk at you about leadership?"

"Oh *yes*, sir."

"What did they tell you it amounted to?"

The boy frowned, trying to remember. Staring at that hillside on the north shore of Sundsråsa. "Well, just that—well, more or less a quality we're supposed to have, sir."

"Like Divine Right, holiness or irresistibility to girls?"

The snotty looked surprised. Nick told him, "It's nothing like that, Cox. No gift of God, and nothing magical about it either. Just common sense. It's not jumping up and shouting "Follow me!" and having all the chaps rush after you because you have this magnetic quality or heroism or something. The reason your instructors never spelt it out is because they're baffled by it themselves because no one ever told *them* either; but not to have this thing is unthinkable, so they daren't look too deeply into it in case they find they haven't got it. . . ." He drew breath. During the shore years, he'd had a lot of time to think about such things. "I'll tell you how you can start working out what it is. First—what made me think of it—this navigation business, as an example. Knowledge and ability, competence— you have to know your stuff. Otherwise you shouldn't be here in the first place, there's no *reason* for you. And your men have got to know that you know it. They'll give you the benefit of the doubt until a time comes when it'll show up one way or the other, and then by God you'd better show it, or else. . . . But there's more to it than just competence. They've got to like you. They've got to feel you're honest and fair in your dealings with them. And for that to come about you've got to like and respect *them*. Anyone who can't, or doesn't, might as well go home. When it works, it works because it's *natural*."

Silence. Staring at the hill. Then: "Any of that make sense to you?"

Cox nodded. He was looking at Nick now, not at the hill. He had a pleased look, as if he'd been given something.

"Yes, it does, sir."

"Think about it, from time to time. If you can really digest it, make use of it, you'll find things tend to go well more often than they go badly. But don't think of it as some kind of trick. It's absolutely basic—to what sort of chap you are, or will be. . . . Better get back to that topmast, now."

"Aye aye, sir. Thank you very much, sir."

Nick focused his glasses on the lookout post again. When he'd been Cox's age he'd had his uncle Hugh to put him straight occasionally. But it had been difficult for Hugh, because Nick and his father were always at loggerheads, and only in much later years had he and his uncle been able to discuss things without a feeling that they were whispering in corners.

Uncle Hugh would be convinced his nephew was dead, by this time.

Still nothing stirring up there. He hoped to God those people were doing what they'd said they'd do. He went back to the binnacle and slung his glasses on one of the spheres.

"I'll be down aft somewhere."

"Aye aye, sir." Brocklehurst added, "Hope that fisherman doesn't run up against any Krauts."

Nick thought Lange was probably quite canny. He looked it. And he'd surely know how to keep his boat hidden, in these fjords. He told Brocklehurst, "Might be nicer for the Krauts if they don't run up against *him*." He went down, avoiding the port side where Metcalf and his team were chopping away with adzes, and walked aft. A Norwegian assistant of Boyensen's and two of *Intent*'s stokers were fixing the steel patch over the engine-room, tightening the bolts all round; and on *Valkyrien*'s stern Kari was watching two

of her crew lowering the second skiff out over the
old ship's starboard side.

"That's a very economical arrangement."

She looked round quickly, startled. He meant
the single pair of davits amidships, between the
two boats' cradles. It could be swung to either
side, to lift either of the boats. Only *Valkyrien*'s
narrow beam that far aft made it either necessary
or mechanically feasible.

"They are going to try out its engine." She
came over to his side. "For tomorrow night when
you need them both."

"Got plenty of petrol for them?"

"Oh, I think so." She looked at her watch.
"My father is ashore a long time. Did you know
we were invited to dinner in your ship's wardroom tonight?"

"I did hear some such rumour."

"Will you be there too?"

"They've invited me."

"Then you will be?"

"I think I'd better let them have you to themselves. I don't want to be greedy and monopolise
you."

"You don't?"

"Well—yes, of course, but—"

"Come too, please?"

"If you put it like *that*—"

"My father says those ribbons you wear on
your shoulder—" she'd perched herself on the

white-painted bulwark—"some are important ones?"

She had a very direct manner. As if they weren't likely to know each other for long and there wasn't time to beat about the bush. Also, she had a way of switching from one subject to another so rapidly that you knew her thoughts must have gone to the new subject while you were still busy with the previous one. Or—in *this* case —she'd been certain that as soon as she said "Come, please?" he'd give in and agree?

He'd told her, "They're from the last war. Too long ago to remember."

"You must have been very young, to have won medals in that war. Do you think your plan can still work, with German ships out there?"

"I am hoping that by tomorrow they'll have achieved whatever their purpose is and be gone on their way."

He would not, he thought, dine in the ward-room this evening.

"You say you are hoping, but do you *think* they will?"

The question was annoying. How the hell could he foresee the enemy's moves when he didn't even know why they'd come here?

"I'd say there's a good hope they'll move on. If they don't, we'll either grab our oil without raising an alarm and then sneak away, or we'll have to fight them on the way out."

"Yes." She nodded. "The oil is necessary. Of course."

The readiness to accept, again. She'd throw out a lot of questions but she wouldn't question a logical conclusion. Wasn't acceptance of logic unusual in a female? To Ilyana, certainly, logic had always been a strictly male weapon to be either ignored or derided or fought to the last shriek. Sarah—well, that was hard to know. With Sarah he'd never really had an argument: except for one very short, almost wordless flare-up, twenty years ago, and they'd ended that in each other's arms. Which was why nowadays she never spoke to him except in front of other people, when she sometimes had to. He felt he knew nothing, now, about Sarah. Fiona? Well, Fiona would accept logic if it worked out in favour of whatever she was after at the time. Otherwise she'd brush it off: "My pet, don't be so *boring* . . ." Fiona had just completed her officers' training course: she was an Ensign now, with one pip on her shoulder. Uncharacteristically proud of the oddity that the MTC drills were patterned exactly on those of the Brigade of Guards: and of the quirk that MTC rankers called their lady officers "Madam" and not "Ma'am" as was done, apparently, in the FANYS, the nursing yeomanry. He'd made her angry by calling it "instant tradition": and by laughing at her totally *illogical* frustration at not being allowed red paint on her nails.

288

This girl—Kari—wouldn't give a damn what she put, or did not put, on her nails.

Why should he think approvingly of that, he wondered? He agreed with Fiona: he *liked* lacquered nails. And he was *not*, definitely, dining with his officers this evening. . . . "Kari, on second thoughts—"

"Here comes my father!"

She ran over to the other side, waving to the motor skiff as it approached from the western end of the little bay. She had a very attractive figure: not a mannequin-type figure like Fiona's, but —eye-catching and eye-holding. . . . Claus Torp was standing up in the boat's sternsheets, waving back to her.

Rear-Admiral Aubrey Wishart pushed the door shut as he passed through into his office; he went straight to the desk and flipped up the intercom switch.

"Any messages?"

"Quite a lot, sir. But one is very urgent and personal—from Admiral Everard. He's telephoned twice, and left a number at which he'd like you to call him back."

She told him the number, and from calls during the last three days he recognised it as a members' extension at Boodle's. He hesitated, drumming the fingers of one hand on the polished desk-top. He'd been at a conference for the last two hours, deputising for his chief; he had a stack of work piled up that needed seeing to, and now on top of it, this. . . .

Which he'd expected, of course. It was a lousy position to be in. He wished to God that Nick had never written that damn letter, putting the old boy in touch with him.

"Ginny—would you come in here, please?"

"Of course, sir."

He was sitting behind the desk when she came in. Third Officer Virginia Casler of the Women's Royal Naval Service was blonde and petite. She was also quick-witted and efficient. He told her, "Sit down for a minute. Something I'd like to explain to you."

She put herself neatly in the chair facing his, and crossed one elegant knee over the other. Smoothing down her skirt: then the small-boned, well-manicured hands relaxed, folded in her lap on top of a file she'd brought in with her. He told her, "I don't like to put a man off with excuses, pretending to be tied up or not here, and I dislike having to ask you to tell such fibs for me. Particularly when it's a man like Hugh Everard. But I do have a very good reason why I'd infinitely prefer not to have to talk to him, at least for a day or two."

"That's about as long as you'll be here, sir, isn't it?"

He nodded. His new appointment had come through. He'd be off almost at once, to join the staff of C-in-C Mediterranean. Third Officer

Casler's grey eyes rested on his face: she seemed patient—sympathetic, he thought—with his obvious unease.

"Hugh Everard's nephew Nick is an old friend of mine. His ship, the destroyer *Intent*, was sunk three days ago, in action with a cruiser believed to be the *Hipper*. Admiral Everard knows this, but won't or can't bring himself to accept it as fact. Nick was very close to him, more like a son than a nephew. So that's bad enough. The old man's wanting news all the time, and there isn't any and I know there won't *be* any. . . . But now on top of it there's something else. In the action at Narvik yesterday morning we lost three destroyers. The communiqué said two, but the three are *Hardy*, *Hunter* and *Hoste*. And serving in *Hoste* was Ordinary Seaman Paul Everard— Nick's son, aged nineteen, first ship. Hugh Everard had taken a shine to his great-nephew too. So—well, you see?"

"Yes." The grey eyes were clouded. "I do. It's—"

"I've been trying to jolly him along about Nick and *Intent*, play up to the wishful thinking. . . . But this other thing—well, we do have reason to believe there was a high proportion of survivors, but—" his hands opened on the desk—"you can only stretch hope and optimism a certain distance. After that—"

"May I make a suggestion, sir?"

He looked at her quickly. Women were such

marvellous creatures to have around when you were tied up in knots. Like oil in jammed machinery. And this one—well, he thought, you've always been a pushover for tiny blondes. Perhaps because one was such a large, ungainly sort of chap oneself. He stared down at his hands on the desk. "I'd be grateful if you would, Ginny."

"I think you should tell him. He's going to find out before long anyway, so keeping it to yourself now isn't really going to save him from it. And if there *are* a lot of survivors—anyway, he's probably a lot tougher than you think. If he's anything like *my* father—"

She'd stopped, catching herself in the act of saying more than was necessary to make the point. Wishart, gazing at a scruffy-looking pigeon which was parading up and down on the stone sill outside his window, thought, She's right. I'm being kind to myself not to him.

"You've got the number. See if they can get him for me, will you?"

"Right, sir. And here's the rest of the intake."

She passed it to him, a file of signals, memos, reports. He stopped her as she reached the door.

"Ginny—thank you."

She'd smiled. And now, skimming through the papers she'd left him, he was thinking of what was new that he could tell Hugh Everard about. Nothing on the blower: but if he met with him this evening—which was what he'd better

292

suggest, if the old boy was staying in town again. . . . One could hardly just state this thing about *Hoste*, flatly over a telephone.

Sir Hugh had won his private campaign, his battle to become a commodore of convoys, at least to the extent that they were putting him through a medical. At sixty-nine, for God's sake: and all right, so he *was* a tough old bird! But what news could he give him? It wasn't easy to remember what was new, what was this morning's crisis and what was last night's, when you were in the middle of it all the time. However, it was a fact that our submarine captains' hands had been untied since the afternoon of the 9th, when an order had gone out that German merchant ships in the Kattegat and Skagerrak could be sunk without warning. You could operate now as the Germans did: but until this moment one had been obliged to surface, issue a warning and give crews time to abandon their ships before torpedoing them. In effect it had meant that if there was any kind of air or surface escort you had to let the target go—to land its troops and guns in Norway. The first man to benefit had been Jackie Slaughter, the ebullient CO of *Sunfish*: he'd had a Hun ship in his periscope when Max Horton's signal had arrived, and all he'd had to do was press the tit. The submarines had been scoring heavily since then. But what other news, while the submarine service was doing most of the hard work? What else to tell Hugh Everard about?

Well, Narvik was the centre of interest now. Admiralty had told the Commander-in-Chief that the recapture of Narvik was to be given top priority. An expeditionary force was being mounted and despatched for that purpose, and until it got there the C-in-C was to ensure that no enemy reinforcements reached the place by sea.

Until . . . How long, one might well ask. The troops should have been there *now*. Why on earth they'd been disembarked in the first place, when they'd been ready and the ships all set to sail, to carry out Plan R4. . . .

The black telephone tinkled, and he reached for it.

"Wishart."

"I have Admiral Sir Hugh Everard on the line, sir."

"Thank you." He put his hand over the mouthpiece, and cleared his throat. "Put him through, please."

"What're you up to, Yank?"

Whacker Harris, in from a spell of guard duty in the snow . . . Rubbing frozen hands together, relishing the schoolhouse's warmth. It was packed to the eaves now, fairly bulging—with another couple of hundred men, here and in the hospital. Paul was squatting in the hallway, cutting up an old motor tyre with a pusser's dirk he'd borrowed from Tom Brierson. He told

Whacker, "Making a pair of shoes. At least, trying to."

"Make me a pair an' all?"

"Okay. Long as you're not in a hurry for 'em."

They wouldn't be the smartest footwear ever seen. Not that that would be likely to attract attention here: men were wearing strips of carpet, curtains, women's underclothes, old sacks. . . .

Twice in the last couple of hours there'd been alarms that German columns were approaching. The first lot had turned out to be survivors from *Hardy*, and the next—the sentries had been about to open fire on them, then heard a shout in English—were British merchant seamen who'd escaped from their German captors during the early-morning battle. They were lucky—they had all their own clothes, uniforms. But there was very little room to move now. A hundred and seventy men from *Hardy*, and forty-seven merchant navy men.

Hardy's captain—Warburton-Lee, who'd led the attack—had been severely wounded when she'd been ambushed by the last two German ships. His last order had been, "Abandon ship. Every man for himself. And good luck." He himself had been *out* of luck: dying. They'd lashed him to a stretcher and the gunner towed him ashore, but he was dead by the time he got there.

The merchant navy group came from several different ships, but they'd been taken prisoner when the Germans had arrived at dawn on the 9th, and held in the *North Cornwall*. There were forty-seven of them, including the *North Cornwall*'s skipper, a Captain Evans. They'd had a ringside view of the battle; in fact they'd been *in* the ring, with ships blowing up and sinking all around them. Then the Germans had ordered them ashore—with one lone Hun to guard them, and not a very bright lad at that. When the boat reached the jetty and he was about to climb ashore, he'd asked one of the sailors to hold his rifle for him.

Whacker Harris, hearing this story for the first time, was convulsed with mirth. Recovering, he suggested, "Might 'a been related to your oppo, Yank. You know—what'sname. Shitface. I mean *Percy*."

Paul glanced up from the tyre. It was a tough thing to cut, and if ever Brierson's knife had had an edge on it, it had lost it now. He said, "Baldy wasn't so bad. He'd have been okay when he'd found his feet."

"Oh, Christ." Harris frowned, embarrassed. "I'd forgot the bugger'd 'ad it."

By rights, Paul thought, *he* should have "had it" too. It was a pure fluke that he was alive. And his father—he wondered. . . . You never *stopped* wondering, really, whatever else you were doing or talking about, the question-mark and the hope and the despondency were there. Extraordinary: such a short while ago, those few days at

296

Mullbergh, good food and bachelor comfort in that creaky old house, big fires and malt whisky, and the two of them sounding each other out, rather cautiously making friends, a little surprised maybe at finding how well they got on; and now in what seemed like a flash here he was in this timber shack with a blanket for a coat and fumbling to make shoes out of some stinking old rubber, and his father was—*might be* a prisoner of war, *might be* dead.

One of the merchant navy people was telling Harris how the Germans had seized Narvik. All over the room men were swapping stories, recounting personal experiences of the last day or so. This one—he was an engineer of sorts—was describing how three Hun destroyers had arrived off the harbour not long after daylight—a little past 5 am. One of the Norwegian coast-defence ships, *Eidsvold*, had been lying in the harbour entrance. She and her sister ship *Norge* were twins born in 1900, antediluvian-looking twin-funnelled gunboats originally classed as "Coast Defence Battleships." *Eidsvold* had flashed an order to the German flotilla leader, *Heidkamp*, that he was to stop: and the Hun commodore had stopped his ships. He'd also sent a boat to the Norwegian, demanding to be allowed to pass into the harbour: demanding surrender, it amounted to. If it wasn't forthcoming the boarding officer was to get himself and his boat out of the way quickly and fire a red Very light. The demand had been rejected, the boat retired and the red flare shot skyward: two torpedoes leapt from the *Heidkamp*'s tubes, blew *Eidsvold* into two halves and killed practically all her crew of more than 250 men. Then they'd sunk *Norge* in a rain of shells followed by two more torpedoes. Only fifty of her company survived. There'd been no warning: Germany and Norway were not at war: the Germans were still claiming to have come as friends and protectors.

Paul said, sawing at his tyre, "I guess this may be the first war in history where we don't have any damned options. I mean we *have* to fight the bastards." He glanced up at the engineer. "You said the garrison commander turned traitor?"

"So they told us. A colonel by the name of Sundlo. One of Quisling's boys."

Harris sniffed. "Sod 'im, then."

"Why not." The engineer nodded. "He ordered the garrison not to resist. The Huns have a general in charge ashore now. We saw him. Twerp by the name of Dietl."

"Sod *'im,* too." Harris eased himself down with his broad back against the wall. "What they givin' us for scoff tonight?"

Claus Torp had arranged that the telephone cables would be blown up near the village of Spillum at 0100 on the 12th. But he had bigger and better proposals too. The men who'd do the job on the telephone wires, if Nick would provide them with firearms, were suggesting they should go on from Spillum to the bridge which spanned Spillumsoren, and if there wasn't a German guard on it they'd go across and make a diversionary attack on Namsos from the east. Probably they'd open fire on a checkpoint which the Huns had set up at some crossroads half a mile outside the town. If there was a guard on the bridge they'd attack that instead. Either way the effect should be to draw enemy troops eastward out of Namsos and divert attention from the harbour while *Intent* was making her approach.

"Not a bad idea." Nick was studying the chart. The bridge over Spillumsoren was half a mile long. "For "bridge", read "causeway", he thought. The village was one mile this side of it and the Namsos road junction half a mile from its other end.

"They'd have to do the cable-cutting a bit earlier, wouldn't they?"

"Half an hour, yes. Or leave one man there, to follow after."

"How will they get away?"

"In the truck, same way they go there. But they go to the mountains after, not to their homes. . . . They all ask one question: when will your British army come?"

"Be nice to know that, wouldn't it?"

"Will you give them some guns?"

It wasn't so simple, when one had to arm three

separate landing-parties already. He asked Torp, "How many men?"

"Five, maybe six."

They weren't going to pin down many Germans for very long in that strength. But if they acted as snipers, from spaced-out positions: and they'd know the lie of the land, which the Huns hadn't had time to learn yet. . . . He nodded. "Five rifles. I'll make a saving by reducing the two flanking parties by one man each."

They were in Nick's day cabin. Knut Lange wasn't back yet; he wasn't likely to show up much before dusk. Nick asked Torp, "How did you leave the arrangements for all this ashore?"

"I arrange that after Knut's boat is coming back to us tomorrow evening, when you are sure what you are doing, I go ashore to them, with the guns or not, as you decide. They will not move to cut the telephones until I am seeing them again first. All right?"

"Yes. Excellent."

"Are you with us tonight, in the dinner-party?"

"No." He hadn't had a chance to tell Kari. Not that *that* should matter. It was the real reason why he wasn't accepting Tommy Trench's invitation: it couldn't be *allowed* to matter. He explained to her father, "Wardroom table's big enough for two extra but not comfortably for more than that. Besides, you're the guests they want. And—"

"It's a pity. Kari—"

300

"—*and*, I've work to do. . . . Now listen, Claus. Assuming the operation tomorrow night goes as we've planned it, don't you agree that if the enemy's still sitting out there and you try to get your ship out, in daylight and at your slow speed, you're certain to be intercepted and captured or sunk?"

Torp shrugged. "I think this ship also. I think you don't get far away from the quay at Namsos."

"I can fight, Claus. I have guns and torpedoes. Also, when your man's done his stuff I can move out at thirty knots. It makes a slight difference, you know."

"I tell you what *I* can do. I can navigate. Through the fjords, the small ones. I have been thinking about this, you see. Instead of going like I was saying before—Rodsundet or Seierstadfjorden—I go through Lokkaren, and across through all the little islands to Svartdalsfjorden and Nordsundet—that will be into Gyltefjorden—"

"You've lost me." Nick went to the table, where he had the chart.

Torp said, "I lose the Boche too, I think. Now —*here* . . ."

Nick dined alone. Tomorrow night, before the attack, he thought he might invite Torp and Kari here again, a quiet supper for the three of them. But solitude tonight was useful, a chance to think over the plan in peace and quiet. He had to try to envisage how things could go wrong, what

301

emergencies might arise and what he'd do to counter them. There was also a need for fore-thought on the question of how he'd handle his ship if he had to fight his way past German destroyers in a narrow fjord. It would be like fighting a battle in a river. Boldness would be the key, he thought: just go straight for them, flat out and no hesitation, hit hard and early, and keep moving fast towards the open sea. Success would build on success: if you could clobber one of them, another might stop or turn back to help him, thus bringing down the odds.

Damn old Torp for his obstinacy. *Valkyrien* was a pretty ship but she wasn't worth men's lives.

"All right, Seymour. I shan't need anything else."

"Aye aye, sir." The leading steward nodded. "Goodnight, sir." But ninety seconds later he was back. "That fishing-boat's 'ere again, sir. Just coming across the bay."

"Right. Thank you."

No reason to move. Trench would have been told, and Torp was with him. The blue boat would berth on *Valkyrien* and Torp would be down here soon to pass on whatever Lange had reported to him. Doomsday stuff, quite possibly. But even if he came to say there was a whole flotilla of Hun destroyers in the fjord, it wouldn't affect the plans. Whatever the situation might be out there now, it would as likely as not have changed by tomorrow morning and changed again by noon; how things looked at this time tomorrow night—*that* would be what counted. At this stage it was a matter of watching trends, trying to see a pattern and understand what the enemy was up to.

10

"OUR friend the Knut's adrift, sir."

Trench said it—somewhat unnecessarily. Nick grunted, and checked the time on his wrist-watch, as if Lange's lateness hadn't occurred to him until now, as if his nerves weren't already racked up tight because of it.

Pacing the quarterdeck. Trench pacing beside him because, tired of his own thoughts which had begun to go in circles, he'd invited his second-in-command to join him.

Five minutes to ten. In one hour he ought to be pulling the hook out of the mud, getting set to move out for the raid on Namsos. And before he could do that, Torp had to be sent ashore to see his wire-cutting friends and then get back aboard again: and depending on what news Lange brought with him when he did come, there might be a need to reshape plans. He was cutting it much too fine for comfort.

Last night, the news had been that in Altfjord was one U-boat and that in Rodsundet were two destroyers. Musical chairs, he'd thought, with a submarine now gate-crashing the party. But there had to be a purpose, a reason: and since then a little of it had begun to show, but last night he'd said to Torp, who'd come down to the cabin with

304

Lange's report, "Let's wait and see what we have out there in the morning, Claus. Who knows— *Scharnhorst* and *Gneisenau* perhaps." He'd teased him: "They know you've got your *Valkyrien* here and they're waiting until they've assembled a force powerful enough to take you on."

"You are so funny you make me want to pump-ship."

"Your wardroom dinner-party will have given you *that* urge. Use my bathroom if you like."

He stole another sight of his watch. 2158. The three minutes had crawled like ten. If Lange didn't come, he told himself, he'd let Torp go ashore at 2230 and he'd weigh at 2300. He couldn't afford to waste any of the short period of darkness; he'd have to assume that the enemy were deployed as they had been at noon—which meant one U-boat and one destroyer alongside each other in Altbotn and one destroyer left at anchor in Rodsundet. Between first light and midday one of the two destroyers who'd spent the night in Rodsundet had gone round into Namsenfjord and then nosed slowly into Altbotn, the inner fjord, and anchored off its western shore; the U-boat had then moved in too, and berthed alongside her. Guesswork suggested that the U-boat was getting assistance of some kind from the destroyer. Or vice versa: but this was less likely, in view of Mohammed having gone to the mountain and not the other way about. But from Nick's point of view the improvement was considerable. The pair holding each other up in Altbotn probably wouldn't be able to get under way very quickly: one of them must have something wrong with her, and the destroyer might not have steam up now. Also, if no alarm or loud noises were made, it should be possible to sneak past them undetected, as they were blind in there to what was happening in Namsenfjord. In fact, having them bottled up in there, one might do them some damage *en passant*. Nip in: a couple of torpedoes: nip out again. During the afternoon he'd been giving it some thought. But Rodsundet too: with only one enemy destroyer there he reckoned his chances of fighting his way out would be better than evens. He knew the German was there, and the German wouldn't know anything until *Intent* hit him. Depending, of course, on how much fuss was kicked up at Namsos before that.

That had been the lunchtime picture. How it might look now was another question. Where the *hell* was Lange?

Three minutes past ten.

He glanced upwards. Cloud cover was still complete. If anything it was thicker than it had been yesterday. So there'd be no bother with a moon. Twenty-five knots would be a maximum speed down-fjord, after the attack, because at full speed the funnel-glow could give them away.

"Rifles and ammo are in *Valkyrien*'s skiff, sir."

That, from Tommy Trench, was a display of nerves. They both knew the skiff was alongside and that Nick had given orders half an hour ago for the weapons to be put in it, to save time when Lange did turn up. He didn't answer Trench. That skiff would be hoisted on *Intent*'s starboard davits, after Torp had run his errand and *Valkyrien* had cast off. The other was already hoisted on the portside davits. On both sides Metcalf's upperdeckmen had riven new falls, fitted new gripes and boat-ropes, cleaned, greased and tested the fire-blackened disengaging gear. Petty Officer Metcalf had worked like ten ordinary men since they'd been in here. Thinking of it, Nick told Trench, "When we're out of here and the dust has settled, I believe we should think about Metcalf going through for chief. Might have a look at his Service Certificate."

"Absolutely, sir."

When we're out of here. . . .

Lange might have run into trouble. Into a Hun destroyer, for instance.

If he didn't come, Nick thought, he'd use Namsenfjord. There'd been three destroyers altogether in Lange's first report, and the whereabouts of the third was currently unknown. If it returned he thought it would more likely join the one in Rodsundet. The one on the other side was there for the U-boat's benefit and there'd be no point in another joining them. Namsenfjord: and if there hadn't been much of a shindy made,

307

stern-first into Altbotn for a crack at those buggers and then away, *fast*, before the Rodsundet ones woke up.

He liked that. It had a certain neatness.

"I hear your guest-night was a success, Tommy."

"Guest-night . . ." Trench swallowed surprise. One was hardly expecting to chat about dinner-parties. He nodded. "I believe it was, sir. We were all sorry you weren't able to—"

"Fishing-boat approaching, sir!"

"—able to be with us."

"I had a lot of stuff to see to." No point in dashing about yet. The blue boat would take a little while to cross the bay. However . . . "Number One, let's have the cable party closed up, and tell Lyte to shorten-in to one and a half shackles. Special Sea Dutymen in half an hour."

"Aye aye, sir. Bosun's mate!"

Intent's engines were in full working order now, according to Torp's translation of Halvard Boyensen's report. Beamish, questioned by Nick, had agreed with it. They'd run a basin-trial this afternoon, at the Norwegian engineer's request; Nick had consented in return for the man's positive assurance that there'd be too little smoke for a German ten miles away to see. In fact, as he'd expected, the wind had backed to north-west and it blew such smoke as there was directly inshore. And the engines had functioned perfectly. Also, by that time the new fore topmast had been

308

stepped and rigged. An interesting evolution, which had taken the whole forenoon. A mast-rope was led from an eyebolt on the foremast top, through the sheave in the heel of the topmast, back up again through a block on the other side of the fore top. Thence it was taken to the capstan on the foc'sl, the slant of it just clearing the fore-front of the bridge and the flare of "B" gundeck. At Trench's order "Sway away!" and with a couple of dozen seamen all around with hemp guys to steady it, the topmast had risen vertically like some variety of the Indian rope trick. After that, things became more complicated: the yards had to be slung up and secured, and the rigging—stays, backstays and shrouds—of two-inch steel-wire rope, set up. Finally there'd been only the lighter work to do, like halyards and wireless gear. It looked like any other topmast now; but such a very short time ago it had been a tree, snow-covered on a Norwegian hillside.

Nick was thinking as he crossed the plank to *Valkyrien* that his feeling of relief at Lange's arrival might have been a trifle premature. There was no knowing what the Norwegian was about to tell them. It might be bloody awful. And even if the fjords were empty, there was still a tricky operation ahead of him at Namsos.

Torp came out of his deckhouse chewing, wiping his mouth on the back of his hand. The same hand went to push his beat-up cap back to a more comfortable angle. He nodded to Nick, still chewing. "About times, he's coming, eh?" Kari came out behind him, and went aft without acknowledging Nick's presence. She'd been reserved in her manner with him all day, and he'd decided against issuing any supper invitations. She was cross with him for not having joined them in the wardroom last night, he supposed: which was silly, and also proof that he'd been wise in not going along.

Sooner or later, he thought, one annoyed them all, one way or another. He hadn't annoyed Fiona yet, though. Perhaps by not giving a damn she was annoyance-proof?

The blue boat was curving round, angling to run in alongside. A Norwegian—the young one, Einar—was hauling the skiff farther for'ard to make room for Lange. Kari appeared suddenly at Nick's side: "We have coffee still hot if you would like some."

"No thank you, Kari. Kind thought, though." Peace-offering? When she smiled she was really breathtaking. And she was calmly prepared to sail this ancient heap six hundred miles, with two old men and a boy for crew. . . . He had a quick, imaginative vision of Fiona faced with any such suggestion, her huge eyes widening as she uttered a characteristic squawk: "My dear sweet man, you must be stark, staring bonkers!" Smiling at the mental picture—Kari meeting the smile and taking it as meant for her, smiling back: an unexpected dividend. . . . Lange's screws were going astern to take the way off his boat: stopped now, the stream of turbulence between the two wooden hulls quietening as crewmen fore and aft tossed lines to Norwegians on *Valkyrien*.

Lange hauled himself out of the doorway in the side of his wheelhouse, and began to yell at Torp. After a dozen words, Kari turned, glanced back at Nick. He thought she looked startled.

"What's he saying?"

She shook her head: still listening. The singsong recitation might have been going on for ever. Then it ended: Torp had swung round, seen Nick, and he was coming over to him.

"You like good news first, or bad?"

"All of it, and for God's sake let's not waste time."

"Okay. In Altbotn is still one U-boat, one destroyer. The U-boat has a big hatch open and the destroyer is lifting battery cells out with its torpedo davit. Maybe smashed battery—bad trouble for a submarine, huh?"

It would make sense. They'd need a surface like a pond's, and that was what they'd found.

"Other side, by Saltkjelvika, is now *two* destroyers."

Two where there had been one, and all three accounted for now. He'd guessed right. And his way out would be via Namsenfjord. With a brief call perhaps at Altbotn.

Torp was grinning at him. "Now some *good* news. In Rodsundet is not *only* the two

311

destroyers. The one that came brought with it an oil tanker and this has anchored too. Big ship— maybe fifteen, sixteen thousand ton."

Kari interrupted: "But with *two* destroyers—"

"Wait." Nick put up a hand to silence her. If there'd been *ten* destroyers that oiler would still have attracted him. But two was acceptable. *And no need to raid Namsos.* If he took them by surprise: which, coming from inside the fjords, ought surely to be possible. . . .

His mind had a picture of that side of it. A snapshot: he'd need to study it closely to extract detail but it was there, complete. The other side —Altbotn—that destroyer would have to be dealt with too. Oiling would take an hour, *after* the tanker was captured, and there'd have been some bangs by that time. Altbotn was less than two miles from the Saltkjelvika anchorage, over that neck of land, and the destroyer would have time to get out and meet *Intent* and the tanker outside, or even to get right round and catch them still alongside, oiling. The U-boat was probably no danger, but the destroyer was.

It could be done. He'd been on his mental toes, keyed up, and everything was whirring and meshing now. It would have to: in the next forty-five minutes there was a hell of a lot of ground to cover.

"Number One—have the rifles taken out of that skiff. Claus, go ashore, please, cancel

312

previous arrangements and get back here as soon as possible."

"Very well."

"Then bring Lange down to my cabin with you. Listen—" he'd stopped the Norwegian as he moved towards the skiff—"I'm going to need your ship and his boat and all your crews, we move out of here at 2300, and you and your people will accept the dispositions I'm about to make. Right?"

"We going to take the tanker?"

"Yes. But we have to eliminate the ships in Altbotn too, so we've got to be in three places at once."

Torp threw a glance at Kari, then looked back at Nick. "Okay. Any way you say." As he climbed over and down to the skiff he called something out to Lange, and the fisherman laughed, glancing round and up at Nick. Nick asked him, "Okay?" and Lange laughed again, raised a thumb: "Hokay!" He had already, when he'd been back here at midday, told Torp that his boat and crew were at Nick's disposal for as long as *Intent* was in the fjords. He didn't want to leave Norway but he'd help out now and he'd join in again when any other British force arrived, he'd said. Kari and he were yelling at each other now, and the other Norwegians were gathering round to listen, while Einar climbed down to join Torp in the skiff.

Nick went over the brow. Ideas developing.

Intent's ship's company were grouped around in fair numbers, ears flapping for the buzz.

"Mr. Opie here?"

"Here, sir." The gunner came from aft; he had a Torpedo Log and Progress Book under his arm. Opie had rather the shape of a praying mantis: skinny, stooped. Eyes so sharp and small that they were like skewers stabbing at you.

"Mr. Opie, I want two depthcharges provided, with wire slings so they can be slung over the stern either of *Valkyrien* or the fishing-boat. I'll let you know in a minute which one. Also, I want two volunteer torpedomen—one of 'em had better be a killick—to go along with them."

Opie said, "*I'll* take charge of that party, sir."

"No, I want you with us. The pair who do go will have to sprint a distance of roughly a mile and a half, possibly being shot at. They're to be warned it'll be a fairly chancy operation. Bloody dangerous, in fact. And I want to see them before we shove off."

Opie nodded, pulling at his nose. It didn't need any stretching. He must have known he wasn't a man to sprint a hundred yards, let alone three thousand. He said, "We'll start getting the gear up, sir."

Nick looked round at Trench. "Tommy—you, Chandler and Brocklehurst—in my cabin, *now*. Chandler's to bring the chart of the fjords with him."

He didn't need the chart to work out the next

314

bit, though. He'd checked over the various distances so often that he had them in his head. From here to Altbotn: just under ten miles. From here to the anchorage at Saltkjelvika: about seventeen. Lange's boat would be the most suitable for Altbotn. So *Valkyrien* should come the other way with *Intent*. Sailing at 11 pm, 2300, and making good five knots—her top speed was six, but it was a rising tide and therefore an inflowing stream—three and a half hours in transit meant that the earliest time for zero hour would be 0230. Then an hour and a half for the fracas and the oiling would make it 0400. Dawn, near enough, no darkness left for the withdrawal. *No bloody use!*

Valkyrien would have to do the job in Altbotn. She wasn't as good for it as the fishing-boat would have been, and Torp, who would obviously insist on participating in that expedition, hadn't the youth or athleticism it was going to call for. But —no option . . . He was in the doorway of his cabin, having thought this out on the way down. Seymour was emerging from the pantry. Nick told him, "Shin up top, would you, ask Mr. Opie to spare me a moment." Seymour and Pete Chandler collided as the navigator came plunging off the ladder into the flat carrying the chart and instruments. Brocklehurst was with him and, dwarfing the GCO from the rear, Tommy Trench, herding them along. Trench said, "I've left Lyte on the bridge, sir. Had to leave the foc'sl to Cox. But he's got PO Granger to keep him on the straight and narrow."

They'd still be shortening-in the cable. And they could shorten it a bit more, now. Mr. Opie followed his nose into the cabin, rapping on the door-jamb as he entered. "Sir?"

"Your charges are to be slung over *Valkyrien*'s counter. With that cut-away stern you'll find it easy enough. You can use our starboard thrower davit to get them over. Haul *Valkyrien* for'ard a few yards if you need to. Wire slings, Mr. Opie, a separate sling for each charge, and a slip on each of them which your torpedomen can knock off quickly and easily. They may be doing it under fire so it must be simple and if possible under cover. Leave the charges set to safe until just before she sails—you can arm them either by hanging over the side or from the skiff. I want shallow settings on the pistols. . . . Is that all clear?"

Opie nodded. "Volunteers are Leading Torpedoman Crouch and Torpedoman Surtees, sir."

"Can they both run?"

"Like bloody riggers, sir. That's why I picked 'em."

"*Picked* them?"

"The whole lot volunteered, sir."

It didn't surprise him. If you told matelots an operation was going to be dangerous they all rushed for it. Before the Zeebrugge raid the

316

recruiters had had practically to beat men off with sticks. He told Opie, "They're to be issued with Tommy guns. Three drums of ammo per gun. Tell the GM, and that he's to see both men know how to use the things. You've got half an hour to be ready, Mr. Opie, so you'd better slap it about a bit."

He turned back into the cabin. Chandler had the chart spread out. Eighteen minutes past ten. He'd been right about those distances, and there was no option as to which of his ragbag squadron did which job. Torp wasn't going to like *Valkyrien* being treated as expendable. He'd have a counter-proposal: Nick could foresee it and he was ready to rule it out. He dropped the dividers on the chart, and told his officers, "Two separate forces. One is *Valkyrien*, the other *Intent* with the fishing-boat. *Valkyrien* as you heard is being equipped with depthcharges slung under her counter and set shallow; she'll drop them under the destroyer and the U-boat who are alongside each other in Altbotn. Here. Torp will no doubt insist on commanding her. He'll need one engine-room hand and one other crewman, Norwegians, and we are providing two torpedomen for the charges. *Valkyrien* should slip and proceed at 2255. That is, in thirty-six minutes' time. At five knots she can easily reach Altbotn and her target by 0100, which is zero hour. You can check exact timings in a minute, pilot. Now—Tommy. The fishing-boat—for short let's call it "blueboat"—

is to be fitted with our own blue stern cluster. Send an LTO over to wire it up. Blueboat will be crewed by Lange and as many of his own men as he needs, and you, Tommy, will go in her to lead the boarding party and perhaps thereafter command the oiler. We shan't just oil from her, you understand, we'll take her with us. Command of her depends on Torp: I'll offer him the job, otherwise it's yours."

If Torp got there, after the Altbotn operation, he'd obviously accept that offer. He'd be the best man for it, it would be a good use of his Norwegians, Nick would get his first lieutenant back, and everyone would be happy. The doubt was whether Torp would get there, after his action on the other side.

Nick told Trench, "Pick twelve men for your boarding party. I'll take at least some of them back from you when we're alongside the oiler later on. As well as the twelve you pick you can have all the surplus Norwegians—around ten of them, probably. Then if Torp assumes command of the oiler he'll have his own chaps as crew. But add a leading stoker to your party, to be ready to work with Beamish when we get alongside. Rifles, bayonets, revolvers—and there's one Tommy gun left—help yourself. You'll need a signalman and he'd better take an Aldis and a pair of semaphore flags with him. And I suppose one telegraphist . . . And they'll stay aboard. But look here, we'll be fighting an action, so for God's sake pick your men in a way that won't cripple us in any one department. It's up to you, because we won't have time to consult on it. Take young Cox with you?"

Trench nodded. "Good idea, sir."

"Lyte can do your jobs—all from the bridge. Torpedo control is going to be important. Is he competent?"

"He is, sir. But I'll have a word with him."

Lyte was Trench's action understudy anyway, so he ought to know the job. If things went as they should they'd have sitting targets anyway. Nick went on, pointing out the route on the chart with the tips of the dividers, "We sail at 2300 and follow blueboat at ten knots through Sundsråsa, over to Lokkaren and up through it, then round this corner into Surviksund and through into Lauvoyfjord. I think you'll find, pilot, that about here—" his pointer stopped on Lauvoy Island, just inside that much wider fjord —"we can reduce by a knot or two, provided we're on schedule. I want to get over to this western coast then and hug it right into the anchorage. In case anyone didn't get the buzz, by the way, the anchorage currently holds two Hun destroyers and one tanker of roughly 15,000 tons."

Henry Brocklehurst raised his eyebrows. "Ah-hah."

"Sorry. As we're a bit rushed I may be missing other points here or there. Stop me if anyone sees

319

any gaps. . . . As I said, pilot, you can work out precise speeds on the various stages, and when Torp's back we'll go over it all with him and Lange. No point bothering Lange on his own, because he doesn't understand English. But his chaps know just how and where the oiler and the destroyers are lying, and we'll get that out of them. What's essential is that everything should happen simultaneously, at 0100: *Valkyrien*'s charges explode here in Altbotn, blueboat puts you and your party into the oiler, Tommy, and I hit the destroyers with torpedoes. Approaches will be dead quiet, slow and not a chink of light. As soon as I've fixed the destroyers I'll berth on the oiler—which will be yours, let's hope, by that time. If not, we'll board and give you some help."

"Fair enough, sir." Trench nodded. "What about Hun prisoners? Lock 'em up?"

Nick rubbed his jaw. "Ship that size could have a crew of—Lord, forty or fifty. Take a lot of guarding, and we're short-handed enough already." He shook his head. "I don't think we can bother with prisoners."

They were all looking at him. Wondering whether that was all the guidance they were going to get. He pointed at the anchorage, the coast near Saltkjelvika.

"Not a very long swim. Couple of hundred yards, in sheltered water?"

"Ah." Trench nodded. "If any of 'em say they

can't swim, I'll put 'em in the forepeak or some hold that's easy to guard."

"I'm sure there won't be time to give lessons." Brocklehurst's contribution raised a laugh. Nick said, "Final point: having put our boarders into the oiler, blueboat will go inshore—about here, but Lange and Torp can fix the spot—to wait for and then embark the party from *Valkyrien*. They'll have beached her somewhere about here—" the south-eastern shore of Altbotn, he was indicating—"and then legged it overland to the beach where blueboat will be waiting."

Contours on the chart showed high ground to the north and to the south of that overland route. It was a valley of sorts and a road ran through it, so presumably it wouldn't be too much of a problem for young, fit men.

He saw Trench glance up: turning, he found Torp in the cabin's doorway. Age fifty-one, and carrying a little weight. Not too clearly one of the "young and fit" brigade. But if he insisted on staying with his ship—which he would. . . .

"All right ashore, Commander?"

"They are disappointed. Here is Knut Lange."

"Come in." Nick looked at Trench. "Better get cracking. Pick your men and arm them, that's the first thing." He told Brocklehurst, "You can help him. Get an LTO over to blueboat with the cluster, to start with. And fill Lyte in on what I've been telling you. As far as gunnery's concerned, I can't spell out what'll happen at zero hour, except

321

that I want to hit with torpedoes first. Just have everything on the top line, right?" The GCO nodded. Nick added, "You can organise your department when we're under way. All right, off you go . . ."

Chandler was bent over the chart, working out speeds and courses. He asked Nick, "We'll have blueboat to follow but we'll have no pilot actually on board, sir?"

"Well." Nick beckoned the Norwegians to come closer to the chart. "We'll have Commander Torp's daughter with us. I gather she knows these fjords as well as he does."

Ten twenty-eight.

Ten thirty-one . . .

Kari had joined them in the day cabin. Torp asked Nick, "Why my *Valkyrien?* Why not his boat?"

Nick explained: because *Valkyrien* couldn't make the distance to Rodsundet and leave them enough hours of darkness to get away before the Stukas came. He'd have preferred it the other way round; the faster, smaller craft would have been more suitable for the dash across Altbotn, and *Valkyrien's* height in the water would have suited the boarding operation better. If the oiler didn't have a gangway or a ladder over her side it might present a problem—an iron wall towering above the boat and no way to scale it. In that event they'd have to wait until *Intent* came alongside. This wasn't a good solution, though, because the tanker's crew would have seen the attack on the destroyers and they'd be ready to repel boarders. One wanted them, if possible, to be sound asleep in their bunks.

Kari was acting as interpreter. Lange mumbled at her, snatched up a signal pad and took Chandler's pencil out of his hand, began to make a sketch. It turned out that he was saying the tanker was a modern ship and very low in comparison to her length. She had a high bridge section amidships and more superstructure aft where the funnel was, but between those two areas of superstructure she had an exceptionally low freeboard. Men could board from the top of the fishing-boat's wheelhouse, and Lange would take some planks to put across.

"Sounds as if he's seen her himself."

"He has. This last trip he went to look, to make certain. It's why he was late returning."

"Well, please tell him I'm very grateful to him." Nick looked at Torp's less-than-happy face. "You dislike the idea of sacrificing your ship. I understand that. I'm very sorry there's no other way of doing it."

"But maybe there is. I make the attack, I turn round and come out again, we have—one hour, one and a half? Easy—I meet you here, near Flottra?"

It was the suggestion he'd expected. He shook

323

his head. "No, Claus. *If* you got away with it, I'd have to find you out there—"

"You don't have to. I go on—right on!"

"But I want my torpedomen back, you see. For one thing because I need them, for another I don't believe you'd get ten miles before you were strafed by German 'planes. You haven't the speed to get away: and we have." He suggested, "You don't *have* to go along in *Valkyrien*, Claus. One of your younger men could do it—or I could provide an officer—Pete Chandler here, for instance—"

"*Valkyrien* is *my* ship, damn it all to hell!"

"It'll be hard going, once you're ashore. Frankly, I'd say it was a job for youngsters, but—"

"One and a quarter sea miles. A little more than two kilometres. I am not yet *falling to bits*, you know!" He was red in the face and glaring. "Okay—how long does it take you to stop, take your men off from me outside?"

"You might not get that far, you see. Once you've dropped those charges, they'll be shooting at you. With only a few hundred yards to go to beach her, you should get away with it, but if you had to go two-thirds of the length of the fjord —and the way they'd *expect* you to be going . . ." He shook his head. "If you got into trouble and I had to come on round and find you, I'd be throwing my own ship away. I'm not prepared to do that. Whereas when you come

324

overland, we're all in one spot together, ready to start off and not stop—*out*, and in darkness."

Torp was silent. Simmering down, seeing the common sense of it. He looked at his daughter, and shrugged. "Man's right." She nodded: but Nick could see she wasn't happy about the job her father was taking on. Nick asked him, "What'll you do—put her on the rocks with her seacocks open?"

Torp suggested, "Perhaps also some of those explosives?"

Fitted charges, with long-enough lengths of fuse to give the five men time to get clear. Half a dozen of them in that old ship's bilges would just about take the bottom out of her. Nick agreed: and his torpedomen could handle that end of it. What he wanted now from Lange was a sketch of the anchorage on the other side, showing exactly where the oiler was anchored and where the destroyers were.

And after that—

Well. One thing at a time . . . But hardly: he was having to think of about *forty* things at a time. He'd had two days to work out the details of the Namsos operation, and he was setting this one up in fifty minutes.

Three minutes past eleven. Eight minutes late, *Valkyrien* was letting go the ropes which had held her to *Intent*. Knut Lange had cast off from *Valkyrien* at five minutes to the hour and dropped

325

astern so that a torpedoman on his boat's bow could set the pistols on the depthcharges which now hung in their wire-rope slings. Then Lange had brought his boat up on *Intent*'s port side, and Trench's boarding party were climbing down a scrambling-net into it. The Norwegians—nine of them—were already in the boat.

Trench wasn't with them yet. He'd be coming up here to report, before they pushed off. Nick went over to the starboard side of the bridge, looked down at the gap of water which had already opened between his ship and *Valkyrien*. Claus Torp was beside the open door of his wheelhouse, chatting to the man inside—a man of about twenty-five, by the name of Larsen. ("Fast runner," Torp had explained. "Strong, too. Carry me and run like hell, I think.") He wasn't only talking to Larsen though, he had Kari facing him from *Intent*'s foc'sl deck, right below the place where Nick was leaning over. She was unhappy, worried for him, and he was keeping up the jokes, teasing her.

She had some reason to be worried, Nick thought. You could hardly expect to pull off a stunt like this one without *some* casualties. And Torp was the most likely candidate. It wasn't only the most odds-against bit of the operation, it was also going to be something of a marathon.

Could he have held him back from it? Stopped him going in his own ship? Nick didn't see how.

He was a highly independent character, not a man to betray his principles.

Torp was staring up at him. Nick shouted across the gap, "Good luck!"

"Look after this woman for me, huh?" Pointing at Kari. Nick looked down, and at the same moment she glanced up: he saw her stiff, unhappy smile. He called to Torp, "We'll keep her safe for you." Rather a daft assurance, he realised: the only way to have ensured her safety would have been to have landed her at Sveodden, *now*. Torp had just passed an order over his shoulder to his man Larsen; *Valkyrien*'s single screw was going astern, sliding her away from the destroyer's side and sending a stream of churned, bubbling water seething forward. But she was clear now, and Torp had stopped the engine. *Valkyrien* still slid astern, with port rudder on to turn her bow out.

Torp's and Kari's gear was in Nick's sleeping cabin aft. It was hers now, and she could use the day-cabin and his bathroom too. At sea he only used the little box just below the bridge.

"Captain, sir?"

Tommy Trench, in his tin hat with "1st Lt" painted on the front of it, and a webbing belt with a .45 revolver in the holster.

"Boarding party embarked and ready to proceed, sir."

"Well done. You've worked wonders. I mean that."

Trench grinned down at him. "Needs must, when the devil drives, sir."

"*What?*"

"Intended, if I may say so, as a compliment. May I tell Lange to carry on, sir?"

"Let *Valkyrien* get well clear first. I'll give you a shout. Best of luck, Tommy."

"Sir." Chandler, coming from the chart-table, interrupted. "Sorry . . . But we must make twelve knots now, sir, to be up to the schedule. Reducing to eight when Lauvoy light's abeam if we're up to it."

"All right. Tommy, see Lange gets that and understands it, will you? Tell you what—ask Kari to translate. She's just down here."

"Twelve knots, reducing to eight at Lauvoy light if we're on time. Aye aye, sir." Trench saluted. "See you alongside *my* oiler, sir." As he moved off, Chief Stoker Beamish clambered into the bridge. He saluted too. "Main engines ready, sir."

"Chief, that's music to the ears."

"Reckon it is that, sir."

"Everything on a split yarn for the oiling?"

"Will be by 0100, sir. Leading Stoker Evans 'as gone with the boat party."

"Boyensen quite happy down there?"

Beamish thought he was. Boyensen would move over to become chief engineer of the oiler, in a couple of hours' time. Meanwhile he was on loan from Torp, to hold Beamish's hand in case anything went wrong or needed adjustment.

Nick told Chandler, "Ring on main engines." He crossed to the starboard side again as *Valkyrien*, her engine chugging ahead and black coal-smoke leaking from that tall funnel, came sliding past at a distance of about thirty feet. Torp saluted breezily, and Nick returned it. He called to Randolph Lyte, "Weigh anchor." The two torpedomen were standing at attention on *Valkyrien*'s stern; Nick took off his cap and waved it at them, and one hand came up in answer. The light was fading rapidly—outlines blurring, hills merging into the background of low cloud. The two depthcharges slung under the old ship's counter looked like dangling testicles.

He'd shown the torpedomen, Crouch and Surtees, photographs in *Jane's Fighting Ships* of modern German destroyers, pointing out the position of searchlights above and abaft their bridges, fixed to the lower part of the foremast at roughly funnel-top height. The searchlight on the Altbotn destroyer would be an obvious menace to the *Valkyrien* party, and if those two could shoot it out with their Thompsons they'd about double their chances of getting away. Men at guns were also worth shooting at, as was anyone on the bridge, and the time to hit them, he'd suggested, would be immediately after the charges had been released, when they were still at close quarters. But the searchlight should be target number one.

Weighing wouldn't take long now. They'd shortened-in to one shackle a few minutes ago. So there were twelve and a half fathoms of cable out, and as there were ten fathoms of water here it left very little slack to be gathered in.

Clanking of the rising cable. Power on the capstan—full, main generator power. *Intent* was reborn. . . .

And *Valkyrien* was crossing her bow, turning to port to head for the gap into the channel which would take them through into Namsenfjord. Torp was up on his wheelhouse roof, already an indistinct figure in the fading light. Nick wondered if he'd thanked Torp enough, for all he'd done for him. Without Torp, *Intent* would still have been out in that open anchorage—Lovik —when the German destroyers had arrived. Helpless, easy meat . . . There hadn't been time for goodbyes and none for thanks either. There *should* have been. The omission niggled in his mind, tinged with the fear that there might not be an opportunity to make it good. Lyte reported, "Cable's up and down, sir."

"Very good." He leant over the port side of the bridge, looking down at the blue boat. Lange was lounging on the canopy of its wheelhouse, and Trench was perched on it near him. Cox, near the stern, had his tin hat slung on his shoulder. Nick called down, "Cast off and carry on, please. Best of luck, all of you." Trench said something to Lange, who gave Nick something between a wave and an offensive gesture; the gleam of his teeth showed up as he smiled. They weren't all that white: just big. . . . Some sailors on *Intent*'s iron deck, letting go the blue boat's ropes on Trench's orders, raised a cheer; Trench called up to Nick, "Knock 'em for six, sir!" A faint blue radiance near the boat's stern showed that the stern cluster had already been switched on. The boat with its low silhouette wouldn't have been easy to follow without it, on a night as dark as this one was going to be.

"Anchor's aweigh, sir."

"Very good." He stepped up behind the binnacle and Chandler moved over to make room for him. Checking the ship's head on the gyro repeater. No hurry, though; he'd wait for the report of "Clear anchor" and by that time the blue boat would have put about the right distance between them. Glancing round, he saw Kari: she was pressed against the port side of the bridge at its after end, near the ten-inch light, and gazing northwards towards a smallish blur and a patch of whitened sea that was all one could see now of *Valkyrien*.

"Kari?"

She was wearing her bright-blue oilskin coat. She came towards him: dark, almost black hair, pale-blue eyes with fear in them. He told her, "Don't worry. Your father's a tough cookie. You'll be entertained with a lot of tall stories from him in about two and a half hours' time."

She smiled, and nodded. "Thank you."

He remembered that she'd offered him a similar reassurance, about Paul. Since then neither of them had mentioned the subject. The anxiety was in his mind but he was keeping it pushed well back, out of the way, where he didn't have to listen to it. He was tempted to tell her that he'd instructed Crouch and Surtees to keep an eye on her father and give him a hand if he needed it. Not to the extent of throwing sound lives after a lost one, but—within reason. . . . Lange's boat was forging out on *Intent*'s bow. Moving slowly, waiting for the destroyer to show signs of following. The swirl of the boat's wake showed up clearly, blued by the lights above it. Getting darker every second: by the time they were through Sundsråsa it would be black. Nice timing, in fact. He heard a shout down on the foc's'l, then Lyte's quiet "Clear anchor, sir."

"Port ten."

"Port ten, sir . . . Ten of port wheel on, sir."

"Slow ahead together."

"Slow ahead together, sir!"

He felt the vibrations, muted at this slow speed, and the turbines' whisper and the soft, slow-speed sucking of the intakes. Then his ship was gathering way.

"Half ahead together. One-two-oh revolutions." Lange would see *Intent*'s bow-wave rise, and put on speed to match.

Eleven-eighteen.

"He's—slicing it a bit short, sir?"

Conning his ship round, following the blue glow, Nick didn't answer Chandler. Lange was certainly cutting corners. They'd passed through Sundsråsa and held that same course for about a mile across the comparatively open water of Namsenfjord, and now the blue boat was leading round to starboard within a schoolboy-cricketer's throw of the island of Ytre Gasoy. Meaning *outer* Gasoy, Kari had explained. Whitewashed rocks looked bright to starboard: he was bringing her round carefully, using only five degrees of wheel. There was not much wind, only a lapping on the black water, enough to take the shine off it. Knowing there were rocks off the north coast of the little island, he shared Chandler's anxiety. All you could see was the broken water, but that was enough to make the hairs stand up on the back of a sailor's neck—if not on a Norwegian fisherman's.

"Don't worry." Kari's voice on his right. "Knut could be doing this with his eyes shut."

"I do hope he isn't." It occurred to him that he and Kari spent a lot of time telling each other not to worry. He bent to the voicepipe: "Midships."

"Midships, sir."

"Meet her." Keeping her on the outer edge of the blue boat's curving wake. "Steer oh-eight-oh." He asked Chandler, "What's our course to pass the next headland, the one to port now?"

"One-oh-five, sir."

Kari said, "He won't cut *that* corner. There is a rock a quarter-mile from the point."

"How very reassuring." Nick told the helmsman, "Starboard five." Lange was edging round again. He'd probably go right round to that one-oh-five, or something near it. "How long is the next leg, pilot?"

"Mile and a half, sir." Chandler added drily, "Depending on whether he's corner-cutting or rock-climbing." Kari giggled, and Nick was glad to hear it. He said into the voicepipe, "Midships." Breeze on the port quarter and astern now, bringing occasional stink of funnel-fumes. Black, quiet water, darkness enshrouding like black flannel. Damp, iced black flannel. "Meet her."

"Meet her, sir—"

"Steady!"

"Steady, sir. One-oh-four—"

"Steer that."

"Steer one-oh-four, sir."

"Meet her" meant putting the wheel the opposite way, to check a swing already imparted to the ship. As the rate of swing slowed you had either to give the helmsman a course to steer, or order "Steady" to inform him that she was at that moment on the course you wanted. A mile and a half at twelve knots would take seven and a half minutes: then there'd be the turn to port into the narrow cleft called Lokkaren, and at the point of entry to it *Intent* and her guide would be less than two miles from German-occupied Namsos.

"Time?"

"Twenty-three fifty, sir."

If it hadn't been for the news which Lange had brought two hours ago, instead of turning into Lokkaren now they'd have been steering farther south and rounding the next headland, Merraneset, to raid Namsos for its oil. Nick wondered whether that might have turned out to be more tricky or less so than the jaunt he was on now. One would never know: it would be something to speculate on in one's old age. If one *had* an old age. All he did know was that the Namsos operation followed immediately by an engagement with superior forces who'd have been actually waiting for him would have been a bit over the odds. He'd have attempted it, because there'd seemed to be no alternative; but now he didn't have to do it he could admit to himself that it had never been a very attractive proposition.

"Steer one-oh-six."

"One-oh-six, sir."

He saw Lyte move from the starboard to the port fore corner of the bridge. Trench had found time—heaven knew how—to run over the torpedo-control system with him, and he'd

335

assured Nick that the sub-lieutenant was "all about" on it. Lyte wouldn't have to cope with the telephone to the director tower: Nick had had a longer lead put on it, so it could be brought here to the binnacle. He could either talk to Brocklehurst himself, or put Chandler on it.

Cold: shivery, bone-penetrating cold, even through a dufflecoat . . . The whitish smear of wake and the blue glow were dead ahead still; he spoke without taking his eyes off it. "How long to the turn, pilot?"

"About one minute, sir."

"Bosun's mate?"

"Yessir?"

"Go round the ship, Marryott, make sure there's not a speck of light showing anywhere. Including cigarettes on the gundecks. Take as long as you like, but make certain of it."

The ship's company had been sent to action stations as soon as the foc's'l had been secured, which had been done by the time they'd been halfway down Sundsråsa. Everything was closed up and ready: they could be meeting Hun destroyers in this fjord—here, *now*. Nothing guaranteed that the Germans would remain where they'd last been seen.

Kari said, "You can see the rock on your port bow."

Chandler put his glasses on it. Nick kept his eyes on the blue cluster: it was a circular arrangement of blue light-bulbs fixed in a sort of shallow

336

box so that it could only be seen from right astern. Lange might alter course at any moment, and he didn't want to overshoot. There was no room or time for errors and corrections or blunderings about, and twelve knots was quite fast enough for negotiating a channel as narrow as the one that was coming next.

"Down five revolutions."

The light had seemed closer suddenly.

"Down five, sir . . . One-three-five revolutions passed and repeated, sir."

Chandler reported, "Rock's abeam, sir, about one cable."

"Very good." His eyes were glued to that blue gleam. This was as close to Namsos as they'd come.

"Port five."

Lange had begun the turn that would take him round into Lokkaren: Nick had seen the light shift away leftwards.

"Midships."

"That rock is slightly *before* the beam, sir."

"Very good." They *were* rock-climbing. . . . He stooped again. "Port five."

The sense of being behind the enemy's lines: silence and darkness emphasised it, that and the knowledge that in a very short time he'd be creeping up on enemy ships which lay meanwhile in sleepy ignorance of his existence. There was a kind of tight-nerved satisfaction in it: just *being* here, armed and ready and on the verge of action

—and unseen, unsuspected. . . . He'd felt it before, more than once, but not for—well, twenty years. There was a kind of poacher's thrill about it. That night off the Belgian coast in 1917, for instance, in a CMB—the modern development of which were called MTBs—en route to snatch some prisoners out of a guard trawler known to the Dover Patrol as "Weary Willie". . . .

"Midships." They'd be past that rock by now.

"Midships . . . Wheel's amidships, sir!"

"Ship's head now, and the course up here, pilot?"

"Course should be oh-one-five, sir. Ship's head —oh-one-eight."

Nick didn't want to look at the compass, if he could avoid it, for the sake of his night vision. He told Jarratt, "Steer oh-one-six."

"Steer oh-one-six, sir."

Chandler informed him, "After a mile and a quarter there's foul ground to starboard, sir, so he'll probably ease over. After that he'll have to come back much more—about ten degrees—to starboard for the slight dog-leg through the narrowest part."

"All right." Chandler had courses, times and distances in his brown-covered navigator's notebook, and a pencil torch so that when he squatted down near the base of the binnacle he could use it inside his coat. For all his stuffiness, Pete Chandler made a useful navigator. And the stuffi-

338

ness might wear off, as he gradually changed from City gent to destroyer man.

"Steer one degree to port."

"One degree to port, sir!"

"Up five revolutions."

"Up five revolutions, sir. Course oh-one-five, sir. One-four-oh revolutions passed and repeated, sir."

It was the feeling of stealth as well as the surrounding quiet that made one talk quietly. As if voices might be heard ashore, or in the next fjord. . . . The Germans in Namsos were lucky. A few of them would have died tonight. Perhaps quite a lot of them. But none of ours, please God. . . . If this trick could be pulled off without casualties—catch them with their pants so far down that only Germans got hurt—*that* would be something!

Torp and the others, plugging down Namsenfjord at this moment: for all five of them to return would be a bit much to hope for. One did still hope, though. . . . Crouch had grinned, and said, "We'll see 'im right, sir, don't worry!" and Surtees had confirmed, "We'll 'elp the geezer out, sir."

Geezer . . . How would one explain that term, to a Norwegian? Literally it meant "old woman". One could hardly imagine anyone less womanish than Claus Torp.

The blue spot was moving left, and he bent

quickly to the voicepipe. "Steer three degrees to port."

"Three degrees to port, sir!"

"Your foul ground coming up, pilot." Lights in cottages on the coast to starboard. It felt like picking one's way through people's back gardens. Kari said, "There are shallows and a small island, and half a mile higher there is a ferry crossing."

"Not crossing now, let's hope."

"I think it won't be operating at night."

"Course one-oh-two, sir."

"Time?"

"Five minutes past midnight, sir."

"How wide is the narrowest bit of this creek, Kari?"

"About—hundred and fifty metres. Higher up. And before it there is a shoal, right in the middle. What is your ship's draught?"

"Twelve-foot six. What's over the shoal?"

"Sixteen, but—"

More, with a rising tide.

"He'll lead us round it, I imagine, sir. Course will still be about oh-one-five. I mean after we've cleared this stuff to starboard."

"Yes, I think so." Kari added, "This would be easy if the lights were burning."

"Steer two degrees to starboard." Nick straightened from the voicepipe. "Except they'd only be burning if your invaders had taken charge of them. Pilot, ship's head now?"

"Oh-one-five—"

"Steer oh-one-five, cox'n."

Lyte reported, "Spar buoy to starboard, sir. Green four-oh, fifty yards."

"It marks the edge of the bad part. Knut will be going to the left of the shoal now. You can make out the high land on your port bow, I think?"

"Yes . . ." There'd be no more than a fifty-yard gap between the shoal and that steep coast-line. Without Lange to follow, this would have been a tricky passage to negotiate. Except that Kari could have brought them through . . . A few minutes later, the high ground to port was so close it seemed you could have leant out from the bridge and touched it. Only for a minute: then the blue glimmer was sliding to the right.

"Starboard five."

"Starboard five, sir . . . Five of starboard wheel on, sir."

Jarratt wouldn't be seeing much, if anything, through his wheelhouse window. He certainly wouldn't see the faint blue glow through sea-misted glass. "Midships."

"Midships, sir!"

"Meet her."

"Meet her, sir . . ."

"Steady!"

"Steady—oh-two-seven, sir!"

"Steer oh-two-eight."

There'd be a gradual widening now, up to the top of the fjordlet. He asked Chandler, "Time?"

"Twelve minutes past, sir."

Forty-eight minutes to zero hour. In that time they had to get around the corner into Surviksundet and through that stretch into Lauvoyfjord and across it to Rodsundet. It seemed like a lot of ground to cover when he pictured the chart in his mind, but it was probably a bit under seven miles.

"Course oh-two-eight, sir."

"Very good. This is a fiddly business, cox'n."

"Seems like it, sir."

Blue light dead ahead, and distance just about the same. The cottages with lit windows to starboard were right by the fjord's edge, a few of them, and the lights were reflected on the dead-flat water. Would Norwegians there be watching them pass? Taking them for Germans? Kari asked him quietly, "Do you mind if I ask a question?"

"Ask away."

"I don't wish to spoil your concentration."

"You won't."

"Will we hear when they explode the depth-charges?"

"Almost certainly."

What one hoped *not* to hear from that direction would be the sound of German guns. *Valkyrien* wouldn't stand up to five-inch shells. One had to hope for confusion, the enemy not knowing what had hit them or where from. If they could smash his searchlight. . . .

Kari murmured, "So we will know they have

342

got that far." Nick was adjusting the course to oh-two-seven, since Lange had drifted off slightly left; he told Kari without taking his eyes off the light, "We'll be busy too by then. I'll want you to be down below."

"Oh, but *please*—"

"There's no question of your remaining on the bridge."

Silence. Except familiar rattles, the steady thrumming of the engines, hoarsely sucking fans. Blue light edging left again: he called down to Jarratt, "Steer oh-two-five."

Cutting *this* corner now. Kari asked him, "May I go in your chartroom, so I can listen to what happens?"

"Yes, you may." She was a terrific girl, he thought. Torp had done a good job in the upbringing of his daughter. He asked her, "Any hazards in this next bit?"

"Not in Surviksundet, down the centre. The only shoal is at the other end and it is ten metres, so it won't bother you."

Chandler muttered, binoculars at his eyes, "He's going round, sir."

"Port five."

Round and into Surviksundet. About three miles of it, with a width of four to five hundred yards all the way through. Three miles at twelve knots—fifteen minutes. Straightening his ship's course into it after a spell of drastic Knut-type corner-cutting, he thought, *After this there's only Lauvoyfjord.* . . .

He wanted to be razor-sharp now. *Had* to be. Eight years pottering about with farm-hands and foresters had had a blunting effect, he suspected. The mind rested, took its time. He hoped he'd sloughed the landsman's skin.

"Up five revolutions."

"Up five revolutions, sir . . . One-four-five revolutions passed and repeated, sir."

He asked Chandler, "Are we up to schedule?"

"Just about, sir. We can check it and adjust speed as necessary at Lauvoy Island. But I *think* —"

"Yes, all right."

In other words, *Don't waffle* . . .

"One mile into Lauvoyfjord—" Kari's voice beside him—"before we come to the island, there is a one-fathom shoal with a marker-buoy on it. I think Knut will leave it close to port."

"Right."

After this—when, touch wood, he'd filled *Intent*'s sound tanks and had possession of the oiler—what next? It was bad luck to count chickens, but one had to think ahead and be ready with the answers. It wouldn't be so long, if all went well, before he was alongside the oiler, with Torp or Trench wanting orders.

Head north, towards Vestfjord?

"Steer two degrees to port."

"Steer two degrees to port, sir!"

344

According to the signal they'd picked up, the one Whitworth had sent *Penelope*, Vestfjord was where the action was. And with a number of destroyers up there the tanker and her cargo would be welcome. So—all right, north. It had the additional advantage of being in the opposite direction to the Hun airfields. Head up towards Narvik—where the 2nd Flotilla's action had been. . . .

"Port five."

"Port five, sir. Five o' port wheel on, sir . . ."

No need, when he made his signal, to mention leaking oil-tanks. After all, he'd have his own replenishments with him. If he reported the leaks they'd send him home. As long as this action left the ship in working order and with a few torpedoes left in her tubes, it would be justified. And they'd certainly want the oil up there.

"Midships and meet her."

"Midships—meet her—"

"Steady!"

"Steady—two-eight-five, sir—"

"Steer that."

Coming out of Surviksundet, entering Lauvoyfjord. Lyte reported from the front of the bridge, "Spar buoy fine on the port bow, sir."

"Ah. Kari's shoal."

Chandler amplified, "Should be three cables south of the eastern end of the island, sir."

At twelve thirty-three it was abeam, forty yards

to port. *Intent* was on a course of 286 degrees. Chandler said, "We're right on time, sir."

Thanks to Knut Lange's short-cuts . . . Two minutes after they'd passed that marker, Lauvoy light structure was three cables' lengths to starboard.

Going like clockwork. Too good to last.

"Blueboat's going round, sir."

"Yes." He put his face down to the voicepipe. "Starboard ten." Then, straightening, "What'll the course be now?"

"Three-three-four, sir. And we ought to be coming down to eight—"

"One hundred revolutions!"

"Hundred revolutions, sir—"

"Midships."

Getting closer now. And Lange had cut his boat's speed too: in fact the light-cluster was brighter, they'd closed up on him a little. It was all right, though. "Steer three-three-four."

This course would take them up close to the western shore, the bulge of land where Lauvoyfjord ran into Rodsundet. The bulge was about one mile below the anchorage where the German ships were lying. The oiler was nearest and the destroyers were about two-thirds of a mile beyond her. All three were lying to single anchors—or had been, when last seen by Lange—and since high water would be at 0414 this morning the inward tidal flow would have them with their bows pointing north, down-fjord.

At twelve-fifty, when *Intent* would be only about one cable's length—200 yards—offshore, she'd be continuing straight ahead while Lange's boat sheered away to port to follow the coastline round the curve into the anchorage to get inshore of the tanker, in a position to board her over her port side. *Intent* would be passing about 400 yards to seaward of her before turning in and closing the enemy destroyers.

Low coastline to port, dimly visible because of its lower edging of white surf. The hills inland weren't discernible even with binoculars.

"Time?"

"Quarter to the hour, sir."

He could hear the swell breaking along that coastline. He'd been too busy watching the blue light and the courses and speeds to have noticed until now the increasing motion on the ship. This north-wester, mild as it was compared to the gale they'd had three days ago, would be blowing straight down Rodsundet and funnelling into Gyltefjorden as well, and they'd be feeling it more as they crept round the bulge.

"Comin' up to 0050, sir."

"Better go down, Kari." He was watching the blue cluster, for it to disappear. At ten minutes to the hour, 0050, in the position they were reaching now, switching the light off would be Lange's signal that he was branching away to port and would no longer serve as guide.

"Has she gone down?"

"She's on her way, sir, yes. Cluster's extinguished, sir!"

The cold, hard rim of the voicepipe cracked his forehead as he stooped and overdid it. "Seven-oh revolutions." He'd straightened. "Sub, for'ard tubes train to port, after tubes starboard. Stand by all tubes."

"Aye aye, sir."

"Give me the director telephone." Chandler put it in his hand. He told Brocklehurst, "Have 'B' gun stand by with one round of starshell and train on red three-oh. Do *not* load yet."

Revs, speed and sound all falling away. The wind was whistling overhead, *Intent* pitching gently, waves slapping at her stem. He didn't want to use starshell: he'd order it only if the targets couldn't be seen without it.

"Large ship at anchor red five-oh, sir!"

Lyte had called it: and the for'ard port-side lookout was only a split second behind him. Brocklehurst's voice came over the telephone: "Oiler bearing two-eight-oh, five hundred yards."

"Our targets should be to the north of her, right inshore." He passed the telephone to Chandler. "Time?"

"Fifty-six, sir."

"Tubes turned out and ready, sir."

Hope to God those bastards haven't shifted. . . .

"Two destroyers to the right of the oiler—red three-five!"

"Port ten."

"Director target!"

"Steer three double-oh. Load all guns with SAP. Give me my glasses, pilot. Time?"

"Fifty-eight, sir." Chandler passed the "load" order to the director tower. Nick called to Lyte, "Sub, tell Mr. Opie I'll turn to starboard in one minute and fire four torpedoes from the for'ard tubes. Can you see both destroyers?"

Lyte had both targets in sight but slightly overlapping. He was talking to Opie now over the torpedo-control telephone. Nick had the enemy in his glasses. *Beitzen* class. Fine-looking ships. They wouldn't look fine for long. After he'd made his turn to starboard they wouldn't be overlapping much either, but they'd present one continuous line of target, which was what he'd planned for in this approach. He asked Chandler, "Time?"

"Fifty-nine, sir."

"Starboard fifteen." He was close enough to be sure of hitting, and swinging now to bring the tubes to bear. Checking the compass. From the west, a rattle of machine-gun fire. Too *soon* . . . Enemy bearing was two-eight-five. He called down, "Steer oh-one-five."

"Steer oh-one-five, sir!"

That *had* been from the direction of Altbotn . . .

349

"Sub—I want four carefully-aimed shots spread over both targets. Don't rush—make sure of it."

"Aye aye, sir." Lyte was hunched behind the sight. With stationary targets the only way he could miss would be if the torpedoes didn't run straight. Which did happen, sometimes. From a westerly direction, shorewards, came a deep, muffled-sounding *whumpf*. Then another. And on the heels of the twin explosions a rattling blare of machine-gun fire. Nick had his glasses on the dim shapes of the enemy destroyers. Silence now: but they'd be stirring, standing-to, alerted by Torp's balloon having gone up a minute early. At any moment there'd be searchlights, starshell, a blaze of gunfire. *Intent*'s swing was slowing as she neared her firing course: with luck Lyte would get the fish away before the enemy woke up enough to—

Searchlight: it flared into life, grew swiftly from the left-hand destroyer, its beam lengthening and at the same time scything round—to search *the shore.* . . .

Lyte snapped, "Fire one!"

11

COMING through the bottleneck from Altfjord into Altbotn, Torp had brought his ship round so close to the point that he'd almost scraped her timbers on it. Then he'd still hugged the rocky shore. By making the most of its cover he'd aimed to have *Valkyrien* within 500 yards of her target before the Germans had a chance of seeing her.

He'd been outside the wheelhouse on the starboard side, at that stage, with Larsen inside at the wheel. Leading Torpedoman Crouch had been close behind him, and Billy Surtees behind Crouch. Surtees was tall and heavily built, a lot bigger than the wiry, curly-headed killick.

Engine thumping like a pulse, a deep heartbeat banging through the old timbers. Knife-cold air: you had to narrow your eyes to slits to be able to look into it without them watering. Black night, with a light here and there in cottage or farmhouse windows. There was one in the curve of bay which they'd just passed, and it looked as if it must have been right down on the beach. Torp had taken her farther out to round that last point because it had some reef fringing it, a visible rock where the white swirled round it and a lot of other broken water. Now he had binoculars at his

351

eyes and he was leaning with his left shoulder against the door-jamb of the wheelhouse; he had an ancient revolver stuck in his belt, a great heavy thing about a foot and a half long. Surtees had queried, eyeing it earlier on, "After elephant, are we?" Broken water again to starboard, Crouch saw. Torp lowered the glasses and turned to look at him, his eyes white and glary-looking in the dark. "Remember what we do?"

"Aye, sir." Crouch confirmed it. "All weighed off."

There was a V-shaped cove ahead, with its open end northwards, facing them, and the Germans were in the widest part of the V. The left-hand arm of it was coastline and the nearer part of the right-hand one was a spur of foul ground, rocks and shallows. Torp's plan was to take *Valkyrien* in between the Germans and the shore and then swing hard a-port to come up across their sterns. As he reached them he'd put his helm over again so that *Valkyrien*'s stern would start a swing inwards towards her victims', and at this point the charges were to be released. The least damage they could do would be to smash the Germans' screws and rudders; in shallow water with the blast bouncing off the bottom of the fjord they might do even better. Internal damage was likely, and there'd be some results too from crashing the two ships together. The submarine's beam tanks, for instance, stood a good chance of getting flattened.

Torp was going to flash a torch aft at Crouch as the signal to knock the slips off the charges. In the stern now with Surtees on his right, Crouch turned half round so as not to miss the flash when it came. Each man had a hand on his own releasing-gear, having located it by feel, by groping for it in the dark. Nobody'd get a *second* chance. One hand on the slip and the other on his sub-machine-gun. After the swing Torp was going to reverse his helm again to steady her and then drive the ship out over the top of that shallow patch. God alone knew how. Well—one might hope that Torp did, too. It was the only way, he'd said, other than by turning up almost alongside the destroyer, beam-on to her, inviting the German gunners to reduce her to matchwood. Crouch hoped the geezer knew his way about it; *Valkyrien*, being a sailing ship, had a deep draught, a keel—she wasn't built for hopping over shallow patches. Torp had said something about the explosions of the depthcharges helping, washing her over.

Peculiar cove. Smashing daughter, though, the one the skipper was keen on. There'd been some bets placed, on the messdecks. He'd said to Surtees, when they'd been chatting on the trip down Namsenfjord, "Nice bit of stuff, that. Don't blame the skipper 'aving a go, eh?" Surtees had looked vague: "Thought it was 'er was after 'im. That's 'ow I 'eard it. . . . Got a missus already, ain't 'e?" Crouch had shaken his head sadly: "Bloody 'ell, don't you know *anything*?"

Ahead, a glow of light, startling in the dark. . . .

He got up higher for a better look. Floodlight of some kind: on a ship's deck. The Hun destroyer's? The light was shaded, shining downwards. Squinting into the icy wind, standing right up and leaning out on Surtees's side, staring out fine on the port bow: he could see men working around that light and a davit in black, curved silhouette. By its position it would be a torpedo davit. The half-lit picture, vague as it was with the flickering shadows, was cut off vertically with knife-edge abruptness where the ship's superstructure for'ard blanked it off. But *Valkyrien* was edging round to starboard, further inshore, now that she'd cleared the reef: she'd be coming in fast towards her still unsuspecting victims. Crouch went back to his place in the stern, Surtees swearing as he kicked his legs in transit and got down on the other side of him. Watch for the flash now. He told Surtees, "Won't be long, Billy-boy. Jerries workin' on the upper, got a light on an' all."

Sharper swing to starboard. And a huge light flaring: searchlight? Jet of brilliance: it had swept *over* them, but there'd been enough spill-off brightness to—

A shout from for'ard. Torp—sounding furious. Crouch put a hand on Surtees' shoulder, pressing

354

him downwards as he passed him. "Stay there now." The light's beam had touched the funnel, swung on, then had second thoughts and started to come back. Crouch scuttled for'ard up the port side; he heard the bark of Torp's old pistol from the wheelhouse doorway. Silly old bugger, might as well fart at it as use that thing. . . . The killick leant with his left arm on top of the port-side bulwark, as a steadying point, aimed his Thompson at the centre of the glare and squeezed its trigger. The gun jumped upwards, as the GM had warned it would: you had to force the barrel down to get it where you wanted. The searchlight was full on them, holding them, and some sort of hooter was blaring from the German. The Tommy shuddering and hammering, its barrel flaming as he brought its stream of .45 slugs down across that blinding glare. Explosion of glass as it smashed and went out. Pitch-black again— worse, he was blinded, couldn't see even his own hands. *Done* it, though. Stumbling aft, groping, pulverising Billy-boy's calves again and *Valkyrien* pounding on, a fine old ship that had never been meant for war, for anything like this. She'd lurched to starboard. Crouch had found the slip entirely by feel. He asked Surtees, "You set?"

"Yeah. Roll on my twelve."

Daft bugger . . . Crouch was beginning to see again. *Valkyrien* heeled to starboard as Larsen shoved the wheel hard a-port and she began her turn in towards the enemy's sterns. Two sterns

355

close together. Using the torpedo davit to plumb the U-boat's midships area they'd had to secure them this way.

"Stand by!"

She'd steadied and she was about to pass close astern of them. The wire slips had to work now, and the slings had not to snag. Crouch couldn't see the enemy, the target, because the old ship's deckhouse was in the way. He wasn't trying to anyway, only watching for the torch-flash. The Norwegian would have to be looking about four ways at once: target to port, rocks to starboard, torch signal towards his stern and what Larsen was doing with the wheel. A machine-gun had opened up and tracer was arching overhead and astern. *Valkyrien* leaned over as she went into her zig to starboard.

The torch flashed, yellowish.

Crouch screamed, "Let's go!" and at the same time struck at the slip in front of him with the stock of his Tommy gun. In the dark he missed it, bouncing off the wire instead: the gun skidded sideways and he'd skinned his knuckles. Surtees yelled, "All gone!" *This* bastard hadn't. He had to feel for the slip again, shove the barrel of the Tommy under its latch and lever it open. It snapped back and the wires' ends whipped away and the charge fell clear. Surtees' gun began to hammer, banging and flaming at lights and men running on the destroyer's upper deck. Crouch put his gun up too and got one short burst off before it jammed.

The German machine-gun had ceased fire. They'd probably be looking for some quite different kind of target: and they wouldn't know anything about the charges yet. Crouch had the pan off his gun and he was working the cocking mechanism to clear it before he put a new one on. The pistols on the charges would be filling with water now and when they'd filled the hydrostatic valves would be triggered by the pressure in them. Meanwhile nobody was shooting, so why give the sods a mark to aim at? He told Surtees, "Hold your fire, Billy!" The first charge exploded and astern the fjord erupted, a huge white mushroom-head lifting, with the German ships in it: then the spread of it travelling outwards lifted *Valkyrien*'s stern and drove her ahead bow-down but with the whole length of her up on the enormous outrushing wave, which passed on under her so that she dropped stern-down, almost under water. A succeeding rush was coming, though, overtaking and slewing her off course and right on round, listing hard to starboard, and the second charge went off with a *boom* that sounded bigger than the first, with another swelling mushroom heading skywards: they heard the roar of the approaching wave just as the old ship rocked back to port, practically on her beam ends. She was in a maelstrom of heavy falling and rushing, oversweeping sea, three-dimensional confusion: spinning her round, the torrent poured right across her, flooded over the bulwarks aft, swirled two feet deep before it drained down. But the engine was still pounding away and she was pitching less already, over smaller waves, follow-ups as the main deluge subsided: it had hit her, mauled her, and swept on. Rolling still but responding to rudder and coming back on course. Astern, the gun began to fire again, something like a twenty-millimetre by the sound of it: but it wasn't shooting in the right direction from any German point of view. *Valkyrien* chugged on: perhaps she *had* been lifted and carried over the shallow patch. The gun ceased fire. It was pitch-black and with any luck the Germans still didn't know what had hit them. It would have done them in, all right, Crouch thought: he muttered, "Lovely grub, eh, Billy?" and Surtees answered, "Ah, very tasty, very sweet." Out of some radio programme. Astern one gun fired once: main armament, one single shot. The crack of it was still echoing round the fjord and surrounding hills when the starshell burst—high and well beyond them, over the land to which *Valkyrien* was pitching over what was now no more than a choppy sea. The shell burst with a sharp thudding sound and the flare appeared and expanded immediately to flood the whole land—and seascape with its harsh magnesium whiteness.

Now they'd seen her. Crash of gunfire astern. Small stuff—pom-poms or Bofors—that kind of thing, and some of it was tracer. Surtees put his gun up, sighted, pressed the trigger: the Thompson banged twice and then jammed. A hand grabbed Crouch's shoulder: Torp yelled with his face down close to him, "Set the charges! Half-minute only, then we beach!" The top of the old hooker's funnel went, flared and soared away in several burning pieces. Explosive shells ripped in flame and flying timber along the port-side strip of deck. Torp had gone for'ard, luckily for him, up the other side. Crouch grabbed Surtees' arm: "Charges!"

They were below, ready to be placed and lit. Arne Martinsen, the stoker-cum-engineer, asked Crouch, "We fix the boggers?" It wasn't clear whether he was referring to Germans or to charges, but an affirmative answered either question. Martinsen was all sweat, coaldust and oil: he'd have stoked her right up by now so she'd have all the steam she needed for this last sprint of hers. There was a crash from up top somewhere: she lurched—either thrown off course or dodging. The fitted charges were all together in an ammo box; he passed three of them to Surtees and took the other three himself. Surtees said, "I'll do port side, right?" They were tin cylinders about a foot long and three inches in diameter, and Crouch had set them up himself before they'd sailed. It wasn't a difficult operation: you slid the explosive into the tin, which it exactly fitted, and the detonator went into an aperture in the end of the explosive. One end of the fuse you poked through the hole in the tin's screw-cap and then crimped into the detonator, and then you screwed the cap on. It was just a tin, now, with the fuse like white washing-line sticking out of it. On the other end of the fuse, whatever length of it was needed, you fitted an igniter, a tube of tin about the size of a small cigarette; the fuse fitted into one end of it and the other end, if you squeezed it with a pair of pliers or by stamping on it, started the fuse burning. It didn't show, but if it was burning properly and you held it against your ear you could hear it fizz.

Crouch lowered his three charges into the bilge along the length of the engine-space, one for'ard and one aft and one between them, and Surtees was doing the same on the other side. They should have been tamped down, really, but the confined space down there would contain the explosion, concentrate it enough, Crouch reckoned. They were leaving the ends of the fuses with igniters on them up on the footplates, ready to be set going. Torp leant in through the hatch: "Is it ready?" Surtees nodded: "Aye, sir."

"Fuses lit?"

Crouch said, arriving at the after end, "We'll light 'em now, sir. Billy—"

"Aye aye." Surtees had the pliers. He went round quickly, squeezing each igniter and checking that it was fizzing, then dropping the whole length of fuse down into the bilge—out of reach, unless you took the plates up. The fuse would burn in water as well as out of it. Arne Martinsen had started up the ladder, leaving the engine unsupervised and lonely, driving itself to its own doom. Crouch pushed Surtees towards the ladder and then followed him up it. Into air even colder than it had been, after the heat below. Surtees asked Crouch, speaking with his mouth against the killick's ear, "Oughter stay with the gaffer, like the skipper said?" The biggest explosion they'd heard yet—enough to crack the fjord wide open. . . . Echoes now. It had been to the east of them—over the land ahead. Now another one exactly like it: this time Crouch saw a flash, a sort of yellow streak, very quick like a light that burns and fuses instantaneously as you press a switch. *Valkyrien* was heeling as she swung to starboard, and a shell burst on her beam —*on land*—a low headland which she was rounding: a fresh starshell had just suspended itself overhead, lighting everything in all directions. Bits of shell or perhaps stones flying, singing away overhead: and another shellburst but astern this time, in the water, he'd heard it scrunch down and then the explosion and after that it was raining, a deluge of heavy rain that stank. They were practically on the beach, he realised. The whole trip across, from dropping the charges to this beach, was only 800 yards. So Torp had said. Five minutes, he'd said it would take them, All we got to do is stay afloat five

361

minutes. Not too hard, huh? Norwegian minutes must be longer than the British kind, Crouch thought. Third huge bang: and the yellow flash again: sure of it now, he bawled at Surtees, "Them's our fish, chum!" Surtees nodded, shouted back, "I reckon." They'd helped look after those torpedoes, done maintenance routines on them. Shells scorched over: a starshell had been fading but another had replaced it. The shells had burst on shore, some way up from the beach. Torp yelled from the wheelhouse door, "Get for'ard, hold to something, *hold on!*" Surtees moved obediently and Crouch, who was ahead of him on the narrow strip of deck, moved too. He didn't want to get too far from the Norwegian. It was still bright as day from that starshell but no more shells had come, not in the last fifteen or twenty seconds. *Valkyrien* lifted, flinging up, smashing and grinding on to rock. Torp had been thrown back—he'd been holding with one arm to the doorway and he'd been swung so that he'd crashed backwards into the side of the wheelhouse. He shouted at Crouch, "I say go *for'ard*, damn it!" He'd given Surtees an almighty shove: Surtees blundered into the killick and they both went on towards the bow. The jolting and bouncing had stopped, and the ship was falling over on to her starboard side, subsiding slowly with the water tending to hold her up. She lurched again and Crouch slipped, fell against the bulwark, down on one knee in the swirl of sea that was pouring over now and also rising from astern, up the slope of deck. Larsen gave him a hand up, then went on ahead, and in fading starshell-light Crouch saw him jump over from the bow. Crouch followed him, thinking he could wait for Torp on the beach rather than hang back now and get sworn at: and Torp's bellow reached him, "Get a bloody move on— *jump!*" Only the way he said it was "yump". Tracer racketed overhead: spraying the beach, now that she wasn't in the bastards' sight? She couldn't be, not in this little cove he'd put her in. Crouch swung his legs over the bulwark, held the Tommy gun up clear of the wet, and slid over, landing in about four feet of icy water. Ahead of him were Martinsen and Larsen, ten- or fifteen-yard gaps between them and between Larsen and himself, and behind him was Surtees and the fellow they were supposed to be looking after. Currently yelling Norwegian: then he put it into English—"There is a stream in front. Follow it to the road then go left and run!" Another starshell: time they gave up that lark, Crouch thought. More shells scrunching over—bursting on land, so they couldn't be aiming for *Valkyrien*. Wouldn't make sense to now in any case. Chocker, probably, wanting to get their own back, teach a lesson to the unruly natives. Martinsen had shouted something back to Torp: he had a high, carrying voice, trained by the need to yell over the sound of engines. He was clear of the water, climbing a steep slope with a gully to the right of it. Larsen was still in the water, the shallows, jogging through it. It was still too deep where Crouch was to move fast and he didn't want to anyway, even though Surtees had managed to stay with the Norwegian back there. *Aching* cold water. More shells—falling to the left, exploding in the shallows, sending up sheets of sea and a hail of stones. Then to the left again, that sort of rasping whistle as they rushed down, the crashes of the explosions and the air alive and humming with flying rock and salt water: and now *more* coming. He thought, *Vindictive bastards!* Then he realised: the new salvo was going to pitch *behind* him—where Surtees and the Norwegian were.

Lange cut his boat's speed. The oiler was a dark mass blacker than the night fifty yards off on the bow. A long, low rectangle with two smaller, upright rectangles on it. One of them was the bridge superstructure and there were lights showing from it. Careless: thought they were all right on the landward side, perhaps. Trench looked down, rapped with his knuckles on Midshipman Cox's tin hat: "Clear about your job, you in there?" Cox said yes, he was. Trench looked past him, at PO Metcalf: "You, Buffer?" Metcalf growled, "I'm the bloke as chucks 'em in the 'oggin, sir." The land was about a hundred and fifty yards to port: on the boat's quarter now as Lange turned directly towards the oiler. Planks were ready on the wheelhouse canopy, to bridge the gap between boat and ship. The boarding party—all in helmets, officers and POs with revolvers and British and Norwegian sailors with rifles—lined both sides of the boat's deck and packed the sternsheets. Riflemen would fix bayonets after they'd boarded.

Trench checked his watch's luminous dial. One minute to zero hour. He leant into the wheelhouse, held up one finger to Lange. The Norwegian blinked at it. "Hokay." His engines were turning over very slowly, just paddling the heavy boat up towards its goal.

"Hey, what's—"

Trench said, "Machine-gun. Keep your voices down, everybody." That gunfire had come from the Altbotn direction. Metcalf grumbled. "Warming the blooming bell, sir?" Translated, his comment was that Torp had launched his attack too soon. Then they heard the first depth-charge go off, a deep explosion like subterranean thunder. Trench watched the oiler, dreading that he might see what he now expected—alarm, lights, men rushing about. Practically holding his breath. Forewarned, a couple of men with rifles could make the boarding operation just about impossible. The second deep and distant *whumpf* came: he said evenly, quietly, "That's both charges. So far so good." His own voice in retrospect sounded as if he might be slightly bored: whereas in fact his heart was beating like a

hammer. More machine-gun fire. *Too damn soon*
. . . If those Huns weren't stirred up by now it
wouldn't be old Torp's fault. He saw a glow of
light to the left of the oiler, silhouetting her
vertical stem and the start of the long, low foc's'l;
the glow had resolved itself into a swivelling
searchlight beam from the destroyer anchorage.
For a second or two the oiler was bathed in its
light as it swept past, then it had gone round to
poke at the beach and coastline of that farther
bay. The lights in the houses ashore, Trench
noticed, had all gone out. Heads under the bed-
clothes too?

This boat hadn't been illuminated at all by the
searchlight: the oiler had shielded it completely.
Which suggested that the inshore approach had
been a wise choice. But surely they *must* wake
up, realise *something* was going on?

Lange's head came out, like a tortoise's out of
its shell. "Hokay?"

The oiler was dead ahead. To the right, the
aftercastle with the funnel growing out of it and
no lights showing in the cabin scuttles would
contain crew's quarters and galley. A few other
things as well. To the left, the bridge superstructure with bridge, chartroom, captain's and
officers' accommodation, W/T office. . . .
Between those two islands of superstructure was
the low tank-top section, with catwalks above it,
where they were going to board. Trench pointed
at that gap, roughly a hundred feet of it.

"There. *Okay.*"

Meaning, Let's get there—quick, before the stupid bastards pull their fingers out. . . .

"Sure!"

So Lange knew *two* English words. . . . He wasn't rushing though. He'd shut the throttles back as far as they'd go, just about. Dead slow, sliding up towards an enemy who was either daft or unpleasantly alert and waiting to see the whites of the intruders' eyes. Trench ran over some of the detail in his mind. Leading Telegraphist Rose would be taking care of the wireless, ensuring that no calls for help went out. Cox would be attending to the clearing of machinery spaces, then leaving guards on the access points and, with Metcalf, searching the rest of the lower compartments and placing more guards as might be necessary. You had to make sure no bloody-minded Hun could slip down to those bottom areas to open seacocks or place a charge. (Germans were scuttle-minded: witness *Graf Spee*, four months ago.) An LTO, electrician, had been detailed to locate the main switchboard and protect it against sabotage. All cabins had to be searched and firearms impounded, documents and code-books in the chartroom and captain's quarters or elsewhere kept safe from destruction.

If there was anyone up on that bridge, Trench thought, he or they might be fully occupied looking out over the bow, towards the destroyers and the searchlight business. With luck, they might . . . he heard a thump—overhead: saw it was starshell, white light spreading. . . . Looking down again quickly, to spare his eyes. Ten yards to go. Too late for the starshell to make much odds, but if it had come five minutes earlier. . . . Sea sloshing noisily, violently, between the boat and the tanker's sheer black side. There were to be no lines put across: Lange would keep the boat alongside by its own power, holding it there until they'd all gone over.

"Stand by!"

He'd called the warning aft just loudly enough for the nearer men to hear and pass it on. Gunfire now from the Altbotn direction was something to be welcomed, to hold the Germans' attention during the next few minutes. Trench was up on the timber canopy and so were Cox and Metcalf and the men who'd be first up behind them, including a killick who'd be taking care of the for'ard end of the ship. Men who'd come slightly later were manoeuvring the heavy planks ready for shoving them over. They wouldn't be entirely steady gangways, with the boat's rise and fall on this swell, but at least the oiler was giving them a lee. Another reason for boarding over this side.

Two Norwegians on the deck below this wheel-house, several feet lower than Trench and others on its roof, were holding up the outboard ends of two planks, as high above their heads as they could reach. They'd launch them upwards and outwards as the boat touched alongside. They were the tallest of the Norwegians.

Three yards—two—one—

"Gangways over!"

The ends of the planks were still bouncing on the oiler's side as Trench rushed over the left-hand one. Other men behind him and on the second plank, and two more bridges crashing over. Not a soul in sight. He was aboard, and no one had shot at him. He grabbed the rail of the catwalk which bridged across the tank-tops in a fore-and-aft direction, hauled himself up on it, ran towards the door into the bridge superstructure: conscious of a whole rush of men behind him, all fast and no noisier than they needed to be. The door was heavy steel, shut and clipped, and he was dragging the clips off. Four, and it still wouldn't open, but Cameron, the killick who was going to lead his party straight through this superstructure and out on to the for'ard section, located a fifth clip low down and heeled it off. The door swung open and they rushed inside, down a short passage, then right into a thwartships passage where, amidships, a ladderway led upwards. Trench went up it. On the next level, cabin doors. Up to the next level with sailors close behind him and the sound of bayonets clicking on to rifles.

He burst into the bridge.

"Get your hands up!"

Three men whipped round to face him: face

his revolver and two levelled rifles with bayonets on them. Signalman Lee hadn't stopped, he'd gone straight through and out into the bridge wing, two other seamen following him. Of the three Germans here two were officers and one was a grey-haired petty officer: one of the officers, a short, stout man, had gold-leafing on the peak of his cap. Trench roared again, "Hands up!" The more junior officer complied. From for'ard came shouting and a single rifle-shot which seemed to have silenced it: Cameron doing his stuff. The PO lunged forward suddenly with some weapon raised above his head: Trench raised the pistol and his finger was tightening on its trigger when the man stopped dead with a bayonet-point about two inches from his throat. All he had in that lifted hand was a pair of binoculars. Now all three had their hands up.

"Captain?"

"Ja." The short one with scrambled eggs on his hat nodded. "I am kapitan." He clicked his heels. Too short and fat to be impressive. "Grossman. I protest—this is unarmed merchant vessel, in passage through neutral waters—"

"Rotten luck." Trench nodded. "Just order your men to surrender, please." The man stood staring at him, trying to look haughty. Trench added, "If they resist they're quite likely to be shot. . . . What's this, Marsham?"

AB Marsham was prodding a youngster in from

the starboard bridge wing, at the point of his bayonet. Some sort of cadet.

"Tryin' to flash a message to the destroyers, sir. Caught 'im in the act."

The newcomer took his place with the others and raised his hands. The captain nodded. "You will not get away. You will see in one moment—"

A flash: huge, yellow, reaching from sea to cloud-level, and with it an explosion that shook the deck they were standing on. One destroyer done for: and all the Germans had swung round to look. Trench allowed it, as an exercise that might take the starch out of them. There was a mass of fire now, flames lighting the base of a pillar of black smoke. He'd only spared it a glance but his impression had been of a destroyer broken in two halves and one of them burning.

"Captain!"

He had the man's attention again. "Will you order your crew to surrender, please?"

A second ringing crash and another leap of fire. No need to look, and the German captain evidently didn't feel he had to either. Behind Trench, Leading Telegraphist Rose reported, "W/T office is locked up, sir. They didn't get no signals out."

"Well done, Rose. You'd better stay there for the time being, keep an eye on it." He raised his gun a little, pointing it at the captain's head. "Well?"

"You take us prisoners?"

"You and your officers, yes. Perhaps a few others. Most of your crew can go ashore." He didn't mention *how* they'd go ashore. Officers were to be held prisoner, Nick had decided, because as highly trained men they were better not returned to the German war machine. There might be some technicians who'd be rated similarly. Outside, a third explosion speared the night with flame, rattled the bridge windows. The German captain had shut his eyes and would probably have shut his ears too if he'd had the necessary equipment. He opened his eyes now, blinking, sad, hard-done-by, noble in defeat. He'd have been a real bastard in victory. He muttered, "I will do as you wish."

"Excuse me, sir?" Leading Steward Seymour announced from the doorway, "Remainder of the officers, sir. Winkled 'em out of their beddy-byes, sir." They filed in, between two fixed bayonets and with Seymour's right behind them —four men of differing ages, shape and sizes but all indignant, confused, frightened. They had coats or dressing-gowns over their pyjamas. Trench waved his pistol: "Over there, and keep your hands up. Stand in line so I can see each one of you. Captain, tell them that in German." He saw a new arrival, an OD named Kelly.

"Sir, report from Leading Seaman Cameron. Forepeak is suitable for prisoners, room for a dozen or more. And I'm to tell you 'e's sent 'is prisoners aft to where the other lot is, sir."

"Thank you, Kelly. And casualties?"

"No, sir. Fired one shot over a bloke's 'ead, and 'e turned all smarmy."

"Fine. Seymour, what about the chartroom?"

"Williamson's in there, sir. Nobody's touched nothing, and there's a safe that's locked still."

Williamson was the CW candidate who was going to become Pete Chandler's tanky. Trench had detailed men and parties for these various jobs mainly during the blue boat's passage through the fjords. It seemed to be working out all right. He looked at the captain again: "Your keys, please. Take them from him, Seymour." And it was time for that broadcast.

But there was another interruption: a stoker, Ackroyd, from Cox's detail. He reported, "From Mr. Cox, sir: engine-room, boiler-room, generator room, shaft tunnel and steering-gear compartment is all clear and secured with guards on upper access points, sir. Crew's quarters likewise cleared, and search of other spaces is continuing. One German seaman killed, sir, and no resistance is now being offered. Main switchboard's under guard and prisoners are being mustered on the upper deck right aft."

"Very good, Ackroyd." It was better than "very good", he thought, it was bloody marvellous. "You'd better report back to Mr. Cox, and tell him that if you or any other stokers can be spared now I'd like you to join Leading Stoker Evans on the oiling preparations."

"Aye aye, sir."

"*Only* if he can spare you."

"I'll explain that, sir."

Ackroyd would have the makings of a killick.
Trench saw that Seymour had the captain's keys:
he told him, "Take those to Williamson. Tell him
to empty the safe, list its contents and parcel
everything up ready for transfer to *Intent*. Then
come back here, please." He told Kelly, "Ask
Leading Seaman Cameron to come up here with
a few hands to escort these officers to their new
quarters."

"Aye aye, sir." Kelly shot away. Trench turned
to the captain.

"Where's your broadcast system worked
from?"

Grossman pointed. There was a switchbox on
the bulkhead with a microphone on a trailing
lead.

"But why is this necessary? You have my ship:
it is not—not *honourable* that a commander
should order his—"

"You'll do it though. *Now*."

He'd gestured with the gun, towards that
corner.

"As a sea officer I ask you, sir—"

"I don't *mind* shooting you, Captain." The
German stared at him: then he moved, sluggishly,
looking aggrieved. Trench said, "Keep an eye on
him, Gilby."

"Aye, sir." Cook Gilby and his bayonet

374

followed the little man to the microphone. Grossman was right, of course, that his ship was now in British control, but lurking in some Teutonic brain might be thoughts of sabotage or other mayhem, and an order from their own CO to surrender could scotch such notions. The German voice was already booming through the ship.

"Sir?" Lee, the signalman, had come in from the wing of the bridge, which connected with the signal deck abaft it. "Beg pardon, sir, but *Intent*'s circling round on our starboard quarter, looks like we might 'ave 'er alongside soon. Should I shine a light down? There's a six-inch each side, I could—"

"No." If the Old Man wanted a light he'd shine his own. *Intent* had no searchlight, thanks to that *Hipper*, but she still had her signal lamps and a ten-inch would serve that purpose. "But—Lee, have you struck the German ensign?"

"Not yet, sir—"

Seymour was back. Trench told him, "Go and give Lee here a hand. I want the German ensign hauled down with a light on it so *Intent* can see it. Then hoist the White Ensign, also with a spotlight on it. All right?"

"Aye aye, sir!"

The captain had finished his speech. Trench went over to the corner before he could leave it, and told him, "Switch it so I can be heard all over the ship, please." Grossman flipped one master-switch up, and nodded: "So." Trench slapped the microphone: it was live, all right. He said into it, "D'you hear there. Petty Officer Metcalf, take four hands as berthing party for *Intent*, starboard side. Leading Stoker Evans, stand by for oiling, starboard side."

"Stop together. Midships."

His orders floated back to him out of the voice-pipe as *Intent* slid up towards the oiler.

"Slow astern port."

Five minutes ago they'd seen the German "State Service" flag—a red rectangle with a black swastika in a white circle in the centre and an eagle-emblem in one corner—come sliding down from the masthead. Nick had said to Kari, "Tommy Trench is giving us a show." A few moments later a White Ensign, floodlit, had risen in place of the German flag. There'd been a round of cheering from the guns' crews, and Kari had clapped her hands. "Bravo!"

She was worried to distraction about her father, and trying hard not to show it.

"Sub—berthing party, port side, and get Beamish moving as soon as we're secured."

"Aye aye, sir!"

Joy, jubilation in the sub-lieutenant's voice. He'd fired *Intent*'s torpedoes, seen three of them hit, seen both enemy destroyers shattered and sunk. Not one shot had been fired at *Intent* during that short, highly conclusive action.

Where the fourth torpedo had gone was a mystery. Dived into the mud, perhaps, if its depth-keeping mechanism had failed, or turned and streaked out to sea if it had been a gyro failure. Failures *did* occur. But those three fish had done the job.

"Stop port."

"Stop port, sir . . . Port engine stopped, sir."

This sweet smell of success might fade when news came of the *Valkyrien* party. There'd been a lot of gunfire during the starshell period. And it mattered enormously about Torp. It had before, but Nick's concern had been partly smothered in the planning of the operation and in uncertainties of other kinds. Now that the objects had been achieved—would soon have been achieved, if there was no unexpected interference now—that anxiety became stronger and more immediate. Not just for Torp's sake, in the way that one was concerned for the safety of the two torpedomen, for instance, but for Kari's and, selfishly, his own. If Torp had come to grief, he —Nick Everard—was going to be stuck with the girl. By his own sense of responsibility for her— whatever *she* had to say about it, he'd fall into the role of—well, foster-father?

The rescue syndrome? The Black Sea and Ilyana, now the Norwegian fjords and Kari?

No connection. Totally different circumstances: and totally different people. Even *he* was different, after twenty years. *Wasn't* he? And whether he cared for her or not—well, to what extent the care was for her, or for her and her father as an entity, the agency he'd been relying on, he couldn't tell. There wasn't time to think about it properly and for the moment it didn't matter anyway.

Heaving lines flew from *Intent*'s side, were caught by men on the tanker's deck. They had torches to help them see what they were doing. Fenders were in place and hemp breasts were slithering out now, dragged over by the heaving lines bent to them. Nick saw Metcalf down there, bawling at a Norwegian to underrun a spring before it got trapped between the two ships' sides, and the Norwegian, understanding no English at all, saw what was needed and did it. Leading Stoker Evans had an oil pipe triced up, dangling from a boom above and ready to be swung over.

Nick told Chandler, "I'm going to pay a call next door, pilot. Look after this end, will you."

"Keep the guns closed up, sir?"

"Yes. We aren't quite out of the wood yet."

The girl asked him, "Shall I go with you?"

"Well, I've things to see to. Better wait here until your father gets back, Kari, then it'll be up to him whether you stay with us or move over to the oiler."

He didn't want her down there when the boat came.

Trench met him at the oiler's side. *Intent* was secured alongside and they'd put a brow across.

378

"Neat job on those destroyers, sir."

He nodded. "What's the score here, Tommy?"

"All in hand, sir. She's the *Tonning*. Naval auxiliary, 14,000 tons, reputedly capable of fourteen to fifteen knots, launched 1938. There's a gun-mounting for'ard but no gun. Six officers—they're under guard in the fore peak—and twenty-eight crew. She has approximately 8,000 tons of oil-fuel in her. Captain's name is Grossman. Inoffensive little chap, knows he's beat, as it were."

"Do we know if they got any distress call out?"

"They did not, sir. We were in the bridge before they knew anything was happening. It's panned out very nicely and our chaps have done a first-class job."

Beamish went hurrying past. Nick asked him, "All right, Chief?"

"Will be, sir, in 'alf a shake. The connections'll do us all right, that was the main 'eadache."

He'd gone on. Nick asked Trench, "Steam up? Ready for the off when we've oiled?"

"Top line, sir, according to Cox. And Boyensen's just gone down to get things in hand. One rather useful thing—or it could be—is that there are two engineers, ERA types or possibly more like Warrants, who say they're Danes and want to join us. They say they were pressed into German service. Will you take a look at them?"

"We certainly need plumbers."

"I meant for *this* ship, not—"

"Naturally. But let's wait for Torp." *Touch wood . . .* "They'll be his crew if we take them on, and he may even talk their lingo, or vice versa."

The oil pipe was across now, linking the two ships. Beamish was back on the destroyer's iron deck with a gaggle of his stokers. Nick asked Trench, "Have you sorted out swimmers and non-swimmers yet?"

"Cox is attending to that detail, sir."

"How has he performed?"

"Well, sir—" Trench smiled, thinking about it—"I'd hesitate to use the expression 'tower of strength' in relation to one of such diminutive stature as Midshipman Cox, but otherwise it might not be inappropriate."

"That's good news. But you've developed rather an ornate turn of phrase, Tommy?"

"It's because I'm happy, I think."

He looked round: Norwegians on the oiler's port side were shouting, pointing out into the dark. Nick heard Lange's name among the less unintelligible sounds.

So the boat was coming. No relief in that: only sharpened anxiety, a preference *not to know*. . . . Trench said, turning back, "There's one thing, sir—I promised Lange he could fill his boat's tank with diesel before we all shove off."

Kari was coming, hurrying across the gangway. Nick nodded to Trench. "Of course. Better warn Beamish, though." Lange was intending to take

380

his boat up through the Leads to Ranenfjord, Mo i Rana, about a hundred and twenty miles north. It was the place from which Torp had fetched *Valkyrien*, there were no Germans there yet and Lange had family near by. Nick was watching Kari as she came up to them.

"I heard the boat was coming."

He'd tried to avoid this, but he was going to have to face it with her. And Torp *might* be in the boat. . . .

He took her arm. "Let's go and meet him."

Over to the port side, ducking under the two catwalks. There were several Norwegians waiting to take the blue boat's lines. Kari pointed, wordlessly: it was the white bow-wave that she'd seen. Watching it as it approached and the boat began to reduce its speed, Nick felt sick with the conviction that her father would not be in it.

The boat was circling into a position from which to come alongside. The Norwegians along the oiler's side waited silently, motionless as statues, watching it approach. You could see their anxiety in that stillness. An arc of white curled shorewards as the boat swept round, rolling on the swell. Then it had steadied, and Nick could see men standing just abaft the wheelhouse door. Two of them. Then there'd be Lange on the wheel and his mechanic crouched in the little engine-space. . . . But he'd *known* this. Right

381

from the start of the operation, when it had become obvious that *Valkyrien* was going to have to do the Altbotn job. There'd been five in the *Valkyrien* party, and Lange and his two men. . . . Kari's hand had tightened on his arm. The boat was slewing in, its starboard screw going astern. More men in sight than had been visible before. Then as it bumped alongside two figures moved to launch a plank across, and almost as it crashed down a large-built man climbed on to it and came shambling over with another man on his back. As he entered the pool of light at the oiler's side Kari pulled herself away from Nick and rushed forward. Claus Torp allowed PO Metcalf to take Surtees off him, and Crouch, following, helped Metcalf in lowering the injured torpedoman to the deck.

Surtees announced for general information, "Two bloody *miles* 'e carted me!"

Crouch told Nick, "Shell-splinter in 'is leg, sir. I thought the both of 'em 'ad 'ad it, till 'e gets up an'—"

"Get him to the sickbay. Pass the word for a stretcher."

Kari was in her father's arms, hugging him, sobbing against his chest. The clinch had been her idea, not his: he'd looked surprised as she'd leapt at him and clasped him. Now he was patting her shoulders as he stared at Nick over her dark head.

"You sank them both, huh?"

"Yes. How about yours?"

"Oh, sure. Well, maybe not *sink*, but—you know . . ." He looked down at his weeping daughter. "What you been doing to this woman —*frightening* her?"

12

THE surface of Ofotfjord gleamed dully under drifting mist. Fir trees formed dark streaks and patches on the high snow-bound slopes and the sky backing the mountains was like dirty cotton-wool. It was a harsh, miserable place, Nick thought, this trap of a fjord where three days ago his son's ship had gone down.

1.30 pm: one German destroyer had already been sunk, although the action had barely started yet. The German had been hiding in Djupvik Bay, on the starboard hand as the British force debouched from the narrows into the wide part of the fjord, and *Warspite*'s Swordfish floatplane, hammering its way up-fjord with the racket of its engine bouncing from the mountain-sides, had radio'd advance warning of its presence. *Bedouin* and *Eskimo* had raced round the headland with guns and tubes ready trained to starboard, and it had needed only a few salvoes to silence the enemy's guns. Then a single torpedo from *Bedouin* had blown his bows off. Finally as *Warspite* steamed by in massive, lordly fashion she'd spared one thunderous blast of fifteen-inch and the already hard-hit enemy turned belly-up and sank.

The echoes died as the force pressed on. Earlier the leading destroyers had streamed their paravanes, minesweeping gear, but no mines had been encountered and they were getting the wires in now, out of the way before the business of destruction started. Leading the force were four of the modern Tribal class—*Bedouin, Cossack, Eskimo* and *Punjabi*—and behind them, screening the battleship which now flew Admiral Whitworth's flag, steamed the smaller destroyers *Hero, Icarus, Kimberley, Forester, Foxhound* and *Intent*. It was a foregone conclusion that when this force withdrew there'd be no German ship left afloat in the Narvik fjords.

Studying that southern coastline, Nick wondered where exactly *Hoste* had sunk. Not far offshore, they'd told him last night. "They" being the captains of two other destroyers who'd come to get oil from *Tonning*. They'd also told him that according to Norwegian accounts quite a number of survivors had got ashore: but later one of them had stumbled into admitting that the ship the Norwegian sources had mentioned had been *Hunter*, whose survivors were reported to have crossed the mountains into Sweden.

So in fact there was *no* news. Except that *Hoste* had been sunk and that before she'd foundered she'd been very badly knocked about. The anxiety was bad now. It had been suppressed, buried under the planning and the action, but now it was in the front of his mind and everything

385

he looked at he was seeing through it. The signals from Admiralty and from C-in-C: or those destroyer captains wringing his hand and showering him with compliments: he'd *felt* none of it.

Last night had been spent off Hamnvik, in Folla, a fjord-complex on the southern side of Vestfjord. The oiler was still there, with Claus Torp as her master and young Lyte in charge of a four-man armed guard on the prisoners. *Tonning* was suckling the fleet's destroyers as they needed it, and in a day or two she was to be moved up to Harstad where a base was being established.

Kari had repeated, last night, "Your son will be all right, Nick. You will see."

"I know." He told her, "You convinced me two days ago."

"Did I really?" He'd nodded. He'd been grateful for her attempt to convince him, that was all, her genuine desire to give him that comfort. But she was looking at him now as if she didn't quite believe him: she was anything but stupid. "I hope I shall meet him one day. With you. Perhaps at your house—" her hand had moved towards a pocket—"of which I forget the name—"

"Mullbergh."

He'd given her his card, given her father one as well, telling them that if ever they came to England they were to make themselves at home there whether or not he himself was around.

Which most likely he would not be, of course. He'd written Sarah's name and the Dower House address and telephone number on the backs of the cards, and also the name of his old butler, Barstow.

"This—" Kari had turned the card over—"Lady Sarah Everard—"

"My stepmother. My father's widow. She has a house—that address I've put there—which is part of the estate."

"Is it very big, your estate?"

"About four thousand acres. I sold off a lot of land a few years ago to raise cash for putting the rest of it in order."

"That is still a great deal of land. And you are all sirs and ladies—"

"I'm a baronet because my father was. My elder brother would have been, instead of me, but he was drowned at Jutland. Paul—" he made himself say this—"Paul will become a baronet when I die. And when a baronet gets married his wife becomes *Lady* Whatsit. It's of no great consequence, Kari, it makes no difference to the sort of people we are."

"I am very happy with the sort of person you are. But I should not like at all to become Lady Whatsit."

"I think I can promise you that you won't."

"Then I *shall* visit you at Mullbergh."

"If I'm not there, you'll make another visit later?"

But the Torps might not come to Britain. Troops were at sea, bound for Narvik from the Clyde and from Scapa Flow. Half a battalion of Scots Guards were in the cruiser *Southampton* and the rest of that Brigade plus another one as well were following in five troopships. If a landing was successful, the Torps might elect to stay; Claus almost certainly would.

All that news had come from the destroyer COs last night. And various other bits of information —such as the cruiser *Penelope* having been sent to find a German tanker reported to be in a fjord fifty miles south of Narvik: there'd been no tanker though, and *Penelope* had hit a rock. Nick wondered if that tanker might have been *Tonning*, missed by *Penelope* because it had moved down to Namsenfjord. It seemed quite likely.

Gunfire ahead. A long way off, though, and drifting smoke was combining with mist patches to blind them. There was also *Warspite*'s lumbering bulk ahead. Nick reached for the director telephone and asked Henry Brockle-hurst, "Can you see anything?"

"Three or possibly four Hun destroyers, sir—fighting a rearguard action by the looks of it, withdrawing towards Narvik. The Tribals and I think it's *Hero* and *Forester* are engaging them. But we've got snow falling up there now and it isn't helping much."

The Germans couldn't withdraw very far. The

fjords behind them were dead-ends. According to what had been said last night there were supposed to be two cruisers somewhere about, and if that was so the destroyers might be falling back to join them. On the other hand *Warspite*'s Swordfish hadn't seen any cruisers or it would have reported them.

Chandler said, "Seems we aren't getting much of a look in, sir."

The comment, in one's present state of frustration, was infuriating. Nick forced himself to answer equably. He said, "Things will probably open out presently."

"But if we're bound to stay astern of the flagship, sir—"

"For the time being, pilot. Not necessarily for ever."

Those *were* the orders. *Intent* was, so to speak, watching the admiral's back for him. And you couldn't blame him if he felt a bit nervous in taking a 31,000-ton battleship up this narrow waterway, if he took all reasonable steps to protect her. One wouldn't blame him in the least —if he hadn't picked on *Intent*. . . .

They'd slipped out of Rodsundet with the oiler just after two-thirty yesterday morning. *Tonning*'s best speed had turned out to be twelve knots, not fourteen, but by six-thirty with fifty miles behind them he'd reckoned he was well enough clear to break wireless silence, and he'd sent for the doctor, Bywater, to come up to the bridge. Nick had been on his high seat in the port for'ard corner, with Chandler at the binnacle and young Cox as assistant OOW. *Intent* had been steering NNE at twelve knots, driving through a low swell and with a light north-west wind on the bow to throw a little spray now and then across the foc'sl, and the oiler ploughing along two cables' lengths astern. Sklinna light-tower had been a pimple on the horizon just abaft the beam to starboard. There'd been no interference, no Stukas coming after them. The cloud-cover would have helped, of course, but he'd been half expecting air activity: the Altbotn destroyer could have got some kind of alarm call out and this had been a weakness in his plan for which he'd had no remedy. The only hope had been that the Altbotn captain might not have guessed at the involvement of a British destroyer: he'd been hit from *Valkyrien* and the attack could have been mounted locally by Norwegians. He couldn't have known until much later, when survivors or men released from the tanker came ashore, what had happened to his two flotilla mates.

Bywater had saluted. "Morning, sir."

"Ah, doctor. How are your patients?"

"Dobbs is very happy to have company, sir. He's mending well. To be honest, I think I must have taken too gloomy a view of his chances in the first place. I mean if he'd been as badly damaged as I thought he *would* have died."

"Better an error that way than the other."

"I suppose so, sir . . . Surtees will be all right. I took a lump of metal out of his thigh—and he's complaining it hurts now and didn't before I got at him. It's a clean wound, though, there shouldn't be any problems."

"Good. Now I've got some *real* work for you." Nick handed him a signal which he'd been drafting. "Read it out, would you, so we can see if it makes sense."

Chandler came closer to hear it. Cox too. Bywater cleared his throat, and read: "To Commander-in-Chief, repeated Vice-Admiral Battlecruiser Squadron and Admiralty. From *Intent*."

That alone would be enough to create a sensation. *Intent* was supposed to have been sunk four days ago. Bywater read on:

"In position 65 degrees 22′ north 11 degrees 36′ east course 020 speed 12 escorting captured oiler *Tonning*, 14,000 tons, with prize crew of Norwegian naval reservists under Lieutenant-Commander Torp Royal Norwegian Naval Reserve and four Royal Navy ratings under Sub-Lieutenant Lyte RN as guard on prisoners. *Tonning* has 8,000 tons marine diesel remaining and is flying White Ensign. Two German Beitzen-class destroyers torpedoed and sunk 0100/12 in Rodsundet 64 degrees 36′ north 11 degrees 16′ east where oiler was taken simultaneously by boarding. Also one destroyer and one U-boat immobilised by depthcharges in Altbotn position

63 degrees 35′ north 11 degrees 13′ east, the charges being dropped from former Norwegian sail-training yacht *Valkyrien* commanded by Lt.-Cdr. Torp. Submit air attack on Altbotn would complete destruction of the two damaged vessels. *Intent* has six torpedoes and 90 per cent ammunition remaining and is now fully operational. Regret have been unable to communicate while in Namsenfjord repairing action damage sustained dawn 8 April. Repairs effected under supervision of Norwegian engineer from *Valkyrien*. Consider *Gauntlet* to have been sunk in same action but have no certain knowledge owing to total loss of visibility when about to attack *Hipper* with torpedoes. *Gauntlet* had rammed enemy and was in sinking condition. Own casualties 8 April one ERA wounded, all other ERAs and Commissioned Engineer and two stokers killed. In Altbotn action this morning one torpedoman was wounded. Both wounded men's condition is satisfactory. Time of origin 0630 GMT/12.

Bywater finished reading. Chandler said, "That's one hell of a signal, sir."

Nick thought so too. He still had a sort of lurking guilt-feeling about the *Gauntlet* action but he didn't think he'd be blamed for it. Not now.

"But one thing, sir—" Chandler's tone was hesitant—"should there be a mention of our leaky fuel-tanks?"

"I'm not absolutely sure they *are* leaking, pilot." He told the doctor, "Get that into cipher,

392

check it very carefully, then tell MacKinnon to bung it out. Mid—you can go down and lend a hand with it."

Signals of congratulation had come in all through the forenoon. There were also orders to escort the oiler into Folla, where she was to anchor. *Intent* was to remain with her, pending receipt of further orders, and another destroyer would arrive off Hamnvik to oil and also to transfer two ERAs to *Intent* on loan. Commander Torp was requested to provide fuelling facilities to destroyers who would be requiring oil during the next twenty-four hours. Commander-in-Chief and Admiralty both sent Commander Torp congratulations on the Altbotn operation and thanks for the assistance rendered to *Intent*.

Nick had signalled his ETA in Folla as 2200/12, and passed all the messages to Claus Torp by light. He was glad that C-in-C and London had had the *nous* to recognise Torp's efforts.

In London a paymaster commander took a copy of *Intent*'s signal to Third Officer Casler in her office.

"Might this extraordinary communication be what your recently departed admiral was hoping for, Ginny?"

She took it from him. By the time she'd skimmed through it, hardly daring to believe her eyes, he'd left the room. She read the signal again more slowly, making sure that she was understanding it, that it did mean what it seemed to mean. Then she reached for the telephone and asked the Admiralty exchange to connect her with a Hampshire number which Aubrey Wishart had left with her. The telephone was answered by a woman with a strident Hampshire accent.

"Is Admiral Sir Hugh Everard there, please?"

"No, he's not. Who'd that be as wants him?"

"This is the Admiralty in London. When do you expect—"

"Why, he's *there*, where *you* are!"

"You mean he's visiting the Admiralty?"

"I'm sure that's what I said, Missus—"

"Thank you very much."

Virginia Casler rang off, and called down to the porters' office at the main entrance. The porters were all retired naval men. Yes: Admiral Everard had arrived half an hour ago, with an appointment in Medical.

"Thank you." She checked her list of departmental extensions, and got through on an internal line. An SBA confirmed that Admiral Everard was there, waiting for a check-up.

"May I speak to him, please? This is Third Officer Casler calling on behalf of Rear-Admiral Wishart."

"I'll see if he can come to the 'phone, Ma'am. May 'ave stripped off like."

"Would that matter terribly?" There was a silence. She added, "I must speak to him. It's very important to him."

Now she had a wait of about a minute. Then: "Admiral Everard here."

"This is Third Officer Casler, sir. I was Admiral Wishart's assistant, but as I think you know he left us yesterday."

"I do know, yes. What is it, Miss Casler?"

"He was anxious that I should contact you if there was any news of your nephew, and—"

"And you've *had* some?"

Quick, excited, suddenly a young, *strong* voice. . . .

Virginia Casler swallowed, nodding. "Yes. It's the most marvellous, *wonderful*—"

She was going to cry. Not was going to, *was* crying. She'd felt a bit emotional when she'd read the signal but now suddenly her eyes were full of it and her voice had gone peculiar. She'd had to pause, struggling for control and annoyed with herself, ashamed, but—

"You *are* telling me that my nephew is alive?"

"Yes."

"His ship was not sunk?"

"*He*'s been doing all the sinking. He's—"

Again, it had stuck in her throat. Swallowing, trying not to weep directly into the receiver, thinking *How ridiculous . . .*

"—been doing the most incredible things, sir. I—oh, I'm sorry, I'm being silly, I—"

"I think you must be a charming and delightful young woman, Miss Casler. Very far from silly. But it might be easier if we were to meet without a telephone in the way? Perhaps after these chaps in here have finished pushing and pulling me about?"

"If you'd ring through when you're free, sir, I could bring this signal—"

"Signal from *Intent?*"

"Yes. If we met down at the main entrance?"

"You really are *most* kind. What extension should I ask for?"

She told him. She added, "It's—a *fantastic* signal . . ."

She'd just managed to get those words out: then she'd fumbled the receiver into its cradle and started looking for a handkerchief. In the medical section Hugh Everard hung up too, smiling to himself. A *young* man's smile . . . He'd fairly fly through this medical now, he thought: then he'd tear down to meet this little Wren girl, who really did sound quite enchanting: and before long—incredibly—he'd be seeing Nick. Nick who might have been dead and by the grace of God was not: and who'd be bound to have quite a yarn to tell! I must not, Hugh thought, get myself sent off into the Atlantic *too* damn soon. . . .

Crouch, leaning over number six tube, jerked his head towards the noise of gunfire up ahead. Banks of carved-up sea peeled away on either side. Way back, even farther back than *Intent* was, a couple of destroyers were ferreting along the coast.

Crouch grumbled to CPO Shaw, the torpedo gunner's mate, "The boats up front's 'ogging all the action. Skipper'll be spitting blood."

Intent was making about twenty knots. *Warspite*'s maximum was twenty-four, and the other destroyers had chased on at more than thirty, so it was hardly surprising that it was distant gunfire they were hearing.

The TGM ignored Crouch's remark. He'd turned to glance up at the ensign, whip-cracking from the mizzen gaff. Joss Bartley muttered as he unwrapped a piece of chewing-gum, "About 'ad our whack down south, ain't we?"

"Not in '*is* book we ain't." Crouch nodded in the direction of the bridge. "Be 'alf berserk up there, I reckon. Specially now 'e's lost 'is Sheila."

Snow swept across the fjord, and there was a lot of smoke as well as swirling fog-patches.

"Aircraft approaching astern, sir, green one-seven-oh, angle of sight two-oh!"

That yell had come from the after lookout on the starboard side. Trench had sprung over to that side of the bridge and he had his glasses trained astern. He told Nick, "Swordfish, sir. About six—eight . . ."

From *Furious*, somewhere off Lofoten. There'd been a signal that they'd be making an attack. Trench amplified, "I think *ten* aircraft, sir. But they're in and out of mist and—"

"All right."

397

Cutting him short . . . In any circumstances, *any* frame of mind, it would have been frustrating to be stuck behind the battleship while other destroyers were off the leash and doing proper destroyer work. The action seemed to be going in two directions now, north-westward towards Herjangsfjord and east to Narvik. Nick heard the roar of engines as the Stringbags flew over, heading for the harbour area. You saw them in glimpses, one or two at a time here and there as they appeared and disappeared through cloud and fog.

Warspite let loose another salvo and its thunder crashed back in echoes from the mountains. The battleship's turrets were trained to port and on the bow, but it was impossible to know what she was shooting at. A second salvo followed that one: then her guns were at rest again while ahead the intensity of destroyer gunfire thickened. The Swordfish had flown on into the murk ahead and quite possibly some of those explosions could be bomb-bursts. There'd be AA guns in it too. For the moment the snow had stopped. The director telephone squawked: Nick reached for it and Brocklehurst told him, "One Hun's gone right up Herjangsfjord, sir, with *Eskimo* chasing him, and there's a group of three that seem to be making for Rombaksfjord."

Nine destroyers up there making hay with them. Avenging *Hardy*, *Hunter*, *Hoste*. Only one out of ten stuck back here where there were *no*

398

Germans. A corollary to that was that there was no danger to *Warspite* from this quarter either. Nick looked round for Herrick.

"Signalman. Make to the admiral, 'Am I to remain in this station.'"

He might have forgotten he had *Intent* sitting here doing nothing when with the action going off in separate directions she could have been making herself useful. It wasn't likely but he *might* have. . . . Four Swordfish, low to the water, were struggling to gain height on their way seaward. *Warspite*'s big guns flamed and roared. Brocklehurst reported, "Enemy destroyer gunfire's slackening, sir. Almost as if they're running out of ammo."

Herrick was clattering that message out on one of the ten-inch lamps, using a big one to beat the soupy visibility. The Germans might be short of ammunition, Nick thought. They'd have used a lot during the 2nd Flotilla's attack on the 10th, and at the end of that battle they'd also lost their ammunition ship. The one with the flames which had risen, according to the BBC, to 3,000 feet. May there have been Germans in those flames, he thought. What about *Hoste*: had *she* burnt? He wasn't sure that his informants last night hadn't known more than they'd told him. Herrick had passed the signal and Nick had seen *Warspite*'s flashed "K" acknowledging it. A yeoman of signals would be taking it to the admiral now. From the north-west,

Herjangsfjord, came the solid *boom* of a torpedo hit, and he guessed it would be *Eskimo* finishing off the one she'd chased up there. He had his glasses trained that way and he heard the clash of the shutter on the lamp as Herrick acknowledged receipt of the admiral's reply. It had been a very short one by the sound of it.

"Sir?" He looked round at the killick. Herrick told him unhappily, "From the admiral, sir— 'Yes'."

Bloody hell . . .

"Director—bridge!"

He answered the telephone. Brocklehurst told him, "one Tribal has been badly hit in Rombaksfjord, sir. Stopped and on fire."

Nothing *Intent* could help with. *Intent* was wet-nurse to a battleship which was here to look for a cruiser—*two* cruisers—which almost certainly were not in these fjords. The Germans never did leave their ships in positions where they'd be vulnerable to attack if they could help it, and it was a fair bet that any cruisers they'd had up here—*if* they'd had any—would be back in German ports by now.

Director telephone again: "There's another destroyer, one we haven't seen before, just coming out of Narvik harbour, sir."

Following *Warspite*, *Intent* was circling to starboard, leaving Narvik off to port. The battleship's guns, trained that way, spurted flame and smoke: swallowing to clear his ears from the concussion, Nick saw three—then four—now *six* destroyers racing towards the newly-emerged enemy. All had their guns firing and the German was surrounded by shell-spouts. And now hits: bursts that blossomed into fires and spread, smoke growing to obscure her. . . . *Warspite*'s guns were quiet again as *Intent* obediently fell into place astern of her. Back near the harbour entrance that German destroyer had rolled over, hung for a half-minute on her side then completed the roll and sunk. There was only smoke there now, and the British ships circling off to port and starboard like wheeling cavalry. Beyond, on the shoreline and the harbour's fringes, shell-bursts had stained the snow in yellow blotches. *Warspite*'s course was now south-west, and Nick guessed they were going to take a look into the mouth of Skjomenfjord for the mythical cruisers. Glancing back over his ship's port quarter he saw *Cossack* plastered under a sudden deluge of German shellfire. Guns from inside the harbour: range point-blank as *Cossack* had nosed up into the narrow entrance.

Warspite was going about again, probably to use her crushing fire-power on that shore battery. *Eskimo* had come tearing out of Herjangsfjord and she was turning in towards Rombaksfjord where enemy ships had run for shelter. They wouldn't find much: *Hero*, *Forester*, *Bedouin* and *Icarus* were dashing in after *Eskimo*. Like a pack of terriers darting around and routing out their quarry. *Warspite* had already reversed her course, and Nick had to let her pass on her way back towards the harbour before he could put his own helm over to turn astern of her.

Shell-spouts out of nowhere rose in a tight group on *Intent*'s bow. The splashes lifted, hung, then disintegrated into a foul-smelling rain which lashed across the bridge as she steamed through the place where the shells had fallen.

"Destroyer red three-five!"

The German had appeared from behind the cover of the point: she'd been hiding in that southern fjord.

"All guns follow director!"

Clang of the fire-gongs: crash of the four-sevens. . . .

If *Warspite* hadn't gone about when she had, the enemy destroyer would have been well placed for a torpedo attack on her.

"Port twenty."

"Port twenty, sir!"

Another salvo ripping over, *down*. . . . Close again. Near-misses like kicks in the ship's ribs as they thumped down and burst and the splashes sprang, one just clear of the quarter but the others abreast the for'ard tubes and collapsing across the iron deck as the ship swung around. Brockle-hurst, with work to do at last, had his guns shooting fast and accurately: his first salvo had gone over but the second lot had hit, a splash of red flame on the side of the German's bridge and others amidships around his funnels as he too swung away under helm. As *Intent* turned, heeling hard to starboard, "X" and "Y" guns were out of the fight only for a few seconds.

Hugh Everard had saved *Warspite*'s bacon for her at Jutland. Nick said into the voicepipe, "Midships." Odd, to think of that. She'd had a couple of very expensive face-lifts since then, of course.

"Torpedoes approaching starboard bow!"

Quickly down to the pipe again: "Port twenty-five."

"Port twenty-five, sir!"

It was the quickest way to get her round because she'd still been swinging. The fish coming at her now would have been intended for the admiral: hence the German's own turn to starboard. They were no danger at all to *Warspite*: *Intent*, in turning to engage and close the enemy, had put herself right in front of them.

"A" and "B" guns were silent now, unable to bear as the ship swung her stern towards the enemy and his torpedoes.

"Midships."

"Midships, sir." "X" and "Y" were still banging away. Cox was aft there, doing Lyte's job. Nick called down to Jarratt, "Meet her."

"Torpedo passing to port, sir!"

And another track to starboard: the lookouts on that side reported it. *Intent* had combed the tracks quite neatly. Nick stooped and called down, "Starboard fifteen." After guns still in action: he'd get "A" and "B" back into it now. The German was circling right around, probably trying to get back into that side fjord. The admiral could hardly expect *Intent* to paddle along astern of him like some bloody duck and let the bastard go. . . .

Warspite let rip. Hearing the crashing thunder of it Nick looked that way and saw her turrets trained to starboard as she muscled in on *his* German. . . .

She'd hit him. Smothering, annihilating. The destroyer exploded upwards in a gush of flame, smoke, escaping steam. Then all smoke, blackness with fire that shot through it like moving scarlet threads. When it cleared there was only litter on the surface.

"Midships. Port fifteen."

"Port fifteen, sir . . ."

"Three hundred revolutions." He needed a few extra knots, to get back into station on that floating fortress. There'd been flashing, some signal coming over. A reprimand for having left his station?

"Fifteen of port wheel on, sir!"

Leading Signalman Herrick reported, "From the admiral, sir—'thank you.'"

"What the hell for?"

Chandler suggested, "For getting between him and that German, sir?"

Nick didn't even glance at him. He bent to

the voicepipe: "Midships." *Warspite* had already been well clear, not in any danger. He was angry, pent-up, feeling the tension like a taut wire in his brain, and knowing at the same time that this *Hoste* business was his own problem, one that he had to face up to on his own, not vent in bad temper on other people. He nodded to Pete Chandler. "You may be right."

There was one good thing. After those near-misses he could now discover that his ship had leaking fuel-tanks.

6.30 pm: withdrawing, and still playing follow-my-leader behind the flagship. Steaming westward at twenty-knots. In the fjords of northern Norway, not one German ship had been left afloat. Four lay shattered on the top end of Rombaksfjord, one in Herjangsfjord, one off the harbour and one inside it, another in Djupvik Bay. Considering the odds they'd faced, the Germans had put up a good fight. Three British destroyers had been damaged. One of them, *Cossack*, was aground but would be refloated before long: her wounded had been transferred to *Warspite*.

The troops which were supposed to be on their way should have been here *now*. German troops were pulling out: you could see them, dark snake-like columns winding away across the snow-slopes.

Broad on the port bow as the ships moved

405

westward towards the narrows, in an estuary which had Ballangen village at its head, an "H" or "I" class destroyer lay close inshore with boats moving between her and the beach. Trench muttered with his glasses on her, "Taking men off shore, sir. I wonder—" he glanced round quickly as he thought of it—"could be survivors from *Hardy* and—"

"It's—possible."

The thought had hit him, explosively, just before it had occurred to Trench. But then a second thought: that there was nothing he could do about it. He'd made one submission in the matter of having to hang around the flagship, and he'd been snubbed for his pains: he didn't want to try again and have it thought he was behaving like a *prima donna*, trading on his successes. Besides—personal anxieties were—well, *that*—personal, and private.

Fear now, as well as anxiety. He'd been left in doubt too long.

"*Warspite*'s flashing!"

Chandler had bawled it, but Herrick was ahead of him and the lamp had clashed before the navigator had shut his mouth. The first word of the message was "Proceed" . . . Release, then, finally? Nick put his glasses up, focusing on the destroyer inshore, in that southern inlet. A lot of men were being brought off. Boatloads of them. He couldn't identify the destroyer.

Trench had begun to read out the message as

the dots and dashes came rippling from *Warspite*'s signal bridge and Herrick acknowledged each completed word with a single flash.

"Proceed — Ballangen — and — join — *Ivanhoe* — embarking — survivors — ex — *Hardy* — *Hoste* — also — merchant — navy — personnel — for — transfer — to — oiler — *Tonning* — stop — You — may — recruit — engineroom — personnel — as — available — and — requisite."

He'd read the last part of it for himself, and as it ended he was ready at the voicepipe. "Three-five-oh revolutions!"

"Three-five-oh revolutions, sir!"

"Port fifteen."

"Port fifteen, sir. Three-five-oh revolutions passed and repeated, sir. Fifteen of port wheel on!"

Turbine-whine rising as the speed built up and *Intent* surged forward: bow-wave lifting, lengthening as she swung away south-westward, pitching out across the battleship's rolling, outspreading wake. Something joyous in that motion and the thrust of speed—as if it came as a relief to the ship herself . . . . Nick called to Trench, "Scrambling nets both sides, Number One. And call away boats' crews."

One dinghy and one purloined skiff.

"Aye aye, sir. Bosun's mate—"

"Midships."

"Midships, sir!"

He checked the compass, and told Jarratt,

407

"Steer two-two-oh." Then he raised his glasses again to study that activity inshore. He warned himself, in dread of what was coming now, Don't count your chickens. . . .

The air was like frozen steel, but he'd begun to sweat. For the first time in twenty years he was aware of being truly, deeply frightened.